THE LABOR MOVEMENT
IN FICTION AND NON-FICTION
AN AMS REPRINT SERIES

THE LONG YEAR

AMS PRESS
NEW YORK

The Long Year

By
ANN CHIDESTER

New York   Charles Scribner's Sons   1946

Library of Congress Cataloging in Publication Data

Chidester, Ann, 1919-
　　The long year.

　　(The Labor movement in fiction and non-fiction)
　　Reprint of the 1946 ed. published by Scribner,
New York.
　　I. Title. II. Series.
PZ3.C4343Lo8　　[PS3505.H745]　　　813'.5'4　　　74-26097
ISBN 0-404-58411-X

Reprinted by arrangement with Charles Scribner's Sons

Reprinted from an original copy in the collections
of the Library Association of Portland and Multnomah
County

From the edition of 1946, New York
First AMS edition published in 1976
Manufactured in the United States of America

AMS PRESS INC.
NEW YORK, N. Y.

FOR
MORGAN
IN MEMORY OF HIS TIME ON EARTH

> ... In the deep room,
> a seagull is flying. ...

CHAPTER ONE:

KAY HASSWELL stood by the window and looked down upon the city street that lay bleary under the golden sun. "Nothing is lost," she thought and watched the dust moving in soft puffs down the low street and thought of the dust as the dust of a man who was himself the city. A man full-grown and weary, a man named New York City. The dust and the sharp sunlight and the goddam heat. The heat was a waxy skin on the wide streets. She could see it thick as fur on the buildings, but in the apartment as she moved through the cool, sterile air, there was little feeling of heat in her. It was Sunday in late May. A few people walked slowly as in a vast dream, a few children played solemnly, quietly in the park across the street. She moved back and forth, a hard-bellied dark woman who moved in a single, knowing way as a dancer or a swimmer or a lazy cat moves. All the while she was talking about herself and her life, and inside herself where her cunning lay working like a persistent crocodile, she knew her own unhappiness. "The thing is—nothing's lost, nothing . . ."

She had decided, after twenty years, to return to her home town of High Falls, and now in her mind she saw her mother standing on the side porch of the old house there. She saw her brother, Hoyt. She saw her father lying on the wicker lounge and heard her mother's calm, commanding voice telling all of them to come to dinner now. She could see the stern outline of her mother's face, hear again the throaty, pleasant sound of her voice that could never be evaded. "Kay, you can play in the yard after dinner—not now." And she remembered how she herself had turned and started to argue and met her mother's quiet, impassive look. None of it was lost—nothing. And she was going back there and start over again in that town. The thing she felt inside was herself—like a diamond lying in the city's heat, herself that had been Kay Hasswell and then Kay Blair and Kay Prokosch and Kay Richter and was now again Kay Hasswell, belonging to no man, alone in the city on a hot Sunday afternoon.

She kept walking across the room talking about herself and her life. She felt all of it there, the diamond hard inside her where she was full of life, like the old gray mare, skittish and full of life. She looked at the big man, Fonn Kelly, sitting in the yellow chair crumpled with the heat. He was young, and she liked to have them young. Then, too, he was always far away from her, watching her, and she could never get near him. She wondered what magic quality ran his big machine, made such a great fighter of him.

"You see," she was saying, "all I do is talk about myself today."

"I like it," he said. His voice was slow and every word was separate from the others. "But if Robert had lived, you wouldn't plan to go back there."

"Oh—Robert," she said. Robert Richter had been dead three weeks. Three weeks were whatever you made them—a year, a day, a moment. She did not believe in thinking of the dead.

"Why go back there?" he asked.

"What?"

"I said, why do you want to go back to that town?"

She moved her hands impatiently, apart and then together. "Maybe I shouldn't talk about it so much." She rubbed her hands together so that the square emerald slipped toward her knuckle and then down again. "Let's go out and have a drink—I'd like to go out and hear some very sad violin music."

He shook his head. "You ought to talk about it, Kay. Besides, I like to listen."

"It was an ugly town."

He waited.

She looked at him seriously. How could she explain it to him? No one could ever know that, and there was no way to tell it—how it was to go far away from your own town and to keep going farther

The Long Year 3

and farther and then suddenly needing to go back there, just to look, just to live there and feel roots there again. "My brother's there. I haven't seen him for years," she said. "He has a family—a son about twenty-four and a girl named Marth. They say she looks like me."

He smiled. "You aren't going back there to see them. You wouldn't walk across the street to see anyone."

"No," she said. "I'd walk across the street to see you."

He kept smiling and watching her.

"At first I thought I couldn't bear the town. My mother died and my brother and his wife tried to take care of me. My brother's wife wasn't like my mother. After my father died, my mother ran everything. We were used to her. When she was gone, my brother didn't know what to do because he needed a woman to tell him what to do. Now, the Depression's hitting him, too. He doesn't know what to do about the factory. My income's been cut terribly, and I know that business. I learned it from my mother. Mamma'd know what to do now. People like Mamma and I can take care of anything if we set our mind to it."

"You said you hated the town," he said.

"Yes, I hated it." She opened the carved ivory box and took out a cigarette and lit it, flicking a heavy silver lighter. "I married Sonny Blair to get out of there. He was awfully sweet—always sang those old college songs. I was almost eighteen then, and there was nothing to do in the town, nothing new, I mean. So I married Sonny."

"I didn't know him."

"He was sweet. Boston was terrible. He lived there with his mother and four sisters—all very weak, cruel women. That's where I learned to hate women."

"I got friends up there," he said.

"Irish?"

"Sure."

That was not her life in Boston—Boston was to be drowned in wads of people, to hear them quote Dear Mamma—Dear Mamma said in 1886 that a blue stocking would never come to any good end, and I've upheld the belief . . . you take a cloth and soak it in goose grease and plaster it to his chest, using good wool . . . and through it all she was drowning, going deeper and deeper. A frightened chicken in a coop, hating those tidy, prune-and-prism-mouthed creatures.

No sense to Boston for her.

She was almost eighteen. She hadn't loved Sonny. She didn't know anything about love until she met Prokosch that time in Vienna, and afterwards she was through with love, too. But Boston was different—at home they talked about Pope Leo and the price of the new virgin timber, white pine, white pine by-products, beeswax candles for the church on Sunday, that Black Irishman, Simon O'Dodd who had loved her—that Simon and a merry go she'd given him. Yes, and in the evenings sitting around to drink a grapey mixture of Dago red wine and the girls in their white dresses moving across the green lawns and the men in their flannels, their shoes off and the water still on their hair to make it lie flat. After Papa died, Mamma was there, everywhere, soft-spoken—how did Mamma get to be right all the time? There was no one in the world, Europe or Africa or South America, no one who had what Mamma had.

"What happened?" he asked. "Don't day-dream, tell me, what happened?"

"Oh. Many things." She smiled and stopped walking across the room. She wore a thin white sports dress and red earrings and red linen sandals with high heels. Her shoes were always beautifully made with narrow soles and high heels, and she walked lightly in them. She was very fond of clothes, and everything she wore had to be the best she could find. She liked knowing there was nothing better.

"I thought I wanted to live in Paris," she said. "I had a quick, nasty divorce from Sonny and bought some new clothes and then modeled on the boats going back and forth. I modeled mostly for Lanvin. But it didn't last. I didn't want it to last. It got soft and easy. I like things to be hard and dangerous."

"That's movie talk," he said.

The Long Year

"No. I can tell you a lot of things have happened to me—but I never belonged *with* anyone or *to* anyone. That's hard to explain to someone like you. You have your fighting, and that's all you ever wanted. But I have nothing for myself except myself. I want to work hard again, Fonn. I used to work very hard every day in the garden in Rio. I worked like an old peasant woman, and at night I slept. Now I don't sleep. I don't seem to want it."

"I see," he said. "You're going home to work?"

"Yes. It was always an old, lazy town. You have to lead those people like stubborn horses and make them drink. And my brother is no one to make anyone do anything. He sits back and lets the place run itself. My people put their blood into it. It killed Mamma. She had arthritis and used to go down there in a wheel chair. I always wanted to be like her—I hated the idea of ending up calm and quiet the way she was—but still, I wanted it."

"You'll never be that way," he said. "Robert told me you had to be every place at one time and own it, too. You'll never be the way your mother was."

She frowned. "I never liked Robert much after the first week or so. He was always so sure everything he did was right. When he drowned out there in the lake, I sat on the shore and waited for them to find him, and it was like a game. I didn't care either way, but they seemed to care—the men looking for him, I mean."

"Well, you'll hate being away from the city," he said.

She shook her head. Her hair was very black but when she shook her head like that, two streaks of gray showed. "The city's ugly now. It's ugly and spiritless with everyone looking hungry and ill-fed." She moved toward the windows. "The grass is yellow. At home we used to have wonderful parties on the lawn under the big green shade trees. It was always clean there. No matter where I went I used to think of that town and how, after Simon O'Dodd died, they hated me." She turned from the window. "I was a kid, and this big Irishman Simon O'Dodd wanted to marry me and keep me in that town. I never said I'd marry him—seriously, I mean—and then he was killed in a plane accident. He was flying over a cornfield and crashed and they said he did it because of me. They always blamed me. God, how I hated those people."

"You ought to stay here."

She did not hear him. "I hated them and I wanted them to accept me. I used to do things to make them like me. An old man named Macbeth—I used to bring him bland puddings, but he never liked me." She sighed. "And now everyone here is sick with lack of money, and I don't like it. Then, I had this letter from my brother about the factory."

"You won't like it," he said.

She shrugged. "I want to go back there and do something with that factory. I need the income, and I want to show my proud, good, fine, conventional brother that I can do it. How soft he is, Fonn— how easily he condemned me! I wonder what they think of me now? That young girl, Martha—she must hate it there, too—the way I once hated it." She lit another cigarette. She was very tired now. She needed a drink or a good party with lots of noise. She'd call up some people and have them come in for cold supper. It would make her forget about the factory, her brother, the town, the whole thing. It was twenty years since she had been there, and she had not seen any part of that country in that time except for a fleeting glimpse from the air where it lay under the mist and the sun. What she needed was to have the people come in and maybe LeGrand would play some Chopin. That was the thing to make her stop thinking.

"You'll see, angel," she said. "Everything'll work out fine. It always does."

"Does it?" He rose and buttoned his white linen jacket over his wide, flat body.

"Don't go. I'll call up LeGrand and the others."

"I hate your little parties."

"That's silly. You know they all adore you. LeGrand says he loves to look at you, just to sit and look at you."

"He talks too much. I suppose some day when you're tired of trying to re-form yourself into the image of your Mamma you'll relax

The Long Year 7

and marry him. He'd keep you under glass." He went out into the small, cool foyer and picked up his white hat.

She laughed at him. She was watching him in a careful, listening manner, her hands behind her back. She could see herself in the mirror, and her hair hung long and black against the white dress and she looked as if nothing could touch her. She knew this was how she appeared to him. She worked hard to keep herself looking like that.

"When will I see you?"

"I don't know," he said.

"Before I leave?"

"I'm going up to the camp tonight with Petey."

"You're angry with me about something, aren't you?"

"How could I be angry with you about anything?" he asked.

She kept smiling at him. She felt that he was terrific in every way, so healthy and strong and never getting involved with anyone. She went to all his fights and sat close to the ring and wore a large red flower in her hair so he could see her easily. She always yelled as loud as she could because she had an actual feeling of being in there and fighting the whole thing through and winning.

"Well—" he said. "Don't meddle too much and have a fine time for yourself."

"Will you come out there sometime?"

"Maybe," he said. He kissed her on the mouth. He kissed like a child, his lips together and dry. "Have fun, Kay."

"Oh, go away!" she said angrily.

He smiled and went out and she heard the elevator begin to hum. She could see him in her mind standing in the elevator blinking in a slow, sleepy fashion when there was nothing slow nor sleepy about him. She could see him going out into the hot street and walking in that soft, effortless way. Probably he would go down toward the cathedral. He usually went that way so he could talk to the pigeons, a grown man like that going to talk to the pigeons. Every Sunday when he was in town he did it, although he never went inside the building but just went there because he liked to stand in open places and because of the pigeons. And the pigeons would look at him, settle under his hand and seem to know what he was saying, but he never spoke words. He made a kind of crooning, musical sound over them. Well, he was a very strange, independent person, and she could never be sure whether he cared at all what happened to her or whether he came to her to be amused.

She moved across the room thinking of him, and then she went into the bedroom and lay across the bed, kicking off her left sandal. She idly picked up the telephone and dialed LeGrand's number. She knew exactly what she would say. She would say she was giving herself a farewell party because she was going back to her own town and to her family there. She thought, to the ghost of Mamma and to the ghost of myself as a child and to the ghost of Simon O'Dodd and to the thousand ghosts of the days I remember and can never quite escape. I will make them like me there and be grateful to me and I will work and be happy, have roots again, be young, be young, always be young . . .

"LeGrand," she said in a low, sleepy voice. "Darling, listen . . . listen . . ."

It was almost eleven in the morning after the supper party. She lay in the low ivory-colored room behind the blinds, and the faint strips of sunlight lay across the floor and walls. It was like the time in Africa waiting for the others to wake—the smooth coolness of the room was like the tent with the strips of sunlight and the dappled movement of the sun on the window edge. Her body lay long and thin and relaxed under the sheet.

The party had gone rather well. LeGrand had saved it because he was in a good mood and had been willing to play all the time. He had been pleased that she was going to her home. He was a sentimentalist—a thin, grave man in quiet suits, very expensive, not foreign or American, unlabeled. Worrying about having to let Carl, his chauffeur, go after all this time. Worried that he might lose her, not knowing that he had never had her—but you mustn't waste anything, not even LeGrand, because there might come a time, God

The Long Year

forbid, but it might come and then you'd need LeGrand—or someone like him.

She got out of bed, pulling the yellow chiffon peignoir over her shoulders, the yellow ribbon untied at her throat. She thrust her feet into yellow satin mules and went into the dressing room and looked at herself carefully. She wiped off the faint traces of night cream and gave her long hair a few quick, hard brushes. Then she opened the blinds and went out into the living room. LeGrand's carnation was still on the piano. She stood in the middle of the room, sniffing the stale air, stretching herself.

When Marie, the maid, came in she smiled her good-morning smile.

"Mr. LeGrand called, Ma'am."

"I know," she said. It's Monday, and on Monday I have luncheon at a Russian restaurant with Mr. LeGrand. Onion soup, a good drink, a fine argument because I'm going to drive across the country alone."

"To Canada?"

"No. I'm going home," and Marie nodded although she did not know where "home" might be. She herself had never thought of any single place as being home, but now that she had decided to go back to High Falls, it seemed that it had always meant home to her. She told Marie to begin packing and then she went through the bedroom and turned on the shower. "I'll build myself a house on the river," she thought. "After a while I'll spend my summers there and all sorts of interesting people like LeGrand and Fonn will come to visit me. The rest of the year I'll go to Rio or Mexico City, some place where there's sun." In this way she would establish a routine of living.

There was never any pleasure in these luncheons with LeGrand. They were always the same, and she knew he would argue with her about driving across the country, about staying in the town. He never wanted her to leave the city or him. She could see the table with its shiny black top and the two Manhattans set carefully in the center of two red-and-white cocktail napkins, a cigarette smoking in the black onyx ash tray, LeGrand touching her hand lightly but strongly so that she would hold her hand still under his. She could sense the dry, cold air in that restaurant and LeGrand's careful eyes surveying the women coming in and out, and she knew that he was her kind of person and that perhaps it was too late, too late to return to the town, but she was going to do that anyhow. The thing was not to have a scene with him. She hated scenes and she was always going through them step by step, knowing the outcome in advance. Not to tease him too much so that his face turned hard and angry, not to lose him entirely.

She pulled on her white gloves. Marie said that Carl was waiting with the car. She looked at herself a moment in the mirror and then went out into the foyer. She saw Robert's fishing hat on the table. It was over three weeks since he had drowned, and she wondered if the hat had been there all that time. She picked it up and put it into the hall closet and went out, smiling.

"Good morning, Carl," she said to the chauffeur. She did not look at him.

"Good morning, Ma'am," he said. He stood very straight in his gray uniform, and she knew he hated her. He hated her because she used to tease him about being unlucky with dice. A small hot wind came across the park as she stepped into the car. She sank back and closed her eyes so that she would not have to look at the people and the buildings lying under the noon sun. This was the last time she would meet LeGrand for luncheon, and she felt a certain pain at the thought. When you left a place, it made you feel useless, defeated . . . she was feeling old, that was the trouble, old into her guts, and she had to have new things around her, young people whose hands were young and not purpled and veined with age. Not that she had any fear of dying nor of what came after, although when she thought of Mamma she knew that Mamma would see her righteously in Hell . . . it was only that she wanted to feel tough and to win again. She had never lost to Sonny Blair because he was a poor college boy not strong enough to break a match. It was Boston that had won from her.

The Long Year 11

Then Prokosch. She had to smile seeing his face—that skinny little guy with the big brain, he had reminded her of a Jesuit she had met during a church mission at home, little lines around his eyes, and never a betrayal of feeling, only a serene, apprehensive look. She remembered how he got up every morning and stood silently before the picture of Masaryk, a hero-worshiper, an honest diplomat. She had lost to him, but no one had ever known it, lost because he had been like Mamma, and there was no way to win with people like that.

And then, listening to the rich, quiet purr of the car, she let her mind go back to Richter, Robert Parsons Richter, journalist and playboy, spending his energies chasing statesmen and tennis balls, and she remembered all the times when she had sat in the white bleachers wishing he'd be dead, fall off the polo pony, kill himself doing a back-flip or half-gainer from a high board.

Oh, well, she had always had a very fine time for herself for twenty years now—a big, full holiday. But, she was through with it and starting over again. Mamma, she thought, in the end you'll have me back in that town among those people, you always wanted me back there, working hard, building Hoyt's ego for him, being kind and mannerly and generous.

Her smile was flat and hard. Well, it wasn't going to be easy, and Lord knew she didn't want it easy, and there was certainly no one to trust here, not LeGrand—possibly Fonn Kelly, but she could never be sure. The maids stole from you—perfume and whiskey and stockings, everything that wasn't locked in a vault or nailed to the floor, and people themselves sucked you dry until you sat there like a husk with your guts aching and your eye sockets bleeding and your hands empty as a jailbird's.

She got out of the car, still smiling. As she went down the steps into the restaurant, she saw LeGrand sitting in his usual place waiting for her. The idea was to keep him waiting as long as she wanted him to wait. The familiarity of all of this made it seem dream-like, and she moved through it lightly, knowing exactly how it would be. At the door, a man in a tan garbardine suit came out and stumbled and brushed against her. He was young and a little tight, and she could smell his sweat as well as the faint, perfumed, harsh odor of liquor. She drew away from him, but he smiled and touched her arm to steady himself. She looked at him and smiled. His was the first happy face she had seen all morning.

Inside, she moved through the cold, dry air. She put out her hands and lowered her voice, "LeGrand . . . darling . . . I'm famished." And she began her last time with him remembering all the other last times from that Saturday with Simon O'Dodd and the other times in Rio, Paris, Vienna, all the places, all the men, all the same little speeches, half humorous, half tragic, turning her head slowly, being wistful, remote, always knowing surely, knowing exactly what she wanted and getting it.

CHAPTER TWO:

It was the first days of June during the summer of 1933. There was little comradeship in the world and almost none in High Falls, Minnesota. Roosevelt was the new president, and the people waited for what he would do. They prayed for him. They read everything that had been written about his life, his sickness, his idealism. They had begun to fret under the dust and the summer heat. What went on in the town concerned them to whatever degree they themselves were involved. What happened five miles down the river, ten miles down the road, a thousand miles across the land—that was nothing to them. Far cities were words to them, not people together. Earth was dust and heat, Time was dead and God was an easy swear word.

The town had green beauty, though. It had two long, sloping hills and a river, many green trees and shrubs that had not as yet yellowed with heat. Everyone there thought it was the only town in the world, but no one ever did anything to make it better. Once, they built a statue. It was to a Lieutenant Stander who had belonged to the First Horse Cavalry. He had been killed on the polo field down at Fort Riley, Kansas—a home-town boy. His father and some businessmen like Hoyt Hasswell took up a collection and raised the statue on the courthouse lawn—a young man on a horse. Every spring, the deputy sheriffs polished bird droppings and tree sap off it.

This was the only place the girl, Marth Hasswell, had ever known. Her father seldom desired to go beyond the town, and she had never thought much about it. She came out of the school and stood in the gymnasium doorway. She wore a pink linen dress that had faded, pink earrings that brought out the new tan of her skin. She stood in the open sun and put one hand over her eyes. After a moment, her friend Barby Leroy came out of the building. Barby was small, quick and dark. She wore a white pique dress and dirty saddle shoes. She could not stand still and kept shaking her head because her hair was thick and hot against her neck and shoulders. There was an intense, worldly quality about her in the way she moved and in the small, bright face.

"I'm scared, Marth," she said.

"Oh, you!" Marth laughed. "You always say that."

"Just the same, that old biddy might flunk me."

"Oh, Barby," Marth said. Barby had a million little worries that were nothing more than nervous energy. "Don't think about it."

"That old biddy hates me. Anyhow—I'm dumb, Marth. I don't care, though."

They both laughed. It was noon. A few people came out of the high school and courthouse across the street. Most of them walked slowly down the hill and stopped at Ferrin's. Barby sat down at the little black-topped table and put her feet on a chair. They ate hamburgers which they washed down with cokes. After a while, Barby said, "I wish Joe was here. That guy." Her mouth trembled.

Marth looked at the floor. She hated to think of Joe and Barby together. They always quarreled. Joe was probably drunk somewhere, down at Mike's fishing shack, or up in the woods. Joe always spoiled everything. He'd spoil the graduation, too. You could never make plans because of him. And yet he had this terrible fascination for Barby. He was all she cared about and never about herself. All the boys were crazy about her but she didn't seem to notice. For her, life was herself and Joe and nothing more.

"Joe'll be there," Marth said.

"Do you think so?"

". . . Sure."

"Marth?"

"What?"

"In a way I hate to think of getting out of school. I'll miss Joe in history every day. Maybe now that we don't have classes together any more, he'll forget—about everything, I mean."

The Long Year

"No," Marth said. "Why, Barby, everyone's crazy about you. We're not old. Gosh, Joe's not the only one for you."

Barby played with a straw. She moved her small, quick fingers over the damp table top. "For me, Joe's the only one," she said slowly. "Please, Marth, don't wish it wouldn't be like this. Don't even *think* things about Joe and me. It might have some power. Macbeth says if you *think* things—"

"Okay. I won't think anything."

Outside Ferrin's it was still very hot, and the cars kept going up and down the hill in a sluggish purring. The girls walked up the hill toward the high school.

"Your aunt coming today?"

Marth shook her head. "Monday, maybe."

"Gee, I wish she'd come for tonight."

"Daddy got a wire. She says she's going to drive, and not to expect her any special time. He's very happy about it. I guess he doesn't like the responsibility for everything—and anyhow, it's *her* factory, too, and she's been getting the money all these years. Daddy's done all the work."

"I'll bet she's wonderful."

"Oh, she is!" Marth said. "She's been everywhere and done everything, I guess. You know how Daddy is—he doesn't like to talk about her much because of all those husbands—"

"It sounds wonderfully wicked. I'll bet none of them here'll appreciate her except us, Marth. You know how stuffy everyone is."

"I don't really know her—except she does send me marvelous presents."

"Think the factory'll be all right then, Marth?"

"Oh, sure. She's a very smart person, and Daddy needs someone to help him."

"Maybe Joe can get a job then. It would be the best thing in the world because that's what he wants, to have a job and work there like other men."

Barby nodded.

They went inside the high school and walked slowly through the old, musty halls past the lockers. They stood in line on the stage. Marth felt a terrible hollowness everywhere. When she looked at the others, there was a shyness already between them. Something she had not counted on was happening.

After rehearsal, Barby went to the library and sat there waiting for Joe. The librarian was taking down the books and packing them away for the summer.

"But, Barby," Marth argued, "we've got to get a bath and dress and do a million things."

"I don't care," Barby said. "I'm going to wait for Joe."

Marth looked at her and then looked away. She walked home slowly, thinking, Now it's happening to Barby, too, the way it happened to my brother. Love is not always lovely clothes, flowers, people dancing in the dark. It's something terrible without sweetness. It's just not the way it ought to be.

Her father was not home yet. Howard, the Negro, was singing in the kitchen and Ophelia, his wife, was slapping the dough into shape for rye bread. Marth went upstairs and took a bath and lay on her bed naked and stared at the ceiling. She felt useless and disappointed and she wondered if her aunt had lain in this same room feeling like this. She looked at the picture of her aunt, the one she always kept on her dressing table. It was an enlarged snapshot of a young girl in riding breeches, an open shirt, squinting into the sun. She smiled gently and ran the tip of her finger lightly over her aunt's face.

CHAPTER THREE:

MIKE HASSWELL went into the boathouse. It was made in two stories, the top one level with the ground. On the top floor, he stored nets, outboard motors, fishing tackle and paddles, cushions, patching equipment, oil cans and other valuables. Now, he stood in the doorway and looked at the tall, blonde girl sleeping on his army cot. She was already very tan and wore a pair of white shorts and a white silk shirt and lay with her arms above her head. He crossed the room and gently slipped the Navajo ring from her finger. She moved a little, smiled and said something.

He was a thin boy with a thin face. He was twenty-five, but he felt older. He wore moccasins and faded trunks. He didn't know the girl's name—Jean or Joan or Joanne. She was one of the "summer girls" who came in and out of his place from June until October, and all of them were the same—young, good-looking, strong and knowing. This one had come earlier than the others. She was from the party last night. Thoughtfully, he bent over and picked up two beer bottles, a match folder and an old jersey. "Joe's," he said and hung the jersey over a wooden saw horse.

He went outside and looked at the ring in the light. It was even better than he had imagined, made of heavy silver and very good turquoise, not greenish but fine blue with no brown stains in it. He went down the dock stairs and entered the lower story of the house where he stored boats and canoes. He polished the ring with an old toothbrush dipped in warm water and soap. He pulled a pair of faded levis over his trunks and found a blue jersey in one of the lockers. He put the ring in his pocket. Then he combed his hair, wetting the comb in the warm river water in the dock bay. While he was combing his hair, the blonde girl came to the top of the stairs and looked down at him thoughtfully.

"H'lo, Jen," he said.

"Joan," she said. She came down the stairs and leaned against the railing. "Going somewhere?"

"I have to go up to the house."

"I thought you never went up there."

"You know too much."

She laughed softly. "I asked around town about you. Everyone knows about you."

He said nothing. He went back into the boathouse and found two socks and sat on the floor to put them on. She stood in the doorway watching him.

"Mike?"

He looked at her and waited.

"Mike, my ring's gone." She held out her hands to show him. There was a white circle on her finger where the ring had been.

"Too bad," he said.

"You took it. I was half awake, and I felt you take it."

"That so?"

"What are you going to do with it?"

"Here," he said. He took the ring out of his pocket. "Take it."

She shook her head. "I don't want it. You can have it. I want you to have it."

"What the hell you make such a fuss about for then?" He slipped the ring into his pocket again.

"Why're you going up there?" she asked.

He grinned. "Women always want to know why. I'm just going, see? I can go up to the house any time I want to. Maybe I'll see the old man and get some money off him. Maybe I go up there to see my kid sister. She's graduating from high school tonight. I might go up there for almost any reason. Now, you'd better scram, honey."

"Joan's my name," she said. "I guess you have so many girls down here—"

"Yeah—yeah," he said. He gave her a gentle push and pulled the big door shut and snapped the Yale lock.

"Will I see you tonight?" she asked.

The Long Year

He looked at her slowly. Her face flushed and she looked away from him. "It's up to you," he said. "It's just up to you, Kid."

She bit her lip. They walked up the steps together and she got into her car, waiting for him. But he walked away. "Got a couple errands to do," he said. He walked thoughtfully, not thinking of the big blonde girl. He never thought about any of the "summer" girls. He was thinking about Joe Connaught and how he ought to do something for Joe, something that would get him out of town. Not just because Joe was Wilma's brother, although that was a part of it. If Joe didn't get a job at the factory soon, probably when Kay came, it would go bad for him. Because of Wilma, he ought to help Joe and then because of the way he and Joe and Rock Macbeth and Mr. Wimmer were friends—but mostly because of Wilma . . .

The thing was, he couldn't go without thinking of Wilma, and he thought of her from the way it began until the way it ended—the time he was coming home from the factory and saw her outside the drugstore and didn't know her, although she knew him. She was a tall, pretty girl with brown hair. He had never seen hair that was really brown until then, but hers was no matter what color she wore with it—plain, deep brown. He liked her right away, better than he'd ever liked anyone. She had a slow, easy laugh, and at first he thought she was happy all the time. Then he fell in love with her.

What was it she said, she said, "Mike, let's not talk to anyone else for two, three days. Just us together."

He liked that idea because it made him feel alone with her on earth. He never asked questions the way he wanted to. He said, "You do as you please, and I won't ask questions, Will." And all the time there was his old man telling him off about her. He remembered the night when his old man had said it out—"a cheap whore operating in Miles City, Montana," the old man had said. And the first thing he thought was that the old man had a mortgage on King Connaught's dry-cleaning place and that would sit hard. The squeeze act, he thought, but it wasn't going to make any difference because he didn't believe it. If she wanted to go away from High Falls and stay away for a couple years, she was smart, see, but that didn't mean she was—well, it didn't mean it. And his father hadn't said anything more but kept looking at him and waiting for him to give in.

"I had a fight with Paw," he said.

"About me, Mike?" she asked.

"I know everything—no one ever has to tell me anything about you, Will—I know."

He remembered sitting in the room behind the Cafe where you could get liquor, and she wore her green jacket and green skirt and the green shoes with leather tongues, Scotch brogans, she said. She began to tell him about it, and all the while he watched Jack, the waiter, going back and forth behind the long table that served as a bar. The light in the room seemed to merge into one big globe of light that hurt back into his head. She kept talking, and he listened to her. She told it straight out like a child telling of going to the zoo and what she saw there, and her hands were very quiet in her lap. All the while the feeling rose inside him, ticking in his ears, and Time stood still, tottered and crashed around him. He felt sick to his stomach.

"Sure, honey," he said. "It doesn't matter."

"I had to tell you, Mike. I mean—your father—"

"Don't worry. I can take care of the old man." He put his hand out to touch hers and then he let it drop on the wet table top. He picked up a pretzel, broke it and then broke another. The pretzels were the world, its convolutions, and elements, and he broke it all strongly between his fingers. "Another drink, Will?"

"No. It tastes raw."

God, he thought, she's beautiful, all right, and I've never seen anyone like her, and he thought of her there sitting in the open windows facing the dirty street, sleeping through the afternoons, walking into town and everyone knowing it—all the bright, pretty girls together. And now she had to tell it to him word for word, and she knew it would make a difference. People said when you were young and loved someone, nothing made a difference, but for now when you

The Long Year

had to exist in this one moment, it made a hell of a difference, all right.

"Let's get out of here," he said gruffly.

"Right now," she said, "right now."

He could remember every moment of it now, putting the money on the table, going out into the dark alley and getting into his car. He had thought at the time how poor the Connaughts were and how terrible it was the bondage people were in, bound to his father for a measly little dry-cleaning shop. She had had enough guts to get out, and she had done the best she could—she might have done a lot worse, taken people blind in some sucker racket. With her looks, she could cheat you and get away with it—only it was hard to take.

And he remembered driving in silence down Chestnut Street and up the hills past her house to the place on the cliffs above the river. She said nothing. He stopped the car in the elm grove and put his arms around her and kissed her. Then they got out of the car and waded in the long, wet grasses. On the opposite side of the river, the land was bright under the moon. He could never remember having a feeling like this, confused, neither big nor small, light nor dark, fierce joy nor deep sadness. He stood with his arms around her and she leaned away from him against the tree.

"Do you believe there was a Mary Magdalene?" she asked.

"Guess so."

"But do you believe it, Mike?"

"Yes. And I don't believe anyone will ever harm you, Will. You're swell—you've been wonderful to the kids—Phil and Mary and Joe and all of them. They won't forget it."

"Yes, they will," she said.

He began to kiss her as if he could not stop. "You belong to me, Will," he said. "Not to anyone else."

"Yes. Yes." Her voice was excited. "I belong to you, Mike."

Maybe she believed it then, maybe she really believed it because she *wanted* to believe it. But always after that, he knew it was because of his father that Wilma left without saying anything. Some days, he thought she might come back to the town. But now, today, he knew it was as if she had died far away from home. Maybe the old man had meant to do him some good, but saying it out like that hadn't helped.

He was better off where he was, not making it harder for the old boy, not making Marth unhappy. Still and all, he missed the old house and the old ways, only he was so goddam bitter inside. He never could feel young the way Rocky Macbeth did. He wondered if Marth felt young, probably she did, young and happy. He hoped she'd grow up, though, and not turn into one of those slick-chick college girls he had once known, maybe grow up and be something for Rock. That was what Rock wanted—to have Marth fight and stay in the town with his old friends, Joe and Mr. Wimmer and himself, Mike.

He took out the ring again and blew on it. It felt small and heavy in his hand. He had taken the back way up the hill, coming in behind the garage. He saw Howard come out of the kitchen and empty the garbage, sniffing as he did it. He whistled softly, and Howard looked up. God, Mike thought, Howard's getting old.

"What you doin' here?" Howard asked, looking over his shoulder at the house. "Now, you don't wanna spoil tonight fer Marth. You know how that girl's been—"

"I brought her a present," he said. He opened his hand and showed him the ring. "See?"

"A-aeeh," Howard said. "That's real pretty now."

"The old man in?"

Howard's face became stern. "Your Paw's upstairs gettin' dressed. He's mighty proud of her graduatin' tonight, so don't you go around—"

"I want to see her, that's all," he said. He went into the house, Howard following him. Ophelia, complaining of her aching back, touched his shoulder affectionately.

"Got some fine apple fritters," she said. "You oughtta try some."

The Long Year 23

"Listen, 'Phelia," he said, "you have some ready for me. On my way out I'll pick them up."

He went into the living room and waited. When he heard Marth coming down the stairs, he stood up and pushed his hand lightly over the stiff, short bristles of his hair. She came down wearing a white housecoat which she held up as she moved. " 'Phelia!" she called, "I can't get the zipper in my slip to go—" She broke off when she saw Mike and then smiled.

"Mike," she said. "I didn't think you'd come."

"No," he said. "I brought you something." He handed her the ring and watched her, smiling, when she tried it on and held it to the light. "It's Navajo," he said.

"Oh, Mike, wherever did you get it? It's wonderful."

"I got it—around," he said. He supposed he ought to say something to her when she was graduating. He remembered how the old man had given him a gold pencil and pen set and a waterproof watch the night he'd graduated, and he'd taken the new car and stayed out all night as a treat. Well, if he had anything to say to her it was that bourgeois America stank, full of grabbiness, always wanting to own and to grab from someone—and maybe to say there was no hope for anyone. Instead, he went over to her and kissed her cheek and said, "Have a good time, Kid."

She held on to his arm. "Stay a while. Daddy wants to see you."

"Got something to do," he said. "You and Rock going out tonight?"

She nodded. "Joe and Barby, too. Why don't you come with us, Mike? Everyone always wants you to come, but you never—"

"No, Kid," he said. He looked around the room again. They hadn't changed it since ten years ago when his mother had died. "Kay coming?"

"Next week," she said.

Then, as he turned, he heard his father close his bedroom door and come down the stairs. He stood in the living room with his hands in his pockets.

"Hello, Paw," he said.

"Hello, Mike," Hoyt said. Marth went over and stood with one arm around him and showed him the ring.

"From Mike," she said. "Isn't it a beauty?"

"Fine," he said. His eyes narrowed, but when he looked at Mike, Mike looked back at him, almost laughing. "You coming to the school, Michael?"

"No," Mike said. "I just came up to bring Marth the ring."

"Everything all right?" Hoyt cleared his throat.

"Fine, Paw."

"Need anything?"

Mike shrugged. "Well, I can use ten-twenty—anything you have on hand."

Hoyt took out his billfold and handed him twenty dollars. Mike did not look at it. He put it carelessly in the small watch pocket in his levis. "Well, guess I'd better go," he said.

"Your aunt's coming next week, Michael," Hoyt said. He wanted to make it clear that this once things ought to be forgotten, whatever it was Mike was always remembering.

"So I hear," Mike said.

"She'll probably want to see you," Hoyt said.

"She knows where I live—anyone can tell her," Mike said. He opened the french doors and closed them quietly, hearing Marth's voice. She was standing close to the old man and saying something to him earnestly. He stopped for a moment, and he heard her voice saying, "He didn't steal it, Daddy. I know he didn't steal it."

He grinned and went to the kitchen door. Ophelia handed him a bag of food. Twice a week, she sent Howard down to the wharf with food for him. He always took anything he could get.

"Thanks, 'Phelia," he said.

"You come round any time, Mike," she said. "Any time you need anythin' you come round here."

"Sure," he said. He held the bundle tightly to him, and then he felt like he was going to cry. He went out and sat in the alley behind the garage. It was a place he always sat when he was a kid and things hadn't been going his way. The thing was that he always messed it up every time he came near the place. Now, the kid would think he was a heel, and the old man would feel hurt all over again. He liked to stir the old man up, but he always felt terrible afterwards. His eyes smarted with tears. "Goddam," he said. "I always make a mess of it."

CHAPTER FOUR:

IN LATER years there were larger graduating classes, but at that time one hundred and forty-four was the largest class in the history of the school, and they made much of it. The class itself had not been exceptional in any way unless you could say Joe Connaught marked that group. He was ahead of his time, already knowing what the rest of them did not suspect. He was confused and afraid, afraid that he would never get a job and have a life such as the men in the town had always had, and he often cried at night, when no one knew it. Most of them in that class believed they would follow the same pattern their people had followed, but Joe was not sure of that.

At seven-thirty, Marth went to the cafeteria to stand in line with the others. Her father drove her down the hill to the school, and on the way they picked up Mr. Wimmer who lived at the hotel on Chestnut Street. He taught economics and sociology, a very intense young man but not without humor. Everyone was already in the cafeteria except Joe and Barby. Joanie Peterson, the valedictorian, stood at the head of the line, twisting her notes and whispering parts of her speech.

"Seen Joe or Barby?" Marth asked.

"No," Joanie said. "Maybe they won't even get here."

"Yes, they will," she said.

"Your aunt coming soon?"

"Next week."

"Oh," Joanie said. "My Dad thought she'd be here this week."

"No," Marth said. "I wish Joe'd come." Then she was sorry she had said that. Everyone knew about Joe and Barby. Some people had to laugh about it and talked about it in an ugly, common way.

The cafeteria was cold and damp and smelled faintly of peanut

The Long Year

butter, leather and orange peelings. Even though it was warm outside it was cool in there, and the class shivered a little and kept talking in low, solemn voices. Mr. Wimmer stood by the doors smiling a little. He had been in the town eight years now, and he liked everything about his work. When he looked at them standing there with their skinny shoulders and their eyes like the eyes of slightly naughty-minded children, he felt inside himself a slow turning of despair. In all ways possible he had tried to prepare these students, and he felt it was no use. He put his hands behind his back.

Marth thought he looked handsome standing that way. She was used to his eccentric ways, slipping in and out of the school, playing his sad Western music as he sat in his room in the hotel.

The class shuffled. Joe and Barby came in and took their places. The Peterson girl looked at them and then began to read her notes. There were more girls than boys in the class. Barby said the world was like that—always more girls than boys. The girls wore white dresses except for Barby. She wore a red dress from Marshall Fields', and her slippers were red with cut steel buckles that caught the light. Mr. Wimmer walked between the two lines. He told a boy to straighten his tie. Joe Connaught had been drinking.

"Joe?" he said.

"Well?"

Marth shivered. She knew that Joe had begun to drink in the late morning, she had seen him squatting down just inside his locker. His locker was the first one from the door in the boys' locker room. He often hunched over a little and drank fast from a bottle. He was older than the rest, and his life had been mean. It was there in his face. When he was happy, he laughed too loudly, feverishly, as if he sought to hold on to it. Other times, he would not look at anyone and walked with a chip on his shoulder.

"Joe," Mr. Wimmer said, "take a good drink of water, a big one. And wash your face."

"Okay," Joe said. He went out into the hall, and when he returned, his thick black hair was wet in front.

"Comb it, Joe," Mr. Wimmer said.

He looked hard at Mr. Wimmer. Barby handed him her comb, but he pretended not to see it and took one from his own pocket and combed his hair. Barby watched this. Marth wanted to yell something. Joe combed his hair slowly, one stroke and then another, and Barby did not breathe in that time.

"Okay, Mr. Wimmer?"

"Okay, Joe," Mr. Wimmer said.

Through the open doors, Marth could see the people coming in slowly, moving in a soft, dreamy murmur, bringing in the summer night. The class straightened its lines.

"All right, now," Mr. Wimmer said. "Try to remember to have some order and dignity. You'll never be students here again. Make it right."

Barby looked at her red sandals and then at Marth. There was a long heavy silence, and then the salutatorian and valedictorian stepped out into the warm, yellowish air in the hall. Outside the auditorium there were two doors, and the girls went in the left door. Marth began to feel everything move again . . . in the beginning, she thought because now her real life was beginning, in the beginning of everything . . .

Inside the auditorium there was the same low, golden light and the feeling of excitement and all the faces turned as one face toward the doors. Marth saw Rocky leaning against the wall. He wore a white shirt and white flannels and he looked at her and smiled.

She wished Mike could be there with Rock—she always thought of her brother being alone, leaning against a tree or sitting on the stone steps of the courthouse tossing pebbles at the war monument and singing dirty songs about it, lying on the docks outside his boathouse.

Now, she walked to the bright, martial music that had no meaning in the room filled with summer night, the women in their summer dresses, the men brown and clean in their summer whites. Barby went up the steps with a worldly, disdainful air, her red dress and her black hair, and there was a slight hum through the crowd. She knew this and liked it. Marth could see her father sitting in the front

The Long Year

row with the rest of the school board. He was too big for the seat and kept trying to sit at an angle, and when this did not work he stuck his legs out straight in front of him and sat at a stiff incline. He was the only man in the room who wore an all-white summer suit.

The speeches were boring, not at all the way she had hoped they'd be. It was just another long moment you had to live through and then be done with, and she could see now that she had been crazy to expect anything. Mike was always trying to tell her this, call a spade a spade he always said. The principal, a beetle-browed, unimaginative man said what he had said every year—that the parents should be proud of such fine children. All the parents liked this part of it, except Joe Connaught's father, King. He shuffled and got red in the face, and Joe's mother, Fran, wept silently into a worn white handkerchief, for they were people of little joy and mammoth grief.

At that moment, Barby's mother came down the aisle. Marth saw Rocky turn his head and then her father turned, too, watching Barby's mother come all the way to the front to sit with the school board. There was the light, quick sound of Barby's mother's heels and the moving of feet as people turned to look at her. She was a small, light woman in a thin green dress with a large white hat trimmed with green flowers that bobbed as she moved. The class on the stage looked at her solemnly and with interest. She settled into her seat and waved at Barby. Barby smiled. Then she waved at Marth. Marth smiled. Then she looked around the auditorium and smiled while she took off her gloves and laid them on her bag. Everyone nodded to her. It was a little, artless ceremony and to be expected of Barby's mother, who was a very rich woman and had not been born in that town. Marth saw her father reach over and pick up one of her gloves. Barby's mother smiled and patted his arm.

The priest got up and said a short prayer about making the days rich as fields of wheat, dedicated to Christ. No one listened. Everyone was thinking of how his feet felt in his best shoes, how much each dress had cost, how long the speeches would last. Only Joe Connaught thought of Christ and His ways. Christ and Gethsemane.

30 The Long Year

Christ was every man at Bull Run and the Marne and every man, sack and barrel of them at Tippecanoe; Christ and John Paul Jones; Christ and Calvin Coolidge—that was a bone to pick on, Christ and Coolidge.

Joanie Peterson's voice was soft and sweet, like the voice of a child praying. She talked about the world this class would make. "We will make a better world," she said. They were saying that all over the country, deep into the South and across the whole land from the edge of the water until the edges of the opposing waters. Joe Connaught leaned forward. Joanie said this class would discover important facts about cancer, the common cold, arthritis. "We will fly to Spain for tea and eat dinner in Shanghai. This is the age of progress, and we are a part of this age."

She was a big blonde girl with glasses. Often in the evenings she went up to the hotel and sat on the porch with Mr. Wimmer. Once she went out with Joe Connaught. She said Joe talked about politics and religion. When she finished speaking, her father, a big, red-faced man named Russian Peterson, clapped very loudly, and she looked at him and smiled.

After that, there was the school song, and they all marched out and stood in the hall. Marth waited for her father. He put his arm around her and kissed her, and she held on to him for a minute, wishing Mike was there. She knew he missed Mike more than he would ever miss her. Everyone stood in little groups on the stairs and in the upper hall, and they kissed and talked about their clothes. Everyone was happy. It was like a big party and much better than the long, worthless ceremony.

"Going out?" Hoyt asked. He was watching Barby's mother moving toward him through the crowd.

"We're all going out."

"Fine."

"I wish Aunt Kay could have come earlier to see this."

"Sure. That would have been fine."

"Daddy?"

"What is it, honey?"

The Long Year

"I'm awfully happy. I feel wonderful."

"You just stay like that," he said.

Barby came with her mother.

"Marth," Mrs. Leroy said, kissing Marth's cheek, a light quick kiss smelling sweetly and expensively of Paris perfume. "Such a dear girl, really—and I tell Barby, you must have a good time tonight to celebrate . . ."

Marth looked at her father. He was smiling at Mrs. Leroy. His coat was white and cool-looking in the dim hall light, and when he stood beside her, she looked even smaller.

"Oh, dear," Mrs. Leroy said, "I hate to have them grow up."

"It happens, Maida," he said.

"Oh, dear, I just hate it . . ."

Barby was not listening to them. She was looking for Joe, and then Joe and Rocky came through the crowd. Everyone wanted to talk to Rock because he had won the district championship for amateur fighters. He had gone to the city to do this. Marth watched him. She never thought of him as a fighter, and she had never seen him in one of the big matches. She thought of him as a boy who came from her town and liked to fight. His hair was light brown, cut very short, and he had an awkward way of moving so that it was difficult to believe he could be so light and quick. He hated to wear suits. He liked to wear trunks and run up and down the hard-packed beaches in the morning.

"Hi, Marth," he said.

"Hi," she said.

"You look like queens," Joe said. "The Red Queen. The White Queen."

Barby laughed and squeezed his arm. Everything was all right now. They walked outside together, and Joe went down the street to get his car, driving up the curb with a quick, daring swish that made the tires whine against the curbstone. It had rained and the streets were still wet, and there were little long seedlings, like caterpillars, lying all around. The air was clean and cool. Marth sat in the back seat with Rock, and Barby sat in the front seat very close to

Joe, forgetting her anger over their quarrel. They were all right so long as they didn't talk or try to make plans. When they fought, Barby always sat quietly and let Joe say anything that came into his head. Her black hair hung heavy against the cracked leather seat. All around them the cars moved out from the curbs and headed toward the city. Joe put his arm around Barby and drew her to him.

Marth buttoned her white flannel coat. The buttons were smooth, made of frosted glass, and they slipped under her fingers. She looked at Rocky. "How was the fight?"

"Okay."

"I've never seen a big one."

"It's the same as a small one."

He did not care to talk, but he always listened, and all sorts of emotions would cross his face. You had to look close to see that. He had a kind of devilish look that was mostly because of wearing his hair so short and then also because he was old Macbeth's son. Macbeth was a dry old man who had retired from the railroad and bought a clothing store on Chestnut Street. He loved fighting more than anything else in the world and taught Rocky all he knew. "Think of Corbett," he'd say when Rocky was warming up at the bag. Rocky had a certain deadly quality when he was fighting in earnest. Other times, when he was doing it around Macbeth's store, it was all in fun and just to be doing it to amuse the old man.

"I want to go sometime," she said. "I want to see a big fight."

"Okay," he said. "Say, Joe, did you listen to that speech tonight?"

"Too damned many speeches," Joe said.

"What Joanie Peterson said, I mean."

"She was awfully good," Barby said. She moved a little away from Joe. He was driving very fast now, past the dim filling station and up the hill that blotted out the view of the town. Now, there was only darkness and pastures and the steady drivel of the tires on the dark, wet pavement.

"I was outside. I heard it through the window," Rock said.

"Geez," Joe said—"the world we make. She had a nerve to get up and talk like that."

The Long Year 33

"Neat, though," Rocky said. He settled back and put his arm up over the seat, and Marth leaned against him, smiling. She thought: Now, I've graduated from high school and tomorrow Aunt Kay comes home.

"Yeah," Joe said. "Words are sure hot air." The car jerked forward until the back door swung off with a loud clatter as it skittled over the pavement.

"You lost the door," Barby said.

"Hell," Joe said.

"Joe, you lost the door."

"I know it."

"Listen, stop the car and we'll get out and pick it up."

"To hell with the door," he said.

Inside the ball room that was made to look like a garden, it was cool and green. Everyone was young there, even the older ones looked younger in that kind of light, younger and fairer, and stronger. Everything there was for pleasure, easy to have and to hold. The band played for Rocky when he came in. Everyone clapped and whistled. He stood with his feet a little apart, smiling. There was a crowd of college kids at the cold-drink stand. One of these crossed the room to get Rocky's autograph on his shirt collar.

"You sure got a punch, Rock," he said with affection.

"Thanks," Rocky said. He wrote his name slowly, flushing because it seemed stupid to him.

"Come to our table, boy."

"No, thanks," Rocky said.

"Aw, Rock," the boy said. He wore an expensive cream-colored jacket, and his hair was carefully rumpled. When he smiled, his eyes looked old and dead. "C'mon, fellah."

"Thanks, anyhow," Rocky said. He began to dance with Marth. She had always danced with him, the days in dancing school above Gramenz' beer hall, the days at the school parties. They played something of Hoagy Carmichael's, and while they played it, the lights melted down until there was only this one long purple shadow over the room. She wondered what he was thinking and why he never told her anything he thought. In the town, people were crazy about him, and many of the men lived more deeply through him and more savagely than they did in their own time. He was used to the way they felt his hands and looked at him carefully and called him big names and talked in a dreamy, gentle way about him.

Joe had a bottle inside his coat. After five or six drinks, he sat at the table and watched Barby dancing with the boy in the cream-colored jacket. He moved his lips in a murmur, as a man in pain, and he was in great pain. He couldn't tell anyone about it. His hands lay hard, tanned, open on the top of the table. When Rocky saw him sitting there alone, he said, "We ought to go back to Joe."

Marth looked at him. The blue shadow around Joe's jaw was coming back. "All right," she said. "Only I wish he and Barby would act like everyone else when they go out. They always fight."

Someone laughed very loud. Two men at the far end of the room got up and danced together. Barby was dancing with the boy in the sport jacket. "I got a belly ache," Joe said. In the low light, his eyes had a brassiness to them. "I got a hell of a belly ache, full up."

"You shouldn't drink like that," Marth said. "That awful stuff." She could not understand him, but all the Connaughts were the same, and everyone said Barby would be in a mess some day. But Barby couldn't help it because she was already into it up to her ears, and that was the worst part of being a young girl and loving someone like Joe. Nobody could help you get out of it.

"I'm not dumb," Joe said. "I got brains, and I know what I want to do. All I want to do is get a job. Last summer no job, this summer no job—maybe no job this winter, maybe no job so long as I live. I mean no good job, just emptying slops or worse."

"Aunt Kay's coming home," Marth said. "Daddy says when she comes, they'll both figure out something."

"They'll close the factory," Joe said. "You'll see."

"Who cares?" Rocky asked. "It can't last forever."

"I care," Joe said. He looked across the room where the college boys' fraternity sat at a long, noisy table blowing little red and yellow

The Long Year

horns. One of the girls wore a white satin dress. She glittered in it. Now the boy and Barby had their arms around each other, and Barby kept turning to look at Joe. Joe's eyes narrowed. The Japanese lanterns had a slow, dull light and the music moved dully through the dark room. Joe wore an old blue serge suit. He was hot.

"Yeah—" he said, "I care. But some day I'm not gonna care."

"I'll get Barby," Rocky said. He brought her back to the table, and she looked at Joe and sat down.

"You spoil everything," she said.

"Sure, sure."

"Oh, Joe," she said.

Marth could not look at either of them. It was too raw and no one should see it there on their faces. She felt tired and dirty, and when she looked at Rocky he took her hand and held it.

"I'm sorry, Barbs," Joe said. "Let's get out of here—let's go to Wildwood. I'm always so damned nasty to you. Be nice to me, Barbs. Just be nice to me."

"Oh, Joe," she said.

After that they drove toward the lake, and on the way home they stopped at Wildwood and rode the Ferris wheel. Rocky and Marth were caught at the top, and they could see all the bright ground spread beneath them, and the people's voices sounded like a faint, sweet music.

"I like the summer," Rocky said. "I like to play tennis and just have a good time with you, Marth."

"I know," she said.

"It's not any different, is it?"

"No," she said.

"I mean, I'm not much and I guess you could have just about anyone you wanted, so I wouldn't blame you if—"

"I don't want it to change," she said. He always seemed a little bit cocky to her, but now she could see he was unhappy. "It's just Joe—he always gets me when he acts like this. He blames Daddy for everything—"

"I guess he's got to blame someone."

"Mr. Wimmer says this is a bad time, and it's everywhere, and we don't need to think it's going to skip us. Daddy's always done everything for the factory—that's his whole life now that Mike's never home."

"I know," he said. "Look, Marth."

"Yes," she said. She held his hand and moved her fingers in his.

He looked at her speechless. He wanted to tell her something, but he was not sure exactly what it was. It was stupid to try to say anything in words because no one ever understood what he meant to say. He hated the feeling that she and everyone else was a stranger, one stranger after another in a line from the time he was born until the day he died. "Look—" he said, perplexed, and she smiled at him, waiting. Then he began to kiss her soft, smooth mouth. He kissed her with quick, breathless kisses, and when the Ferris wheel stopped for them, he was still kissing her. She had never kissed him back like this, and it made him feel that she knew how much he needed her. Then he heard the man who operated the machine. The man was laughing a great, hoggish laugh. He drew away from Marth. She was not angry or ashamed, but he was ashamed. Not for himself to be caught like this but for that big, hoggish man and his big, hoggish laughter. Everything was spoiled by people like that. They never knew the truth about anything. His eyes burned with tears. He wanted to hit the man in his red face. A few people were standing around. Some of them smiled gently at him. He looked away from the man and saw the gentleness on their faces. He took Marth's hand, and they ran among the people, losing themselves in the crowd, running from the man and his thick laughter.

The night thinned to gray, and the lights of the car were dim in the grayness. Rocky fell asleep, and after a while Marth moved closer to him and slept, too. When she woke, the car had stopped in the drive outside her own house. The house looked big, white, fragile with its front tower and the intricate latticework around the porch. She had never been out this late, and it seemed stupid to be sitting in Joe's car in the thin gray light. Rocky's suit was rumpled. She tried to smooth the jacket for him.

The Long Year

" 'Night, Barby—Joe," she said.

They looked at her as if she were a stranger. "Oh—night," they said.

"See you tomorrow?" Rocky said.

"Sure," she said. She went upstairs, knelt by the window and saw him walking down the sidewalk toward Chestnut Street. He lived with his father in old rooms above the store. She often went up there on Saturdays and read the funnies and played checkers with Macbeth or Rock. "I love him," she said softly. "I really think I'm in love with him." She rubbed her hand against her cheek. When she turned on her lamp, she looked at the picture of her aunt. "Yes," she said, "I think I love him, and it's going to be all right, not the way it is with Barby—or like Mike and Wilma. It's going to be wonderful." Her aunt seemed to look back at her with a wide, knowing look. She smiled and turned off the light and lay fully dressed across her bed, kicking off her left sandal and swinging her leg back and forth.

CHAPTER FIVE:

HOWARD, the Negro, had worked in the house with his fat wife, 'Phelia, for almost nine years. Every morning at six o'clock, he came in from his place above the garage that had once been a carriage house. Every morning at the same time, he came softly into the kitchen, luring his niece, the wicked Teresita, luring her with murmured threats. "Sling you over the head with a hatchet, you wicked, sleepin girl," he'd say. And Teresita, giggling and sleepy and lazy, would come slowly, shivering in the early morning air, desiring the warmth of her forsaken bed. She liked gay places, high living, parties and sleek uniforms, and there was nothing in town to satisfy these desires. Howard worried over her, remembering all her former scrapes. "You an God are far apart," he'd say. "I worry about that."

"I don't see why 'Phelia can't get up and put on the coffee herself."

"Her feet hurt. Her back hurts," he said.

"I know it," she said, "but so does my feet hurt, an my back's fair ready to bust."

"Hush, now," he said. He had no age to him—just a little, skinny black man with hair turning gray, and when he did anything he loved doing it. This morning, he went out and took the paper out of its rack and read the headlines and the funnies, standing in the lower hall. Then he put it on the dining room table, carefully folded. He went to the kitchen and wiped off the plates with a warm towel and set the table. Teresita stood dreaming over the coffee. Howard gave her a poke. "You better git a move on you. Mrs. Leroy's been reprimandin' me because yer always late. You start out from here soon enough, but yer always late."

"I'm not gonna run myself to death," she said.

"You don't try to better yourself at all," he sighed.

The Long Year

"Hunh—you wait till this woman comes, this Kay, an' you'll be too tired out yerself to tell me what to do. She's gonna work you to death. You never had a woman here to work fer, doin' as you please all the time—you just wait."

"Hunh yerself," he said. "I do my work fine, woman or no woman."

"I hear tell she's a wicked one," she said, laughing.

"You hold yer tongue," he said. He went up the back stairs and knocked on the door of the big front bedroom.

"Seven-thirty, Mr. Hasswell," he said.

"I know, I know."

Howard frowned. He liked to be appreciated, and no one appreciated him in the morning. "I'm just tellin' you, that's all," he muttered and went down the back stairs.

"Maybe she'll come today," Teresita said.

"Who?"

"Miss Kay Hasswell."

"That's not her name. She's a married lady."

Teresita laughed. "She's been married three times, an' she calls herself Miss. Everyone says so."

"Get a move on you and tell 'Phelia she better get up just in case and maybe put on something looks like a uniform. And don't be late at Mrs. Leroy's. She thinks I don't send you off in time."

"I'm no good," Teresita giggled. She ran across the back lawn. He sat down on the kitchen stool, staring at the coffee bubbling in the glass percolator. Upstairs, he could hear the heavy sounds of Mr. Hasswell walking in his bedroom. He rubbed his hands together and stood very straight looking at himself in the bright lid of the stove. He could see himself plainly. He pulled his body stiff and saluted himself gravely in the manner of a musical comedy soldier, bowing a little from the waist. "Yes, my capitan," he said soberly and began to take out the frypans for bacon and eggs.

Hoyt came down the stairs and sat at the head of the table looking out across the lawn, toward the factory. He hated eating breakfast alone, but now since Mike had left the house, he had been eating alone every morning. He left the house before Marth was awake, but sometimes when she got up merely to have breakfast with him, he felt entirely happy. He wondered if Kay had changed—in the old days, she was always the first one up. He supposed she was used to having breakfast in bed now. He frowned—it was difficult to remember anything about her because she had always been changeable, whatever kind of person she wanted to be for that moment. His wife had disliked Kay. He himself had never really liked her or felt at ease with her.

"Any calls?" he asked Howard.

Howard poured the coffee. "No, sir," he said. "Expect Miss Kay today?"

"I've been expecting her for a week," he said. It was like her not to give a definite time of arrival. She never understood how things like that kept people on edge, gave them nothing definite to cling to.

"Front bedroom's all cleaned and fixed," Howard said. "We put them fancy bath salts and things in that bathroom for her."

"Fine," he said. "I expect she won't find many things changed."

"She never saw Marth, did she?"

"No," he said. He smiled. "You know, Howard, Marth's a lot like her—she looks like her and every once in a while she does something that reminds me of my sister."

"That so, Mr. Hasswell?"

Hoyt sighed. He remembered that day when Simon O'Dodd died and his wife stood in the middle of the living room and Kay sat on the low stool by the fireplace. She wore a candy-striped dress, and she sat with her hands in her lap, smiling and not saying anything, but he had the feeling there was something dreadfully wrong with her. His wife used to say that, "She's plotting against everyone. She knows too much, and she's not human." And that day his wife and his sister stared at each other in hate and anger. His wife said that Kay did it with her high-handed ways. "Nothing in this town's good enough for her," his wife said. His wife had been small and blonde, and when she got angry her skin reddened, and her voice became

The Long Year 41

high and very shrill. Kay sat there smiling, and he looked first at his wife and then at Kay and he knew that, of the two, his tie with Kay was the stronger, although not at all pleasant. It had something to do with all the days when he was growing up and everyone kept telling him to take care of her. His mother had been the one to say that: "Take care of her and try to keep her believing in God." And Kay had never believed in God. She had Mamma to believe in and that was enough. And that one day, that day Simon O'Dodd crashed the old plane up on Monson's Ridge, his sister had laughed over it, saying she had nothing to do with it. Had she ever said she'd marry Simon, that Irishman. Had she ever said she'd marry anyone? She had looked at his wife—he could hear her voice, soft now, and she herself looking like a child, her soft voice saying, "Don't worry, Amy. I may never marry anyone and live here forever and take my share of the factory without working for it. Who knows about the factory? Not Hoyt. I'm the one learned it from Mamma. Hoyt needs apron strings—not yours—*Mamma's* apron strings, *my* apron strings."

He never forgot it, hearing it put that way. And later he had blamed himself when she divorced Sonny. "I shouldn't have let her marry him," he had said, but his wife had laughed. "She does what she pleases to do." Maybe that was true. He wanted Kay to come home because everything was in a terrible mess and he needed someone who knew the business, someone to take part of the responsibility, he needed a woman in his house, maybe she'd do something about Mike, maybe she'd help him with Marth when Marth needed it. He didn't have her cleverness at getting inside people.

Howard came in with the eggs. He sat down by the kitchen door and waited. He always did this, just to be in the room so that Hoyt could talk to him if he wanted to. While he was sitting like that, he saw the big red Packard swing up the drive. The woman wore a printed scarf and a blue linen coat. She got out of the car and took off the scarf and shook her head. She looked young and ambitious. "Oh-oh," he said softly. He did not like ambitious women—he liked them lazy and full of humor and stuffed into corsets. He buttoned his jacket. Ain't a decent hour to come home after twenny years, he muttered. Just like she'd been down to the corner store for a loaf of bread. He saw her stoop and pull at the lawn spray, and then he heard her turn it on.

"She's here," he said.

Hoyt raised his head. "What?" He saw the car in the drive and got up and opened the door. When he looked at her he forgot anything he had ever thought about her. He went out on the porch and opened his arms and tears came to his eyes. "Kay—Kay," he said.

She ran lightly up the porch steps, laughing a little and pushing the fine, loose hair out of her eyes. "Look at you," she said softly, going into his arms. He was heavier than she had remembered him, and his face seemed to her weaker, and she thought: The poor old boy's forgotten everything. He's going to cry.

He looked at her, holding her wrists. "Welcome home, Kay," he said. "Twenty years."

She moved into the house, looking around her, slipping out of her coat. Howard took it, smiling.

"This is Howard," Hoyt said.

"Hello, Howard," she said softly. The house hadn't changed, not even the living room.

"You see," Hoyt said. "Nothing's changed."

She smiled. The room was very ugly, uglier than she had remembered it, ugly and cluttered.

"Twenty years," he said again. "And you look the same."

"No," she said. She touched the gray streak in her hair.

"I like that," he said.

"I don't. I hate it. And I'm too thin. New York always makes me get thin. And besides, no one's ever the same. Oh, I always thought of seeing Mamma here—I thought if I walked in it would be like seeing Mamma again."

"I know," he said. This moved him, and he blew his nose violently. She wasn't so terrible, after all, remembering Mamma that way.

"Go up and wake Marth," he said to Howard.

The Long Year

"I'm starved," Kay said. She tossed her scarf on the hall table and went into the dining room and sat at the foot of the table. "Pour me some coffee, darling."

He smiled and called to 'Phelia and 'Phelia brought in a cup and plate and the silver and set another place for Marth. Kay sat in silence watching her.

"This is 'Phelia," Hoyt said. "She's a wonderful cook."

"Hello, 'Phelia," she said. "I hope you can cook French things. I love French pastries and no one but the French can make soup."

"I cook Southern style," 'Phelia said and went back into the kitchen.

Hoyt laughed. "You've lost your touch," he said.

She smiled at him. "Look at you," she said again. "Honestly, I've thought so often of coming back here and meeting your kids. I suppose they're the only ones on earth, very polite like you, very soft-spoken the way Mamma'd like them to be."

"Why—no," he said. "I don't think they're like me at all."

"Tell me," she said. "Is it bad down at the factory?"

"Oh—no, not so bad. I guess the times are bad everywhere, and this can't go on forever."

"Oh—really," she said, and then she changed her mind about talking about it so soon. "I suppose we ought to say all the things people say when they haven't seen each other for a long time—about the places they've been, things that have happened?"

"Just to have you here is enough," he said. "You look so fine, Kay. I always knew you'd look like this. And you've been happy, haven't you?"

"Sometimes," she said. "Have you?"

"Most of the time," he said.

"I do so want to see the kids. I've never seen Marth."

"Well—Mike's not here, but Marth's getting dressed. School just let out and she's been catching up on sleep."

"Let me go up," she said. "Let me go up and see her alone. I do so want to see my old room."

"She has that now," he said.

"May I go up, darling?"

"Why, of course," he said. He was pleased with her enthusiasm. He wished Mike could be here, could forget all that mess about Wilma. Mike was a good-looking, smart boy—she'd like Mike. Maybe later on, when he told her about Mike, she'd help him.

She ran up the stairs, and he could hear her in the hall. She stood for a moment by herself wondering that this house was where she was born and had once lived—it smelled the way she imagined it always smelled, of paint, house dust and summer morning. When she stopped at the door of her old room, she stood for a moment and ran her hand over the wood panel, smiling. Who said a person could never go back? She remembered standing here that last day holding Sonny's roses and listening to the dead silence between Hoyt and his wife, after she had told them she was going to run away with Sonny that very day. Who said a person should never go back?

She tapped lightly on the door.

"Come in," Marth said. She was sitting on the edge of the bed pulling on her stockings. Young girl pulling on her stockings, blue dress, the soft babyish look of the dark hair that curled slightly at the ends—Kay thought, It's myself as I was then, exactly as I was.

"Listen, Teresita—" Marth began, without looking up.

"Hello, Marth," Kay said. She stood with one hand on the door.

Marth looked up, her eyes going wide. "Yes," she said. She stood up, and one stocking fell around her ankle. "Aunt Kay," she said.

Kay put out her hand. "Come here," she said. She took the girl's hand, holding it warmly and then she put her arm around her and sat down on the bed. "How pretty you are, darling," she said.

Marth smiled. "I'm so glad you decided to come," she said. "Daddy's glad, too."

"Yes—of course," Kay said. She was looking at the room. She had forgotten that anyone could be so young as this girl, and for a moment everything about the girl and the room hurt her. "This was my room. I had the bed exactly as it is now."

"Yes," Marth said. "That's why—we have it here, too."

"And some of these books are mine."

The Long Year 45

"Yes," Marth said.

"Look at us," she said. "See how we are in the mirror."

"I know," Marth said. She saw how their hair grew in the same way and it both shocked and delighted her to know that she looked like someone else. "I used to want to be like you," she said.

"You did—you really did that?"

"Oh, yes," Marth said. "I always thought of you here in this room and then everyone talked to me about you. I felt like I knew you."

"That's good," she said. She took out her lipstick and ran it quickly, expertly over her mouth without looking in the mirror. "Do hurry, darling. I'm starved, and there's so much to do. I want to do a million things."

Marth laughed and pulled on her stocking.

Kay smiled. The kid was just a baby, a big, awkward baby with no sense and a big heart she wore on her sleeve for everyone to see. She'd have to get over that and learn a few things about clothes and how to wear that lovely hair.

"Kay! Marth!" Hoyt came halfway up the stairs, and they went out into the hall, their arms around each other. When he saw them standing like that, he felt suddenly happy. "Come on and have breakfast," he said.

"You see," Kay said. "Marth and I are friends already." She touched the girl's cheek lightly. Everything was going to work out all right. "When will I see Mike?" She sat at the table and began at once to eat her bacon.

"Oh, Mike stays at his docks," Marth said. "He has a boat business."

"I thought he was with you, Hoyt."

Hoyt put down his fork. "Mike's a fine boy," he said. "He's young, that's all, and he has an idea that he wants to work there. I'm hoping—Kay, you have a way with people—and—I thought—"

"Oh-ho," she laughed. "He's a handful."

"Mike's a fine, bright boy," he said. He frowned.

Marth sat watching her aunt eat. She ate quickly, neatly, with apparent relish. Whenever their eyes met, she smiled, and when she smiled she looked very beautiful, like someone who was used to being beautiful and so never thought about it.

"I want to change," she said. "And then I want to go down to the factory. Do you work down there, Marth?"

"No," Marth said. "Usually I play tennis with Rocky."

"Rocky's Macbeth's boy," Hoyt said.

"I'll bet he's a number," Kay said. "I thought Macbeth was dead."

"No," Hoyt said. "He married that year when—when you left, and then he had this boy right off."

"Old Macbeth," she said.

"Rocky's a fighter," Marth said. She leaned forward. "He's a very well known fighter."

"I see," she said. She looked at Marth. She saw a lot of things—Myself and Simon O'Dodd, she thought, and she'll have to get over it, get away from here, the poor baby.

"Would you like me to stay home today, Kay? Perhaps I could help you, and we could talk and drive around town," Hoyt said. That was what he wanted to do, show her the old places and talk about the factory.

"Why no," she said. She seemed surprised. "You go down to the factory the same as usual."

"You don't come home every day, you know."

"I'll come down there later, Hoyt. I thought maybe I could have that little office Mamma used to have—that is, if no one's using it."

"It's a filing room," he said. "I thought you'd want the one across from me."

"No," she said.

"Well, I can have a desk moved into that little office, I guess."

"Yes," she said. "A desk and some file cases and I'll want to look at the reports. Do we still have a contract with Runner Mallinson?"

"Yes," he said. "How did you remember that?"

"I remember all of it," she said. She felt the girl watching her, marveling, and she sank easily into her role. "Don't worry, Hoyt. Between the two of us, we'll really do something."

The Long Year

He got up and came over to her and kissed her cheek. "I'm glad you're home," he said. "I'm very glad."

"So am I," Marth said.

She smiled at both of them, held Marth's hand and looked into her brother's face. He doesn't change, she thought. Mamma should see him, he never changes. And then she began to drink her hot coffee and to eat her toast. She wanted to get started at once, have her bags unpacked, do something about that living room. Then she'd walk down Chestnut Street and look it over, just to look at it again.

CHAPTER SIX:

IN EVERY TOWN there is a street where people hang out and where they go almost every day in their lives either to talk or to drink or to shop or just to be going somewhere. In High Falls, the name of this street was Chestnut Street. None of the streets in that town had names like Camino del Monte Sol or Street of Seven Angels or Via de Junipero Serra. The streets there were Elm, Pine, Maple, Laurel—Chestnut, and Chestnut was not the widest, coolest, best street of all. It was the narrowest, dirtiest, lost in a little place, forgotten except by those who lived on it.

It began at the edge of the water where no one could truly see its beginnings. It was down there where Mike had his wharves and houses in the curve of the bay. Every morning he sat in the sun mending nets or scraping a canoe or unwinding tackle, winter or summer, he sat there. Now, he wore trunks, dark glasses and a crushed sailor cap, and he sat cross-legged. Joe lay on the dock beside him. They could see Rocky running on the beach. They watched him.

"Dammit," Joe said thickly, "someone died in my mouth last night."

Mike looked at him thoughtfully, scratching a mosquito bite on his thigh. All the Connaughts looked alike, dark or merry depending on their moods. Mary Connaught looked like that, too. Whenever he saw her, it made him grin to think his father had given her a job in the office, trying to make up for everything else. He couldn't see where it made up for anything. "Barby won't like it if she finds out you come down here every night after you leave her."

Joe shrugged. "She knows." He sat up and wet his comb in the water and smoothed down his hair. "Gee, I'm sorry about last night. Wouldn't blame you and Rock if you got fed up."

"No," Mike said. "Only you certainly get stinko. Why don't you come in this business with me? It's not hard work, and we could make ends meet."

"I can't, Mike."

"You think you'll get a job at the factory?"

"I've got to wait and see—just to see if there's a chance."

Mike shook his head. "No. Listen to me, Joe."

"I'm listening. I know all about it."

"You won't leave on account of Barby?"

"Maybe."

Mike kicked his foot hard against the bottom of the small boathouse. It moved a little, and the kicking made a deep, hollow sound. He ought to do something about Joe because Joe wasn't getting anywhere like this. When he talked he always looked at his feet, the sidewalk or a blade of grass as if to conceal himself in his deep concentration on these.

"I've got to talk to you about this, Joe."

"Go ahead."

"My aunt won't change much. She's no better than anyone else, smarter maybe, but it won't help."

"I'm not leavin' the kid."

"Barby can—"

"Not Barby," he said angrily. "She can take anything I got to give her. It's Lindy. I'm not leavin' him to get kicked around the old man's house. Already he works like he's ninety-five. They never know if he's hungry or dirty or aches or anything. There were always too many kids at home." He thought of the old house and the way the boards in the porch had fallen through and how the steps hung off the porch and how when you sat down at a meal, there was never enough to go around. He thought of his father's brother, Parnell, that big, hulking idiot working on the presses, slobbering his food, taking up space in the house, somebody always having to take turns sleeping with him. And then his old man—never having enough time to notice how the house was falling apart, doing a lousy job at the dry-cleaning business if it hadn't been for his mother. There were just too many of them for what they had, never enough to go around. Never a moment's peace in the house to sit down and read or to listen to the radio or to go to a place of your own. No one had a separate place, and the kid, Lindy, the baby, was always hiding under the porch, just to be alone. No one with sense would have so many kids and then run a lousy dry-cleaning business with no snap to it. There wasn't a chance for any of them. No wonder Wilma had pulled out like this, never letting the folks know, and going her way. That was a tough one, sending home money all the time, and the folks bragging it around that she was so good to them. How could he leave Lindy there when there was no one to take care of him, not even Mary because she had too much to do when she came home from work, a house to clean, cooking, looking after the babies that were still younger than Lindy, the ones without any personalities or sense to them yet—and Parnell besides. No, he could not leave.

"What about you and Barby?" Mike asked.

He puckered his mouth. "That's something else again, Mike." He looked toward the beach. "That old bugger, Rock, 's got up some real steam."

"Yeah," Mike said. "He's fighting Balaban on the fourteenth."

"That's a cinch."

"You know Rock—he never thinks it will be. He always hopes the guy'll turn out to be another Fonn Kelly and really give him a battle. Besides, he likes to train. Macbeth wouldn't let him stop anyhow."

"Joe—listen, if you ever change your mind—"

"Sure," Joe said. He lay back on the wharf and closed his eyes. How could he change his mind? It was always the same, the kid Lindy needed someone, they all needed someone. It was a shame the old man had to go around looking so defeated. It was a shame his mother had to look so old all the time, too. The whole damned setup was a dirty, rotten shame. He ought to get his pins under him and repair the porch and paint the house and do a million things. But he

The Long Year 51

knew he wouldn't—he would never do any of those things that he ought to do.

From Mike's the street opened wider over the railroad tracks where the C. St. P. M. & O. whistled through once a day. Here the dust and the slashing weeds clouded the hot afternoons. But, it was always Chestnut Street there from the edge of the water to the mind's end, every town has the same and everyone born there, who has lived there, knows it and remembers it clearly from the water's edge to its end in the hills. Across the tracks, among the slashing weeds and to the corner where Macbeth had his store.

Macbeth sat in his round-backed chair contemplating the slow, beautiful progress of the red ant on the sidewalk. He marvelled at how the ant was made and how the ant endured and how the ant knew his place and was in it and did not turn from it or seek beyond it. Each day, it was an ant or a fly walking on the faded brick wall, a beetle, a bug, a bug, a beetle and another after that. Behind him, the dusty windows of the old building opened into the long, dark, deep room with men's clothing hung on long racks. Inside was the narrow, high varnished counter, the old cash register with a bell like a fire gong, the sink and rise of the old floor, back to the end of the building where again the dusty windows looked out on a dark alley. In the cleared space between the suits and the windows was a tumbling mat and a new wood floor the size of a fighting ring. Rocky did his exercises there, skipping rope, punching the bag, shadow-boxing, working on dumb-bells. The men sat around on old packing crates watching with a light in their eyes that said: "This is living beauty, and this is myself as well. It's wonderful to see. I would rather see this man than have a million dollars or sleep with Garbo. This is what it is, by God."

Macbeth rose and pulled the lever that let down the faded awnings. He sneezed several times from the dust. Now, in a moment, he would go inside and do some yoga. It kept his belly muscles strong and enough blood in his head, but for these few minutes he would sit in the chair and close his eyes and let his spirit go off by itself. He sat. He felt the sun. He tasted the dust. He was a skinny, reddish man with thin lips and sharp blue eyes, and there was a narrowness to him—narrowness in his bullet-shaped head, in his hands, in his shoulders.

He held his breath, letting it out slowly and felt the widening of his feet. They seemed to dissolve into a watery substance and then at once the sun came inside him, and he contained it well and that which was himself, truly, rose and went off alone.

After a time, Joe, wandering around looking for Lindy, stopped at the corner and smiled at Macbeth. "Hello, Macbeth," he said.

"Go away, Boy."

"Is your soul in Chicago?"

"No."

"Fine," Joe said.

Well, he looked ridiculous sitting there with his soul gone from him, but he delighted everyone who saw him there. There, with his fine gold watch from the railroad company which he never used but carried in a red plush box in his hip pocket. There, with his sandy head bent and his little squinty eyes closed and all the big, chuckling power inside him. There he sat and lived in himself and got more power, like an engine feeding from a vast tank, like a great moose lapping at the waters of an endless river, but Lord Above, what a funny old guy, really. Something from Mars.

"See where Kay Hasswell come home this morning. Her car's in the driveway."

"Ummm."

"Remember her?"

Macbeth opened his eyes. "I remember her—running around with Simon O'Dodd, and him as weak as water when she was with him. She hated us here. Wonder why she's come home now—must be because it's rotten everywhere else."

"Didn't you like her?"

"Not much."

Joe watched the red ant carrying a piece of bread crumb. "I got to go down there," he said. "I've got to get some work somewhere."

The Long Year 53

Macbeth said nothing. His eyes were closed, and his soul had gone from him.

From Macbeth's, Chestnut Street started up the hill past the post office on one side, the Cafe on the other. From time to time, the Cafe changed hands, but it never changed in any other way. There was here, as at Macbeth's, a dusty, old, worn, torn, lost air. It was clean and smelled faintly of varnish and sawdust, and in the room behind the front room, you could get bathtub gin, corn and homemade beer brewed in the town. It was known as tiger pee. Everyone knew about that room and no one believed in prohibition and no one cared about that law.

Next to the Cafe was King Connaught's place with a baby in an old rusty buggy and Parnell Connaught, the half-wit, sitting by the presser and watching it as he had watched for thirty years. A big burden to Fran Connaught, everyone said, but when he looked at her out of his sad, stupid eyes, they could bite off their tongues for saying that. Fran and King were big, slow, sad people with worries, and in the hot summer days, they always came outside and stood on their makeshift porch and sighed over this or that. Inside, the pressers also made a soft, sighing noise in the hot, damp room.

Even early in the morning, the street outside Macbeth's, outside the Cafe, the dry cleaner's, the newspaper office, the post office—the whole narrow, forgotten street was full of those who waited—waiting for the mail, for night, for something to drink, for someone to drive them up the hill, for a color, a sound, a face, a voice. Some waited day upon day, long forgotten why or for whom or for what they waited, but they waited now as people whose whole life was to stand there, rain or shine, not caring but only to stand and wait in this dreamless dream.

Joe parked his car by the filling station and walked to the Cafe. He saw his mother standing out on the porch, and then she called to him.

"You—you didn't come home again," she said. Her eyes were very bright and full of tears, and she sighed and wiped her face in a round, uncaring movement.

"Yeah," he said. "I stayed at Mike's."

"You oughtta come home, Joe. It worries your father."

"Not much," he said.

"Oh—I don't know—" She sighed again and wiped her face. She had a beautiful build, everyone said, but she was always tired or hurt or worried about the kids, and to her Chestnut Street was an ache in her bones, a bleeding at her heart, sleepless nights—nothing more than these.

"Where's Lindy?" he asked. He wanted to do things for her so she wouldn't look like poor white trash, that was how she looked. He ought to be able to do something for her, for all of them—look at Wilma, she tried, and what the hell?—"

"He was here a few minutes ago," she said.

Mrs. Amos stuck her head out of the newspaper office. "He's here working good, honest work, Joe," she said.

"Okay—I was just askin'."

He moved away, hearing her talk to his mother. She was full of many crusades and never seemed to tire of them nor to tire of explaining them. She wrote editorials against the Mid-western Power Company, about the road that ought to be straightened, because the curve there was dangerous, about what was happening in Chicago or New York. People thought she was a little mad to care so much about these small, unimportant things. Yes, she was nuts—that big old woman, coming from nowhere, wearing her black dresses, never seen away from her desk.

They all belonged on that street—they were full of dreams, dead or dying or struggling. They sighed, and their sighs were lost in the sighs of the others—Fran with her worries, Joe with his youth, Mrs. Amos with her crusades. There at the widest part of the street by the filling station, the newspaper office, the dry-cleaning place.

Beyond the newspaper office was a newer building, built shortly after the war. The young lawyers, dentists, real estate and insurance

The Long Year 55

men had their offices in this building. One lawyer thought Chestnut Street was a big joke, and he always laughed over it. "Michigan Boulevard," he said. "Fifth Avenue," he said. "Hollywood and Vine," he said.

This young lawyer, Johnnie Evans, was a crook. He did not like being that kind of lawyer but he did it well and easily, a natural talent with him. But sometimes he felt a sickness inside him, and he wanted to get away from himself. He was nice looking and wore smart clothes and had a fine, bright mind. From his window, he could see the green hills under the sun, the water moving under the bridge. He had a fierce ache inside to say to hell with this racket and to hell with everything. He wanted to go out in the hills, swim in the deep water, have a good time for himself.

In the mornings he was sharp with the office girl. He could never remember her name although she had been working for him over a year now. In the old days when he was just starting out, a pretty girl made him look out the window to see how she walked and maybe guess at the color of her eyes. It was a pleasure that had often filled the morning for him, but now he had clients, all with sour faces, and it was no pleasure to look at these, God knew. And there was so little time now to look at pretty girls although he loved the way they walked, their sweet, childish faces, the colors of their lipsticks.

He had few friends in the town. His college friends had forgotten him. His clients came from other towns or from the city. High Falls had not disowned him or even shown any dislike for him. His office was nice, they said, and he was neat, polite and friendly enough, but then there was another lawyer on Chestnut Street who still had spittoons in his office and who chewed tobacco and kept white mice in his file case. His name was Walt Purdy, and he was the town's lawyer.

At first, Johnnie Evans had been for the town in every way, but when the people did not accept him, what was he to do? Afterwards, other people came to him, and he grew busy with no time to look at young girls. But a small part of himself still hoped, and it was this that sighed along with all the other lost sighs of that street.

The seepy, seepy whisper beneath cracked sidewalks, the total melancholy and blueness of nights along the street, the little cries that no one heard.

Now, he looked out upon the street, up the hill toward Hasswell's. He could see the red car in the drive. "So the Hasswell woman's home," he said.

"Yes," the girl said.

"I suppose she doesn't like it now that the place isn't coining it for her. Does she think she can wave a wand over it?"

"I guess so," the girl said without interest. She worked for him because he paid well and because there was no one else to work for. By turns she disliked and pitied him.

"Purdy's their lawyer," he said. That guy with the white mice, slobbering all over himself like a half-wit. "That guy's their lawyer." He frowned, and then he saw his face in the window, frowning hard. He thought it a strange face, surely not his. He turned away from the window, from the street, from the hills and the river. He began to go about his business of the day.

The street became active around eleven o'clock. A few people went in and out of Macbeth's. Some summer people parked across the tracks and rented canoes from Mike. Mrs. Amos called across the street to the filling station. A thick, clouded mist of heat emanated from the dry-cleaning place. Joe came out of the Cafe, got into his car and roared up the hill, driving more slowly past Hasswell's, looking at the red Packard, whistling softly through his teeth. Then he drove to the end of the street, to the end of Chestnut Street, where it dwindled into a path and was lost in the tall grasses. Joe lay down and slept in the shade of his car.

CHAPTER SEVEN:

HOWARD WAS a family man. That was his life, and he had always worked for family men. Any foreign element he both feared and resented, and so with a stubborn, set face he carried the bags up to the front bedroom. Kay began at once to unpack. She liked to do things for herself. Really, it was much better to let Marie go because now she felt free of everything and everyone. This room had been Mamma's and she recalled the times when, in the early morning, she had crossed the hall in her bare feet and crawled into bed with Mamma, warming her feet against Mamma's back. She remembered the times when, after running all evening in a game of Go Sheep Go, she'd come into this room and lie across the bed and watch Mamma brushing her long hair.

Marth had changed to a pair of white tennis shorts, and she came into the room and helped her unpack.

"Really, darling," Kay said, "I can do it."

"I want to help," Marth said. "I love to look at clothes."

Howard set the last bag at the foot of the bed. "Seems that's all," he said. "You havin' a trunk, Ma'am?"

"Yes—sometime soon, I imagine. Thank you, Howard." She knew he didn't like her. Carl, LeGrand's man, had never liked her, either.

"Have you ever been to Savannah, Howard?" she asked.

"No, ma'am. My old Pap came from down there, though."

"Savannah's lovely, very warm all the time and very sweet-smelling."

"Howard's always lived North," Marth said. She was holding a neatly folded pile of lingerie, holding it lightly, amazed at the way it was made, at the laces and the feeling of the satin.

"Let's leave the other bags," Kay said. "I want to take a shower and go to the office."

Howard, going out, said, "Rock's waitin', Marth."

"All right," Marth said. "I promised to play tennis with him, but if you'd like me to go with you—"

"No," Kay said.

"I wish you'd come down and meet Rock. Everyone in town thinks he's wonderful. He's a prizefighter, you know."

"Some other time, darling," Kay said. She smiled. "Have a good game."

"Will you play with us some day?"

"Of course," she said. "We'll have marvelous times together, Marth." She began to undress, and then she went to the window and looked down to see Marth and the boy crossing the drive. He looked large and terribly young to her, and when she saw his face, she thought: He's not bad-looking. She's got taste, but he's probably nothing at all, not a real fighter like Fonn. You get a fighter like Fonn once in a hundred years, they say, like getting a singer like Marian Anderson once in a hundred years.

She took a shower, dressed slowly in a blue linen suit. She wore a small, crushed linen hat to match and earrings and a twisted silver bracelet she had bought in Italy. Then she went downstairs and stood in the living room. Mamma used to sit there by the fireplace knitting sleeveless sweaters for Hoyt, she thought. He always grew so fast, she had to knit one after the other. She went over to the fireplace and took the vase off the mantel and put it in a drawer beneath the bookcase. Howard came into the room and looked at her.

"This room is very ugly, Howard."

"I guess we're used to it, Ma'am," he said.

"It needs yellow in it, lots of yellow."

She went into the kitchen, running her hand over the top of the buffet. She hated old-fashioned buffets. 'Phelia was scrubbing the back porch. She said nothing but looked up at Kay with expressionless eyes.

"What time is dinner?" Kay asked.

"Six," Howard said. "Less 'Phelia gets a bad ache in her back."

"Six is a good time. When my mother was alive, we always ate at

The Long Year 59

six." She drew on her gloves and went outside and started down the drive. Howard stood in the doorway watching her, and she called over her shoulder to him, "Put my car in, will you, Howard?"

"Yes, ma'am," he said.

She walked down the street past the hotel. She saw the man sitting on the steps with his accordion. He wore a wide-brimmed black Stetson and a pair of scabby cowboy boots, and he was playing a slow, sad song. When he saw her, he nodded his head. "Hello," he said.

"Hello."

"You're Kay Hasswell."

She stopped. "Yes." He was young and attractive, and there was something about him that pleased her at once, an air of being where he wanted to be, in his own place and time.

"Everyone in town's been going past your house this morning trying to get a look at you."

"Take a look," she said.

"I'm Gene Wimmer. I'm a teacher here."

"I believe it," she said. She walked away from him, giving him a quick nod. She turned down Chestnut Street still smiling. Here was the old place she remembered best no matter where she went—it was always at the bottom of everything. Moving down it, she felt a curious lightness. It was amazing how much real energy she had when she was alone like this, how much she could think in one mortal second, how brave she felt. She saw the little man sleeping in front of the clothing store, and she saw that one eye was open.

"Macbeth," she said. "You old devil, Macbeth."

"Yep," he said. "I heard you come home, Kay."

"Were you surprised?"

"No. Nothin' surprises me."

"What have you been doing all this time?"

"Been no place except the seven-mile run on the peanut express. That's all the world I've seen and it's enough. Now, I own this place here. Mostly, I sleep a lot and philosophize. Got a fine boy, though, Kay, finest fighter on this earth."

"I saw him from a distance this morning."

"He's too young for you."

She laughed.

"What you come for, Kay?"

"Why, I came to help in the factory. I can't let it sit there like an old, dying turtle, Macbeth."

He cackled. "Everyone thinks you're gonna help them. They'd think that about anyone who'd come back here from such a distance."

"The people here. What do they know?"

"Some, like me, know a lot. Take Gene Wimmer, teaches school here, an' Russian Peterson, the foreman, an' my boy and some of his friends. That old Greek, Mrs. Amos, on the newspaper an' Howard, that colored fellah—they know something."

"Don't you ever take a bath, Macbeth?" she asked.

"Satiddys," he said. "Go away, Kay. I want to sleep."

She laughed at him and recrossed the street. She saw herself, very elegant and clean on this old dirty street. She was the only one in the whole place who was not dying of a terrible disease of the mind, she alone of all of them had sureness in her, the kind of sureness Mamma always had. The rest of them were lost—the buildings, the streets, the people walking on the streets were already molested by the uselessness of their own lives, devoured by the cancer of their own despair. She was outside of this, herself, belonging wherever she chose to belong.

She wondered why she always listened to Macbeth. She used to think of him, and once, in Vienna, Prokosch had brought home a professor of economics, a little red man like Macbeth, and she had thought if you put them together in the same room you wouldn't have been able to tell the difference. As a young girl she had always laughed at him, so full of old jokes and stories. She could not understand then why, when she left town, she remembered him best of all, but now she saw that he was like the town—past his usefulness, dirty, old, useless, lost. She sighed. Everything was the same—the same old street, the same old stink, the same old buildings and people.

The Long Year 61

She walked across Main Street slowly, and she saw the people watching her, and she walked even more slowly, letting them take a good look. Something curled up in scorn inside herself that they would waste so much time looking at anyone. That is the trouble, the whole trouble, they look and sleep and eat and talk, and if they put half that energy into their work, things would go better. They are like blind sheep waiting for someone to lead them out of the valley, out of one valley into another. I would not give a good horse for ninety percent of these people, talking and idling their lives away when there is a world to own, an apple to eat, an earth to inherit.

She took a low path to the swamp. Now, there was a stink to remember, the odor of hot iron from the foundry, the dryness and wetness which were entirely two different smells coming from the swamp, the dustiness of the sun on the gray stucco sheds, the river itself. She turned toward the office building. A few men standing outside the number one warehouse looked at her. She went into the cool building. A young girl in a white blouse was sitting at the switchboard.

"I'm Kay Hasswell," she said, smiling. "My office is going to be in the small room at the end of the hall."

"Yes, Miss Hasswell," the girl said. Her eyes were taking in the dress, earrings and small, lovely sandals. "Mr. Hasswell's had it ready since early this morning."

"Thank you," Kay said softly. "And who are you?"

"I'm Mary Connaught."

"Oh—yes," she said in the same soft voice.

She walked through the big office where the stenographers and accountants worked. She could see Hoyt sitting at his desk in his own office which had glass on two sides. She waved to him but went by quickly. She entered the small office and sat at the desk and tested the chair for height. Then she went over to the file cases and opened them and saw that as yet there was nothing in them. After that, she opened the top drawer of her desk. Inside were several stacks of bond paper, a letter opener that had belonged to her mother, as a souvenir of the World's Fair in St. Louis, some engraved stationery, an inkwell, ruler and a few paper clips. She unsnapped her bracelet and dropped it into the drawer.

On top of the desk was an inter-office phone, an outside phone and a large new green blotter. Through the window, she could see the group of men still standing by the warehouse. They were big men, and she recognized Olds and the foreman, Russian Peterson. It amused her for a moment to sit there watching the slow, clumsy gestures of Russian's big hands. She knew he was talking about her, and she could see the men shake their heads, and one of them angrily got up from where he sat leaning against the building. He shouted something in anger and went into the warehouse.

She rolled up the sleeves of her linen blouse. Her arms looked white and sickly to her. Usually by now she was tan all over except for a thin mark across her nose from the sunglasses.

She picked up the inter-office phone. "Give me Mr. Hasswell," she said crisply. She could see the Connaught girl pull the plugs up and then make the connection.

"Hoyt?"

"Yes, Kay," he said in a patient, smooth voice. "Everything all right?"

"No," she said. "Really, darling, I need the reports for the last two years—maybe three years. I want an estimate on cancellations and productions. What about the contracts we have with that old Greek woman who owns the newspaper—Mrs. Amos—did we cancel the advertising? Listen, darling, I want something in here besides furniture and telephones."

"Sure, I was only waiting—"

"Do we still retain Walt Purdy, that keeper of white mice?"

"Well, yes, you see—"

"Isn't there a younger man? Honestly, I don't understand—"

"There's Johnnie Evans, but we've never had him."

"I think this Connaught girl would make a good secretary."

"Now, I wouldn't do that, Kay."

"Why not, darling?"

The Long Year 63

"She's used to the switchboard."

"She can type, can't she, and take dictation?"

"Yes, but the Connaughts mean trouble, Kay."

"I like her looks." The world ought to be full of people like that Connaught child, young and strong and beautiful. "Send her to me, then. Also, Hoyt, I seriously want to know what's going on here."

"Nothing's going on," he said. "You have a suspicious attitude, Kay. Nothing's happening."

"Don't be a fool, Hoyt," she snapped. When he started to say something, she dropped the receiver. Really, he was an awful fool. She got up and walked the length of the small room. She knew about this business, she used to sit there with Mamma reading contracts and figures and estimates, writing wires in her slow, large hand, answering the telephone. She knew the price of good virgin timber. Right now, she could put the vari-colored pins on the map to mark timber that was being cut, new timber, virgin timber.

She sat down, turned around in the chair, drummed her fingers over the top of the desk. Hoyt came in with the Connaught girl. "Mary will work for you now, Kay. I thought maybe you might like to come into the office and I'll show you how the land lies."

"No," she said.

His heavy face flushed. "Well—it's a job to get everything you want together."

"I'm patient, Hoyt." Her manner softened. "Right at first I'll want to see all of it on paper, and then afterwards, of course, I'll have to get some help from you. After all, you *do* know the business better than I."

"Mamma used to say no one knew it as well as you did, Kay."

She thought, Well, that's true. "Here, Mary—I've written down a list of things I want. Get them for me, please."

"Yes, Miss Hasswell." She gave Hoyt a sly, malicious smile.

"Good," Kay said. "You see, Mary will take care of me. You go along, now, darling—"

"But I thought you'd like me to explain a few things. I called Walt Purdy, and he says—"

"That terrible old man."

"He's a good lawyer."

"I had no idea we still retained him."

"But I sent you all the letters and documents and photostatic copies."

"At that time it pleased me to do nothing more than cash the checks. I had no idea this factory was so small. How many men have we laid off?"

"A hundred in all."

"How many are there?"

"About a thousand—nine hundred and eighty-six to be exact, and that includes the office staff."

"We'll have to get rid of them."

He frowned. "I've been thinking about that." He dug his hands into his pockets and rocked back and forth on the thick, solid soles of his well-made shoes. "I thought if we laid off five hundred—"

"You're dreaming."

"But we've always kept the factory open."

"This is different. Don't you understand? I've seen it everywhere. I know that it's bigger than you dream it is."

He sat down heavily and shook his head. He understood a few things, and in his own time he felt that he had done well to run the factory for over twenty years. He had been a good, fair mayor, a good president of the Rotary and the Lions Club and a good president of the school board. The people of the town seemed to like him—at least to prefer that he take the responsibility of everything for them. "We can afford to lose money for a while, Kay," he said.

"Include me out of that," she said. Her face hardened. When she looked at him she thought, Mamma would hate to see him this soft. Mamma had always despised negation. "This is a big thing, it's everywhere. They say Roosevelt is going to try to do something. When Repeal goes through in this State, it'll help, but it's a drop in the bucket—in more ways than one. The people will get relief as soon as the thing is well-organized. It's just that this town happens to be one of the last places to feel the pinch."

The Long Year 65

"But, Kay," he said wearily, "if we lay off so many men, what can they do?"

"Twiddle their thumbs for a while. That's about how much ingenuity they have. What do people do—they find answers."

"The men here have families. There won't be anything for them." His eyes clouded over with tears. His big, full lips were bitten with nervousness. He touched her hand. "You see, the people aren't used to not working."

"It's the same in Chicago and San Francisco and New York."

"But, *here* they've always worked."

"Hoyt," she said, "we could lose money for a while, but in the end it would be no solution. We've got to save what we can. If we lose the factory, we aren't helping the people, are we?"

"No."

"And if we lose our own money, that's no help either."

"I guess not."

"You've got to close the factory."

He stood up. "It's a shame, though, isn't it, Kay?"

"Yes," she said.

He paused at the door. "You know, Kay, I'm very glad you came home. At first, I couldn't see it because we never got along very well—"

"Oh, things like that pass," she said gently.

"Well, now it seems two heads are better than one."

"Of course," she said. She watched him go toward his office. Then she saw Mary Connaught coming with her arms full of papers. She smiled and lit a cigarette. She wondered if Fonn would believe her if she told him about this. She pushed up her sleeves and began to sort the heap of papers. "There's going to be the devil to pay, Mary," she said. Might as well let her think she was a conspirator. "Yes," she said, "I guess everyone in the world will hate me for this."

"Oh, no, Miss Hasswell," Mary said, looking at her with admiring, friendly eyes.

"You'll see. Eventually, everyone hates that person who wants to do him a good turn. That's the way the world works." She laughed. She wondered if Mamma could see her. Mamma's Heaven had always been very high, a definite place; probably she was looking down from it. She'd be pleased to know that things were beginning to move again.

CHAPTER EIGHT:

MARTH AND ROCKY sat at the far end of the tennis court, under the shade trees that hung over the wire fence of the court. No one else was playing because of the heat. They were drinking lemonade from paper cups and eating cold chicken sandwiches that 'Phelia had made for them. Several times each week they came down to the court that was behind the factory office building. They usually played tennis very hard for two hours and then had their lunch and went swimming.

Rocky was putting his racket into the brace.

"Tell me, Rock," Marth said. "Why doesn't Joe go up to the courthouse and get relief? Everyone says that's what the office is for."

"Pride," Rocky said. "Joe could never do that."

"What'll he do then?"

"I don't know," Rocky said.

"It's terrible for Barby."

"No. It's not so bad for her. It's hardest on Joe. And on a lot of fellows that won't go up there. A hundred men got laid off last month. I'll bet no more than ten of them went up to the relief office. In a town like this that's always worked, going to the relief office isn't easy."

"But, Daddy said it wasn't shameful. He said if things got bad, a lot of people'd go there. And besides, the President is going to do something about it."

"I feel sorry for that man," he said.

"For Daddy?"

"No, the President." He screwed the brace tight and then began to put her racket in its brace. "Everyone thinks he can do all of it.

Mr. Wimmer says the people have got to do it themselves, not just that one man." Usually, he didn't talk so much, but of late he had begun to feel the need to say whatever came into his mind. He wanted her to know everything about him, what he thought, how he felt about fighting and about his old man and about the town and his friends—Mike, Joe, Gene Wimmer. He thought she ought to know everything about him so that they could always share their lives. The strange part of it was that he had always known her, as long as he could remember, and when he thought of her, he never thought of her in one single moment of remembering—he remembered each time separately. He remembered when she had been sick with pneumonia all that time and he'd go up to the house and sit in her room and talk to her. Outside it had been snowing, and in the room that had been stripped of everything except the bed and the bare dresser, in the room it had been very warm and moist from the steamer that had to be kept going. He remembered her lying there and waiting for him to tell her everything that had happened in school that day, and how her hand had felt heavy, lifeless in his. It had made him ache inside himself because he could not help her, and ever since then whenever he wanted to help her and could not, he felt the same ache.

"You ever remember the time you had pneumonia?" he asked.

"Sure," she said. She looked at him in a sidelong, appraising fashion.

"I never kissed anyone until then," he said.

"I know," she said. "It was always different after that, Rock."

"Yes," he said.

"I never kissed anyone else—never."

"Didn't you?"

"Not even at parties when we had kissing games." For a moment the sun was unbearably hot, and she could not look at him. "Do you suppose it's like this with everyone?"

"No," he said. "Just us."

"I mean—when Mike loved Wilma Connaught?"

"Maybe. Maybe it was pretty good but not *exactly* like this." He

The Long Year

knew how she liked to talk about everything, to think of how it was with other people.

"I wonder if it's like this with Barby and Joe."

"Probably not," he said gently. He smiled at her. He opened the lunch basket and took out an orange and began to peel it carefully, not breaking the skin except at the top. She watched him.

"Barby's having a tough time, though. She and Joe want to get married, and he can't get a job, and he hates it. Do you think he—well, you know—does he go with other girls—like when he's at Mike's?"

"Stop it," he said. "Don't think like that."

"Well—"

"That's Joe's business."

"You never want to tell me anything."

"Here, eat half this orange."

She sighed and took it, stuffing the whole half in her mouth to quench her thirst. During the summer, she felt thirsty all the time and it was because she had to keep moving, doing something.

"You're a pig," he said.

"Do you think Mike does?"

"Does what?" He handed her his handkerchief, and she wiped off her chin.

"You know—with those girls that hang around there?"

"How would I know?"

"You know, all right."

"Listen," he said. "I'm only interested in us, not in anyone else, see."

"If you get to be a very famous fighter—like Fonn Kelly—do you think we can come back here and spend the summers and swim and play tennis?"

"I'll never be a fighter like him."

"Yes, you will."

"No," he said. "He's the best fighter in the world. There's nothing like it. You have to be pretty great and have something inside you—I don't know—"

"Oh, Rock," she said. "You can be like that."

He smiled and touched her hair. "You're prejudiced."

"Sure, what'll you do then—I mean, if you don't make a lot of money fighting?"

"I'll do something." He stood up and gathered the wax paper from their sandwiches. He picked up their rackets, two tennis balls, the little rubber bag with Marth's suit. "Don't worry about that."

"Will you work for Daddy?"

"No," he said. "I guess not."

"I suppose you could do something about the store. It's really an awful place, and everyone says—"

"No," he said. "I'll find out what to do, and then I'll do it, but right now I want to be a fighter and work around the store and stay here. I like it here."

She smiled and took her racket and walked with him, holding his hand and swinging her arm a little. "I'm very happy, Rock," she said. "Aunt Kay's home, and that's wonderful and there's vacation and nothing to do but have fun. And Rock, I *do* think you're going to like her—she's wonderfully dressed and so darned nice and just exactly as I wanted her to be. I'm *sure* she's going to do something to help Daddy. She says she is."

"Do you always talk so much?"

"No," she said. "Just with you." She began to run out of the court and around the office building toward the beach. He ran after her. He could see Kay in her office, the blue dress and her quick, sure movements, nothing more. As he ran, he saw Marth stop and turn and wave to someone. It was Johnnie Evans in his gray convertible. "Wonder what he's doing down here," he thought. "Old Purdy's their lawyer—I wonder if—" He frowned but kept on running toward Marth until he caught up with her.

"What's your hurry?"

"I'm hot. I want to swim."

He caught her wrist. "Stop a minute."

She stood still. He put his hand on her shoulder and then around her neck under her hair and pulled her to him and kissed her. She

The Long Year 71

was breathing hard from running and she leaned against him, smiling when he let her go.

"There," he said.

"Thank you *very* much," she said.

They walked toward the beach. "That was Johnnie Evans," she said.

"Do you think—?"

"Oh, no," she said. "Daddy wouldn't let anyone but Mr. Purdy be his lawyer. Grandma got Mr. Purdy, and Mike told me once that Grandma'd turn over in her grave if anyone let Mr. Purdy go."

"Just the same—"

"Oh, no, Rock—really, she's not like that. She's—well, she's *very* beautiful and *kind* and I know you'll be crazy about her."

"Sure," he said, but he did not think so—from what he'd heard, he wasn't so sure she was like that at all, beautiful maybe, but probably not very kind or good.

Mike and Joe got out of Joe's car. Joe had parked on the other side of the warehouse where the men could not see him. He didn't want to make it any harder on Mike.

Mike looked at Joe. "Take it easy," he said.

"I hate asking women for anything."

"It's the thing to do," he said. "My old man's gone to the Rotary meeting, and she's alone in there. You can do it."

"All right," Joe said. He wore a clean white shirt and a pair of Mike's white ducks. He had combed his hair several times that morning. He wasn't going to ask for any favor, just a job, and he had a right to a job, being both strong and willing. It wasn't as if he was any dumb guy and couldn't learn or that he was some lazy Joe scared of work. He knew work, he'd worked all the days of his life, hadn't he, on the pressers or passing papers or harvesting ice during winter vacations, doing anything came his way and doing it damned well. "I'm not asking any favors," he said.

"All right," Mike said. He put his hands into the pockets of his levis. He hadn't been near the place in over three years now, not since that business about Wilma. He walked into the outer office, holding the door for Joe. When Mary Connaught saw him, she looked first at Joe and then at him.

"What's the matter, Joe?" she asked.

"Nothing," Mike said. "I just came down to see my aunt."

"Oh," she said.

"Take it easy, Mary," Joe said.

"I thought maybe you two were up to something."

"Nuts," Joe said. "How's Lindy?"

She shrugged. "You ought to know. You see more of him than the rest of us do."

"He working for Mrs. Amos today?"

"Same as always," she said.

"He oughtn't to work for her. She's a saint, but she works everyone to death."

"Let's go in, Joe," Mike said.

"I'd better tell her you're coming," Mary said. "She doesn't like to be interrupted."

"Go ahead, put on the swank," Mike said.

"Well, I don't want to—"

"It's all right," he said. "You got your job to do."

He watched her knock at Kay's door and then open it. She wasn't anything like Wilma. None of them were like Wilma or had what Wilma had, they all looked thicker and not quite so gay. It wasn't just because he was prejudiced, it was something anyone could tell at first glance, anyone who ever knew Wilma. He saw Kay get up, and then she stood a little outside her office and motioned to them.

"Dammit," Joe said.

"Now, look," Mike said, "I didn't come down here for nothing. Act decent, and she'll be glad to have you. You'll see."

"You don't need to play games," Joe said, but he walked stiffly, carefully beside Mike.

"It's good of you to come, Michael," Kay said. She drew him into her office and kissed him, and he grinned and kissed her very hard on her cheek. He liked the smell of her a lot better than the way she

The Long Year 73

looked, she looked like Marth only there was a difference, and it was the difference that made him decide she'd be a cold one in bed. That was the way he always thought when he met a woman.

"You look fine, Michael."

"This is my friend, Joe Connaught. You remember the Connaughts, that's Mary out there, Joe's sister."

"Yes, of course," she said. "Sit down, Joe."

"Thank you," Joe said.

"What can I do for you?" she asked. She thought, it's begun, one or the other of them wants a job, and I'll have to handle it carefully. And she looked at Mike, thinking, He's not soft, this one's not soft like Hoyt, this one's more like Mamma than any of us.

"Well, I came down to see you," Mike said. "I don't go up to the house much except when I need food or money."

"I see," she said. "You and Hoyt."

"Yeah," he said. He was surprised. "You think fast," he said.

"Thank you," she said.

"I came for a job," Joe said.

"Damn you, Joe," Mike laughed. "Joe's got no finesse."

"That's what I came for," Joe said abruptly.

"I see," she said. "And you've been here before, haven't you, Joe?"

"Yes," he said uneasily.

"You don't look as if you're lacking in ambition."

"Joe's very smart," Mike said. "He was just about the smartest in his class. You ask Mr. Wimmer. Mr. Wimmer says no one can out think Joe when he sets his mind to it."

"I believe that," she said.

"I don't care what kind of job," Joe said.

"I know," she said. She got up and opened the file case and took out a manila folder, opened it and laid it on the desk for Joe to see. "This is a rough estimate, Joe," she said. She leaned over him, one hand close to his. He did not look at her. "You see here what percentage of business was cancelled last year. Take this contract with Runner Mallinson. He used to be our biggest buyer. He cancelled ninety-one percent of his business this year." She ran her finger down the line. "You see, this is the amount of stock by carload we now have at hand—and this is the amount that is ordered."

"Yeah," Joe said, "but I don't care what kind of work."

She sat down facing them. Mike picked up the folder, scanned it, put it back on her desk.

"I don't know what to say," she said. "I would like to help you. I like young people, and I'd like to help your friend, Michael."

"It's okay," Joe said gruffly. "We aren't asking for any favors."

"Hell," Mike said. "You're in for a tough time. Everyone thinks you can work miracles."

"Maybe I can," she said. "I'll tell you what I'll do—I have an ace up my sleeve. In—say, six months, if you'll come back, Joe, I may possibly be able to give you something."

"Six months," he said. "I'll be damned if I'll sit around on my fanny six months."

"I'm sorry," she said.

"Thanks, anyhow," Mike said.

"I hope to get down to see your place, Michael."

"Any time. We usually have parties at night. Don't come if you can't swim, though, because someone always falls in the river."

"I can swim," she said. She went to the door with them. "Shall I tell your father you came?"

"Don't care if you do. Don't care if you don't," Mike said. He walked behind Joe. Let her look, he thought, let her take a good look at me and then go yelling to him that I ought to dress up, I ought to work here, I ought to do this, do that. But, secretly, he thought she wouldn't say anything. She was too smart to say anything unless she had a reason for it.

"You coming home tonight, Joe?" Mary asked.

Joe did not hear her.

"Probably not," Mike said.

He followed Joe and got into the car. At first the car would not start and then when it did, Joe backed it up until he hit the wire fence of the tennis court.

"What'll you do?" Mike asked.

"I'll do something," Joe said. "Don't you worry about that."

"God, I'm sorry."

"You couldn't help it," Joe said.

"She's a smooth one, too. She makes you feel she can do anything."

"She's all right, I guess."

"No," Mike said. "If the old man doesn't watch out, she'll own the joint. I know dames like that."

Joe said nothing. He drove over the bumpy swamp road, down the beach toward Mike's place.

"Rock and Marth are swimming," Mike said.

Still, Joe did not look at the river or at anything. He was going to think of something, there was that kid from the city who had told him of a good deal, a good deal, if you weren't scared of taking a chance, and he wasn't scared of taking a chance. He could do anything, but he wasn't going to sit around waiting for a fine woman to make room for him in that factory, not so long as he was alive and kicking.

"Take it easy, for Gawd's sake," Mike said. "You're bumping the guts out of me."

Joe slowed down. "Okay," he said. "Okay." He was talking to himself, making up his mind.

CHAPTER NINE:

FOR THE PEOPLE of that town, that was the craziest week they had ever known. Everything happened in one big burst so that afterwards they thought of it as being much longer than a single week, a month at least. The heat began in earnest that Sunday afternoon, and the people did not bother to fret under it. They moved through it in a kind of pale, apprehensive sadness. They had one thing that kept going through their minds that now Kay Hasswell was home, and everything would have to be all right. Even Hoyt had begun to have that idea. He sat on Mrs. Leroy's porch drinking Tom Collinses. Kay had taken the car out early in the morning and gone up to the farm to ride with Johnnie Evans. He thought if she was worried, she'd go down to the office. I guess she's not worried, although Mamma never showed it. Mamma always let on everything was going full steam even when she knew things were letting down —but of course, they never let down like this.

Marth and Rocky walked on the bridge. You could smell the heat. It went down like shafts into the water, changing it to a strange, hot copper. That afternoon the people walked in the park along Mike's docks. They still wore their Sunday clothes. Even the smallest children seemed to be waiting. They talked about Kay Hasswell, and tried to remember her as a girl, but only a few of them—Macbeth, Russian Peterson and his friend, Olds—only these few remembered about her and Simon O'Dodd. The others remembered the parties she had given and the way she always dressed and the things they'd read or heard about her. They found much business now to do on the street that went by Hasswell's house. They looked at the house, waited, felt a vast, relentless fear sour

The Long Year

and shrink into raw terror inside them. They did not know what they feared. It was only that they feared.

During the lunch hour on Monday, the men stood around and talked about her. Their talk was at first aimless.

"I hear she pays two hundred dollars for her hats, mind you," Olds said. His glass eye was round and large with the wonder of such a thing.

"It's too much," Russian Peterson said. He said it with finality. "I would say it's a sin."

They nodded their heads. "It's a sin, all right."

"She'll do nothing," Russian said. He had worked in the factory since he was fifteen. He ran the largest saw and had lost two fingers in two different accidents. This had happened because of someone else's carelessness in sending faulty timber through the saw. He was never careless. It was partly because of his fingers and partly because of his bigness that the men always listened to him.

"We ought to talk to her," they said. "We ought to do it, and by Jesus, I'll do it."

"Okay," they said, and their mouths felt hot with the slowness of that one word. At first they had griped when their wages were cut, and then at the second cut, they had griped less. Now, when their jobs were threatened, they did not feel they dared to gripe. "Yes, you do it," they said. "You're the one to do it, Russian."

They stood against the gray stucco wall, and the youngest of them was even as the oldest. There was no sound left in them, no movement, no other thought. They felt that perhaps the uncertainty might be better than the certain knowledge. They watched with fear and trembling and a desire to call out and bring Russian back into the warehouse. He crossed the open place where the grass grew yellow in the heat, and he stood outside the door of the office building. Above the door, the two large air vents made a cool, sucking sound. He took off his cap, wiped his forehead and brushed the sawdust from his overalls. He felt no fear, felt nothing, not even an urge to open the door. If he could have his choice at that moment, it would be to stay there like a big, sweating animal. But he pushed open the door and went into the outer office.

"Hello, Mary," he said.

"Hello," she said. She was very busy. He noticed that although she was hurrying, there was no sweat on her because here in this building it was always cool.

"I would like to see Hoyt," he said.

"You'd better see her."

"Kay?"

"She's Miss Hasswell."

"I thought she was married."

"She calls herself that anyhow," she said patiently. "And she's the one to see."

"I worked for Hoyt all this time."

"Maybe so, but if you're smart you'll see her." She bent forward and spoke in a low voice. "She knows everything. She knows just about everything there is to know."

"She does?" hopefully.

She put down the neat stack of papers. "But I'll tell *him* you're here."

He felt crowded in this low office room, and there was no place to sit. Mary came out of Hoyt's office. "You can go in," she said.

"Thanks, Mary." When she passed him, he laid his hand on her arm. "How's Joe these days?"

"He's all right. I guess he drinks—we almost never see him—but he seems all right otherwise."

"He'll snap out of it," he said gently. He went into the office where Hoyt sat. Hoyt stood up and held out his hand. "Fine to see you, Russian."

Russian shook the hand. "I came to find out if we're to be laid off, Hoyt," he said.

"Sit down, man," Hoyt said. He cleared his throat and moved some papers on his desk.

"The men want to know," Russian said.

Hoyt took a deep breath. "It's not so simple as that, Russian. It's

The Long Year 79

a very hard thing for us to decide." He put the tips of his fingers together. Russian felt terrible to see him there not saying anything but searching around for something to say. "It's understandable, of course, that the men would want to know."

"They sent me to find out."

Hoyt frowned. "I don't know what to tell you, Russian. We've been working awfully hard, but you see things aren't going the way they should for us, either. There are no orders, plenty of cancellations, though. Perhaps there's a chance the government will do some building, and if we get contracts, it would certainly help."

Russian watched him get up and stand by the windows behind his desk, looking toward the foundry. He had always thought of Hoyt as being an impressive man like a preacher or a governor, but now in some way he had changed. He was all right when everything was going like oil—then he was as strong as the men who worked for him. Now when the men under him were like so much wind pudding, he was like them as well. Russian rose.

"I can tell them you don't know."

"Yes," Hoyt said. "That might be the best thing to do."

"All right," Russian said.

"You might—you just might have a talk with my sister. She has some idea. I don't know—" He spread out his hands and looked at them. "You might ask her about it."

"I'll do that," Russian said. "Thank you, Hoyt."

"Come in any time," Hoyt said.

"Thanks, Hoyt."

He went out into the hall, looked around the office. They all were very busy doing things with small machines and papers. Usually when he came here he was impressed—but not today. They seemed like children cutting up paper dolls on a rainy day. It was not a real kind of work, and it would not stop this thing that was happening. He walked slowly down the hall where he could see the woman moving around the small office that had once been a file room. Inside, Johnnie Evans, the lawyer, was sitting on the edge of the desk talking very fast and moving his hands. So,

Russian thought, it's true about him, he's going to take Purdy's place. I suppose she thinks he's young and good-looking, but he'll never be as good as Purdy. Damn her stinking hide. He let the breath go out of him, and then he went to the door, rapped on it, and the woman looked up. He saw her face clearly for the first time—her wide, sparkling eyes, the full mouth, the high cheek bones and the skin that was very thin and untanned. She motioned for him to open the door.

"Yes?" she said.

"I'm Peterson, the foreman in the shop. Russian Peterson."

"Oh, of course," she said. "I remember you very well—come in, won't you, Russian?"

She turned to Johnnie Evans. "I'll see you this evening, Johnnie?"

"Sure, Kay," he said. He nodded to Russian and then went out as he had been told.

At first, Russian could not believe that this woman had ever come from the town even though he could remember her when she was about the age of Marth Hasswell. But this woman was too fine, too delicate, and the perfume from her filled the room so that he seemed to breathe inside that smell. It was not of flowers or sun or water but a queer tart odor that went down inside him, all around him, making it difficult for him to breathe. He kept his eyes on her as he would keep his eyes on a hunted deer or a brook trout.

"Well, Russian," she said. She wore a heavy silk blouse with the sleeves rolled up. She began to take some papers out of the file case.

"I came for the men," he said. He didn't want to look at her any more. Sweat broke out on the backs of his hands. "I came because the men want to know what's gonna happen."

"I see."

"Yes."

"They want to know."

He nodded. "It's hard on them to wait with one hundred men already laid off."

The Long Year

She looked at him and smiled. "What do you want me to say?"

This puzzled him. He didn't *want* her to say anything. He just wanted to know. "They want to know, that's all," he said firmly. He was not going to play at being polite or clever. He didn't know how to do that.

She shrugged.

"Will there be work next week?"

"Who knows? I tell you, my brother has kept this place open too long without good reason. We've lost a great amount of money. No business is run in such a fashion."

"We do good work."

"I know that—but someone has to buy the good work."

He looked out at the people in the office, the old girls who had been there as long as he could remember. "Doesn't it tell in those papers—somewhere? So the men could know about next week and this winter?"

"No."

"They think—the men all think you'll do something."

"They do?" She arched her eyebrows.

"Yeah," he said heavily. "They think so."

"Well—," she said. With deliberation she stacked the papers on the small, crude desk. With slowness, she turned and looked at him out of her amazing eyes, and he suddenly wanted more than anything to get up and run like a crazy man from that room. Something inside him was deadened in that moment to pain or anger. "It is a time for everyone, Russian," she said. "Do you understand this? Some people rise when everyone else falls. But I do not intend to fall."

He did not care about this talk. He didn't want to know anything more about her than he already remembered, that business with Simon O'Dodd, a finer boy never lived than Simon, and then to crash up there on Monson's Ridge. "Will there be work?" he asked doggedly.

"Oh, now." She made an impatient gesture. She was not accustomed to such bluntness. "Everyone will know soon enough."

"All right," he said. He nodded to her and went outside and stood in the hot, unmoving air and wondered what there was to say to the men now. One of them came out of the long, gray warehouse and called to him, and he moved heavily in that direction. Once inside the warehouse, he stood facing the men.

"I don't know," he said at once, shaking his head slowly. "No one will say anything."

"Did you see Hoyt?"

"I saw him."

"Well—?"

"He doesn't know."

"What about her?"

He looked over their heads. "She's quite a woman," he said.

"Yeah, but what does she say?"

"Nothing—except that she's lucky."

"Doesn't she know anything about the business? What'd she come back here for?"

"Oh, she knows the business all right. You can tell that just watching her."

"Yeah, but is she good—is she doing the right things?" They did not know why this was important except that they had once heard Mr. Wimmer ask that about someone. One good person would know what to do in the face of every situation, and then they could follow that person and do the same.

Russian wet his lips and stared hard at the floor where he could see the dusty shoes of the men. He looked from one pair to another and then to another, and he knew each pair. "I think she's a smart one. Like a fox. Like a big, black bird," he said.

"Ah, smart," they said. They turned away in disgust. "Russian, you should've found out something."

"She's damned good-looking," he said. He went off toward his machine that was now silent. He kept the saw very clean and often polished it several times a week although it was almost always idle now. Some of the men went with him and asked him more questions.

The Long Year

"We've got to tell our families something definite," they said.

Then he told them word for word as he remembered it, but he had a peculiar, frightened, dazed feeling. He remembered once feeling like this when his boy had died, the only boy he'd had, and this boy had died when he was seven days old, and then it was like this, something he could not understand. Finally he said, "She ought to have stayed away from here, I guess. I don't think she belongs here any more."

They nodded their heads. "But she owns her share of this place."

"She doesn't own me," he said. "No one owns me." His voice rose harshly, and the men stood looking at him. He was a great, slow creature, certain in all his ways, calm as a well-oiled machine. But now, suddenly, he was full of anger and trying to fight something. They didn't know what it was, but he was yelling like that to fight against it. All day, he was angry, and the men stayed away from him. But they, like him, were confused with their anger and fear, and they could see nothing but this fear all around them— fear of fear, not fear of being hurt or humiliated or alone or dying —just fear of fear—and it was everywhere, tangible, lying in the open sun, under the shadows of the plank piles, everywhere. After work that day, they did not linger in the halls or outside the buildings but each went home quietly and pretended to be calm about the whole matter. But their wives were not deceived.

Russian's house was small, set back from the wide street, neatly painted and had a nice, compact look to it. He had bought it on time payments, and now he had owned it outright for two years. He could see his wife moving around the kitchen and then in the living room. He went inside and hung up his hat and coat and called to her.

"Anyone home?"

She came at once from the kitchen and kissed his cheek. She was a thin woman and had grown up on a farm south of town. She always looked the same to him, young and friendly and busy. Her lips were warm and smooth against his cheek.

"Tired, dear?"

"Yep," he said. He sat down in his cracked leather chair that had worn a thin spot in the carpet near the Atwater-Kent radio. He turned it on. He slouched down and picked up the paper that was always left by his chair. He turned at once to the editorials. "Where are the kids?"

"What, dear?" She came to the doorway.

"The kids—where are they?"

"Oh, Joanie went up to the hotel to see Mr. Wimmer. Peggy's swimming, I suppose."

"She's not very strong. I don't think she should swim so much."

"You tell her, then. She'll listen to you."

"Umph," he said and read the editorial. He liked that old Greek woman, and he liked what she had to say. Now, she wanted the road beyond the river bridge straightened. She said it was condemned. She said the turn there was at an angle of eighty-two degrees. He frowned. "Goddamit to hell," he said. "Did you read what Mrs. Amos says here? She says that road's got an angle of eighty-two degrees."

"I know," his wife said. "Every time we go up there, I'm afraid. Why doesn't someone do something about it?"

"No one ever will," he said. "That road's been that way since I came here."

"How was it at the factory today?"

"The same."

"Did—did Miss Hasswell have anything to say?"

"No. I went to see her, but she doesn't know."

"I suppose not."

"No one knows," he said.

She sat for a moment on the arm of his chair. "David?" She was the only one who called him by his proper name. He liked to have her do that.

"What?"

"I'm not afraid."

"There, now," he said. "There's nothing to be afraid of."

"I mean, if you don't have work, we can get by. We have this

The Long Year

house, and everyone says—Mrs. Amos says, anyhow—that the government will have a good program of relief."

"I never took any relief from anyone."

"But the Olds' boy has a job on the roads for the county."

"Not me," he said. "I know my own kind of work, and I'll not take a relief job."

"I don't know why. We're no better than the Olds boy."

"No," he said angrily. "Even on relief, they can't make ends meet at Olds' place what with the girl having babies and always so sick. Olds was talking about it today."

"Why don't we walk up there this evening?"

"Why, sure," he said. "That's fine."

They smiled at each other. He was quick in his anger, but she was seldom angry and waited for his moods to pass.

"I wish the kids'd come home." He got up and went out on the porch. His older girl, Joanie, was a smart one, and he was proud of that, but at times it frightened him. He had heard of nice, smart girls like Joanie going away to school and getting new ideas and not caring about her folks. He liked things the way they were now —or the way they had been before he felt this terrible fear about his job. It was nice to have a house of his own, and he was lucky to have a wife like Jo. He didn't want to lose any of it.

He wished the child, Peggy, would come. She was the one of his heart, small and fragile and very pretty. He worried about her all the time for fear she'd get sick and then she wouldn't have anything to go on. As he stood thinking about her, he saw her coming slowly up the street swinging her bathing suit. He walked toward her.

"He-llo, Pa-pa," she said. Her face was burned from the sun, and her hair lay flat and wet.

"You look like a drowned sunfish, Baby," he said. He picked her up and carried her into the house. He'd make her go to bed early and talk to her about swimming such a long time. He held her lightly against him, her thin arm around his neck. Nothing was going to hurt her, she'd have anything she wanted. By Christ— by Christ—

CHAPTER TEN:

Joe Connaught stood on the lawn outside Barby's house. He was tired of fighting against what he knew was inevitable. He wanted to relax and have a life like everyone else, to be happy with Barby. He loved Barby. He knew this because he always wanted to be with her even when he knew they would quarrel. He put his arms around her and held her close to him and they stood there holding fast to each other and not saying anything. It was late, and the town was quiet except for an occasional car that passed them and turned up the river road.

"Barb?"

"Uh-hunh."

"Gee, I hate to quarrel all the time. Rock and Marth don't quarrel, and I'm tired of it."

"So am I."

They sat down on the wide stone steps. He held her against him. The house was very big and quiet behind them and even at this hour a light fragrance came from it. They always had flowers in their house. One day she had showed all of it to him, all the rooms from the attic to the cellar, and it had amazed him that there could be so much of everything in one house. Now, thinking about it, it made him feel like kicking someone, not anyone in particular but maybe Hoyt Hasswell or that smooth dame, Kay.

"This is a hell of a business," he said.

She waited, not moving, scarcely breathing, but leaning against him very quietly.

"Listen, Barby, I'm no good for you."

"Don't say that, Joe. I don't like to hear you say it about yourself. Besides, it's not true."

The Long Year

"Marth thinks I'm trouble for you. She doesn't say it exactly, but she *thinks* it."

"She doesn't know. I'm the lucky one, Joe." She put her arm around him. She was thin. He could feel her thinness against him. "Gee, Joe."

"Listen, Blue-eyes," he said. "I got enough troubles."

"I'm no baby," she said.

"I know," but he thought, Gee, she's a baby. Look at this house. Look at the way her mother's always making her drink milk and keeps her clothes for her and never lets her get her hands into smelly old dishwater. She's a baby, all right, but in a way she's smart, too. She never asks for anything. We fight and all that, but she never asks for anything. God, I don't know what to do. No one ever knows, I guess, but me, I'll never know no matter what happens. I just have too many messes on my hands now.

"Tell me, Joe," she said.

"Look, it's two lives. I have one life with you and then I have another life, too."

"I don't care."

"I'm not good for you, Sweets. I'm not good for anyone. Every gabber in this town knows about Joe Connaught. You can't—"

"I know, too," she said. "I know how you are and how you take care of Lindy and how you always want to make money to help your folks. These are bad times, everyone says, but Joe, I know how you are—"

"Ah, Barbs," he said. He nuzzled her cheek softly. He held her as if she were his child, his own tender baby. But instead at this moment he felt like a child himself, clinging to the coolest and loveliest part of his life. He loved all of her, the way she was angry and the way she walked as if she owned the whole damned world and the marvelous, clean smell of her. That was all HER. HER. She was for him no matter what anyone said, and they all had plenty to say, gabble-gabble all over the whole place all the time. When he was away from her, he felt that it was right, but he was never happy and there was this crazy longing for her that made him feel hungry all the time. No food ended that kind of hunger.

"You're really my girl, Barby. You're a devil and you're terribly spoiled, but you're my girl."

"We could be together," she said wistfully. She ran her finger along the scar under his chin where he had ripped it open in a skiing accident when he was ten. That always felt wonderful to have her do that.

"You wouldn't like it," he said.

"Joe?"

"What?"

"I wouldn't ask you to do anything."

"Like what?"

"Like to stop drinking."

He laughed softly in the darkness. "Maybe not at first, but later on you would."

"No."

"And always wanting to know where I was and where I'm going and making plans to go to the movies or dancing and then I wouldn't be there."

She shook her head. "I wouldn't ask any questions. I'd just be happy with you."

"And what about when I went away?"

"Honestly, I'd be all right. I'd just wait for you."

He sat up, leaning against the porch railing. "A swell life for you. Your mother'd be crazy about that. I can't even get a job from Kay Hasswell, and today I went around to see Monte on the garbage wagon, and even that filthy bastard gave it to me right out. There isn't anything. Can't you see how that'd sit with your mother?"

"She had her way when she wanted it."

He stood up, moved across the lawn, and she sat watching him. "That was different. Look at what your father did for her. Barby, this is a big thing, a Depression, and it's not gonna pass over quick like that. Ever since that run we had on the bank it's been

The Long Year 89

getting worse. I was there. I saw it—all those people crowding into the place like they were ready to kill each other. This isn't a good time for guys like me."

"I don't see what that's got to do with us."

"Sweets—" he began, and then he saw it was useless to try to tell her. How could she know about things like this? Living in her clean, safe world, she couldn't know. "How old are you, Barbs?"

"You know—seventeen."

"Sure—seventeen." He blew out his breath. "Geez," he breathed. He walked around the lawn. He touched the willow tree that slung its shadow over the garden. He touched the brick wall. Then he sat down in the white lawn chair. "Come on," he said. She came and sat in the chair with him, and he held her, wanting to hold her that way forever because she was the best part of his life. She was always so clean, just right, and nothing else was clean or right for him—nothing except Barby.

"Joe—will I see you?"

"Maybe."

"When?"

"Whenever I can make it. Maybe I'll have to go out of town, but I'll come back."

"You mean go away this week?"

"Maybe."

"Oh," she said.

He walked with her up the steps of the porch and then he kissed her gently. She didn't move. He went across the wide lawn that was gold in splotches from the moon, dark patterns from the trees, soft under his feet. He closed the garden gate, and he heard her go into the house. "God," he said. "Mother of God."

He let the car slide, dead engine, down the hill. He didn't want to go home or go down to Mike's or see anyone. Tomorrow there was another little business for him to do, and he wasn't going to think about it now. He drove the car toward the cliffs and off the main highway onto the narrow, bumpy road that was overgrown with tall grasses. He drove by instinct, without seeing the road, and he did not have to see it because it was all known to him. He parked the car under the elm tree in the meadow, and then he took off his jacket and spread it over his shoulders and lay, huddled, in the car. His fists were clenched tight and he smelled the leather, the faint odor of Barby's cologne. After a long time, he fell into a light, nervous sleep and did not waken until the sun was over the river. Then he got out of the car and began to walk down the road that led to the lip of the cliff. The road dwindled and was lost in the underbrush. He stepped awkwardly over the brush and walked in the grasses and finally found a small thread of a path. When he came to the water, he stopped and scooped up some clear water and washed his face. After that he combed his hair and tightened his tie. He walked slowly, and his hands were clenched in his pockets.

When he saw the cabin near the marsh, he walked more slowly. You could hardly tell that the cabin was there because of the color of it and the way it was sunk into the shoulder of that one hill. He walked even more slowly because he did not want to get there too soon. As he moved toward the shack, he knew that he was being watched. He had never been watched before, and now he could feel that person looking at him. He took his hands out of his pockets and began to swagger a little. He stopped by the big oak tree that gnarled its roots down the slope toward the shack. He whistled three times, once low, once high and a third time an unbroken, high note. While he waited he kept his mouth puckered to whistle again. But a man came out of the cabin. He was a little man, dark and swarthy and heavy on his feet. He came up the slope and looked at Joe. Joe had never seen this man, and he didn't move. He wasn't going to do anything wrong—the man he had dealt with was taller, with mottled red skin, better dressed than this one and not so pleasant to look at.

"Connaught, hey?"

"Yeah," he drawled.

"You look better in the daylight."

"I never saw you before."

The Long Year

"No, but I saw you. And I say you look better in the daylight."

"I'm no Ramon Novarro."

"No smart cracks," he said nervously.

"I speak my mind," Joe said.

He was scared of this little man and of the other one. This little man had eyes like dried grapes. He was scared, but he figured he'd get used to it, and so he followed him into the cabin, swaggering. Inside there was an old kitchen table and three chairs. The other man, the one with the mottled skin, got up when Joe came in and shook hands. He wore a very bright tie and a gold tie clasp with the initials A.J.G. "This is Amory," the little man said. "My name's Vance—just Vance."

Joe said nothing.

Amory said, "Sit down, Kid." He shoved a pack of cigarettes toward him. "I like your looks," he said. "I think you'll work out fine."

"If I get paid, I'll work all right," he said.

Amory laughed. He was trying to be jolly. His laughter made Joe feel sick. He knew he didn't look good to these guys, and he felt tough and dirty. He wasn't going to think about Barby or Mike or Rock or the kid, Lindy—of any of them. A fellow had to take from the lowest branch of the tree when he was hungry and too tired to climb. Well, it was that way for him, and Barby was not in it. He was in it alone. She and the others were somewhere else, something else again—

"You ever shoot a gun?" Amory asked.

He narrowed his eyes. He could feel the other one, Vance, watching him. "No," he said.

"Well, Vance'll teach you."

"I shot a BB gun and I used to hunt pheasants, but I never shot to kill a man."

"Don't worry," Amory said. "You won't have to. That's why we got you. You've got brains, and you're a cool number. Why, you're ready-made for this kind of business."

The little dark man, Vance, moved in toward the table.

"Now let's see," Amory began, "we ought to work the southern part of the State this week—" Joe followed his yellowed finger across the map, bent forward and began to listen carefully—that was the only way he'd make a go of this, to listen and to wait . . .

CHAPTER ELEVEN:

Whenever Kay dressed to go any place, she had a keen feeling of excitement. She never got over that no matter how many places she went nor how many people she met. You never knew what would happen, and if you kept yourself truly ready for anything, it was really marvelous what could happen. Now, in this week that she had been in the town, she had begun to feel at ease, to know exactly how she would handle everything—Hoyt, the girl, the house, the factory. She smiled when she thought of Mike, let him go his way, soon enough he'd learn or get tired of going his own way or love someone else. She understood about loving that way, as she herself had once loved Prokosch, but in the end you got a hold of yourself. Mike would get a hold of himself.

She kept going back and forth into Marth's room. The girl was curious. Despite her apparent love of clothes, she had no natural talent for them. "Good Lord," she said, "you can't wear those stockings to Maida's garden party. They're too thick—or something. Really, darling—"

"Well, I don't know," Marth said. "If I could go without stockings, with just nice, smooth, tan legs—that would be best."

"Try it, try it," she said eagerly. "You must develop some kind of feeling for clothes, darling. It's merely a matter of being clever and understanding what you need for yourself. Think of the intelligent women who've made a life study of nothing but clothes. Give it some thought—more than just liking."

Marth looked at her in the mirror of her dressing table. "I'll never be able to do it—the way you can, Kay. Barby could, though."

Kay laughed. She bent over and kissed Marth's cheek. She felt very happy today. In the morning, LeGrand had called her from

New York. His manner had been teasing and gentle. He wondered when she was coming back, wasn't a week enough? Everything was going exactly as she wanted it to go.

On the way to the garden party, they saw Lindy, Joe's kid brother. He was sitting in the baseball field. It was dusty there, and he was sitting on third base. A few draggling yellow flowers and dandelions grew around that place. He waved to them, a skinny, forlorn little boy in clothes that were shabby and too large for him.

"Joe's kid brother," Marth said.

"The place is ugly," Kay said. "I see it a thousand times. There's something terrifying and ugly about a little boy sitting in a dusty ball field all alone on Sunday afternoon."

"He's really a wonderful kid. He works for Mrs. Amos on the newspaper. Rocky says he bets no one in this whole town knows as much as Lindy Connaught."

"Nonsense," she said. She pushed her foot hard on the gas. The big red car picked up speed, tore down the narrow street, roared heavily, hungrily up the hill, kicking up a great cloud of hot, gassy dust. Marth could hear her father's laughter while they were still outside the house. He always went to Mrs. Leroy's parties very early and was the last one to leave. It was the only social event of any importance in the town. The factory people who were on the office staff, the foremen, the summer guests at the hotel, the teachers, a few people from the city, summer people from their places on the river, and a few of Barby's friends. The others usually tried to pretend it was nothing and they wouldn't go to Maida Leroy's party even if they were asked. But it was a slap on the face to them.

The house was newly decorated, and there were flowers everywhere. In the garden, a few people sat at the small, round lawn tables under striped lawn umbrellas. Joanie Peterson played the piano in the sun room. She played Gershwin, Strauss and Greig, sitting in the far corner of the sun room so that the music went out into the garden. Every year it was the same.

"Hello, darling," Kay said to Johnnie Evans. She took his arm

The Long Year 95

and walked into the garden. She kissed Maida's cheek. She looked with critical, sour eyes at Maida's new dress. "Darling, Maida," she said.

"Kay, it's—it's heavenly to have you home again. I do hope we'll see a lot of you."

"Kay's very busy," Hoyt said.

"Oh, dear," Maida sighed, "you were always such a hard-working person, Kay, and you always had so much fun—"

"It's nice to be here," she said. She wondered where Marth had gone, and she looked around and saw her sitting with Mr. Wimmer. She wondered why everyone quoted this man and tried to talk with him, even her brother quoted him. She saw Russian Peterson standing at the far end of the garden. "I want to talk to Russian, Johnnie," she said. "He doesn't like me, you know. I can just hear him shouting it out: 'She's a sinful woman. She's a sinful woman.'"

Johnnie smiled affectionately at her. "You're crazy. He's not like that at all."

Russian held the teacup with skill. He had grace and cleverness in his crippled hands. His wife looked solemnly at Kay and Johnnie Evans. "Oh, dear," she said, "she's coming over here." With worn, reddened fingers she tried to smooth down her hair and her cheap, homemade dress.

"She's no one," he said. He touched her shoulder. Under his touch, her shoulder was hard and bony. He smiled and tried to look at ease. He could hear Joanie playing in the house. He felt that he was better than anyone there, he worked hard and he had a fine family and he took care of his own.

"He-llo, Russian," Kay said warmly.

"Hello," he said. "You remember my wife, Miss Hasswell."

His wife nodded.

"Why, yes," Kay said. "I remember you very well. Your name was Jo Anderson."

The woman looked at her with calm blue eyes. For a moment a young, pleased expression crossed her face and died. "Yes," she said dully.

"I remember when you used to bring eggs to our house. I was a terrible child, always wanting to ride on your cart."

"Yes," the woman said again.

"You used to have a big farm up on the river, didn't you?"

"That was a very long time ago," Russian said. He kept his hand on his wife's shoulder.

"Not so long," Kay said. She smiled at them. They looked like those peasants she used to see on the road from Praha up to the Skoda. Every morning when she went driving, she would see those peasants, they called themselves farmers or agrarians, but to her they were peasants with dull, hopeless expressions, large and slow-witted. Those two, Russian and his wife, didn't look at all like Americans to her. America was big cities and wonderful little shops and oysters in the halfshell and imported wines, linens, silks, woolens, caviar, perfumes. These people could be from any place in Europe, any rural district—only they did not seem so clever as the farmers of Normandy or the ones in Austria.

Johnnie Evans surveyed her with amused eyes. "You should be an actress," he said. "You have a different face for everyone, depending on what you want from them and what kind of people they are."

She tapped his arm playfully. "You're too clever."

"My face is my fortune," he said.

"No—I don't think so." Then she saw Mr. Wimmer come into the garden again. He wore a dark suit, and there was a faint smudge of ink across his forehead. When he saw her, he smiled. He was carrying a cup of tea and three small sandwiches. As he moved toward her, one of the sandwiches fell on the grass. "Wouldn't you know?" he said. "Hate to waste anything," he said. Across the garden, Mrs. Leroy's high, childish voice rose. She was having a fine time airing her troubles about Teresita. "If it weren't for Howard, that girl would never come to work. She drinks too. She drinks and dances out there in the middle of the night. I've spoken to Howard, but he doesn't seem to be able to stop her."

"Teresita's in the wrong place," Kay said.

The Long Year

"No," Mr. Wimmer said. "There isn't any *right* place for her."

"Really?"

"Is it pleasant to return to your home town after such a long time?" he asked.

"Yes," she said. "I haven't thought much about it, but I guess it is."

"You've been too busy to know," Johnnie said. Beside Mr. Wimmer he seemed poised and dapper.

Marth came across the garden with Barby and Rocky. They waved to Kay and then sat under the willow tree, and Mr. Wimmer went to sit with them. Kay looked at them, thinking of the other times when they had parties on their lawn and Mamma made quarts of hand-turned ice cream, and she thought: It wasn't like this, though. It was better. We didn't think about anything but having a good time, except how to make the boys do what we wanted them to do, Simon and then Sonny, sitting out there on the lawn. We were terribly young, it makes me hurt inside to think how young we were and how little we knew—innocent, Mamma said. "You're young and innocent, Kay, and there's no harm in that. Keep it that way for a while." But Mamma had not understood her driving need to change it all, the whole thing, the way of life, the place, everything.

She sat at one of the tables and talked to the men from the factory. She talked about crops and places she had seen in Africa and South America and Europe. She talked about the old days when she had gone North to the timber land and helped with the marking of trees. Occasionally, she would look toward Mr. Wimmer and his group, all of them talking earnestly and eating sandwiches and pink and white wafers. The men looked at her with solemn, blank eyes. They were waiting for her to say something about the factory, and she held it away from them like bait, biding her time. She had to do this in her own way. She told little stories, and they laughed at the proper places. Her manner explained that she belonged to them, this was like the old days—she had really never, in spirit, left the town.

When she went into the house, Johnnie followed her. She stopped at the piano, watching Joanie Peterson play, not hearing the music or even caring to hear it.

"You play beautifully," she said. "You know, I have a very dear friend—LeGrand, Robert LeGrand—perhaps, you've heard of him?"

"Yes," Joanie said. "I saw his picture in *Etude*."

"Some time when he comes to visit me here—you must meet him."

"Yes," the girl said. She smiled wistfully.

"Let's go somewhere," Johnnie Evans said. "I find this sort of thing very dull."

"Don't be silly," she laughed. "I have to go to the office."

"You're just saying that."

He went into the living room with her. He put his arms around her and kissed her on the mouth. She closed her eyes and then stood away from him. "These people are interesting," she said. "Look at them out there. They don't have any fun at this party. They have to get dressed in their best clothes, and they hate it. Why do they come, there is no pleasure in it for them. You see, they can't get pleasure out of anything. They're heavy clods of earth, not young but full of defeat and death."

"No," he said. "I remember when they were young. Only now they're worried."

"What help is that—to worry?"

"They can't stop worrying."

She said nothing. She leaned against the french doors. They were dusty. The people moved in the dusk of the garden beyond the room. She could hear them talking. They talked loudly with much laughter, but somehow it wasn't the same as in the old days. The people had changed so that even in their social lives there was too much reality, no real flare for drama or color. In the old days when Sonny used to come to the house with all the big, clean college boys in their blue coats and white flannels, there had never been a lack of color or drama. They were always looking for something

The Long Year

and singing of it and dreaming of it. They had as much liquor as they wanted and big, open cars, and whenever they got drunk, it was fun. Now, when you saw a drunken man on the streets, it was nothing like a party. It was sickness. That was the trouble with prohibition of any kind, it didn't work because people wore off their hides trying to find a way out of it. Prokosch had explained this to her, and now she understood how it was. Soon, probably by the end of the year, the State would have Repeal, but why did everyone have to take it so seriously? Why couldn't they make a big joke of it, a party, a secret, gay time? No—it had to be a thing of politics and sociology.

She was watching Russian and Mr. Wimmer. Mr. Wimmer looked tall and thin beside the big, slow-moving man. Russian was moving his hands apart as if he were telling a fish story. Mr. Wimmer stood hunched over a little. He had a very nice head and a good profile. All right, she thought, let them stay by themselves and be exclusive, it's what they want, but none of them can do anything without me. They admit it, too, they can't do anything without me, and some day they'll know it.

"Listen, Loveliness," Johnnie said, "let's go somewhere."

"Where?"

"Dancing—anywhere."

"All right," she said. "Let's get out of here."

"Oh, darling," Maida said, coming into the room, her chiffon handkerchief trailing from her fingertips. "Don't go." She stood in the middle of the room, holding a tray of sandwiches in one hand and a silver dish of pink and white wafers. "I can't get Teresita out of the kitchen. She's spilled on her uniform, and she's so fussy about uniforms, they've got to fit like paper on a wall. Darlings—don't go—so many things coming at one time . . ."

"That Teresita," Kay laughed.

"Oh, she's really a wonderful cook and quite attractive. I'm lucky to have her even though she's hard to manage. I just never know how to manage her." She sighed. "I wish you'd do something with Barby, Kay. She does admire you so, you know, and I wish you'd do something for her. She isn't the same child she used to be. You remember, Johnnie?"

"Yes," he said. "Barby's always been a very gay, social creature."

"Oh, dear, yes," Maida said, "but now she isn't much fun. She's utterly wasted on that Connaught boy. Have you met him, Kay? He's a friend of Mike Hasswell—my, that *is* a tragedy for poor, darling Hoyt."

"Yes," Kay said. "I know Joe Connaught."

"Of course, he's nice looking, but really, Kay, I wish you'd stay. Everyone wants to talk to you."

"I have to go now, Maida."

"Oh, dear—"

"I promised Johnnie."

"You're a heel, Johnnie," Maida said. She had always liked him and thought that his reputation was greatly exaggerated. She liked clever people, and after all he came from a very good family and had gone to a fine university, and even if the majority of people in town didn't care much for him, she liked him. And Hoyt liked him, too. She always asked Walt Purdy to come to these little gatherings, but now for several years he had not been going anywhere, and maybe it was just as well—because she wasn't sure if he liked Johnnie. Not that he'd ever said anything, but Johnnie was awfully sweet and attractive, and even if he was almost ten years younger than Kay, Kay really didn't look her age at all, and she had a wonderful way with men. She must have a way with them, after all, to have had three perfectly good husbands, and God only knew how many lovers, probably beginning that summer with poor Simon O'Dodd. "Yes," she said, "you're a very nice heel, Johnnie."

"Okay," he laughed, "so I'm a heel."

They ran down the steps. Kay's soft, thin dress caught in the bridal wreath bushes along the walk. She laughed for no reason at all. When she got into the car, she could see Barby and Mr. Wimmer looking at her over the garden wall.

"Tell Marth I'm leaving!" she called to them.

The Long Year 101

"Okay," Mr. Wimmer said. "Have fun."

She tried to think of something to say to him, but then she merely waved. He waved back, but Barby was looking off down the road. The people were talking and laughing in the garden. She could hear them even above the sound of the motor. She reached over and switched on the radio and they drove fast in the big, heavy red car.

"Johnnie? Do you know this Greek woman, Mrs. Amos?"

"Yes," he said. "I'm in love with her. She's massive, and everything she does is massive. You can't help being in love with her. She's great, really great."

"Do you read her editorials?"

"Sure. Everyone does. Why?"

"She had some very snide remarks to make about people giving garden parties and wasting all that food, cutting off crusts from the bread to make fancy sandwiches—all sorts of things—saying that garden parties were like a kick in the belly to people who were starving."

"I read that."

"Now, I know very well Hoyt has a mortgage on that paper. It seems to me he ought to do something about it. First she wants the road changed. Then she wants people to put in their own electric and gas system—"death to the utility companies," she says. "Things like that can cause trouble."

He grinned. "You've forgotten about living here. Everyone reads what she has to say, but no one ever does anything. That's the way it is."

She sat with her hands in her lap, very still, but her mind was racing. "Nevertheless, I think a thing like that's dangerous. When the men are out of work, they'll read all of that and have plenty of idle time to work up false enthusiasm for whatever she advocates."

"Oh, I wouldn't say that. Besides, a newspaper that has pressure from its owners isn't really a paper. It's an echo of whatever the owners think."

"Really, now," she sniffed. "How can you talk that way? You're too much of a realist—"

"It's the truth, though," he said. "If you want to get the real brains of the town, don't pick on Mrs. Amos. She's smart enough and has a lot to say, but the people she talks with, her friends, are the ones behind it. Gene Wimmer and Macbeth. They're the only liberals and internationalists in the town." He liked to talk to someone who was intelligent and had something to say. He thought, This one's got a marvelous mind, and she lives her own secret life, and I think she's dangerous. She'd do anything to get her own way; kill a man—I wonder how many men she's killed already, not outright to bleed them or knife them and leave them dead on the pavement or in their bedrooms, but to kill by ignoring or changing or demanding from them. She could do it. She's that kind.

"Who is this Mr. Wimmer?"

"He's not anyone. He came here seven, eight years ago as a teacher and made his home here. He's a wonderful teacher."

"Do you know him well?"

"No—no, I guess no one knows him well. Maybe those kids do—Mike Hasswell and Joe Connaught and young Macbeth. Probably Marth knows him as well as any of them."

"I shouldn't think he'd be—well, very complicated."

"He's not your type," he said. "I'm your type."

"Perhaps," she laughed. "I've never really decided. Perhaps he's my type. He's very attractive."

"He doesn't like women. He just likes to teach and to visit. He goes around and visits in the factory and up to the newspaper office, all around."

"A man like that must know the town very well."

"Let's not talk about Gene Wimmer," he said.

"I'm really not interested," she said. "It's just that I have to know what's going on here—" But she was thinking, I suppose that's what a poet is, a man who goes around and listens to people and talks to them and doesn't want to do anything but his work. I

The Long Year 103

suppose that's what Prokosch meant when he said I didn't understand the poetry of living, the substance of life ... All things are like molasses, running together until there is no point of separation, Praha and New York and High Falls ... all as one and the same thing ...

Mr. Wimmer had always lived in this same room in the hotel since he had first come to the town. The room was small and overlooked a narrow alley. In the mornings, the laundry men used to sit outside the kitchen door and smoke and drink their morning beers, throwing the bottle caps up against the screened kitchen windows. On Saturdays during the school year, he went down there and sat with them and had a beer or two. Almost every night during the summer, he stayed in his room and played the accordion. He had learned how to play by listening to music on the radio. Mostly, he liked to play Western ballads and songs about Mexico. He wore a blue satin shirt from a mail-order house, a pair of tooled cowboy boots he had won in a crap game and a touring rodeo unit in the city, a black Stetson Macbeth had ordered especially for him from Chicago.

He had never been in the West, but it was his dream to go there some day. He thought he would find himself a girl who knew how to cook and wasn't afraid of cows or horses, and he would go out West and live. He didn't especially care about making his fortune there, all he wanted to do was to live near or in the mountains and to fish in the clear mountain streams.

When he had nothing to read and was tired of being alone, he usually went down to Mike's boathouse. Sometimes he and Mike, Rock and Joe went up to the filling station and sat there and talked. There was no place he could go that was as much his own as this town, and so even during the summer vacations, he did not desire to leave this place. He took extension courses in political science, philosophy and economics. Most of the summer he walked around the town and talked and walked in the hills and spent some time on the river, fishing or swimming. Until now, he had never felt any lack of companionship in his life because he had many friends and he had his work, but now he began to feel his need for this woman.

He had known girls in his classes at the university, but he had never thought of loving any of them. He had known girls on farms and in his own classes, but his relationship with these had been friendly and almost paternal, and he had not felt that he was missing anything. That first day, though, when he had seen her coming down the street, a woman like no woman he had ever known, he had thought: I'll bet she smokes and uses one of those little ivory-and-gold cigarette holders and holds it between her thumb and forefinger—that had been his first thought about her. After that, he thought of her in many ways, and his thoughts were not separate but continuous, so that he discovered that underneath everything he said and did there was an underlying current of thought about this woman.

Before this, he had thought a lot about theories of teaching, that had consumed his mind. Then, after a while, he knew there was no rule as to how a person should teach, just to tell the students the truth, truth was white, untruth was black. He didn't have any ambitions to have a big degree or to make money or to wear fine clothes. Of course, there was the matter of living in the Far West, some place in the Rockies, probably the Jackson Hole country, but other than that he had no desires—until he saw Kay that first day. But then, he forgot any dreams he might have had, and he had the dream of love. He began to find it in his sleep. Sometimes it was a girl, about six years old. This girl went whizzing up and down the sidewalk on a small red bicycle. She had red ribbons in her hair. Another time, the dream was a woman who was lying naked on a bed. She was lying on a hand-knitted afghan, and except for a pair of blue-and-white knitted slippers, she was totally naked. She was very beautiful and real to him. Once the dream was himself alone. That was the worst dream because there was nothing to see except himself on a doorstep. He wore a blue serge

The Long Year

suit such as Joe wore and he sat on a doorstep waiting. That was all he ever did in this dream, he waited and waited and nothing happened, and he was alone there.

He never spoke of this to anyone. He wasn't afraid of being laughed at, but he thought that in one of these dreams he would see himself or the child on the bike or the naked woman and then he would know what the dream meant. When he went to bed at night, he would say a quick prayer, Lord let me know what the dream means. But he never knew except that he understood that each dream was a dream of life, one was waiting, one was going away fast, and the other lay still and waited for him.

He thought, too, he might have these dreams because he was alone so much. It was the first time he had ever desired anyone to be with him all the time, but now he thought that he would like to have Kay Hasswell with him. He always planned what he would say to her when he met her on the street or in the hotel lobby or around the factory, but when he saw her he immediately forgot what he had planned to say. His manner toward her was quiet and humorous because she pleased him, and it was some kind of joke—the way they talked to each other. She knew. He was certain that she knew, felt it under everything they said. "Look here," he would say to her in his mind, "look here, now, I'm not such a bad sort, and we could get along fine. Look here, now—" But, he never said it, and he supposed he never would say anything like that to her because she didn't need it. She didn't need anyone but herself. He could see that. Still—some day, he might say it.

CHAPTER TWELVE:

THAT MORNING, the men in the station were having a bad time with a big Mack truck. Lindy and Joe Connaught went down the hill in Joe's car, and Joe stopped and let the kid out and then went on his own way. After a time, Mr. Wimmer and Mike and Rocky came along, and Lindy called to them. "They're havin' a hell of a time with this here truck," he said.

The men kept walking around the truck, shaking their heads and cursing. One of them crawled under it and lay there for a long time. All the men were excited about this truck and angry with the driver.

"You don't feed her enough oil," Mike said. "You got to feed them oil or they burn out."

"I feed her enough," the driver said, but he knew he didn't have a chance against all of them. They acted like the truck was a horse that he'd kicked or whipped. They made him crawl under the truck and poke around and shook their fists at him, shouting curses. After a time, they all sat down on the cement driveway and leaned against the station and tried to think of something to be done about that big, dead truck. They reached no conclusion. Rock went over to the truck and sat in it and tried the motor, but it would not turn over. Then they all were angrier than before. Mike watched him, smoking his cigarette the way Joe did, hard between his lips with a little frown when he sucked on it. Macbeth came out of the post office and sat on the curb looking at the truck. After a while, someone down the street stuck a nickel into the juke box. Johnnie Evans came out of his office and got into Kay's red convertible.

"Where's Marth?" Mr. Wimmer asked.

"Probably with Kay. They're lookin' fer a place on the river so she can build a house up there."

The Long Year

"You don't say," Macbeth said. He ambled over to the truck and looked under the hood, sniffing the odor of hot grease, dust and alcohol. He pushed his fingers into the intestines of the motor, touched the wires gently, holding his ear close to them. "That damned woman's going to build herself a palace, I bet. She always wanted a palace and a throne and a lot of vassals." He belched and stood away from the motor, looking at it carefully. "Might try her now," he said.

"Go on, try her," Mike said to the driver.

"Nuts," the driver said. He got in, and the big engine suddenly turned over and roared. The truck started up the hill, racing its motor, and then going easily enough. Soon the sound died, and the men around the filling station sat down in the sun, and it was then, at that moment, that Gene Wimmer saw the men coming down the street like a dark cloud, together, moving in silence. They looked pale and walked in their working clothes, their hands in their pockets. Mr. Wimmer said nothing and did not move. He already knew what it was.

"What's the matter?" Macbeth asked.

"We've been laid off," Russian said. "All of us, every man down to the washroom boy."

"It's come," Macbeth said. "I knew it. Man doesn't know whether to shit or go blind."

"We've got to go somewheres," Olds said.

"Chicago, maybe," someone said.

"Yeah—Chicago," Russian said. There was a dull, stunned look across his face, and in his mind there was a heaviness, and in his big, solid body a worm feasted on his spirit. Everything he said came slowly, heavily from his mouth in confusion.

The men were as silent as one man in misery. They did not seem to want to move now that they were together in the shade of the filling station. The weariness was inside them and in their shoes and in their hands and over their shoulders like a black rock.

"Chicago's worse," Mr. Wimmer said. "I saw some pictures over at the newspaper office. Things are always worse in cities."

There was a long silence. Russian shifted his weight. "Been in this town since I was knee-high to a grasshopper."

"Me, too," they said. "Yeah—me, too."

One of the Hickory boys said, "I been to Chicago once. Had a lot of money to spend free as anything, but it didn't matter much. The place was crowded, an' everyone lived in a real small apartment, sleepin an eatin in the same room."

The men turned toward him. "Here we got our own houses," they said. "We got them anyhow."

"You can fish," Olds said. His glass eye was not the same color as the other one. Rock remembered when they were children, Olds would make that eye pop for them. Now it was there like a small, shining, uncertain button in his narrow, red face. "Everything'll open in the Fall. The factory never closed before."

"No," Mr. Wimmer said. "I don't think so."

"I don't think so neither," Russian said. "She said she'd keep on a few watchmen, but she didn't say the place would open up very soon. She didn't make any promise."

"Maybe there's somethin' at the prison." From where they stood, they could make out the reddish buildings of the cell block standing on the cliff above the swamp.

Mr. Wimmer said, "The prison's cut down on its staff, too."

"Yeah," Russian said. "That's right."

"The factory won't open," Mike said angrily. "You guys should use your heads. Why, every week or so Mrs. Amos has been telling you in the newspaper, but you didn't care if they were standing in the streets in Chicago, dying where they stood."

"Shut up, Mike," Rock said. It was hard enough on the men, he thought, without Mike throwing it in their teeth—Mike never had hope for anyone, not the smallest grain to offer the poor dying old crows. And it hurt to look at Russian Peterson—of course, he'd be one of the few to be kept on, but that wouldn't help. It would be hard on a man like Russian when the rest—Olds, the Hickory boys were still out of work. He saw Marth coming down the hill in Kay's red car, and he went to the curb and she stopped.

The Long Year   109

He leaned against the car. The metal was very hot. How cool she looks, cool and pretty and the way girls should look, without any cares but to run around town in a slick car. I could never give her that.

"What's the matter?" she asked. "Look at the men standing around."

"They've been fired," he said. "The factory is closed."

"Oh, no!" she said. Tears came into her eyes. "But Kay said only last night she'd do something soon."

"Not right now," he said gently. "But Mr. Wimmer says it's bad and everyone's going to be poor, but it isn't the worst thing that can happen to them."

"Oh, Lord," she said. "What about their families? It's just about the worst thing—and poor Daddy—the factory's never been closed. I think I'll hurry down there." She looked at the men. "You don't think they'll riot, do you?"

He frowned. "Whatever gave you that idea?"

"Well, Kay said that sometimes men riot when they don't have everything their own way."

"Goddamit," he said. "You ought to use your head."

"I only mentioned it."

"They won't riot," he said. He moved away from the car.

"Good-bye, Rock," she said.

He did not hear her.

Well, she thought, Kay said they might riot, and I don't see why he got so mad just because I mentioned it. *I* don't really think they will, but then they've never been out of work before. Her mind was confused. The town had always been the place for her, really swell, and all the people in it had seemed like her friends, and she had always felt glad to be there. But now—now, looking at the men, she remembered that one time when she was going to St. Mark's and on the way home, where the old Greeley school had been, the Ku Klux Klan had burned an effigy of the Pope. She wondered why she remembered it now, after all this time.

And yet, to love the town alone and for itself, just to sleep there and walk on the streets was enough to have happiness in that town. In the early morning, she used to wake up and see the factory from her window, and the house in its silence was her own. In the cold grayish light, she'd see Macbeth taking his morning walk beyond the swamp, there by the pools of water, the green tufts, the boggish, smoky smell, all gray, and the morning mist hanging over the swamp and the factory. It was not real, but a thing half seen, contained inside her, in the bones, far away from earth. She could not imagine what it would be like to leave the town, and now for several days she had had the pressing knowledge that she *would* leave it. She must ask Rock about that, if he felt that soon he would leave there.

The men together like that, Russian and Olds and all of them, standing in this one manner, their hands in their pockets and their big, working shoulders hunched over. Even though it was terribly hot they stood unmoving and did not take off their jackets—they looked gray and cold. When one of them breathed, all of them breathed, and when one shifted his weight, the others did the same. Why? she thought. What's different in them now that was not there before this time?

She turned the car down the factory road.

Rock watched the car until it was out of sight. She's a big baby, he thought, she ought to get rid of all those ideas—she ought to do something, and I should help her do it, now—quickly—whatever it is . . ."

Russian said, "Mike, you hear anything—I mean, you hear what Hoyt thinks about this?"

"Hell, no, Russian. You know better than to ask me. Ask Mr. Wimmer."

"It's all over the country," Mr. Wimmer said.

"Why?" they wanted to know.

"I don't know why," he said. "We did it to ourselves. The country is ours."

"Yeah," Russian said heavily. "It's ours, all right."

"I could go down there," Mr. Wimmer said slowly. "Probably,

The Long Year

it won't do much good, but I can find out what she—Miss Hasswell thinks."

No one said anything. They merely looked at him, and he stood up and looked at them. There were more of them now, and their voices as he moved away were mournful and did not belong to the world of daylight. It was a weird sound. In the night, it might have been different, but with the sun out like that and the faces of the men clear, it was too unreal and a part of the human fables that should not have been seen so clearly. No one should look at the faces of those men slit open like apples and revealing the hidden, darkening fruit . . .

The factory that noon lay silent beside the hot swamp, nothing moved there, and this made the place seem smaller, older and shabbier. Marth stood for a moment outside the office building. She could hear her father's voice and then Kay's. She wondered what her father would do now that the factory was closed, and she could not remember a time when he had not gone there. She went into the outer office. Mary Connaught was sitting at the typewriter erasing an error. She looked up.

"Mary, are you staying?"

"Someone's got to," Mary said. "I'm working for Miss Hasswell."

"Where's Daddy?"

"In her office."

"It—it's funny around here now, isn't it?"

Mary nodded. "I feel terrible, Marth."

"Yes."

"What will everyone do?"

"I don't know." She felt like crying. She looked at the rows of typewriters and adding machines with their black covers pulled neatly over them, at the cleared desks and the silent ceiling fans. "I don't know."

"Miss Hasswell's *very* hopeful," Mary said. She sounded like Kay when she said that.

"She'll do it, Mary," Marth said. "You'll see."

"I know that."

"Will you be here alone?"

"No. She says we'll have to keep some sort of staff and the men in the engine room and some night watchmen."

"Oh," she said. "That's not very many." She walked toward Kay's office and opened the door. Her father was sitting in the far corner by the file cases.

"Come in, darling," Kay said. "Did the sky fall on your head?"

"I—I saw the men," she said.

"Where are they? Did they go home?" Hoyt asked.

"They're up at the filling station—most of them." Now, sitting in the small office, it seemed that her father filled the place. He held his hands open on his big knees, and he was sweating heavily. Kay looked very cool, though. She sat at her desk, her chair swung around to face them. She wore a pale yellow dress and earrings and yellow-and-brown sandals.

"How many men will come back?" she asked.

"About twenty-five," Kay said.

At that moment, Marth felt that her aunt was far away from them, farther away than she herself was. Her aunt belonged totally to the precious, isolated world of women, possessing all the mysterious, calm airs of that world. She saw many things and told only what it pleased her to tell, and her manner was neither arrogant nor humble, only calm. She had the feeling that her aunt would know what to do and was planning already to do it.

"What'll we do now, Daddy?"

"Nothing, honey. Just wait."

Kay said, "You wait for things, Hoyt."

"What else is there?" he asked.

"There are always ways."

"Mr. Wimmer says things won't pick up. He told us so last year."

"What does he know?" Hoyt asked.

"Daddy, that's his business. He knows economics and sociology."

The Long Year

"Apparently," Kay said dryly, "apparently this Mr. Wimmer is quite an oracle."

"Everyone listens to him," Marth said.

Kay laughed. Her laughter was light and easy in the small, grim room, and she was the only light, easy one in the whole town. "Perhaps this man Wimmer does know. He's quite attractive. Perhaps Mike knows, too. But Mike is bitter. You should never have let him get so bitter, Hoyt."

"I had nothing to do with it," Hoyt said.

"He's up at the station, too," Marth said. She touched Kay's hand. "What is everyone going to do, Kay?"

"People endure. Look at the Chinese. They eat bark and roots. They manage to survive."

"We're not Chinese," Hoyt said.

"What do you hear, Marth?" Kay asked.

"Nothing," Marth said. "Just what I told you—the men are up there and Mike and Rock and Mr. Wimmer are with them, and they aren't going to riot."

"Aren't they?" Kay asked.

"Rock says they aren't." She was looking out the window at Howard sleeping in her father's car. It was hot out there, but in here it was cool. Then she saw Mr. Wimmer coming down the street, and she heard him open the door and talk to Mary. She wondered if he had gone up to the woods and thought about this. He liked to walk in the woods and think, and often when she and Rock were on picnics up there, they could hear him crashing around in the underbrush, whistling softly under his breath.

He came into the office without knocking. "Well," he said, "the men are laid off, and they're not taking to the idea kindly." He pushed back his Stetson. He did not look at any of them except Kay.

"Don't worry, Gene," Hoyt said.

"Bull," he said. "Naturally, everyone's worried. Only, if they could understand about it, it might make it easier for them."

"Is there something to understand?" Kay asked. She put her hand on Marth's arm, and Marth leaned a little toward her.

"Sure," he said.

"What?"

"Why, there's a rhythm to things, and now we go down or we rise. It's a time of death and resurrection."

"A sermon," Kay said. "I've heard men talk like that before." She smiled at him. She thought, He's younger than Prokosch, but he talks the same.

"Very fine," Hoyt said. He was embarrassed. The boy was thin and poor, a teacher in the town, full of words and ideas, but it was different when you had a business to run—you didn't have time for words and ideas.

"There's more," Mr. Wimmer said.

"Go on, then," Kay said. "Get it off your chest here and forget it."

He looked at her sharply. "You don't know how it is to be a man who desires nothing but to work and take care of his family. Poverty is ugly only to those with ugly minds, but sickness, hunger and infidelity and the hard face of cheapness are something else again. There are traitors among us. We are betrayed by softness. We are betrayed by good foods and rich lands and poor leaders."

"All right," she said. "We are betrayed."

"When people are idle, they do many things they would not otherwise do."

"Rock says the men won't riot," Marth said.

"That means," Kay said slowly—"Hoyt, that means, with the factory closed, we'll have the people on our hands. People become dangerous. Do you understand that now?"

"We don't have trouble here, Kay," he said patiently. "I told you they have trouble in cities but not here."

"Darling," she said sharply, "it doesn't matter where—cities, towns, countries—it's the same everywhere."

"You'll see," Hoyt said. He spoke to Mr. Wimmer. "We're people of business, Gene, and we like to listen to you. But now we have

The Long Year 115

things to do—we have to talk to the board of directors at the bank and we have to talk with Walt Purdy—"

"Johnnie Evans has some fine ideas," Kay said.

"Yes—Johnnie Evans," Hoyt said. He did not look at Marth, and when she started to say something, he said, "I tell you, Gene. You stick to your classroom and let the factory alone. Your classroom's your place."

Little twinkles of humor came into Mr. Wimmer's eyes. "The world's my classroom," he said.

Hoyt snorted. Kay rose and ran her fingers lightly through her hair. She looked very young to Marth. "This is interesting, but it has nothing to do with the factory. The people will have to take their medicine the same as the rest of us will."

"It's too bad," Mr. Wimmer said. "If they had had a union here, they might have been more prepared—but to come down to work in the morning and then read a notice about it—that makes it harder."

"A union is no solution," Hoyt said.

"A *good* union," he said.

Kay said, "I know your kind very well. You have fine talk, and you do nothing."

"Perhaps," he said. He was still smiling at her. "But Johnnie Evans won't help you much."

Hoyt said, "People don't like Johnnie Evans, Kay."

"I like him," she said. "I like him very much."

Marth said, "I thought Mr. Purdy was Grandma's lawyer—"

"I like him," Kay said sharply. Then she lowered her voice. "He's very clever, darling, and we need a clever lawyer."

"He's supposed to be kind of a crook," Marth said.

"My darling, who isn't?"

"I'm not," Mr. Wimmer said.

"You're a big baby," she said in a slow, warm voice. "I can see that."

"No," he said quietly. He was leaning against the wall, and he bent down and rubbed a worn spot on his knee—a shabby young man with a young, angular face. "Guess I'll go out and pick up my accordion," he said. "I only dropped by to see what was happening."

"Let's hope you're satisfied," Kay said.

"No," he said. "Not yet." He stopped just outside her door. "Do you call yourself *Miss* Hasswell?"

"That's my name."

"I just wondered, that's all."

Hoyt watched him going up the street, his hat on the back of his head. "What was that all about, may I ask?"

Kay laughed. "He's really very simple but dangerous, you know. It doesn't hurt to have him on our side."

"It's easy for men like that to talk—no responsibilities, young fellows like Gene."

"I've called in the salesmen, Hoyt—as you suggested."

He had not remembered suggesting that. "Uh—fine," he said.

"I thought we could meet with them tomorrow. They ought to get in by then."

"Fine."

"I think I'll go home now," Marth said. "I brought your car for you, Kay."

"Thanks, darling," Kay said. She put her hand on Marth's shoulder. "You look tired, Baby. Haven't you and your fine friend been getting along so well?"

"Oh—Rock. We never fight."

"Well, you and I ought to have some fun next week, go shopping and ask Barby and have a very good time. How about that?"

"Do that, honey," Hoyt said. "You don't have any fun."

"I don't feel like fun," she said.

Kay patted her arm. "There, now, this doesn't concern you. This is *our* problem, not yours, and you ought to have a good time now."

"Nobody else is having a good time," she said.

"We'll ask Barby, too," Kay said.

"All right," she said.

The Long Year

"Darling, don't look like that. You make me feel awful—and you make your father feel awful, too."

Marth blinked. "I'm sorry," she said. "I didn't think it was anyone's fault."

"Of course not," Hoyt said. "You go along, now, honey."

She went outside and got into the car with Howard. He woke up, yawning.

"Let's go for a drive, Howard," she said.

"Sure thing."

"Go anywhere," she said. "Up the river, maybe."

"Okay," he said. "You got a stummick ache?"

"You can call it that," she said. She wondered if Kay would build her house on the river now, and she wondered why, suddenly, the town seemed different to her and if this was what Rock meant when he said, "You want peaches and cream, Marth. Can't you be satisfied with the way things really are and see them that way?" But she didn't see any harm in wanting everything to be very nice for everyone. She shook her head. It hurt to think, it hurt terribly suddenly so that she could not look out the window but lay back against the seat with her eyes closed. Why was Rock angry with her because she had said that about the riot? She listened to Howard humming under his breath. The car turned off the main highway and drove along the river.

"I wish I was twenty-five," she said aloud. "Twenty-three anyhow, and then maybe I'd know something."

That day, in the late afternoon, the sun went down, and the evening was still and cool, almost cold. Up on the hill, Velma, Olds' daughter-in-law, ran out of the house. She ran into the alley and stood there yelling. "I don't care! I don't care!" she kept yelling. "I'm just sick and tired of it—vegetable stew, vegetable stew. I'm sick of sittin' in there all day!" She was nineteen now and pregnant, and her young husband, Smut Olds, had once been foreman at the paint factory. He had been among the first hundred laid off down there, and now he was working four hours a day on the county roads. He looked like his father, angular and quiet. In the dim light of the evening, he saw his wife's face, and she seemed old and sick to him. She was sick, and she knew her own sickness. When she looked at her husband, he was not young, either. This was her third child. The two little girls sat in the kitchen listening to her screams, and the younger one, who was eleven months, began to cry.

Smut Olds went out into the alley and tried to say something to her, but she would not listen.

"It's more'n a person can bear," she said. "I'm sick of all of it."

"Look, Velma, c'mon in the house. Paw oughtta be here soon. Someone'll hear you out here."

"No," she said hoarsely. "Let 'em hear me. Paw got laid off today, too, and what's he got to live off of? An' us with one kid after the other. Don't you touch me, Smut Olds. I hate you 'n' the house 'n' even yer nice old Paw. That's how rotten I feel. Don't you ever touch me again, Smut Olds."

"Aw right," he said wearily. "Onny come into the house now, Velma."

"No! No!" she screamed.

"Paw's comin', an' I won't have him lookin' at you like this." He grabbed her wrist and dragged her screaming toward the house. When she fought him, he hit her hard on the side of the face, and then she came with him, crying harshly all the while. They went into the gray, unpainted house and then there was thick silence around the house and in the old alley. The baby stopped crying. The men in the valley outside the filling station moved quietly, saying nothing, ashamed to go home, too weary to move, and the silence lay around them and through them like a mortal sickness.

Russian and Olds walked slowly up the street.

"I guess the wife'll be worried," Russian said.

"Yeah," Olds said. "I s'pose the girl knows."

"Velma?"

The Long Year 119

"She always knows," he said painfully. "I dunno how, but she always gets news even before it happens."

"She's a nice girl," Russian said.

"Young," Olds said. "It's no fun."

Russian cleared his throat. "How—how does Smut like it workin' on the roads?"

"He don't like it none," Olds said. "He don't say much, but he kinna speaks around it. He says it ain't like real work, even if it's hard, 'cause you got the idea this here work's made to order. But I guess most of 'em aren't fussy, glad to have it, whatever it brings in. But Smut, now, he's used to doin' fine work his own way 'gardless of the pay. He's lot like you, Russian, got to do very fine work no matter what."

"It's too bad," Russian said.

Olds looked at him. "You'll be one that stays on. You oughtta be one. You been there a long time, an' yer one of the big foremen."

"I don't know," he said. He was thinking how his wife had talked—they'd get along no matter, but she didn't know. She'd never been poor, without food, crazy with worry. But he had been that way and remembered it even when he tried to forget it, remembered it with bitterness, and for a long time he couldn't bring himself to vote, although his mind called him a fool not to vote. It was that he kept a hankering knowledge inside himself that if you were smart you put in good men for office, and he had the feeling then that he'd never vote because even being smart didn't help.

"Yer lucky, too," Olds said. "You put by for yourself."

"Not much," he said. "I got the house."

"I got the house, too," Olds said. As they came up the hill, he heard his daughter-in-law's voice and then his son's and then the baby crying. Now, in a moment, everything was very still again. "God Almighty," he said.

Russian raised his eyebrows. "They don't get along?"

"They get along fine," Olds said. "It's just bad like this at times —can't say I blame her. The house ain't smart lookin' on the inside and she tries her best, then the babies ain't trained yet an' she can't seem to keep up with all of it. Kids eat a powerful lot. Orange juice. Cod-liver oil. Butter. Milk. You know."

"Yeah," Russian said. "Maybe this time she'll make herself a boy."

Olds smiled. "I got the feelin'," he said. "I got the feelin' this one's a boy." He cocked his head a little to one side and squinted his good eye. "Come in a minute, Russian."

Russian looked toward his own house. The street was empty. "Well, I should get on my way." But he thought: Poor guy doesn't want to go in there by himself and tell it to them even if they know it. "Sure. I'll come in for a minute or so."

They walked around the back of the house. The tomato plants were already watered, and when they walked into the low-ceilinged kitchen, Smuts was quietly eating his supper, holding the older baby on his lap. She squealed when she saw Olds, and he took her, holding her wiggling against him. "Wet Pants Olds," he said. "That's a name for her."

Velma, bent over the sink, sniffled. "I can't keep her dry, Paw."

"I know," he said. "Sit down, Russian."

Smut looked at Russian. His voice was careful, controlled. "You have some stew?" he asked.

"No, thanks, Smut," he said. Goddam, the boy looked busted to pieces, puny, tubercular, maybe. "On my way home," he said.

Velma turned away from the sink. "Sit down, Paw. Take the load off yer feet."

He cawed with laughter. "Yer the one should take off the load," he said sitting down. The child pulled his nose and he tickled her feet. "Hear the news?" he asked.

"Yeah," Smut said. "Velma tole me."

"No surprise," Russian said.

Velma said, "You'll get back there, Russian. She says she's gonna keep a few of the older ones. Smut couldn't be one of those—he never had a chancet down there. Now, if he'd gone inta that business with my sister's hubby like I wanted—"

The Long Year 121

"Shut yer big mouth," Smut said. "I'm no crook. Maybe I'm lazy, but I don't go crooked jist because there ain't work."

"I like that!" she said.

"Take it easy, Velma," Olds said. "We know about Roy." He turned to Russian. "Roy's got some neat racket in the city. Can't seem to name it, though, when you ask him."

"Anyhow, he takes care of his own," Velma said. She straightened up, holding her hand to her back. In the other room, the smaller child fretted. Russian stood up. "I'll see you in the morning," he said.

"Might as well go down there and find out anything new," Olds said.

Smut looked up, he was moving the food in his mouth, trying to swallow it. He washed it down with water. "If things don't break for you, Russian," he said, "you kin come lean on a goddam shovel with the rest of us charity workers."

"It's no charity, boy," he said slowly, "to work on a road. I know that." For a moment, his eyes met Smut's and then Smut looked down at his plate. "Come over some night, you and Velma," he said. "Let Olds sit with the kids. We got some fine hard cider."

"He never goes," Velma said. She smiled at Russian. "He's tired all the time, but maybe some night we can make it."

"We'll make it," Smut said.

Olds continued to sit holding the child and talking to her. Then Russian walked toward his own house. He stood by the gate. He always liked to stand by the gate and see his wife moving inside the house. Now, Joanie was lying on the porch swing, kicking it back and forth and reading by the low, bleary light of a bridge lamp.

"That you, Pa-pa?"

"It's me," he said. He closed the porch door behind him. "What's that you're reading now, Baby?"

"Poetry," she said.

"Poetry? Well, I'm damned."

She got up and stood holding his arm. "Papa, you're *not* to worry, understand? I've been waiting out here to tell you that. We all talked about it, and you're just simply *not* to worry."

"Not to worry, hey?" he laughed. He bent down and kissed her and smoothed her hair. He loved to touch their hair, so fine and smooth, and it made him wonder how he could have children like this. "Where's Peg?"

"She's helping Mother. We're having shortcake for supper."

"Fine," he said. She took his cap and lunch bucket. He hung his jacket on the rack and went out to the kitchen. "Well," he said, "I guess I'm pretty late."

His wife kissed him. "David," she said—nothing else but that—just his name.

He put his hands into his pocket and looked at his younger child. "Well?" he said.

She giggled. "Pa-pa," she sighed. "You always act like you're angry with me."

"Come kiss me then," he said.

She felt lighter than ever in his arms, and for a moment, looking over her shoulder at his wife, he thought he could not say what he had to say.

His wife said, "We know all about it. Mr. Wimmer dropped by this afternoon, and he said to tell you Miss Hasswell's keeping on about twenty-five of the oldest and highest ranking men."

"Yeah?"

"Even so, we wouldn't have to worry," she said.

"We could eat vegetable stew like the Olds, I suppose."

"Yes," she said briskly. "Let go of Papa, Peg, and put the chairs to the table. And besides that, David, there's no reason on earth why I couldn't do work the way I did before we were married. Mrs. Hickory told me she intends to take in washing."

"My God," he said. "Whose washing?" There were times when he felt that women were too much for him to understand. They were so terribly calm about big things, and the smallest thing would send them into a spin.

The Long Year

"Let's not talk about it," she said. "It gives the children poor stomachs to talk about things like that when they're eating."

He went to the kitchen sink and washed his hands with lava soap. He looked at himself in the mirror. Well, maybe she would take him back. But somehow, he could not forget Smut Olds' face and the girl, Velma—she could easily be his girl, either of his girls —and the vegetable stew with hunks of undercooked potato and the kid without a decent dress to her name and Olds himself being too afraid and too ashamed to go into the house alone. He dried his hands and turned and took the dish of potato salad from his wife and carried it into the dining room. "I asked Smut and Velma to come over some night. It's the only place they ever go now, and she's fond of going out just to be going somewhere."

"Yes," she said, "and I'll make some ice cream. They like ice cream."

The children looked at them. Then they looked at each other, their light, blonde-skinned faces solemn and still frightened. They had heard the men downtown and had gone there to look at them. They had seen all of it.

"Pa-pa?" Joanie said.

"Say your grace," he said.

"But, Papa—"

"I know, I know," he said. He folded his hands and said grace. He did not believe there was a God, but he prayed to whatever there might be inside himself or inside Kay Hasswell or Hoyt. Whatever there was, he would pray to that.

CHAPTER THIRTEEN:

THE MEN continued to stand outside the filling station every day and sometimes until midnight. Maybe there were fifty of them, sixty even, and they were silent as a single man who does not wish to be heard breathing. They stood in the moonlight as well, their faces ghostly in that light, their hands at their sides. Once in a while, they would talk in a low, expressionless fashion. The women walked up and down Chestnut Street in their thin, cheap summer dresses, and they spoke among themselves softly about their men and what each had said he would do, but they did not go near the men.

The salesmen came back to the town from Cleveland, Birmingham, Seattle and New York. They were tired men with shabby brief cases. They stayed in the hotel and sat in the lobby talking to Kay. She went down there every night.

Marth lay on her bed, listening to Kay moving in her own room just beyond the bathroom. In a moment, Kay would come into the room and talk and then go to the hotel, sitting with Johnnie Evans and the salesmen. Afterwards, she would come back to the house and change to go out with Johnnie. The summer had already begun to die, and some days were like autumn although it was still late July. "There is a sickness in the land," Mr. Wimmer had said, "and now it's in the air as well."

She could hear Kay moving around the room, touching the many delicate, foggy bottles on her dressing table, moving languidly as if Time were a little thing, a penny to be dropped and left to lie forgotten.

"Darling?"

Marth stirred. "What?"

The Long Year

Kay came through the bathroom and stood in the door. She wore a green dress with no trimmings, no other color except the deepness of the green, a simple dress made as a leaf is made, with supreme care and sureness, without anything except the leaf itself.

"What's the matter, Marth?"

"Nothing."

"You and Rock?"

Marth shook her head. "He's busy. He's training."

"Don't you go down there to watch him?"

"Tomorrow," she said. "I guess I'll go down there tomorrow."

Kay's eyes narrowed, and she held her earrings in the palm of her hand, rolling them back and forth so they caught and held the light. "Darling, do you really like it here?"

"Sure."

"Why?"

"I don't know. I just do."

"Doesn't it frighten you—a little? It always frightened me when I was eighteen."

"No," Marth lied. It was true that now it had begun to frighten her in many ways, seen and unseen. Everything was going wrong, and in the mornings, you never knew what was going to happen that day. It was not the same—nothing was the same, not even Rock. What made Rock so angry with her? She felt terrible about that because it was as if Rock waited for her to do something on her own and she never knew quite what it was he wanted her to do.

"Yes," Kay said. "It's beginning with you, too. I can see it— just as it was with me."

Marth was watching her put on the earrings. She did it without effort or thought, and when she moved her head they were like living things on her ears. She looked young, young as Marth except more knowing in every way.

"I'm not like you, Kay," she said.

"You don't know."

"Nothing's beginning with me."

"Hah," Kay said, turning quickly. She lit a cigarette. Her hands were very sure.

Marth thought: I can never be sure like that. I'll never know as much as she does or be able to work as hard. I'll never see as much as she's seen or have any of the things she's had—maybe Barby will, but I'll never be that lucky.

"I know," Kay said. "It will begin with you and then this town will not hold you any more. This town is small-time, darling."

"How?"

"Rocky Macbeth for one."

"No," she said.

Kay let out a puff of blue smoke. She sat on the edge of Marth's bed, her legs crossed, and one green sandal moving in a careful pattern over the rug. "Darling, in this town it's one thing to be a fighter, but outside—say, against a man like Fonn Kelly, he would be nothing. You don't want to mess up your life with someone like Rock even though he's attractive and pleasant. Ten years from now, you'll think he was neither pleasant nor attractive. So—you see—you'll leave here the way I left."

"I'm not scared, Kay."

"You lie," she said softly. 'I know you lie, darling." She was laughing, and suddenly everything about her was frightening— the broad white forehead and the eyes and the movement of her head and hands. She felt that perhaps everyone else was blind except Kay, and Kay saw clearly, step by step, what she must do. She thought in this moment of how her father did not know what to do and waited for Kay to decide, and she herself was frightened of what was happening here because she had never lived through anything like this, a war or a famine or anything.

"Rocky's a good fighter," she said. "Everyone says so."

Kay shrugged. "Sure. But against a man like Fonn Kelly—that's something else again, darling."

"Maybe later on he could do it, though."

"I know Fonn Kelly, and he takes things, whatever he wants.

The Long Year

He took the title with hardly an effort. Rock is not that kind of man nor that kind of fighter."

Marth lay back on the bed. She would go down to the beach tomorrow and watch Rock train, and it would be the same as always. "Let me alone, Kay," she said.

"About Rock, you mean?" Kay asked.

"Yes."

"I know, darling, but believe me, I'm right. He's not for you. He's small-time, small-change."

Marth raised herself on one elbow. She looked at her aunt and saw there in that moment that, in the end, Kay would be right. "What's big-time, Kay?"

Kay laughed. "Wonderful things, darling. Furs and champagne and going places and always having a very wonderful feeling of being alive and having whatever you choose to have. You don't care if there is a hell or a heaven."

"I see," she said. "But there must be a trick somewhere."

"Of course," Kay said. "You have to go away from here, darling. That's what you have to do. You have to have money and strength —most people are very weak, you have no idea how weak. Outside this town, there is freedom and anything you want. Do you think I came back here because I loved this place? No. I came back to make money, to work hard, to lead a few blind people, and afterwards I'll leave here and go wherever I choose to go."

"It sounds—hard."

"Hard?"

"Difficult, I mean. You have to go away, and I guess I'd hate to leave here and leave Daddy and Rock and Barbs and everyone."

"We could go away together. Would you like that?"

"Yes," she said. "I think I'd like that." She was really very tired of the town and of the men in the streets, of the long winters and the ugliness that she now saw everywhere. She wanted to live in Kay's world, in the carnival or the parade or in whatever people like that lived.

She smiled. "Kay—what about you and Johnnie Evans?"

"Oh, darling—nothing about Johnnie Evans and me."

"People say—"

"Oh, that."

Marth thought that before this no one had paid much attention to Johnnie Evans, but now that he was with Kay, they all pretended that he had belonged to the town always and that they did not want Kay to hurt him, and they talked about the days when she had gone around with Simon O'Dodd. Macbeth said, "The thing repeats itself. Women like that never get tired."

"Today," Kay said, "when I went to my office, someone had been there. Everything was overturned, papers on the floor, but nothing was gone. How stupid! On the streets, the people look at me as if I've sinned against them, but I expected that."

"I think you'd better be careful. Mr. Wimmer says when a man is out of work and hungry and cold and angry, he doesn't see clearly."

"When the factory opens again, they'll come crawling. They always do, people like that."

"I've never seen anyone here crawl."

"Wait and see," Kay said. She rose. "I have to go down to the hotel and talk to Rice McLeod. He's the only smart salesman in the outfit." She was used to sitting in the lobby talking, to having meetings in her small office. She liked the salesmen, but she did not think they knew the score. They were too interested in making ends meet, lacking imagination and enterprise. Around eleven o'clock, while she sat in the lobby talking, Mr. Wimmer came downstairs. He bought a pack of Camels at the desk. When he saw her, he came over to her, holding his accordion lightly so that with every step a faint air of music, hardly more than a scent, came from the accordion.

"Big business?" he asked.

" 'Lo, Gene," Johnnie Evans said.

"Hello, Johnnie," he said, but he kept looking at Kay. He knew about women like this although he had never seen one before. This was a woman of sharpness and treachery, of elegance, little thin

The Long Year

ankles, hands that moved in a deceitfully soft fashion. "Want to go dancing, Miss Hasswell?"

"Now?" She was always surprised because he was like Prokosch although Prokosch had been European in every way, and yet this man was like him in manner, in thought, and in a curious expression that was a thing of neither manner nor thought.

"Sure—now," he said.

"I'm busy."

"Go away, Gene," Johnnie said. He had no time for Mr. Wimmer. This was a shabby guy, a small-town teacher, a little crazy in his ways.

"I know a place," Gene said.

"Please," she said.

"Some other time, then?"

"No."

"You're not getting anywhere with this business, you might as well come with me."

"I know what to do," she said simply.

"I wonder," he said. He rolled away on his cowboy boots. He kept looking at the woman with affection. He played a sad, sweet, mourning song of lost love. He wandered across the lobby and spoke to some of the salesmen and then he saw Marth walking down the hill and went out to her.

"See Rock?" she asked.

"No," he said.

They went down the hill and sat on the steps of the newspaper office, and Rock, hearing the music, left the store and sat with them.

"Where's Joe?" Mr. Wimmer asked. "I saw him around town today."

"Probably drinking his head off down at the Cafe."

"We ought to go down and get him," Mr. Wimmer said.

"No," Rock said. "He doesn't want anyone."

"It's no use anyhow," Marth said. She turned and look at Mr. Wimmer. "Would you say this town's dead?" she asked.

"Yes," he said.

"Why does a town die?"

He thought about it. "When it doesn't belong to the people, it dies—and it doesn't belong to the world any more. When the people don't care about being farmers or lumber men or weavers and become makers of money."

"I see," she said. Upstairs, she could hear Mrs. Amos' invalid sister yelling. She was mad about the heat and mad about the way her dress stuck to her bottom and she didn't like asparagus for supper. Mrs. Amos said something in a low, humorous voice, and in a moment, there was no sound at all. In the valley where the heat of high noon was still coming off the water, it was suddenly more than just heat, a kind of shadow seemed to have settled in a liquid pattern over everything. Mr. Wimmer began to play and sing softly,

> "I'm gonna leave ole Texas now,
> They have no use fer the long-horned cow,
> They've plowed and fenced my cattle range,
> The people there are all so strange . . ."

In the dim street light, the men stood silently outside the filling station. Marth saw Russian go into the Cafe alone.

"Rock?"

"Ummm."

"You training tomorrow?"

"Sure. Same as always."

"Couldn't I come down to the beach and watch?"

"Don't see why not."

She put her hand in his, but his hand did not tighten. He looked at her curiously.

"Please, Rock," she said. She thought maybe it would be better to go home and take a bath and wait for Kay. Then they'd lie on the bed and talk or Kay would sit in the middle of the bed brushing her hair and talking. That's what she wanted to do, get away from everything here. Mr. Wimmer got up.

The Long Year

"Night, Kids," he said.

"Night," they said. They watched him going up toward the hotel, not playing but walking in silence.

"What's the matter, Rock?"

"Nothing—nothing at all."

"I love you still," she said.

"Do you?"

"Don't you believe me?"

"I don't think you know what it means," he said.

"Damn you to hell," she said suddenly. She pulled away from him and began to run up the hill after Mr. Wimmer. She'd go home and take a bath . . . that was the solution, take a bath and wait for Kay to come.

Rocky Macbeth saw the whole thing when it happened. He could not have missed it unless he was blind or dead, and he was neither. He was sitting on the beach that morning. He was sitting where the beach sloped into the rock piles beneath the highroad, at that spot where the road curved eighty-two degrees. He was sitting there taking the sand out of his toenails. To do this, he used a small green twig which he had sharpened with a Boy Scout knife. The twig was still soft and pithy and so did not prick his skin. He carefully went under the nails and rubbed his feet until there was a feeling of blood, bone and skin coming alive. He always took good care of his feet because they belonged to his fighting. They were his balance, the same as his heart was his balance for his timing. As Macbeth had taught him, he was careful of his feet and his heart.

So, he was sitting there cleaning his toenails when the little green jitney came down the hill. It was newly painted so that the green was bright, but it was not a new Ford—probably a '29 model. The other car was heavier and very new, but it was hard-worn. It came over the bridge in a low roar that flattened it to the earth. It made a sweeping twist like a big wounded creature, and it crashed into the little green jitney. The jitney was light but with power that came from good care, but still it was light, and it flew into the air, high into the hill above the river. As it flew, it spilled its contents—a man in a striped overall and a child in a faded blue wash dress. One of the child's patent-leather shoes rolled over the hill and landed near Rocky. He picked it up and carried it carefully up the hill where the two bodies lay, the man and the child, angel-spread on the summer grasses above the river rocks.

He passed the other car. It was crumpled up against the two big trees that crooked over the river cliff. The horn was jammed and kept playing, "The Campbells are coming, tra-la-lala . . ." and it played this in a sick, grinding tone over and over. One of the men was spilled out on the pavement and lay in a wide streak of amber liquid. Rocky walked over to the road, dipped his finger in it and smelled it. "Bourbon," he said. "Goddam bourbon." The man moved, opened his eyes and said something.

"Get me out of this stinkin' hole," he said.

Rocky looked at him. "Later," he said. He walked away and climbed the cliff to where the others lay.

"Like angels," he said, "like angels, just like angels." The man's face was not marked, although his body lay twisted, and his left arm was under him, his face turned sideways. His eyes were open, bright blue, and his hair was a light, golden color, and his face was very smooth and closely shaved. "Going to town with eggs and vegetables," Rocky said. "That was all they meant to do."

The child lay on her back, and nothing had touched her although she was dead. He knew this without bending over to feel her small beat dead under his fingers. Her eyes were closed, and one hand was outflung, open. He lifted her foot and carefully put on the slipper, buttoning the strap. After that he looked at her, smoothed her hair and bent down and kissed her warm cheek. He started down the cliff, and then he heard the car, and he saw Marth driving across the bridge. In the sun, the red car looked dark brown. He waited for her on the beach. She stopped by the wrecked car. The

The Long Year

man had fallen farther out, lay sprawled on the pavement, his fingers moving in the stream of liquor.

"Rock," she said. "He's—he's alive."

"The others are dead," he said.

"Do something," she said. "You ought to do something."

"I'm going down to the beach shack and call the police," he said.

She kept looking at the man. She bent over him and loosened his collar. He looked at her, moaning.

"Don't touch him," Rocky said.

"But, Rock—"

"Don't touch him," he said. "He broke his neck. He knows it, too. Just let him alone."

She began to shake all over. Rocky slid down to the beach and set out running toward the beach house. She watched him go. The man had sunk into a state where he moved his fingers but his eyes were closed and he did not seem to want to say anything. She looked through the door. The other man sagged over the wheel, not breathing but bleeding through the mouth. "We should've fixed this road," she said. "We should've done that. We ought to —we ought to—" She crossed the road and leaned against the car, looking down toward the beach. Death was terrible. You ought to have a very good time because you never knew when it would happen, even the smallest thing like driving a car over a bridge, or maybe dropping dead the way her own mother had dropped dead in the flower garden when a minute before that she had been standing at a telephone in the hall. Kay was right. Go away from the town, have fun, don't think about anything except having a very good time . . .

"Rock," she said. He was coming up the cliff.

"They'll be here in a minute," he said.

"Did you—did you get an ambulance?"

"I guess so," he said. "I told the cop there was one guy pretty much alive." He took her hand. "The others are up here," he said.

"I—I don't want to look."

"A man and his little girl," he said. He began to climb up the cliff, holding her hand. Her hand was cold, and she didn't seem to know what she was doing. He said, "See. They were on their way to town, this man and his little girl—farmers. The stuff's all scattered over the beach, radishes and lettuce and tomatoes and cartons of fine, big eggs—all smashed." He felt the man's eyes upon them. Marth stood very still, looking at the man and the child, her mouth working, not crying or not trying to say anything, but feeling loose and cold and terribly hurt inside. He bent over the man, and he seemed to see all the substance of life moving away there, sinking down deeply into the jewelled jelly substance, sinking away from the light. "Making a journey," he said. "He's making a long journey." He wanted to say something to them, to the child as she lay there, something that would be a bon voyage, but he did not know what to say. He thought they were beautiful lying there, not ugly like the other men.

"We ought to do something," she said.

"There's nothing to do, angel."

"They look—different."

"Sure." He put his arm around her. "This isn't terrible, Marth. This man and his little girl aren't terrible even though they're dead."

"Please," she said. "Let's go down. That man—"

"All right," he said.

They went down to the road. He picked up a crumpled piece of road guard, and threw it to the side of the road in the slow, glistening, sweet-smelling liquor that flowed from the car.

"Rotgut," Rocky said. "They bring it across the border." He flipped open the man's ostrich-leather billfold. Inside, there was a picture of a blonde woman in a fox neckpiece. She was standing outside a Spanish-type house. In the other compartment, there was nothing but a piece of thin paper and the man's name: Harold Oldfarm, 2784 Palace Road, Dallas, Texas.

"Look at the dame," he said. He handed the billfold to her.

"No," she said.

"Why not?"

The Long Year 135

"It's like spying. It belongs to him."

"Oh—him," he said. "He died a million years ago anyhow."

"How can you be like this?"

"Like what?"

"As if it doesn't matter."

He said nothing. He felt sad because she did not understand what he was trying to tell her. She used to be a nice, bright kid who wanted to see everything and have a good time and be calm and friendly, but now she was fighting everything there was in the world, everything that she did not want to acknowledge was there. She was always going to the city with Kay, driving around in the red Packard, and when he wanted her to understand about the man and the child, she thought it was terrible.

"Look," he said, "you'd better go. They'll be here any time now."

"Yes," she said. "I guess I'll go." She started the car.

"Marth," he said.

She was crying. She turned and looked at him. He went over to the car, leaned against its hot side and kissed her on the mouth, and her lips trembled with her crying. "I'm sorry," he said. "I guess it's terrible."

"That man—that man," she said. She pushed him away from her and started the car with a quick, hard grinding of the wheels on the tar road. She could see him standing beside the car and then going up the cliff. As she crossed the bridge, the police car and the hearse with AMBULANCE printed on a white card started toward her across the bridge. She could still see Rock standing on the cliff. She wondered what it was he had tried to tell her about death and how he knew about it—perhaps fighting had taught him something about death, but she could not help thinking it was terrible. I'll go down to the office and maybe Kay and I can go up-river and walk around and try to find a place for her house, she thought, but she could not stop seeing the car and that man lying on the pavement—and then the others, the man and the child. She wondered if Rock knew them, if he had known that child. For a moment, when he was looking down at them, she had thought, he knows them very well. I think he knows them . . . Why? Why hadn't they straightened that road, someone, her father or Mrs. Amos at the newspaper or Mr. Wimmer or any of them?

She turned down the factory road and stopped the car and leaned over the side and was sick into the tall weeds beside the road. Sick and hot, a slow, hot turning in her stomach, behind her eyes—an amber, liquid turning behind her eyes . . . She had never been afraid like this, maybe to live was to be afraid, was Kay afraid, was Daddy afraid, was Rock afraid when he got into the ring? What did people do when those they loved died, and what did you say in the short time you had, what did you say to someone you loved—to Daddy, to Kay, to Mike—to Rock? Whatever did you say to make the fear less in them and in yourself?

She wiped her mouth. She wasn't going to cry. The crying was inside her now. She could feel it there.

Olds was almost always working in his garden when Russian went to work in the evenings. He was night watchman now, and there was nothing to do but read detective magazines and walk around the empty factory or go out to the engine room and talk with the engineer. Now, he seldom stopped for any length of time when he saw Olds in his garden. Olds had nothing to do, and he had begun to look like a man who has nothing to do. Also, he felt that Olds might think it strange his having the job of night watchman when there were so few still working—but, of course, he'd been there a longer time and was a foreman and after all, Olds had been there only seventeen years and wasn't a foreman and wasn't really very strong.

"Hey!" Olds said. He straightened up, wiping the sweat off his face onto his sleeve. "You hear 'bout the accident?"

"Yeah," Russian said. "I went down there. Kind of a mess. They say them two guys were bootleggers." Olds did not seem unhappy about not having a job. He was actually having a fine time with his tomatoes. "Well," we ought to have straightened that road,

The Long Year 137

Gawd knows Miz Amos told us about it enough times, two-three times every year."

"Sure," Olds said. He popped out his glass eye and rubbed it dry on his shirt sleeve. "Always get sweat over so's I can't see out of it," he laughed.

"How are things?"

"Fine, fine," Olds said. "Smut's been havin' a little trouble goin' to sleep on the job. He says all of 'em want to sleep anyhow, do it first chance they get, an' he says it's catchin'. He don't like to sleep on the job." He popped his eye back in. "You kin sleep on yours, too, hey?"

"No," Russian said. "I don't do that."

"Aw, don't be so touchy. I was only kiddin'."

"You got the damndest sense of humor," he said.

"Well, for Christ sakes, I onny said—"

"I know what you said. Well, I'm not getting foreman's wages down there, and it's not easy just sittin' around. I keep thinkin' how I'm gyppin' that woman, though."

"What woman?" Olds was surprised.

"Hasswell, Kay Hasswell."

"Oh—her." He sniffed. "She don't know you're gyppin' her none."

"Hell, she don't. It eats her hide to have to keep a guard down there. She'd like to do it all herself so's she wouldn't have to pay any of it out."

Olds said nothing. He was tying the tomato plants to the poles.

"Guess I'd better go," Russian said. Goddam that road, he was thinking. You'd think we'd have done something about it. It's our road.

"Yeah," Olds said.

Russian walked stiffly away. What the hell was the matter? If you were one of the lucky ones to keep a job, the others hated it, and if you were one of the unlucky ones you wouldn't hate the ones that had a job. It just happened that way. He had kids, too, and he had his own place, and he was going to do anything he could to keep them. What was the matter with that? No reason why you couldn't get someone to have a drink now and then with you and maybe sit around the Cafe and talk like old times, and you wouldn't mind buying a drink for someone else, a ten-cent beer or something.

He shook his head. Some things he couldn't understand—the road, the people who had always been his friends, something that was happening inside himself, too. He walked slowly, sweating, trying to think, frowning with the effort of thinking.

CHAPTER FOURTEEN:

MARTH BEGAN to fall into the routine of going to the city with Barby and Kay. The decorators had come to redecorate their living room. That had lasted for three days, and now the living room was more like rooms she had seen in furniture stores—very long and spacious with a low coffee table, and all the old furniture was changed, covered and redone. She and Kay and Barby went to the city to buy new lamps and new draperies, and after that, they went just to be going. They sat in the front seat of Kay's car and drove very fast to the city, leaving early in the morning and often spending the entire week-end at the Beldon Hotel. Before this, on Saturdays, she always played tennis with Rock, but now she explained it to him.

"I like going," she said. "I like all of it, sitting in the hotel and buying new clothes and having fun."

"That's all right," he said.

"You're not angry, Rock?"

"Hell, no."

"I mean—well, I just want to do this for a while."

"It's all right," he said, and he thought: She'll get over it. She's got to get over going around like the whole town's a big dream to her. I can't get near her when she's like this, and I want her to belong here with me and not with Kay, running all over town, buying every which of a thing she sees. "It's all right. I'll go down to Mike's after I get through in the store."

"Kiss me, then."

"Why?"

"To prove you aren't angry."

He laughed. "I don't kiss you to prove anything."

"Please, Rock," she said.

"All right." He kissed her cheek and held her close to him a moment. "Go on, then," he said. "Don't stick around here or you'll never get to the city."

She knew he didn't like it. He liked to have everything the way it had always been, but a girl couldn't be the same all the time. A girl had to get around and make something of herself and be someone. And Rock would understand after a while, why he'd *have* to understand, that was all. And he would, he would.

They always had lunch at the Beldon. They sat in the grill, and sometimes Johnnie Evans would meet them, and they would sit at one of the little round tables in the low, dark room and eat slowly and talk. Every time, she and Barby would try to order something new, but Kay always had the same omelet, salad and green tea and Roquefort cheese and crackers. Barby and Marth sat close together, bent over the menu. The people came and went in the big room, their richness all around them.

"It's like at Lake Louise," Barby said. That was the only trip she had ever made, and she liked to compare everything with that. "People looking so wonderful and rich, like they have all the time in the world. No one in High Falls ever has any time except to work—or, the way it is now, to *worry* about work."

Marth looked at the people. They wore lovely, colorful dresses, and the men were all brown and lean and carried sun glasses which they tapped against their thighs as they walked. At no time did the true heart of the city come into that place. There was always music, even in the mornings when it came from grates in the wall—Viennese waltzes and musical-comedy tunes and summer songs. At noon, the string quartet played in the grill and a few people in sport clothes danced on the small floor. Whenever Johnnie Evans came to have lunch with them, he would dance once with Barby and once with her and the rest of the time with Kay. Barby and Marth sat there watching them.

"I think they look marvelous together," Barby said. "I don't care what people say. He's crazy about her and she loves him, too."

"He's okay," Marth said. "I guess he's not really a good lawyer,

The Long Year

but Kay says he's modern. Mr. Purdy's not modern. But I like Johnnie."

"Do you think she's in love with him?"

"I don't know."

"No—now when I look at her, I don't think she is," Barby said wisely. "Not the way I love Joe. You can tell she always has her own way and she doesn't get hurt. I mean—if Johnnie did anything to hurt her, she'd know how to take care of herself. Maybe, she'd just laugh."

"No—she wouldn't laugh, but she'd get over it."

"She'd laugh," Barby said. "I wish I could be like that."

"I'd like to be able to wear clothes the way she does. Honestly, Rock makes me kind of mad—he doesn't think it matters *what* a girl wears." She was watching Kay. Now, Kay moved away from Johnnie and said something to him and then moved close to him again. "She's had a lot of men in love with her. Daddy says when she married her first husband—Sonny Blair—there were lots of girls who wanted him. She took him."

"Everyone says she made Simon O'Dodd kill himself, though. You know Macbeth says that, Marth."

"Oh—Macbeth!"

"Just the same, that's what I'd like—I mean to go away like she did. Mamma'd help Joe if we once got away to San Francisco or some place like that. I know she'd help us then."

"Joe wouldn't stand for it."

"If I could be like Kay, I'd know what to do. I'd never have any trouble with Joe."

No one else danced as well as Kay and Johnnie. Almost every night during the summer, they came to the city and danced. Sometimes they met friends of Johnnie and went out to the country club or went sailing. Marth wondered what it was that made them seem so exactly right for each other, it was something they shared and had nothing to do with the fact that Johnnie was a small-town lawyer and Kay was a person of many travels and many different kinds of living.

They came back to the table. "What's on the program for today?" he asked.

"Shopping," Marth said. "I want to buy a white linen dress. Irish linen with emerald-green trim."

"I just want to shop," Barby said. "Let's go to Millner s, Kay."

"Of course," Kay said. "We'll buy some hats there. I want a new hat, a black one with a veil and some flowers or fruit or something."

"Yes," they said, "let's do that."

Johnnie grinned. "Women," he said.

Millner's was a little shop on St. Peter Street. The woman who owned it was small, chic, and wore her hair lacquered high on her head, a startling new fashion that Barby had once tried. She said it made her look like a washwoman, but on this woman it was dramatic. She also wore amazing earrings, large and comical —sometimes they were hats with dangling blue and yellow flowers. Sometimes they were red globes that caught the light or little donkeys drawing flower carts or ballet dancers with tiny sequined skirts that bobbed whenever she walked fast or turned her head. She was thin and sharp with a thin, sharp face, and she spoke with an accent which she said was French.

"It's Polish," Kay said. "She wants you to believe it's French because no one but the French can make hats that are worth anything."

"Mother gets hers in New York," Barby said.

"New York," Kay said. "That's something else again—but not as good as France for hats."

Inside Millner's was like no place Marth had ever known. The carpet was blue and deep, and there were little mirrors everywhere, and the women sat around in the deep pink chairs and crossed their legs and smoked and watched the models go back and forth. Behind the main room were rows of fitting rooms. These were all in pastel colors, and the air there was full of many faint, bewildering perfumes. The hats were kept in transparent boxes, like flowers, and there were many of them. Mme. Millner herself would bring them out and put them on the table and then make a ceremony of lifting them tenderly from their boxes and holding them gently in her red lacquered fingers. She would turn them and talk about them as if they were her beloved children. "This one, my dear Miss 'Asswell—this one is a lovely bebee. I myself made it in the morning when I was feeling 'eavenlee and delicious—*mais oui* . . ."

"Yes," Kay said. "Go on."

"We 'ave such love-lee ones, you 'ave no idea. My dears," she assumed an air of conspiracy, of most profound secrecy, "in black baku, and a small one with sequins for the evening."

Kay sat back in the pink plush chair smoking and watching the woman, and then she ceased to watch and instead looked at the girls. She had to smile. They were so easily taken in by all of this. They loved it—that pimply-faced, fake woman making two hundred percent on every hat, slaving her own workroom girls for a pittance, eking out the blood from turnips, so to speak. But in a way, she herself lived in the newness of this place again. She remembered herself and how she, as a young girl, had always loved the heavy material and the marvelous, creamy laces and the hand-stitched satin negligees—so many things.

The models came in from the little rooms wearing pale, late-summer dresses, the wonderful cruise clothes, imported tweeds, cherry-colored cashmeres. It was in this way that the town and the men standing outside the filling station—all of that was blotted out for them as they went from one small shop to another. They were all the same, small and exclusive, glassed-in and clean, and Marth wondered how she would dare to keep such wonderful clothes in the windows where it seemed that you could reach out and hold them forever.

Kay bought straw hats from Nassau and others for winter evenings and blobs of bright-colored beads, fragile shoes. They went into one shop that had all these elegant, fragile shoes hidden away in a large room behind the main one. They sat down in big deep chairs and a man in striped trousers went back and forth holding the shoes up for them to see, all made narrow with high heels and the look of glass shoes. Glass was everywhere—in the man's eyes, in the glitter of the sun on the jewelry cases, in the light across patent leathers. There was nothing but this brittleness, brittleness of glass and shells and porcelain.

Kay's manner was neither grand nor bored. The salesgirls buzzed around her and admired and made gentle pattings along the shoulders of a new dress, swung the mirror around to show the whole room and themselves in the center of it.

"I like that little thing you have in the window," Kay said in her cool, remote voice. "May I see it, please?"

"Oh, yes, ma'am," the clerk would say, "it's one of our finest imports." It was as if nothing made in this country was quite good enough, Marth thought, as if coming across so much space made it better. Then the buyer herself would come and talk about the lines of it, the material, and Kay would sit quietly listening and smiling. Then she would buy it and something else—viyellan flannel or shantung or sharkskin, very heavy and smooth, or some thin stuff that was like the stuff of cobwebs—or perhaps a linen with multi-colored blocked linen flowers.

She bought peasant scarves, chunky rings and perfumes that came in heavy bottles with crusted gold stoppers. She bought more hats and wispy veils and wide bracelets of fruity little balls that were like water bubbles.

"Darling," she would say to Marth or Barby, "that looks horrible. You ought to have it in yellow, something sunny and new and exciting. Here, let me show you."

When they were with her, everything went as they wanted it to go. Afterwards, they had tea at the Beldon. They sat in the big room, and a waiter named Harry always served them, and they each had a little silver pot with a large engraved "B" on it. In autumn, the women had begun to wear furs and let them slip elegantly over the backs of their chairs, and the men wore tweeds and bright ties. Johnnie almost always met them and brought someone with him —young, hard sportsmen with names like Penn or Bix or Barney. Then they would stay for dinner and dancing and drive home in

The Long Year

the early morning with Kay and Johnnie in one car, and Marth and Barby and the two boys in the other.

After that, they began to stay overnight. At first, Barby did not like to do this. She would go up to the room and sit on the bed and smoke, but she wouldn't promise to stay overnight. "I'll get Bix to take me home," she said. Bix Lawrence was Johnnie's best friend. "Joe always tries to come up to the house later," she said. "I ought to go home."

"Why?" Kay asked. "Why must you spoil it for yourself, darling?"

"Well, Joe . . ."

"And if he *doesn't* come?"

"I ought to be there, just in case."

Kay smiled gently. She took Barby's hand and held it. "Listen, Barby, you can't do things like this. It's a constant defeat, sitting around waiting for Joe. Don't you see?"

"But I said I'd be there."

"I know, I know," she said softly. "But life goes on. You'd be surprised how it goes on in spite of everything, and you're young. There's so much to do and see, and it's stupid to sit around waiting for him."

Barby said nothing. She took out her handkerchief and blew her nose and then twisted the handkerchief.

"We do have so much fun, Barbs," Marth said. "Stay and sleep in your slip."

"Sure," Barby said. "I always like to be with you. But then I think of Joe back there."

"Oh, really, Barby," Kay said.

"He probably won't come anyhow," Marth said. 'You know Joe. And if he does come, he can always go down to Mike's. He and Rock like to go down there."

"Let's forget the town, darling," Kay said.

But Marth did not care for any of the boys Johnnie brought with him. They were good dancers, and they had a way of talking so that if you heard one of them you had heard all of them. This one, Bix Lawrence, came every time because of Barby. He would dance with her all evening without saying much. He sat and looked at her and then danced with her and maybe would kiss her goodnight, but that was all there ever was.

"Bix knows," Barby said. "I told him about Joe."

"Don't tell me you told him!" Marth said.

"Well, I like him—so naturally I had to tell him."

Usually, there was someone new for Marth, and it gave her a delightful feeling that now she was getting around, she knew a lot of people outside the town. She tried to tell Rock about this so that he would understand and not disapprove every time she broke a Saturday date with him.

"You see," she said, "it's like taking a long trip even though it's not very far, but it's so different from here—it really takes your breath away to be with Kay. We have so much fun."

"I didn't say you shouldn't have fun," he said.

"I don't think you like Kay. That's why you act so gloomy every time I go."

"I like her. Only I wish you wouldn't go around with Johnnie Evans and his crowd. Then there's nothing for Joe and me to do on Saturday nights but go down to Mike's. I miss you."

"I miss you, too," she said. "Let's not fight over it."

"I'm not fighting."

"Be nice to me, Rock. We never used to fight like this." She thought: I can't explain to him about the white dress with the pleated skirt and the hat to match with red flowers on it and shoes with red buckles and thick heels painted red and long, tropical beads that jangle whenever I walk. And everything is always better because of the slow, easy way we do it when we're with Kay—the little shops smell so wonderfully of those perfumes— "My Delight," "Scarlet Slipper" and "From Noon to Heaven." Saturday afternoons will always be that to me: the wistful perfumes, the musty smell of hot tea and flowers, the dimness of the Beldon with the women coming in and out in a wonderful, peaceful, gay harmony as if nothing else mattered.

"I love it so," she said. "I do love it so."

The Long Year

"All right," Rock said. "So you love it."

"But, Rock—look how it is here—the men stand around, and they don't look at you any more. They look at their feet. With Kay, it's not that way. She wants to build her house on the river. She always knows where to go and what to do. She doesn't look dark or gloomy. She makes you happy." Life wasn't just the town, the way he thought it was—the town and going into the ring to fight and coming out and then sitting on the beach with Macbeth and listening to Macbeth make up quotes he blamed on Shakespeare. Besides, it was always different for women. He ought to know that.

"It's just that you don't like Kay," she said, finally. "You never want me to be with her."

He said nothing. He looked at her for a moment and then took her in his arms. "Don't leave me," he said. "That's all—don't ever leave me."

She drew away from him. "But, Rock—"

"No," he said. "Even if Kay wants you to go with her, don't go, Marth. If you do, it's all over between us. I know it is."

"Couldn't I just go to Cuba or some place? After all, Rock, you don't expect me to stay here forever."

"Why not?"

"Well—you aren't, are you?"

"I don't know," he said. He drew away from her. He was thinking of Mike and how Mike had changed when Wilma left, and he thought that he might change like that. It might do something to his fighting, too, and at the same time, he knew nothing lasted or stood still even though you wanted it to.

She didn't know what to say to him. He wanted her to decide now, and she wasn't ready to decide. "I don't see why you have to make it sound so terrible, like I'm leaving you forever or something. Oh, Rock—everything used to be so darned perfect, and now look—I don't know why, but now the town is different and we're different, and I just don't know what to do."

"Okay," he said. His voice was low, harsh. "You **want** me to give you all the things Kay has had. Why? Do you think she's happy—a nice, tall, gutty woman with a laugh you can never forget and a way of talking that makes everyone else feel like a fool? Do you think no man's ever mattered to her enough to make her eat her insides out to be with him again? I'm not dumb, Marth. You get one thing or the other but not both." He walked down the sidewalk heavily, his heels making a hard, angry sound.

She bit her lip. Now, he'll go down to Mike's and later on Joe'll come and they'll have a party down there with those "summer girls" they're always talking about. You meet them on the streets and they give you a snickering, knowing look and you almost die. Not Rock, though—not Rock down there— She had never been jealous before, and it surprised her when she stopped and said, Why, I'm jealous, that's what. I care what he does.

When Kay came, she went into her room and watched her cream her face. She did this expertly, and finished off by running her fingers over her eyebrows.

"Do you like Johnnie, Kay?"

Kay went into the bathroom and brushed her teeth. "My darling, he's a very smart, attractive young man. There are several million like him, but in this case he is useful to me. I intend to send him to Chicago to pull out some very neat plums for me—government building contracts."

"But don't you care for him?"

"He's fun," she said. She put on a yellow nightgown with wide shoulder straps.

"No one here liked him much except a few people like Mrs. Leroy."

"I don't see that the town likes many people."

"Oh, I don't know."

"Who, for example? Certainly not your father."

"Yes, they do. They like him in a kind of funny way because he grew up here and knows about them and they can trust him."

"Who else, then?"

"Mr. Wimmer. He's strange and booky and he kind of sits around

The Long Year   149

here all summer and thinks, but everyone likes him. It's because he's wise and they respect him for it."

"He's dangerous."

"Oh, but Kay—"

"Men like that always are. Who else do they like?"

"Mike, I guess. They think he's crazy but they like him."

"Personally," she sniffed, "I think he and that Connaught boy and your precious Rocky are tramps. What does Mr. Wimmer talk about?"

"Oh—ideas, mostly. Municipal heating and electricity and getting the power company out of here so we can have one of our own—unions. Things like that. Besides, Rock works hard. He's no tramp, Kay."

Kay came over to the bed and began to rub the back of Marth's neck. "I wish I wouldn't fight with him," she said.

"It's probably good for him."

"It spoils everything."

"Darling, you'll be all right."

"Will I?"

"Of course."

"Do you think I will?"

"I *know* it."

"I mean, Kay," she rolled over on her back, "I don't want to be just anyone, another girl in this town. I—you know what I want."

"I know—but, darling, you can get what you want many times, but sometimes when you have all the saying and all the doing, you lose."

"You don't lose out, do you?"

Kay laughed. Her eyes were very bright in the low bedroom light. She raised her hands above her head and lay back on the bed. "Me—I guess I win . . ." It sounded like a wise thing to say. "Or at least I tell myself I win . . ." She could never remember when she hadn't won except that time with Prokosch. What was it he said, something about everything in a woman but the one thing that mattered, humanity? "Without humanity, Kay, you're dead," he had said, and she knew what he meant because she had seen all the kinds of death there were, the Riviera Death, the Switzerland Death, there were as many kinds of death as there were people—only in her case, she would name her own kind of dying in her own time.

"I don't want to go away to school," Marth was saying. "I want to go when you go."

"We'll arrange that," she said, but she didn't want to talk about it now. She had forgotten how young people were completely involved in their own lives, nothing else, just themselves. "Go to bed now," she said. "We'll talk about it later." God, she thought, I'm beginning to be bored again . . .

CHAPTER FIFTEEN:

BY THE TIME of the first real snowstorm in November, thirty-five men were working at the factory in the engine room and in the office and as guards. These went to work very early before anyone else was up, half-ashamed that they were working and the others were not. Russian Peterson and Hickory, the engineer, were the only ones who worked at night. He and the others felt as if they faced an enemy whose face was not known to them, and this for them was a vague, secret kind of war. They were always fighting something unseen, unknown, unyielding.

The men in their idleness looked at the few who still worked and did not know these any longer. Maybe these men were their enemies, the cause of their trouble—maybe the factory was the unsleeping, mortal foe, maybe it was Hoyt Hasswell or that sister of his in the big red Packard. Mrs. Amos wrote about it in the paper and named their enemy as that which lay sleeping in their hearts, deep in their minds, under the softening of their idle palms, but they laughed at her. So, in this small, invisible, bloodless war, there was no name for the battle, not Harpers Ferry nor Tippecanoe nor Bunker Hill. There was only a certain amount of talk, a growing restlessness and dissension, much bitterness, anger, infidelity, tragedy of all kinds that man can make for himself.

During the late days of summer, they had talked hopefully of Roosevelt, having no understanding of the vastness of this lack of work. And after a time, they ceased to think about work and thought only of many grievances, imagined and real. They clung to what money they had and suddenly spent it in a moment's savage foolishness.

But Joe had money. Joe had plenty of money, another new car, a good suit of clothes. He walked around his empty house, thought of the family up at the shop, the kids playing or at school. He hated the house for its stink, the ugly wallpaper chipping off the halls, the creaking old brass beds, the rattle and stink and poverty of the place. He pulled on a new tie and looked at himself in the mirror and started down the stairs. Then, as he turned on the landing, he heard the kid in the kitchen. He went down the rest of the stairs softly and saw the kid, Lindy, standing on the kitchen chair holding the big sugar bowl. He saw him take out some coins, look at them and then put them in his pocket.

"Kid," he said.

Lindy turned, holding the sugar bowl. "Hi, Joe," he said.

"Put it back," he said.

"The sugar bowl, hanh?"

"The dough," he said.

"You can damned well go and—"

"Can it!" he said. He took the kid's thin arm and pulled his hand from his pocket. The kid clenched the money in his fist. "Give," he said, twisting his arm, but the kid held on for a moment longer. He pried his fingers apart and dropped the money into the sugar bowl and put the sugar bowl on the shelf where it belonged. "I ought to kick the tar outta you, Lindy," he said gently.

The kid was trying his arm. "When I get as big as you, I'll do that to you, you louse."

"Listen," he said, still holding to the kid so he wouldn't run away. "What you wanna do that for?"

"I'm hungry," he said bluntly. "Well, I'm hungry all the time, an I thought I'd get me somethin really good, a hamburger with and some ice cream and stuff. An', Christ, you ain't been aroun' here for two weeks now, and I'm starved."

"Whatcha do with all that money?"

"That? I give part of it to Maw, like you very well know."

"Listen, Kid, you don't want to take things out of the sugar bowl. You don't want to end up jail bait. Now, I tell you—" he opened his billfold. "I'll give you a dollar now and a dollar every Saturday

The Long Year

to spend like you want, understand—and no snitching." He thought: the damned baby, how in hell can he help snitching? I'd do that, too. I know what he wants. He wants a square meal and a good bed that's warm and someone around to take care of him, to keep his clothes right— "Say, go upstairs and put on that old blue sweater of mine."

"The football one that Rock give ya?"

"Sure—it's too big, but it's warm, and you can roll the sleeves."

The kid gave him a light, quick punch on the chest. He tapped him back, not hard but feeling how slight, skinny, small the kid was. Gawd, he loved that kid, though, couldn't help it with his skinny, old-man face. "You working hard?" he asked.

"I clean the linotypes now," he said. "That Miz Amos, she's swell to me."

"She better," he said.

He went down to the Cafe. The men were sitting around in the bar room, just sitting and talking, but when he came in, they stopped talking and gave him a sharp look. He went up to the bar. "Straight," he said. "Good ole straight rotgut." He turned. "Anyone gonna drink with me? It's on me today."

Russian got up slowly. "No," he said. "It's one on you an' one on me."

Russian was the only one who'd drink with him. The others had no money, and he had plenty, rolling loose in his pocket as if it were nothing—well, hell, it wasn't anything, just green paper stuff.

"All I ever wanted was to work in the factory," he said. "That's all. Once they had the money an' I didn't. So now they know how I felt. Now they know." He wasn't worrying for them, not he, and he could look boldly into their faces, see them old, unshaven, weak, skinny, scornful, full of pity for themselves. "Hah," he said to them, the outlines against the wall, tipping the chairs back, leaning against the walls, slouched. He said, "Why don't you help yourselves, then?"

"Shut your mouth, Kid," one of them said.

Russian's hand was heavy on his arm. "Nothing to fight against," he said.

"You can fish, can't you? You can harvest ice and work on the roads and get relief? Naw—you're gonna let your wives do washing for Hasswells or Leroys or someone like that, break their backs makin' babies for you, while you sit around feeling sorry for yourselves."

"Keep it quiet," Russian said. "They're good men, Joe."

"I spit at good men," he said. "What do they pray for? 'Let me have food, oh, Lord in Heaven, let me have a little sleep in a warm bed and let me have, let me have.' That's all they care. Just about letting themselves have." He lowered his voice, turning toward Russian. "The earth rots under them. They sleep like sick dogs in the mud."

"Okay, Joe," Russian said. He put his hand on Joe's shoulder, sliding it around him, and with his other hand he hit him neatly, sharply. "Fool kid," he said.

"Watcha do that for?" Olds asked. He helped him drag Joe to the corner and prop him up between a table and the wall. "You shouldn't hit the kid."

Russian looked around him. "If I hadn't, someone else would have," he said. "He'll be all right."

It was almost dark when Joe came to. He did not move except to let his eyes go over the room. No one was looking at him. It was funny as hell, he thought, because no matter what you did, you lost in the end.

His days were curious as the days of a man who has not slept and therefore goes through each day in the deepest dream. His senses were hammered flat, stunned, and he saw no single shape with outline or color, just a dim blur of it. Inside him where there had once been a cancerous fury of anger, there was now only hollowness, an open wound gushing his blood back into the earth. He could never bring the feeling of *being* back into himself, never since that day when he had asked Kay Hasswell for a job. He did not *feel* what it was to be, to live, walk, sleep, cry, be angry. Even when he made the face of anger and spoke angry words for Rock, Mike or Mr. Wimmer, it was no good. And he had lost the feeling of belonging to them, the image of loveliness was gone forever, the world he desired was a memory past resurrection. When he spoke the words of his enormous anger, they were far away from him, hollow, useless and making little hollow, useless sounds as when you throw stones into a deep well. The lands of his desire were faded from his memory. The visions of his days were as the visions of a sleeper deep in his sleep . . .

He went to the washroom and gulped some cold water and bathed his face. He drove up the hill to Barby's in his new car. When he got out, he stopped and carefully brushed the front fender with his handkerchief. Then he stood back and looked at it, smiled and began to whistle as he walked toward the house. Barby came out on the glassed-in porch. She wore a yellow flannel dress and yellow kid sandals. She had been shopping again with Kay Hasswell.

"Hi, Sweets," he said.

"Hello, Joe."

He sat down on the porch swing. "See anything new?"

She looked at him. "No."

"Not me," he said. He pointed to his car, standing under the street light. "New car," he said.

For a minute, she didn't say anything. Then she said, "You got a job, didn't you, Joe?"

"In a way." He had thought he would feel happy about this, but he was not. She looked thin and tired to him, and she sat with her chin in her hand and looked at the car.

"Did you decide to go into business with Mike?"

"No."

"Oh."

"Not with Mike." He thought: Now she'll ask me a lot of questions. Instead, she seemed suddenly very happy, willing to accept anything he wanted her to.

"Came around last Saturday," he said.

"No one told me."

"I told Teresita."

"Oh, that Teresita."

"You weren't here."

"But, Joe, I told you I was going over to the city with Kay and Marth because you said you weren't sure you could make it. Then some people came with Johnnie Evans and we stayed and danced."

"I don't remember you told me about that." He held her hand, looking at it. "Who'd you dance with?"

"Some fellow named Bix Lawrence."

"He's always there. Is he a good dancer?"

"Not very. Why?"

"I just asked, that's all."

"Joe, I wouldn't have gone if—"

"It's okay. I want you to go," he lied. "I guess I do as I please without asking you."

"He wasn't a good dancer at all, Joe, and I don't like him. I just like the music, and Kay and Marth are fun to go with."

He looked at her, and the resentment went down inside him. Just because he felt rotten he didn't need to make her feel that way, too. He put his arms around her. "I'm sorry, Blue Eyes," he said.

"Come in and have some hot chocolate."

"Where's everyone?"

"Mamma's gone to Hasswell's. Kay gave a dinner party, and Teresita went up to help. She'd do anything for Kay."

They went into the kitchen. It always made him think of Holland, what Holland must be like with large kitchens painted yellow and yellow and red tulips stencilled on the cupboards. The best times were when they were alone like this, although he hated hot chocolate, it was too thick in his mouth. He pretended to like it and ate two cookies to make it taste better. She was certainly going to make a hell of a cook, a hell of a swell of a cook.

"Aren't you having any?"

"I like to watch you."

She seemed pale, though, and he knew what it was. They were always after her, her Mamma and old man Hasswell or some of her relatives, even Marth. She'd never say what they said to her, but he knew. When she was pale, she looked smaller and thinner. He got up and put his hands on her arms, and she stood close to him.

The Long Year 157

She smiled and moved her head from side to side, holding tight to him. After a while, they went out and got into the car, and he drove along the river. It wasn't cold now, just pleasant and white, and they sat in the car looking at the river, which had not as yet begun to freeze. If you half-closed your eyes the land was copper-colored over there.

"You've got some money now, haven't you, Joe?"

"Yeah," he said. He pressed his face into the soft, clean stuff of her polo coat. "We could do it okay now. We could do it, and no one would know and then later on we could tell them and have another kind of wedding if you want—and maybe go away and take Lindy with us."

"Could we?"

"That's what I'm telling you, honey."

She was trembling. "Could we, really? Then it would be okay—to be the way we are, I mean." She felt him change, his mood turning from tenderness to anger. "Oh, darling, not that way—it's just that it always seems a little like cheating, like not belonging with other people."

"Yeah," he said shortly.

"Joe, look at me. I won't ask questions—ever. I'll just be with you whenever we can and the other times I'll think about you and in a way it'll be almost as if we're together all the time."

In the low light of the dashboard, he could see that her face was flushed as if she were going to cry, and when he put his arms around her she was still trembling. He began to kiss her, to invade her world, to sink deep into the dream of loveliness that he desired to own forever. She held tight to him, moving a little against him.

"No please, Joe, not here—no—" she said.

He needed her. "Yes," he said, still holding her lightly but firmly. "Barby—Barby, listen to me . . ."

After an age of moving between the earth and the heavens, the moon came out again and he held her away from him, and she was crying. He thought he was crying, too, but there were no tears, only the crying inside him. He didn't know what to say to her. "Oh, Jesus," he said. "Look, Barby, what do you want?"

She shook her head. "I—Joe, when can we get married?"

"Soon, Baby," he said. "Maybe after the next time with Amory, maybe if I'm careful and don't let on what I'm planning to do, maybe I can get out of it and we could go away somewhere, West or North."

She smiled through her tears and blew her nose. "I'm awful, Joe."

"No—you're wonderful."

"I wish I knew more, though. Maybe I could help you."

"You help a lot. You're my sweet baby. That's what matters. When I'm with you, nothing else is real."

She laughed at him. She was his old girl when she laughed. Everything might work out after all. He could move slowly and watch out and wait for the break. "Geez, honey, I hate to think of anything happening to you when I'm away like this."

"S-ssh," she said. "I don't care what anyone says to me. I'm not that way."

He couldn't tell her in words. He wanted to tell her how he had to make that damned money—it wasn't easy or safe. He wanted to tell her how happy she made him and how he loved her and Lindy as a man loved the best things in his life. He felt soft and easy inside himself.

"We'll get married and go away," she was saying.

"Sure, Kid," he said. "Whatever you want." He thought: I wish we could do it here and now, openly, and have a house of our own and sleep on the screen porch on summer nights and I could work at the factory. Nothing fancy, only I'm sick of going around with my tail dragging. A guy should have what he wants once in a while, but this is no time for it—maybe there'll be a time for it but never for me, not for me, not ever for me. I know it.

He pretended to listen to her, but instead he was listening to the moving of his blood along his veins, to the blood circling himself like smoke unseen. He had no sure knowledge that he was alive in this time. He was remembering a time he had almost forgotten—where?

The Long Year 159

in a movie? in a book? Sometime when he had seen himself lying in a pool of blood, the slow, surging rhythm of it pouring out of himself. He shivered and reached for Barby, drawing her to him. He started the car and drove very fast so that the motor roared. He tried to remember where he had found this car—he couldn't quite remember except that Amory said to take it and shut up about it, take it . . .

CHAPTER SIXTEEN:

MARTH RAN up the stairs and went into Kay's room. Kay was getting dressed to go out with Johnnie. She was putting perfume behind her ears and on her wrists. She looked smooth and rested although she had been working all day. Marth leaned against the wall, breathless.

"Was that Johnnie just came in, darling?"

"No," she said. "You can't imagine."

Kay smiled. "President Roosevelt?"

"Don't laugh, Kay. It's old Walt Purdy."

"Oh?" She raised her eyebrows. She wore a soft blue wool dress made with a very low neckline. She wore a brilliant diamond clip and earrings to match, and these were separately alive like water and the heat of the earth. "I do hope he hasn't brought any white mice," she said.

"He looks awful."

"He always does."

"No—" Marth said slowly, "he looks—well, his eyes are red and he shakes."

"He's an old man," Kay said. She got up and pulled her coat over her shoulders. "Johnnie and I are going to the Flame Room."

Marth sighed. "You're never serious. Walt's come to see you."

"Why should I be serious? Where's your father?"

"He went out. He said he thought he'd go up to Leroy's."

"Oh, well!—I know what Walt Purdy wants. He's angry with me." She smiled gently. "Really, Martha, you are becoming so kind of desperate about everything. Walt Purdy's a harmless old geezer."

"I know, but—"

"And look at yourself in the mirror. You have a frowning look, little lines in your forehead."

The Long Year

Marth looked at herself. "My face is dirty, too," she said.

"You see! Now, don't worry, darling, I'll handle Walt as easy as anything."

"But, Kay, Daddy used to say that Grandma would turn over in her grave if we ever let Walt Purdy go."

"Go wash your face," she said.

"All right," Marth said. She felt like a dirty child, and all her love suddenly rushed to the surface. She touched Kay's hand. "Have fun, Kay."

"Yes, certainly," Kay said, kissing her cheek. The poor baby, she thought, the poor lost little kid, she doesn't know anything and it's time she got out of here, but I'll go next fall after the house is finished and things get under way. And even if Mamma said she'd keep Walt Purdy on forever, she didn't know there was going to be a time like this, and I'm certainly not going to have that dirty old man telling me what to do—arguing and bickering and making it harder for me.

She walked down the stairs slowly, her coat swinging from her shoulders. She was putting on her gloves, at the same time her brain was working on what to say to Walt Purdy. She had been avoiding him for over three weeks, since she had sent him that letter of dismissal. He was sitting in the living room, a dirty old man in a corduroy hunting jacket. He had his feet up on the footstool. He rose slowly, grunting with the effort. Everything about him was decaying—his teeth, his gnarled, empurpled hands, his fingernails stained with nicotine. Only the crafty eye, blue and fierce, looked out of his weathered face. She was aware of his cunning and skill. She put out her hand.

"Hello, Walt," she said. "I've been wanting to see you."

"Yep," he said. "I betcha." He sat down again and put his feet on the stool. She stood, drawing on her gloves. He motioned to the chair by the fireplace. A few dying embers glowed in the grate.

"See you done over the livin' room," he said. "Looks fine."

"Well, Hoyt needs someone to take care of him, you know. He

doesn't realize how ugly this place was merely because he had no one to take care of such things for him."

"Saw him goin' inta Leroy's place so figured I could see you alone, Kay."

"Fine, Walt," she said. "But I haven't much time."

"You've got enough," he said.

She sat down, feeling the dying warmth of the fire. Her coat slid from her shoulders. She pulled her other glove on and then took them off again. "Well? What's so important that you had to ferret me out like this?"

He hunched his shoulders, leaning forward. "You never liked me much, did ya now?"

"No," she said.

"I never liked you neither, even when you were a kid hanging around the office all the time."

"That's that, then," she said. "What do you want me to do?"

"Tell me the truth."

"Oh?"

"What made you write me that letter when I was spittin' distance from your office?"

"It seemed more businesslike." She could already see exactly how the conversation would go. She could manage. She did not want to think too much about Mamma and get involved in any soft, tender feeling for the old man. She hated it when the one opposing her was old and helpless. She liked them tough and armed in their youth.

"Hoyt know you decided to let me out like this?"

"I've mentioned it to him many times. Certainly you've been aware that Johnnie Evans has been called in and retained."

"Yeah," he said. "I ain't been called to any meetings, and when Hoyt meets me on the street, he looks like a sick cat. I know. You like to murder people like that, Kay. You always did. Simon O'Dodd was just a beginnin' for you. I know your kind. You ain't so damned original."

"Please," she said. "What do you want to know?"

The Long Year

"I want to hear you say it," he said. His voice rose shrill and quaking and he pointed a trembling finger at her. "I want you to say it out, the words, and me to hear them myself."

"That seems silly."

He shook his head. His hair was dirty gray. He had once been a good-looking man, and he might be one now if he ever took a bath. Most of the time he studied books, read Caesar and old Greek things that everyone else had forgotten about, but she supposed he liked the way he lived or he wouldn't live that way.

"Johnnie Evans is younger, Walt," she said. "We need a younger man with ideas." She lit a cigarette, holding the case out to him, but he shook his head. She snapped it shut smartly with a final strong air of being in full possession of this whole matter. She blew out the dry, blue smoke. "I'm sure you can understand that."

"No," he said. "Time has always been my friend. Just the other night, I was talkin' to Gene Wimmer about this letter of yours, an' he said the thing for me to do was to talk to you and make you say it right out—'Walt, you're too damned old an' your mental capacities aren't what they used to be.' Gene said he didn't think you could say that to me."

"Gene Wimmer?" She rose and stood by the fireplace, leaning against it. She kicked the glowering log deeper into the fire where it sparked up and began to burn. Why was Gene Wimmer in everything? If she said yes, he'd say the answer was no. If she said black, he'd say white. Just like Prokosch. It was annoying. "Nevertheless," she said, "We are retaining Johnnie Evans. He will go to Chicago at the right time and get what I want. I want some good contracts and he'll get them for me."

"A drop in the bucket," he said.

"It may be more. The government's going to do some healthy building, and the way I have things lined up—well, that's my affair. You ought to sit back now and take it easy, Walt. You must be tired."

"Hadn't noticed it."

"There's no sense in arguing." She threw her cigarette into the fire, picked up her gloves, brown alligator bag, her mink coat. She put the coat around her shoulders again. He was staring into the fire.

"I remember your mother," he said. "She was a fine woman, warm and honest." He looked at her. "I want to warn you, Kay."

"What now?"

"You think I'm a crazy old man."

"No. I didn't say that. I just think it's over for you."

"Just the same, let me tell you something."

"Go ahead."

"The people won't like it."

"Like what?" She smiled at him. "You mean they won't like it because we've taken on Johnnie Evans?"

"No." There was sweat on his forehead. He put his trembling hands into his pocket. "I mean, you can get the contracts, but you don't dare cut down—make just any kind of frames, any kind of pulleys, the cheapest and easiest thing. You won't get by with it even if you do open the factory to almost full production. People can do a lot to you, Kay, and if they don't like the kind of work you're putting out—"

"Nonsense," she said. "Everything's been done to me that will ever be done. I'm through with caring what people do or say. All I want is to open the factory again."

"For the money?"

"If you like it that way—yes. I don't see why one should be ashamed of saying what's true. I admit that I want the money. It's true of everyone."

"You'll have to leave here in the end—the way you left before. They'll run you out one way or another, and you'll leave like you've left everywhere."

She said nothing.

He rose, a big man for his age. "I've been the Hasswells' lawyer for fifty years, almost from the beginning of my career. It makes fifty years seem wasted and useless."

She touched his arm. "It's business, Walt."

The Long Year

He moved from her. "You don't need to pretend you're sorry, Kay. You've got it the way you want it, leave it at that." He brought out a small, white mouse. "This is Ursula," he said. "She's a good mouse. Macbeth say she's got the personality of a dowager—maybe a bubble dancer's."

"I hate mice."

The mouse lay still in the man's big, tough hand, its eyes pink and bright. Its coat was very clean and white, and the mouse itself was delicate, soft, warm with life, huge with life. He stroked it, looking ta Kay. "A mouse is a small thing in a big world. He can get lost or find himself. He's humble, he works hard, he's nice to look at. Can't say the same of most folks I know."

"It's getting late, Walt. I hear Johnnie outside. Come down to see me whenever you feel like it."

"No thanks," he said.

"Care for a ride?"

He shook his head. "No," he said. 'Thanks for seeing me."

She said nothing.

He went out, and she heard him speak to Johnnie. When she looked out the window, he was going down the street, walking at a slow, awkward pace as if he were blind. Johnnie came in, standing in the hall slapping his hat against his hand. A fine light film of snow had begun to fall.

"What's the matter with Walt?"

"Nothing."

"Yes there is."

She sighed. "He merely doesn't like the way things are going. That's all. You could hardly expect him to like it—a young man coming into his shoes like this."

"You told me you had dismissed him long ago."

"I did, but I just wrote him formally several weeks ago. He knew, of course, but I had to talk Hoyt into it. You know how Hoyt clings to these old people that Mamma put in office."

"What did you tell him?"

"Who?"

"Mr. Purdy."

"I told him the truth."

"You mean—you told him he was too old and dirty and you'd be ashamed to send him to Chicago? Did you tell him you weren't sure you could push him around the way you can push me—"

"Stop that, darling." She moved toward him. She looked at him in a moment of silence. "Do I push you around?"

"Sometimes I'm not so sure that you don't," he said. "My God"—he looked at her sharply—"I suppose when you're through with me, you'll write me a letter and do it neatly—coldly like that."

"Don't have a scene, darling."

"But, my God, Kay—"

"Oh, come on," she said. "Let's get out of here."

Sometime during that evening, Walt Purdy shot himself in his office. In the early morning, Mr. Wimmer and Russian were walking by and saw him there at his desk. His file cases were upset. They found a bucket behind the desk. Twenty little white mice were lying dead on a wool blanket in the bucket. They all looked alike, very delicate, clean and totally dead. There was a wistful, lingering odor of chloroform, and the big old man lay with his head on the desk, the gun on the floor beside him. It was an antique gun, a seven repeater. Everyone in town knew that gun. Walt had bought it off an Indian agent when he was a young fellow opening his law office, and now he had shot himself with it. The people would not believe it.

"What in hell's the matter around here?" Russian asked. "Nothing's going right." He looked down at the body. He wondered if anyone in town had ever really known this man—he had been kind and shy and withdrawn, and he wondered if he had hated living alone like that. "I'll bet he had these white mice to keep him company," he said. "Dammit, Mr. Wimmer, *she* did it. I know she did it."

"Who?" Mr. Wimmer asked.

"Her—that Kay Hasswell."

The Long Year

"He shot himself, Russian. It was up to him."

"She did it, though," Russian said. "I can remember Simon O'Dodd. She did that, too."

"How did she do this?" he asked.

"She let him off at the factory an' took on that pretty boy, Johnnie Evans. Can you imagine how that made Purdy feel?"

Mr. Wimmer said nothing. He stood watching Russian go toward the Cafe.

That early in the morning, a few prison guards sat around the walls, lounged at the table. Russian would never drink with the prison men. He didn't like them nor the kind of work they did. He saw Joe at the bar and went up and stood near him. He seldom went directly home from the factory. In fact, he spent little time home now. For some reason, he was too restless to stay there.

"Let's drink," he said. "Let's drink a toast to Walt Purdy, Joe."

"No," Joe said. "I don't drink to any man who's dead—no matter who he is."

"She did it, though," Russian said. "Sure as if she took the shot herself."

"You didn't see it. You weren't there. You don't know what he thought. Maybe he was being sensible."

Russian's eyes glinted in the low light. "Figure it out," he said. "She got Johnnie Evans for a lawyer. She gets him so crazy about her he can't tell his left from his right."

"It's a free country."

"You sure must like her, Boy."

"No, I don't like her. I couldn't get a job off her, but I just think you got a hold of a crazy idea."

"As long as Hoyt was running things, he and Purdy got on fine. Now, Hoyt goes down there and hasn't anything to do so he comes back and works jigsaw puzzles or goes up to Leroy's or sleeps. She made old Purdy feel useless and old. She could do that to anyone."

"Just the same, I wouldn't beat my gums too hard about it. It's not healthy letting an idea like that get around."

"It's the God's truth."

"Where'll it get you to tell it around like that?"

He leaned heavily against the wall, seeing all of it: poor old Purdy dead in his office with those white mice dead in the bucket—her dancing her golden slippers off at the Flame Room—and Walt Purdy dead as a three-day-caught fish. It made him mad as a hornet to think of her looking so respectable and clean, as if she had nothing to do with it, but he knew—he knew— He was angry, too, because none of the men stood together against her. Used to be you could have a nice talk at noon hour, sit around together, but now you couldn't talk to anyone, scared the other guy might cheat you out of a job if he worked too hard, did too much. Why couldn't everyone get together and do something the way pioneers did, pulling together instead of standing around or sitting around on their fat asses praying for Roosevelt? Why couldn't they go back to the old days? "A stinkin' time," he said aloud and took a long, hot swallow of whiskey.

Several days later, Hoyt Hasswell sat alone at the breakfast table. "Where's my sister, Howard?"

"She went to the office already," Howard said. "She said to tell you that."

Hoyt ate his breakfast slowly. The truth was that for the first time in all these years, he was in no special hurry to get to the office. He had two helpings of everything merely to forestall the moment when he would have to go down there. At last he admitted that the factory could exist without him. It made him feel terribly old although he was only forty-six. He tried to figure it out. At first, Kay had come to him to ask about this or that, and finally she had ceased to come at all. He knew there was no reason for him to go near the place except that if you started your life in one place, you or something inside went back to that place, and there was no help for it.

He put on his coat and went out to the car. He supposed Marth was with her, they were always together now. He wondered if he

The Long Year 169

ought to have insisted that she go away to school. The only thing was that she had objected to it, and he didn't want to make her unhappy. Bad enough to have Mike down there in his river shack in the dead of winter. Bad enough— Howard held the door for him. He looked at Howard. Howard's face was cold, and his lips were cracked. "Guess I'll sit in front, Howard."

Kay's car was not at the factory although he could see from the tracks in the snow that she had been there earlier—probably looking for land for her house. She wanted to build it in the spring. He went into his office, sat at the desk, stared into space. He had the same powerless feeling he had had in the days when Mamma had been alive, sitting in the small office running everything, yelling through the open door at him, "Hoyt! Hoyt—where are you, Son?"

While he was thinking about Mamma, he heard the red convertible roar up the circular drive outside the office. He saw Kay jump from the car. She wore a tan polo coat, and when she ran the coat flapped open revealing a red wool dress with black frogs down the front, a kind of Russian affair, he supposed. It must be wonderful for a woman to be so full of energy like that, but it annoyed him, too. She came into the building hurriedly, spoke to Mary, waved to him and went at once to her office. He kept hoping she might come in to ask him about what to do with the stuff in Warehouse Number Nine or if he had checked with Russian about the East gate—the one that they had broken into last night. No one had ever damaged any of the factory property. It made him feel that perhaps she was right, they were outnumbered, and if the men in the town suddenly decided—but, of course, it was nonsense, pure nonsense, she got ideas like that from living in cities and among foreigners all the time.

Then he heard her coming down the hall, the click of her heels. She walked like a man, very firm and with certainty, and when you did not see her, you thought it might be a small, light man walking that way with cleats on his heels. He pretended to be engrossed in a stack of old letters, but all the while he kept watching her move in the outer office, walking among the desks, opening drawers, slamming them shut. Finally she came to his door and opened it.

"Hello, darling," she said.

"Good morning, Kay," he said.

"You shouldn't come down so early," she said. She sat on the corner of his desk, swinging her legs, smoking. "Really, darling, you ought to get more rest—or take a vacation. Now's the time for it. It's my turn to worry about things."

"Oh, I don't mind. I'm used to it."

"I know, but even so—" She had a thoughtful, worried air. She smoked. "Apparently, Russian doesn't know about the East gate," she said. "Must have happened some time between three and four in the morning when he was checking the West side."

"I see," he said.

She was silent again, looking out the window.

"What's wrong?"

"Nothing."

"I think so—"

"Well," she said slowly, "Marth says that everyone seems to think I'm involved in Purdy's death."

"That's silly."

"Of course. But they think because I let him out—"

"You did that?"

"Well, I told you we had to let him go."

"But I thought it was only temporary. That's what you told me."

"It's done," she said. "Anyhow, Marth was very upset about it and said everyone around town is talking."

"I don't like Marth involved in these things."

"Don't worry. She and Barby have some times together, and in the fall when I go, I'll take Marth with me. But the main thing now is that the men stand round and brood. They stare back at you as if you were to blame."

"I'm sure they know how hard you work—"

"You think everyone's a Rotarian—Brother we are one. Christ was

The Long Year 171

the first Rotarian, all of that—but you're wrong, Hoyt. The men are spoiling for a fight, and this business about Purdy doesn't help any. Then they've got Mr. Wimmer to listen to them and to tell them— well, whatever Mr. Wimmer *does* tell them. He's a radical, and he'd do anything to put some of his ideas into effect. Last night, two men were in a knife fight in the Cafe. The east gate was broken."

Even so, he knew these people, and they were hard-working, honest people, harmless. She had always, even as a child, had the idea that the people were against her.

"They're all right," he said.

She shook her head. She put her hand over his. "That Gene Wimmer talks too much."

"He's harmless enough."

She rose and began to walk back and forth, smoking nervously. "Harmless. They listen to him. I've known men like that, and once they can get enough people together they can do anything. They might even be able to take this place from us. We're outnumbered, and by the time they got the State guard out—who knows? He's against us. I can feel it. These—these idealists and radicals are in the limelight during bad times like these. We might wake up and find the place burned down around us."

He understood how she felt because it was partly how he felt now, thinking about everything she had mentioned. "Wimmer has a lot of friends here."

"I know that, but he'd get out."

"It wouldn't be easy. He likes it here."

"I know, I know."

He watched her, waiting. She's got the solution in her mind already, he thought, or she wouldn't have mentioned this to him.

She said, "The people are spoiling for excitement. They'd turn on him as easily as not if they had the chance." She looked at him. "You're on the school board, aren't you?"

"I'm president of it, but that doesn't mean anything."

"Doesn't it?"

He shook his head.

"It could mean a lot, Hoyt."

That was all she said. She smiled and went out of the office. He could hear her heels going toward her own office. He kept drumming the table nervously with his fingers. At noon, he was still sitting there thinking. Suddenly, for the first time, he was afraid of these people whom he knew so well. He had to admit there was something in their faces, in the faces of the women, too—they looked gaunt, feverish, desperate. When the men worked they had no time for fighting or drinking or plotting together. He did not understand this Depression, although both Mr. Wimmer and Walt Purdy had explained it to him a number of times, still he did not truly grasp what it was about. He was just there to run the place when there was work. Still, he was one man against so many. It was a very good idea to have them think of something besides the factory, and if Mr. Wimmer was gone, they would have no leader, no one smart enough to give them ideas. "Maybe," he said softly, "maybe Kay's right." After all, he could easily persuade the members of the board—Russian was scared about his job, Maida was his friend, the others—

He picked up the telephone. Now, he had something to do.

CHAPTER SEVENTEEN:

THE SCHOOL board, four men and a woman, thick through the middle and full of her own thickness, met in a special room in the school. The room was for them alone. Every time Russian went there, he was more and more pleased with it. It was not like the old days when everyone had to study in one big, bare room with a coal stove and everyone sweating like hell or shivering like hell. The board room was small, panelled in white pine. A long table almost filled the room. Around the table were five very grand green leather chairs. At the head of the table Hoyt Hasswell always sat. He wore a blue serge suit and a white shirt. The others did the same. Mrs. Leroy always dressed for the occasions, wearing her bagette diamond and her blue sapphire. Russian sat at one side of him, and Tom Hickory, the treasurer, sat on the other side. Otis Hickory and Meyer Holland, a veterinarian from up-river and Mrs. Leroy sat at the other end of the table.

Russian wiped his hand slowly across his face. "Mr. Wimmer's a good teacher and a fine man. I kind of hate to do anything against him."

"Russian," Hoyt said, "listen to me. We are not *doing* anything to him. We are doing what we were elected to do."

"All right," Russian said, "but we're putting him out of a job. My kids were crazy about him."

"I think most of us will agree that Mr. Wimmer's been popular," Hoyt said in his best Rotarian manner.

Mrs. Leroy smiled her dazzling smile. She wore a gray woolen suit and a red-and-green owl with glittering eyes pinned to her lapel. When she moved, the owl's eyes blinked. "Oh, dear," she said wistfully, "I don't see why we have to do things like this."

"Maida," Hoyt said, "we aren't doing anything."

"He's such a sweet man. I adore the way he plays the accordion."

"That has nothing to do with it. We can't have him teaching radical ideas in the school. You know that."

"It's—it's all too big for me," she sighed.

Tom Hickory, an old man with a goatee, rubbed his hand over his eyes. "I don't get this. Wimmer's been here eight years, and he's been teachin' the same stuff every year."

"You don't understand," Hoyt said. "It is in times like this that we cannot tolerate such things. It's not good for the students here. In other times, it might not matter, but now—"

Mrs. Leroy said, "I just thought he mentioned it—Communism, I mean—so the children would know what it's about."

Hoyt cleared his throat. "Look at it this way. We all know he's got strange ideas, don't we?"

The Hickory boys nodded. "Sure," they said.

"We don't want Communism or any of those ideas to get a hold here."

Russian asked, "What's the difference between Communism and Democracy? I suppose there must be some difference, but no one's ever told me."

Mrs. Leroy said, "I'm not sure except what you read in the papers. It's something dreadful, I guess."

Russian said, "They burn churches and throw bombs and don't want anyone to own property, as far as I can see. It's not our way. It would mean you couldn't own your house, Mrs. Leroy—if people like that got hold of this town. I think that's the difference."

Mrs. Leroy thought. Only Meyer Holland, the veterinarian, said nothing. Usually, he did whatever the others did.

"Well," Mrs. Leroy said, "my husband left me that house. I guess it would be a terrible thing to let Communists get hold of our town, and I must admit—Mr. Wimmer talks a lot and people like to listen to him."

Hoyt nodded. "You see?"

Tom Hilton said, "But how can we get rid of him, now? He's a smart man."

The Long Year

Hoyt said, "He's coming here in a few minutes, and we'll ask him some questions in a kind way, of course. We want to be fair. And if he says he'd like to resign, we'll agree to accept the resignation. That will make things neater, easier for us."

"All right," Russian said. He didn't like the idea, but he felt that Hoyt wasn't running this—Kay Hasswell was the one—and it wouldn't do him any good to try to stop it. "I guess it's something we've got to do."

Every day, Gene Wimmer had adventures, everything was an adventure and a miracle to him. He loved the town, he loved to teach school there. He had never been to a meeting of the school board, but he thought perhaps they were interested in some of his ideas on the cooperative system of truck gardening and dairy farming. He was working on his doctorate about cooperatives. As he walked toward the school, he planned what he would say about this so that it would be simple and still not an insult to their intelligence or vanity.

He stood in the school hall for a moment, looking at himself in the windows of the trophy case. He admired the trophies, reading the names on them, some he knew, some had a dreary, lost sound.

As he was standing there, Hoyt came out into the hall. "Come in, Gene," he said. He held out his hand in a friendly way, and Mr. Wimmer went into the room ahead of him. The five members of the board sat at the polished table. He could see their faces in the surface. Mrs. Leroy smiled and held out her hand. He shook it, feeling the big diamond scratch against his palm. Tom Hickory, the treasurer, was absorbed in a report, kept pulling at his beard, his eyes lowered to the paper. Russian grunted. Usually he was very friendly, but now he looked away. There was no place to sit, so he stood at one end of the table, leaning against the wall near Mrs. Leroy. They all looked at him, and in each he read that which was not pleasant but for which he had as yet no name.

Hoyt stood at the head of the table. Everyone turned at once to look at him. "Now," he said, "we're going to talk over this matter."

He sat down. No one spoke. Mr. Wimmer blinked his eyes in the low, greenish light. He thought it was funny—the men sitting there as if they knew something and that pretty, foolish, lovely woman who was always so gay trying to look serious now. Hoyt shuffled some papers, cleared his throat. When he raised his eyes, the others turned again in a single movement and looked at him.

Hoyt said, "Gene, we've been hearing things about you."

The others nodded their heads.

Mr. Wimmer waited.

"We've been hearing that you're a Communist, Gene." His voice was sad, resigned.

"Oh, I see," he said. He put his hands behind him, braced them flat against the wall. It was difficult not to smile. It was just a word, Communism, just a word to him and never a desired way of life, but he thought they knew nothing about what the word meant. They handed it around like a hunk of hot lead. All of this was like a comedy he had seen that had to do with superstitious mountain folks.

"We can't have that here, Gene," Hoyt said.

He said, "I suppose not." There ought to be something witty to say to show that this was a bad dream or a farce with a happy ending. Still, in the end it would not matter what he said. He smelled the death here, lying in pools around the room, pools like blood. For a moment, he could not breathe.

Russian said, "Are you one, Gene?"

He said, "No—I don't think so."

Mrs. Leroy said, "I'm a Republican. I've always known it."

Meyer Holland said in a slow, drawling voice, "That's no answer, Mr. Wimmer."

He smiled and said nothing.

Hoyt said, "I don't understand you, Gene."

Finally he said, "Well, some things about Communism sound fine. They're good. Some things about Democracy are wonderful, the idea I mean, but then people change it because of their natures."

The Long Year

Mrs. Leroy said, "You really mustn't say things about Democracy, Mr. Wimmer."

He didn't say anything. He felt curiously, looking at their faces, that their eyes were like those of a doll, shoe-button or glass eyes, unseeing. He was the fallen fox, cornered. He looked at the woman. He always believed in women, believed in their gentleness and mother-natures, but Maida Leroy was confused. He had thought to teach all the days of his life in this town, to live here all the time except for going West once. His mind reached out for a reason for this, and he thought of Kay Hasswell at once, but he could not understand why she'd want to get him out of here. Why?

Hoyt asked, "You mentioned Communism in your class, didn't you?"

"Yes."

"You also praised the cooperative system of dairy farming in Sweden. You said that it could work out well here, didn't you?"

"That's in the text. When the students ask me, I tell them what I believe to be true."

Tom Hickory said, "You know we don't believe in things like that here."

He said nothing.

Hoyt shook his head. "We can't have instability and flossy words in our school systems in these times, Gene."

"No, sir, we can't," the Hickory boys said. Russian said nothing.

He looked at Mrs. Leroy. There were tears in her eyes. She was nervously twisting her ring.

Hoyt said, "I tell you what, Gene. We don't wish to make it hard for you. You think over what we've said, and if you want to resign at once, we'll accept your resignation and give you a fine recommendation. No hard feelings."

Mr. Wimmer looked at him silently. What was there to say?

"You hear me, Gene?"

"I heard you," he said.

They had expected some sort of argument from him, at least a speech, and now they met only silence. He looked terribly young to them at that moment, silent and young, and there was still something warm and friendly that made them feel sad to do this to him.

Russian said, "Mr. Wimmer, you ought to tell us what you think."

In that instant, he was angry at them. He wanted to tear them apart, to knock some sense into their heads, to make them see something in the vision of their days, their faces so still and dead, their lips solid without the warmth of life. He wanted to turn their spirits inward to look upon themselves, and everything he knew passed through him, and he was speechless, finding no words to tell them of man's time on earth, of the thousand images to which they were stone-blind, of the earth itself and the heart of it, the hearts of everyone in the darkness. What could he say?

"It was good of you to tell me anyhow," he said. "You could have made it harder for me."

"But look here now," Russian said. "You can say what you please. A man's got a right to speak for himself."

"Yes," he said. "Well—I'll tell you this—a teacher has to do what he thinks is right. A nice building doesn't make a good school. It's there to see. No one ever truly sees the teacher. He knows himself, but no one else sees him. You can't tell a teacher what he must say or how he must say it. In the end, you'd have mouthpieces for yourselves and nothing more. The school belongs to everyone in the town instead of a few of you to make it easier for the others to forget. You give your children nothing, though, if you tell the teacher how he must teach." That was all he wanted to say. He buttoned his coat and left the building.

He walked swiftly down the winter street. The snow was beginning again. Somewhere far off, he heard the snow plow working. He went down Chestnut Street. He saw Johnnie Evans come out of the office building with Kay, moving in the grayish air. She wore a red coat. They were arguing, and he heard her voice. He stood back against the building.

"All right," she was saying. "Only you'll have to be cleverer than that in Chicago."

The Long Year 179

"You don't care what I think of this, Kay?"

"No," she shook her head. "I don't give a damn."

He could see Johnnie's face in the light as he helped her into the car. It was how he himself felt. He shivered and walked toward the river. The water was frozen, lying black and glittering under the cold winter moon. He turned toward the beach where the winds had swept the snow into a ridge. The beach sands lay flat and hard under the wind.

Now, if he could think of everything that had happened to him, that he had said or done, he might have a reason for this. He felt suddenly alone, there was no one with whom he could recall these times on earth, no one had ever shared his life. He had come here and found it like a home, always a place to which he would return, and that was what he had desired more than anything except to teach the kids. He didn't mind now if he lost face with them, the idea scarcely occurred to him. He minded, though, if because of this they would cease to believe what he had said to them.

He could not explain the change that had come here, all over the country, so that the face of the country was strange to him now. The pioneer was in his grave, the dream of the pioneer was dead, and the children of the pioneer sat in buildings making long speeches and died a thousand times over with the weight of their own voices. Well, he thought, the land was here even before the people came to infest it, and no one knows what America is—they say it's a melting pot of this and that, and then they say it's the biggest dream anyone ever had, but now it's lost and no one remembers that it was a great, wonderful, innocent dream, the biggest circus idea a man could have—now it's lost—maybe forever, maybe for only this time.

He thought of Kay Hasswell in her red coat. It was like a splash of living blood in the snow, like seeing a wonderfully warm and rich-smelling house flower through a window. He could understand how, if you loved your country, it was like loving a woman—and if you loved someone or some country, you could understand how others did the same. Yes, the thing was everywhere, this business of loving and belonging, and he had missed part of it.

He stumbled along the beach. As he turned the bend and came into the open, flat part, he heard Rocky running, and he knew at once it was Rocky. As soon as he came into the last stretch he could see his face clearly in the moonlight. The snow turned blue and the night itself was not black but a marvelously deep shade of blue.

"Hello, Rock!" he called.

Rock came up to him, running slowly, not panting or even breathing hard. He flashed a small light and wiped his nose on his jacket. He wore a pair of old flannels and a windbreaker, and tennis shoes. The snow was thick in his hair. He bent over and shook his head, running the flat of his hand over it. "Want to run awhile, Gene?"

"Sure."

Wimmer took off his coat and put it under the pier, and he and the boy ran up and down the winter beach, not fast, but in an easy loping manner. After two turns, he slowed down, and they sat on the pier and clapped their hands together. The wind rose on the river, lifted the ghostly visions of snow.

"Storm coming," Rocky said.

"You can smell it."

"Russian said you were in for it tonight. He told Paw."

"I guess so," Wimmer said. "I guess I was in for it."

"Didn't Russian say anything for you?"

"Why, no," he said, surprised.

"Well, the old boy's scared about his job. He's not the way he used to be, and I guess no one is. He can't think about anything except to hang on to the job. You can't blame him for that."

"No," he said. It was strange that he didn't feel unhappy about it. He felt that a teacher was a teacher no matter where he went or what he did. Some people were mechanics or circus riders or doctors, and he was a teacher. It was not a great problem once it was settled in a person.

The Long Year

"You going to do it?"
"Do what?"
"Resign?"
"No."
"They'll kick you out."
"Yes, I guess they will, but they'll be the ones to do it. I won't help them."

Rocky buttoned his jacket under his chin. "Got up a good speed tonight," he said.

"You fighting Saturday?"
"Brownie McMahon—at the arena."
"Is he a flash?"
"I don't know. Maybe he is. That's what the handlers all say, and you can usually get the real drift of a thing from them. But, he doesn't care much. Maybe he's a flash."
"Does Marth like it when you fight?"

He laughed. "She doesn't know anything about it. She thinks if you win, it's swell. I've been lucky, haven't lost a fight. Kay Hasswell knows Fonn Kelly. She says he's really something. I never saw him except in news reels, but you can't expect to come up against a guy like that. I keep hoping, but I never get anyone like him."

"I suppose not."

They each lit a cigarette, holding the flame close in the curve of their hands. They sat well back on the pier that had been swept clean by the wind. They sat in the shelter of the hill.

"You like women, Gene?"
"Some."
"What kind?"
"There isn't any kind. They're each different."
"How about—Kay Hasswell?"

"I like her fine," he said. He smiled in the darkness. The boy was uncanny. He thought again of the red coat, the red blood, the red flower, the little flame, the woman alone. He thought of her in all the ways he imagined her to be, and he smiled gently.

"Paw says she's a terror."

"We don't know," he said. "She's different from anyone here."

"She's the one who wants you to get out. Russian said so. He told Paw she's behind it. She can wrap Hoyt around her little finger."

"I know," he said. "What about you, Rock—you like women?"

"Just Marth. It's funny, though, the times when Mike and Joe and I'd go hunting and stay up North. All we think about is women, like we were used to whoring around all the time, but when we came down from the woods, we forgot about it. I mean, you see them round, and you take it easier. Only up there in the woods, we'd sit in the cabin and drink beers and talk about women. It was pretty rough, I guess, but that's how it was."

"Unhunh," he said.

They got up and walked slowly down the beach.

"Only thing is you can't let it matter too much," Rocky said. "You can't let it be the thing to decide you because then they got their teeth in you. Paw says you can't let a woman get her teeth in you or you get like a woman, too."

They could see Macbeth inside the store. He was sleeping on the counter near the clothes rack. He had been reading and now he was asleep, living in whatever he had just read.

"What'll you do?" Rocky asked.

"Thought I'd stay around a while. You know Walt Purdy's old farm up-river. His sister wants to sell it cheap. I'd like living up there."

"Yeah," he said.

"Look at Macbeth," he laughed. "He's an old cat."

"Look at the old man," Rocky said. "Now I've got to carry him to bed. Every night I've got to carry him. He weighs like a feather and sleeps like a baby. What an old man!"

Mr. Wimmer laughed Then he walked off down the street toward the hotel Joe's new car was outside the Cafe. He looked at it from all angles, touching it, bending down to read the license plate. He shook his head. Outside the dry-cleaning place, he saw the dog. The dog was sitting there as if he had never been another

The Long Year

place nor known another town. He was an old stray creature, shivering, and he looked out of his enormous eyes mournfully.

"Hello, Jawrge," Mr. Wimmer said.

The dog got up, his bones cracking. He sniffed Mr. Wimmer's shoes. His stringy tail whacked the sidewalk.

"All right, come along, Jawrge."

It was a very strange business, he thought. How people eat their guts out trying to have things the way they want them to be, and in the end they die and someone else changes it over to suit himself. Everything was continuous like the girl on the baking-powder can, going on forever, repeating itself. He supposed there was a native wisdom which acknowledged that love was the animal heart set free—he believed love and freedom were the same thing, always the same—and this native wisdom was a rock seeking its natural bed, an eye turning toward the light, everything together in its best natural state.

He walked along the empty street, the dog following him. He took him into the hotel, and the dog slept in his room. For some reason, he felt less lonely, and in the morning when he woke and found the dog lying there, it was not unusual in any way. "Hello, there, Jawrge," he said.

CHAPTER EIGHTEEN:

AFTER THE board meeting, the others stood in the hall talking, but Russian set out at once for his home. As he walked up the hill toward his house, he saw Olds come out and stand in the street, shivering.

"Hey!" he called. "What's the matter?"

Olds slapped himself hard, trying to keep warm. "Smut ain't come home," he said. "She's started to come along, and Smut ain't come home."

"Maybe he's working late."

"No," Olds said. "He didn't come home last night neither."

He looked at Olds sharply. "He's run off, maybe."

Olds nodded. "That's what I figgered. It got to be too much for him, I guess. A young guy like Smut's jist so tough and no tougher."

"He'll come back," he said.

"Been to the board meetin'?"

"Yeah." He moistened his lips. "Say, Olds, you'll probably hear it around soon enough, but tonight—at the meeting, we decided to let Gene Wimmer go."

"Zat so? Go where? Sendin' him to a convention?"

"No," he said patiently. Goddamit, he knows, and he wants to make me say it out. "We asked him to resign. Give up the job."

"Oh," Olds said. "Don't reckon he'll like it much. He's pretty fond of teachin' here."

"Oh, he didn't have much choice."

"What'd he do?"

"He taught radical ideas."

Olds thought about it, jumping up and down, a ridiculous, skinny little guy trying to keep warm. "What's radical ideas?"

The Long Year

"Communism and Socialism and stuff like that."

"Oh. Well, I guess a young man's got a right to want to change the world here and there."

"This is different," he persisted. "This is dangerous."

"Oh. Even so, people aren't gonna like it much, Russian. They'll take it hard, and you'll find yourself in a pot of trouble."

"No, I don't think so. Folks'll talk a lot, but there won't be trouble."

"You always liked him, Russian."

"Don't you understand, it's not a matter of liking or not liking—"

"It's a matter of keepin' your job, hey?"

"Maybe," he said shortly. He wondered why Olds didn't mind not having a job. Here it was early November and they'd been let out in late June. You'd think by now Olds would begin to take it harder than ever before, but he didn't seem to mind much.

"Send for the doctor?" he asked.

"Not yet. She says she'll tell me when to go for him. He's waitin' up at his house, though." He was excited. "I hope it's a boy. Smut'll like it if it's a boy. 'Course he's crazy about the girls, too, but it might help a little—"

"Uh hunh," Russian said. He didn't want to stand there in the cold talking to Olds about his new grandchild. "See you later," he said. He hurried toward his house. Inside it was warm. The windows were steamed. His wife was ironing in the kitchen. The man on the radio was explaining something about South American music. South America was a pink place on the map to him. He switched off the radio and went out to the kitchen.

"You're home early, dear," she said.

He nodded. "Time the kids got in from the late show," he said. He did not have much money to spare for such things, but he could never say no to them. Besides, they had to keep a guard at the factory, didn't they? No escaping that.

"Smut Olds hasn't come home for a couple days," he said. "Velma's started to have pains, too."

"Smut? You mean he's run off."

"Yes," he said.

"Oh, no!" she said. She put down her iron, and rubbed the back of her neck. "That's terrible, that young boy running off."

"Olds says it was too much for him."

"Poor boy," she said. "Do you want a glass of milk? There's some on ice."

"Not tonight," he said. He went in and sat by the radio and started to read the paper. He always read what Mrs. Amos had to say first. Now, she was giving statistics on municipal gas and light. While he was reading that, the two children came in from the movie. He always thought of them as children, even Joanie, who was eighteen now. Somehow, she still retained much of her childhood appearance and manner.

"Pa-pa," she said.

"Humm?" He did not look at her but stayed behind his paper. Joanie was a smart one. He was proud of that, but at times, such as now, it frightened him.

"Papa," she said insistently.

"Now what?" he asked. He put down his paper and looked at her.

"Papa, everyone says Mr. Wimmer got fired."

He could hear his wife put down the iron suddenly. It clicked against the metal heat plate. Then he heard her slam the lids on the kitchen range.

"That so?" he said.

The girl came over to him and took the paper gently from him. The younger child stood there looking at him. She seemed smaller and prettier than usual, and again he found it hard to believe she was his. He was not that lucky.

"Papa?"

"Now, Joanie, honey, you're out of the high school. It doesn't matter to you. I've been mighty proud of you getting out first in your class. A big class, too, and there was my Joanie up there making a speech. That was a very big night for your old Papa."

The Long Year

The younger child went into the kitchen and came back with her mother. They both stood in the doorway looking at him. He put his feet together hard, heavily on the floor.

"Papa, is it true?" she asked. She was not going to be put off.

"He'll give in his resignation," he said slowly.

"Oh." She sat down on the footstool. She sighed. "He was the best teacher I ever had."

"He'll go somewhere else and teach. You'll see. I felt it there. He would not give up teaching more than I'd give up my work."

"All right, Papa," she said. She did not kiss him. The younger child came over and kissed him, but she would not look at him.

"You could've done something, Papa," she said in a small whisper. It was her smallness and quietness that he loved, and now she was using these against him. He could feel that they were all against him. He listened to her going up the stairs slowly, and then he heard them talking in their room. He turned up the radio, and still he could imagine their quiet talk. His wife came in again and began to write her weekly letter to her family. He stood her silence for a long time—that silence that was in the house and outside in the night. Finally, he turned down the radio and went to the foot of the stairs.

"You two get into bed now," he said. "Stop that talking."

"We aren't talking, Papa," Joanie said.

He walked into the kitchen and took a drink of water. Then he returned to the living room. "Women," he said. "It's always women! They could do no better."

His wife put down her pen. "Yes," she said. "We could do better."

"There wasn't any choice, Jo," he said.

She was silent, looking at him. He would not look at her. Let her think what she chose to think, it couldn't be helped now. Besides, what good would it have done to speak against Hoyt? They all knew who held the purse strings there. "I tell you, Jo, Kay Hasswell doesn't want him around. She thinks he's too popular and might stir up trouble. He talks a lot, too, and everyone listens to him and you have to admit if he had his way we'd have had union contracts all along."

"Better to listen to him than to her, and as for the union idea—it's true you've always had better than union pay till this happened, but you never knew what other men in factories thought or what they were doing in other places. So, it's easier to sit around and do what comes easiest and listen to Kay Hasswell."

"She owns part of the factory, remember that, and that's my job. He owns nothing."

"You talk like a sick man."

He looked at her sharply. "Sick?"

"Sick, yes. Inside where it's worst. I suppose you think you've done right to let that young man go for no reason than that Kay Hasswell's got a feeling the men might turn on her. This is an awful thing you've done tonight, Russian."

"I've done nothing but what I had to do."

"You are with them—with them and Mrs. Leroy, foolish little jackrabbit that she is. And you helped them."

"I did what I had to do."

"He's a young man and a fine teacher, and God knows there are few enough of them in any time. To do this to him is a cruel thing. He won't leave the town. Joanie knows that, too. He won't leave here because he feels at home here, and he'll find a way to stay. Then what will Kay Hasswell—and the rest of you—what will you do then? What else can you do?"

"He'll leave town."

"No. I don't think he will."

"Yes—yes, he'll send in his resignation and leave." He felt now that it had all been stupid; there was no proof the man was a Communist, and what if he was, wasn't everyone free to have his own thoughts on government—there was only what Hoyt said to make you think he might be one. Still, he could do nothing to change it now or to help himself. Kay Hasswell was the one. She

The Long Year

had Hoyt under her thumb, all of them under her thumb, doing what she wanted them to do from that first day.

He went over to his wife and put his arm around her. She stood very still, away from him in her own mind. "Listen to me, Mamma," he said. "I want to keep my job down there. They will let me off only if I do something to make her think I should go, and then she'd talk Hoyt into it. Right now, she believes it's better to have me in the factory working than outside it not working. And I need to be down there. I—I wouldn't know what to do if I didn't have work every day."

"We could make out," she said stiffly. "We could make out same as the rest of them—little Velma and that poor boy, Smut Olds."

His face reddened with anger, and he pushed her away. "Women! This is a thing for men to decide." He stamped out into the hall and put on his coat and went out into the night. He walked toward the factory and stood outside the last warehouse, near the swamp that lay frozen under the snow. While he was standing there, he saw Mr. Wimmer go toward the hotel with the gray dog. He remembered something he had read as a child, that not even a sparrow could fall without his fall being marked. He had always wondered what that meant. Maybe it meant that everyone was like the sparrow, that everyone was the same, no more than a sparrow, no less than a sparrow. Someone would hold you to blame if you stepped on another, even if you did it in secret. He put his big, cold, trembling hand over his mouth and chin. He wiped his hand strongly across his mouth. There was a bitter, sad moaning, dying inside him, and he began to cry out there behind the warehouse. He turned against the rough stone walk, crusted with ice and snow, and he cried in anger and confusion. Then when he heard the guard who took his place one night a week, he turned and ran quickly over the swamp road and up toward the Cafe. He had not cried like that since his younger girl had been sick with polio, and then he had cried for hours without stopping. He wondered if this wasn't worse in every way, even worse than having his child near death. "Yes," he said, "I guess—there's not much use. I'm not the way I was once, I'm getting old and sick and I'm not much good —not much good at all . . ."

Olds' grandson was born early that morning. During that day almost every man in the town wandered up the hill and came into the house and stood in the kitchen looking at the baby. They didn't have much to say. They looked at the baby and went away. No baby in that town was as important as Olds' new grandson. No one knew why this was so. God, things were bad, probably the worst time on earth, but seeing the new baby made them think that despite what happened for them, there was a continuous flow of hope, of people inhabiting the town. Anyhow, there was nothing much to do that day and they liked the old guy, Olds, and they wanted to see the kid. Olds moved the blanket around a little so they could see the small, red, blind face. And they looked at the baby in blank silence and went away in the same silence.

They felt no anger because Mr. Wimmer no longer had a position at the school. That was the way things were, they said. No one stood a chance. They were sorry about it, sure, but then you were up against something hidden and powerful and the best you could do was to hold on and not let it matter too much, that was the only thing left to do.

Olds said, "You think Mr. Wimmer's going away?"

"No," they said. "He says he wants to buy the old Purdy farm up-river. Not a very good place, but it seems he don't want much."

Olds thought about that. His daughter-in-law lay on the cot in the kitchen. The other two children were up at Russian's. The house was very clean and warm. Outside he could see people slipping slowly up and down the hill, the children coming from school and sliding along the smooth, icy places. He sat in the kitchen by the stove watching the baby and wondering about Gene Wimmer.

"Velma?"

She opened her eyes. Now, she looked very young, like a kitten, lying still and warm.

The Long Year

"This one's the best-lookin' baby you've had."

She nodded. "Smut'll be glad. You wait, Paw. Smut'll come home after a while an' things'll work out for us."

"You know, I wouldn't mind if this one grew up to be like Mr. Wimmer. I been thinkin' about him. He's a nice young man, full of guts, not tough exactly but—strong. That's what you'd say —strong."

"He talks nice, too," she said. "A swell fellow. Once he danced with me at a school dance. It was just like he danced with one of the teachers. He asked me how I liked his freshman class an' what I was gonna do after I graduated. I didn't know I was gonna quit an' marry Smut then. Gee, he was nice to me, Paw."

"He oughtta be. Yer a nice, good girl, Velma, onny it seems like I never think to tell you."

She closed her eyes. "I'm tired. I'm so tired," she said and was asleep almost at once.

He picked up the baby and held him. It was the first good thing that had happened to him since the factory had closed. "Listen, Robert," he murmured, and he began to tell the baby about the farm he had once lived on as a boy and the days at Chateau Thierry and the time he grew a watermelon the size of a barrel.

CHAPTER NINETEEN:

In the language of his father and the town, Mike Hasswell called himself a tramp and a bum. In his own eyes, he was a free man who lived in life, endured, waited, did a number of things, all rather well. He was not sorry for his life nor afraid of leaving the earth. He had nothing on his mind—slept when he was sleepy, ate when he was hungry, liked to sniff at things, flowers and people and water and air. There was nothing he especially wanted to be, but he could understand how Rock wanted to be a fighter and Gene wanted to be a good teacher. He would choose to *be* Mr. Wimmer if he had a choice, but he would not deliberately set out to be like him. He preferred to live day by day, fully, conscious of his time, with humor and bravery—to hell with the rest.

He had ideas. Sometimes these stunned him. His dream of love had come true. He had wanted to love someone beautiful and to remember it, live in the shade of it forever. Anything else that came his way was gravy. When he grew old, he would be like Macbeth, remembering things, watching everything, feeling the days slipping from him. He learned in the nights when he walked through the sleeping town. It was never any good for him to try to sleep. He felt he had a sad destiny, because he saw it in his sleep, the dark face of it, the reality of it. His destiny was a boy standing outside store windows, seeing the people inside. The boy did not desire to enter because that was not his place to be, but there was no one outside the windows with him. He was alone there, and that was his destiny. So, it was no good for him to try to sleep and end up dreaming this dream.

Instead, he threw drinking parties with the "summer girls" and a few of the river people, the bargemen and campers. Other times he walked the streets looking at the silent houses, listening to the crickets and the frogs in the swamp, watching for a small, golden spark of life somewhere. Sometimes, it was a firefly that ricocheted toward the shadowy trees. Often it was the light the night cop used walking down Chestnut—or it was the light in the newspaper office where Mrs. Amos worked. He never went in there but stood outside watching her. She had a wonderful, secret life, knew everything that happened although she never left the building. In a way, it was sneaky of him to stand there on the street watching her, but he saw her truly then. He used to make up names for her —no one knew her first name—"Elizabeth," he said. Sometimes he said Elizabeth and other times he said Margaret or Frances.

He loved the town when he was alone in it, thinking of the people in their beds in their own houses. He liked to think of the women with their hair spread out over their white pillows and their bodies relaxed after the day, and when he thought of their faces, sleeping, each face was Wilma's and each house was hers and each child in his bed was her child. Then he saw her easily as if she walked with him, alone in the town. "Will," he said, "you old sweet girl, Will."

He walked past Macbeth's store. Macbeth sat under the naked light, sitting in the lotus position, wearing a pair of striped cotton shorts, his eyes closed, hands turned upwards as if to catch the falling leaves. That crazy old man, Macbeth, bringing his gifts of incense and myrrh up and down Chestnut Street. The street was silent and dim except for Macbeth's light. He walked slowly, his heels making sharp clicks. Most of the snow had vanished except on the ridges of the street where it had crusted with coal dust and dirt. He supposed the night cop slept—there was only one now.

As he walked past the post office, he saw the man. He did not see him truly so much as he felt him there, and then he saw his shadow. He was standing inside the door. Mike pretended not to see him, walking quickly, heavily, clicking on the cold, misted sidewalks. The quiet air moved around him. He scuffed through a pile of winter ashes in the gutter. He saw the car down the street, nosed toward the hotel. He heard the low, live humming of its motor. The car was another living creature in the night. He came abreast of it and saw Joe, knowing it was Joe because of the way his hair grew, thick and curly in the front. Joe stood with one hand in his pocket, the other on the door, not moving.

"Hey, Joe," softly.

"Yeah?"

"Waitin for someone?"

"Maybe."

"Look, Joe."

"Just waitin'," Joe said. He put his hand hard on Mike's arm. "Scram out of here," he said. Mike could see his face, and he thought, All the days of my life with this kid, Joe Connaught.

"No," Mike said.

"Lissen, Mike, get goin' now."

"No," he said again and felt the slow rising excitement inside and knew that wherever the enemy was, the enemy was never Joe. "I'm staying right here. Will always said—"

"Will's gone, and you'd better go, too. We're friends. So get out of here."

"If you're in some mess, I'm with you. Just to make sure no one pulls a fast one."

"I make my own breaks," Joe said. He kept turning his head nervously trying to see through the darkness and mist. Mike stood a little away from him; he didn't want to get into a fight with Joe. There was a low whistle and then the sound of running feet. Joe whistled softly. "God's sake, Mike, get out of here."

Mike laughed softly. "Can't." He felt neither brave nor curious, only that Joe shouldn't be here alone. Joe turned quickly and struck out at him, and Mike ducked, felt it go over his head, close. Then something flashed darkly, and Joe's voice changed. It was not his voice but a way of speaking he had learned, expressionless, flat, cold, and hard. "Get going, now," he said. "I've got a gun on you."

"I'm staying," Mike said.

Joe hesitated and then got into the car, pulling the door shut. He

The Long Year

speeded the motor and then opened the door again. "If you stand still, they might not notice—get back toward the building. I don't use a gun on anyone, Mike."

He started to say something, but the men were closer. There was an angry whispering. He stepped into the car.

"That's right, get in, fellah," the shorter one said, giving him a push.

"Don't shove me, mister."

"Shut up," Joe said.

The tall man said nothing.

The short man said, "Who's this guy?"

"He came by," Joe said. He eased the car forward. Mike sat beside him, the two men in back breathing hard.

Mike felt a sharp pain in his guts—maybe fear—he couldn't name it, but he didn't care except that Joe got out of this and soon. He could hear the money crackling as they folded it and stuffed it into the small duffel bags. Joe drove slowly down the street, turned on his lights and headed for the river.

"Step on it," the tall one said. Mike tried to place the voice—young, thin, deceptive. He'd like a look at their faces. This one was the boss. "Slow down at the bridge, understand, Joe?"

"Oke," Joe said. He drove very fast, turning off the main road through the park toward the bridge. That looked like he was making time. Then Mike felt the gun slide across the seat and his leg, and he reached out for the cold short barrel. It felt small and heavy, a little thing with enough to kill six men. A gun was nothing, it didn't prove anything. He shoved it toward Joe. He'd wait for something better.

They came to the bridge. Joe slowed down, the men spoke in rough voices. The boss asked, "Is this guy important?"

"Naw," Joe said. "A stumble bum."

"He's important," the other man said. "He's seen us."

"That makes it tough," the boss said. "You ought to be more careful, Joe." His voice purred.

"D'ya want me to kill him right on the street, hunh?"

"You got to use your head, Joe."

Joe breathed slowly, and Mike listened to him. Suddenly, Joe twisted the car, and Mike kicked the door open and fell out. There was one shot, a quiet, muffled shot, sweet, like the ping when you shoot a bean on a tin roof, anything tin. Neat. Quiet. Final. Sharp. It was silly and slight, a thing like that. Mike felt himself go down, melt onto the bridge that was damp and cold from night air and river mist. It was Spring coming slowly on the river, the ice moving in floes, melting as it moved. The mist seemed terribly thick to him, like rich pudding, thick and gooey. In all his life on the river, he had never known the mist to be so thick on his face and against his eyes and in his throat.

The car still veered, making a savage whining of tires, gripping and sliding on the asphalt. There was another shot and nothing else but the rising groan of the car gaining speed. Mike sat with his shoulders hunched. His left hand was inside his old leather jacket, his hand was warm and wet. He felt light, dizzy-light, drifting, ghostly. He wanted to laugh. He felt fine, though, not sick, and there was no special ache as there was when you broke a bone or someone cracked you over the head. There was just this light, high feeling—pretty good.

He heard Joe speak, and he tried to move to see, to come back into himself, but he could not and did not really want to. It was just to prove something—he had forgotten what—but it was to prove it that he tried to come back. Joe was beside him, dragging himself closer.

"Damn you to hell, Mike."

"Aw, Joe—we messed it up, didn't we?"

"Loused it up fine," Joe said gruffly. His left arm hung like a broken wing. "They think we're done for, Mike. They won't come back. Don't worry, I'll tell all of this— Boy, I'll talk from here to Kingdom Come, you'll see. I didn't figure on this. That's the God's truth. Don't care what happens now, but I'll straighten it out for you, Mike."

"Joe," Mike sighed. He could see the small, prickly bridge lights

The Long Year 197

flagging in the dark waters. They were amber and blue. The bridge turned under him, wheeled on its separate axis, all around him it grew warm and thin. "C'm here."

Joe dragged himself closer, put his arm around him and felt Mike's body slump a little. He held tight with his arm across the wide shoulder under the dirty leather jacket.

"We guys—all of us had a swell time, hey?"

"Stop it."

"Remember the times my old man—took us hunting?"

"Sure."

"Will said I should look out for you—Joe. I just talked and boozed and made the girls, never did anything."

"You gonna die now, Mike?" Joe's fingers tightened on his shoulder.

"Feels like it, very warm for May. That's a song, too." He turned in the golden light and saw himself, felt himself pivot in his world, turn back, pass through the place from which he had come. It was a conscious journey for him, without time or destiny. "Will was swell, Joe."

"Swellest girl I ever knew."

"You—you're a good friend, Joe."

Joe swallowed, inside he was crying hard.

"I'm not sore any more—not at the old man, you tell him— probably okay guy." The breath went out of him slowly, he felt the last one rise inside him high as the highest bird and then he sank more deeply than he had ever gone in sleep or sickness. "Will —the green coat . . . the green coat . . ." and in this lengthy dream of weight and color, everything ordered itself as it should be, in artlessness and in innocence, in every way that a child has come, in this way, he went as well . . .

Joe felt the wetness come from Mike onto his shirt. He thought, I used to think about sitting in a pool of my own blood, but this is Mike's, Mike's life, Mike here with me. He tried to see his face, but he could not. His leg hurt into his groin, his arm had no feeling, the only hurt was inside himself, a terrible mortal hurt.

Far away, he saw the vision of the three of them—Mike, Rock, himself—on the river, sometimes Mr. Wimmer. Mike and Rock. Mike and Wilma. Marth and Barby. Himself and Barby. The day going to the factory to get a job from Kay Hasswell, like two small boys going to a candy store: give me three licorice, one peppermint, and a root beer barrel.

A light above him went out and came back again. He held Mike more closely and turned his face into his shoulder so that the lights would not get into his dead face. He did not know how long it was before the car came and the man got out, another man and another one, and then someone tried to take Mike from him, but he would not let them—Mike, his friend. The words these men spoke were far away, a murmur, a low sigh, but when they hit him hard across the face, he began to cry although he did not feel it much. He was shivering and crying like a dopey baby. He looked into the eyes above him, and they were the eyes of the woman. "I'm sorry, I'm sorry," he said and reached out for her with his bad arm. "Miss Hasswell—I'm sorry, please help me, I'm sorry." He expected her to do something, she was always doing something, but she did nothing but move away from him. Then the blackness began at his feet and came to his knees and he walked in it, stumbling. It sucked at him. He sat in the car shivering and crying, waiting for it to come over his face. When he felt it around his throat, he opened his mouth and took a good raw breath and sank down into it. "Mike—Mike, listen, listen . . ."

The men stood on the bridge. Johnnie Evans walked around the place where Mike's body lay, crumpled, his legs bent and his one hand turned open, empty. He snapped on his flashlights. "Joe dragged himself," he said.

"Look here," Russian said. "You can see where the car skidded. You can see it plain."

The night cop said, "The ambulance'll be here in a minute, Miss Hasswell."

Kay shivered, put her hands deeper into the pockets of her polo

# The Long Year 199

coat. "The ambulance will be here in a minute, Hoyt," she said. He put out his hand to her and she took it. Death in the afternoon, she thought, death in the evening, young death, old death, death seen and unseen. It is here in this town, everywhere, all kinds of it.

Hoyt looked down at Mike's face. "I didn't know—he was so old," he said aloud. He thought: He's dreaming there, like the times he sat in the back seat of the car and fell asleep when we went fishing at Big Lake and Millelacs, a big, long boy in khaki shorts sleeping, his skinny arm for a pillow, not caring about the bumps or the railroad tracks but sleeping peacefully in the back seat of the car. We never knew each other, and I was wrong. I should've let him alone about that girl, it was for him to decide. I should've—I should've— "We must find Marth," he said. "Where's Marth?" his voice rising shrill.

"Oh, God," Kay said.

The hearse came, the white ambulance sign stuck hastily under the windshield wiper. Two men got out. "Yessir, Mr. Hasswell," they said. One of them bent to pick up Mike.

"No," he said. He let go of Kay's hand. "I'll do it," he said. He picked up the boy and carried him to the ambulance and laid him on the cot inside. He pulled his jacket together, zipped it and took out his handkerchief and rubbed the drying blood off the boy's chin. Then he got inside and sat on the floor beside the cot. Kay got in beside him. Mr. Wimmer came to the door.

"Marth's up at the house," he said. "Rock went up there."

"Thank you," Kay said. "Thank you, Mr. Wimmer." She looked at him. He put out his hand, pulled her polo coat down over her knees. "Oh, God," she said when he closed the door. She shook her head. She was crying now, crying very hard, her lips were puffed and chapped. She bent her head over Mike. It was Spain she remembered, the young matador, eighteen years old, no older, the one who had danced so well at the fiesta ball—they brought him off the arena like that, lying just so, the people not particularly saddened by it, only a momentary lull and then everything beginning again. Prokosch had gone out and come back in a little while saying the boy was dead. She thought: Mr. Wimmer ought to know something to say, something to make it easy. Truth should be comforting and he ought to say some big, true thing to us. It is because we are outnumbered here—Mr. Wimmer and his people on one side and only a few of us on the other side, and that's how things can happen to Mike—because he *did* belong with us, would've come to us in the end. Everyone chooses sides against us.

Hoyt reached out and held her to him. "Don't cry," he said. "Please don't cry." His voice was flat, his eyeballs felt terribly dry and unmoving. He held the trembling body of his sister to him. What had he done wrong to have this happen to him? He was being punished, the way Mamma used to threaten—If you steal, Hoyt, you'll pay for it twice and maybe as much as a thousand times, if you lie, Hoyt, you'll see lies in everything that's said to you so long as you lie—if you dishonor your family, Hoyt, you will be dishonored—if you steal, if you lie, if you dishonor . . .

The ambulance crossed the railroad tracks. The boy's body rolled a little and Hoyt put out his hand and held it still on the white cot.

The cop and Johnnie Evans picked up Joe and put him in the police car. He lay crooked, crying on the floor.

"He'll be okay," Johnnie said. "The Connaughts are tough. Probably busted his wrist."

"Maybe he killed Mike," the cop said.

Mr. Wimmer spoke out of the shadows. "They were friends. Joe wouldn't kill Mike." The men turned and looked at him, and the cop felt ashamed for saying that. The cars turned and went up the hill toward the hospital.

A little boy ran out of the park. He wore a leather jacket over his pajamas. He was trying to zip up the jacket. He went out and stood under the bridge lights. It was Lindy Connaught. Mr. Wimmer stood in the darkness watching him. Lindy looked down

The Long Year

into the water, then he moved back into the park. "Gosh—must've been a big fight out here or somethin'—a big fight or somethin'."

He ran home and got into his warm bed, but he couldn't go to sleep. He wanted to wake up his mother and ask her about the siren and all the cars down at the bridge. Joe would know. Tomorrow Joe would tell him what it was about. Joe always knew. He burrowed deeper into his warm bed.

Then he heard the telephone ring, and his mother went down the stairs in a hurry. Someone came to the door, too, he heard them talking, and suddenly the lights in the hall were on and the lights downstairs. He could see them shining on the bare, hard, cold lawn. He heard his mother's voice rise into a scream, and his father's voice, and then his sisters and his brothers went down the stairs. But no one came to him. If they didn't want to come for him, he didn't care, they were always keeping things from him, about where babies came from and how to shoot dice and how to smoke and where to get the biggest fish. He found out, though. He lay on his back and looked out the window and moved his finger to trace the big dipper. After a long while, he fell asleep with his hands flung above his head. One of them was smeared a little, dark and sticky, where he had touched the railing near the bridge.

Marth walked back and forth in the living room. "I don't believe it, Rock. I just don't believe it." She wore a pale blue flannel robe, and her white rabbit slippers stuck to the rug when she walked. Rock watched her. He could hear the ambulance siren coming up the hill. "You didn't see it happen, Rock. You didn't touch him or anything—to know."

"No."

"There's some kind of mistake, Rock."

"Mr. Wimmer sent me here. Your father and Kay were up at Leroy's and they called them and they went down there. They said you should stay here and wait with me. They know it's true."

She shook her head. "I don't— Things like that—"

He watched her and waited. Before this, he had told himself she wasn't anything like Kay and didn't even look like her, but now he saw that she did. She had the same kind of hair and her eyes were like that, very bright and quick to see everything, and she was built like that, too—tall and narrow-hipped. And her voice—that was where she was most like Kay, because her voice was always low, but you could hear her well. It carried. Still, she never yelled, not even on the tennis court, and you had the feeling that if you stood closer to her you could hear her better. Yes, she was like Kay, nice-looking and animated and full of energy. It did not seem right that now when she was so young she should already be so much like the older woman.

"Mike's dead, Marth," he said. "It's true." He kept rubbing his forefinger against his thumb where it was dirty and sweaty and the dirt rolled off like dead skin.

"But, Rock—" She bit her lip. Then she sat in her father's chair, huddled, her head on her wrist, feeling her own life there. Mike. Dead. She thought of a boy in a Scout uniform whittling soap statues of the discus thrower and the Parthenon for Latin class. A boy handy at changing washers in the bathroom fawcet, lying on the floor listening to radio serials, going away to college and coming home wearing a sheep-lined coat, a fraternity pin, driving a red roadster. That time down at the drugstore when she saw him in the booth with Wilma and she wondered what made him seem different, just sitting there that way with Wilma in her green coat. And the other times—bringing her the Navajo ring. She heard how he took it from one of his girls. She had wondered how he could do a thing like that, and now Rock said he was dead out there on the bridge, like those two men that time and the others lying on the cliff in the grass, dead.

"No," she said. She waited for him to tell her something so that she would know why Mike had to die like that. His round, reddish face was puckered with worry, and his lips kept moving wordless. "Where was he going?" she asked.

"I don't know. Joe knows, probably."

The Long Year 203

"Oh—Joe. It should've been Joe. He doesn't care about anything. What happens to him is—"

"Don't say that," he said harshly. God, she ought to get some sense in her head, so damned sweet and pretty. He loved her no matter how she was, but she ought to get some sense. "Mike was tired of the boat business, of all of it."

"I wish—I wish Kay and Daddy would come."

"Want me to go?"

"No." She ought to cry about Mike. Everyone cried when things like this happened, but she couldn't. The worst was for poor Daddy, poor old Daddy. Kay would know, though—she'd know what to say to help him because she had seen everything and knew about everything. "Where are they? They ought to be here. What makes it so long? I just can't believe it—that I won't see him around. They ought to come. They ought to be here."

There was nothing he could say to her. Look darling, things go on. Look darling, I knew Mike better than most, and I can't believe he won't be around any more. Death is still a word to me. But I knew him and how he hated the spats he was always having with his old man and that business with Wilma—how he could never figure out why it had to go wrong for him. Maybe it's not all over for Mike, wherever he is, he feels grand about everything. I'd like to think that, but look, darling, there's nothing I can say except to believe me and stop wanting Kay, want me, listen to me. Death isn't much at all—sometimes, it came near me, that time with Rush Miller at the Stadium in the first Golden Glove match with Macbeth yelling his throat raw as beef. I felt it come damned close that time, never a time since then. So, maybe it's just a little thing for Mike, and tomorrow it will begin to be easier for you. We ought to go down and see Lindy, that kid without Joe—but darling, please don't keep asking for Kay, ask for me.

Marth rose, rubbing the back of her neck under her black, loose hair. "Maybe someone did it. Kay says we're outnumbered here. Somebody wants to get even with us."

"Outnumbered? Who's outnumbered?"

"Us. Kay and Daddy and me—because the factory's closed."

"All men are the same in varying degrees. No one's outnumbered. Don't get ideas like this, darling." He put his arms around her, but she stood rigid within them, a kind of rigidity all through her. She smelled of pine soap, and she was warm from her bath, but when he touched her face, her skin seemed cold.

She shook her head. "I don't know. But, Rocky, *why* do these things happen here? I mean, in Chicago, or somewhere, you read about these things happening, but not here." She had begun to cry. She kept moving her head a little against his shoulder, crying for herself because she wanted to see Mike alive once more and see him clearly and know what he was like.

But, he thought: I'm not helping her. She'll listen to Kay, whatever Kay says, but she won't know what I want to tell her. I can't tell her until she finds out for herself, sees it in a dream or touches it closely, and then she'll know it's not terrible—a moment of farewell, a journey, something that she will know and understand truly like how to angle a man so he opens himself for you and you can come in quickly and neatly. But I can't tell her a thing is science, always. Kay'll use the right words, and she'll know what Kay means, but she won't understand me—not now, anyhow. Maybe later but not now.

CHAPTER TWENTY:

Mike was buried in the family lot in the Catholic Cemetery. That place was dry, sandy ground, and almost at once it flattened over his grave. The flowers wilted there and on the grave of his mother. A small marble headstone marked where he lay. MICHAEL DAMIEN HASSWELL (1909–1934). That year, spring was cold until suddenly it turned hot and dry overnight in early May.

Marth and Rocky took charge of the boathouse. Almost every day, Russian and Olds went fishing. Mr. Wimmer worked the Purdy farm and came into town several afternoons each week. He dipped the net into the minnow trough and poured minnows into Russian's scabby green pail which he shoved under the rear seat of the old rowboat.

"You'll see," Russian said, "this is the beginning. Young men can't get jobs. They run away from home like Smut or they get into messes the way Joe did—cause a lot of trouble and worry."

Rocky said, "Joe *tried* to get a job. You ought to remember that."

Olds said, "Smut'll come home. Wait'll he sees Robert. Robert's smarter'n Smut ever was." He got into the boat. Marth handed him his pole. He took it carefully, holding the spinner under his thumb. It was a cheap spinner and never worked right, but it was all right for river fishing. "Sunfish," he said. "I promised Velma sunfish."

"Jesus," Russian said. "The season's not open, and they fined Wilcox ten bucks last week. Besides, you're never lucky, an' how you can have the gall to promise Velma sunnies—"

"She believes me." Olds laughed. "You got a mood on is all."

Marth sat on the wharf, tying her sneakers. "Just the same, Russian's right. Nothing's going the way it should." She was thinking of Mike and now Joe up there in jail and Barby sitting in the garden eating out her heart, and her father complaining about his stomach, walking aimlessly about the house and puttering with his tulips.

Mr. Wimmer smiled. The dog, Jawrge, yawned and slept. "Look," Mr. Wimmer said, "there is the miracle of light, of water—of Life itself, a million miracles everywhere. One can believe there will finally be the miracle of goodness in this town. It would be wrong and poor of you to join the ranks of unbelievers—they are too many as it is."

"Do you believe that some day—"

"Yes," he said.

"It's not a bad town," Rock said. "When I was a kid—"

"Oh, it's different when you're a kid, Rock," she said.

"Maybe," Russian said. He went back to the storeroom for the oars, the dock springing under his weight. "Seems everything's changed."

"Yeah," Marth said. She looked across the still, copper water. Now everyone wanted Joe's blood, and the reporters were coming in every day, making a big thing of this. They stayed at the hotel—quick, skinny, hard men who always smoked and wore old, shiny suits. Every day the deputies took Joe to the city to identify suspects, but still the two men had not been found. The people stood outside the jail to get a glimpse of Joe when he walked from the courthouse to the car. He looked fine, neither unhappy nor worried, and they could not stand this. They yelled at him and it seemed to make them feel better to call him names.

"You'll see," Mr. Wimmer said. "We are not a bad kind of people, Marth."

"Speak for yourself," Russian said. He got into the boat, and Rock gave it a push with his foot. Russian pulled hard, and the boat shot across the dock bay. "Just the same, they'll get Joe's blood. The poor, damned-fool kid."

"Joe's a good boy," Olds said.

"I don't know," Russian frowned. "Seems as if we always expected him to get into messes, and so he did—almost like we wished it on him."

The Long Year

"Naw. If he couldda got a job—"

"He went to see her. He got down on his knees to her, almost. But she wouldn't give him a chance."

"You hate her, that's all," Olds said. He stood up in the boat, made a long cast and sat down again. River fishing was for him. Once he went trout fishing, but that was work, having to walk around and cast all the time. Best to let the fool fish come after it if they wanted it, no sense tossing it right smack into their rubbery old mouths. "Yeah—you don't like her an' so you blame her for everything. Mr. Wimmer gettin' fired you blamed on her an' you're the one's on the school board. She ain't on it."

"I already explained it to you." He jerked his line. The fish had nibbled the bait. "You don't understand about that woman. Ever since she come here, we've had trouble. She don't care what happens to us so she holds the cards every time, jist so she holds them. We don't stand a chance."

Olds belched. "Bring any beer?"

"Under the seat."

"Seems to me people got themselves to take care of no matter what she says or does. Maybe she's a bitch. Velma says so. Women always know about other women. But, anyhow, we gotta take care of ourselves."

"Mark my words, she'll do a lot before she's through."

Olds shrugged. "Can't do nothin' to me." Olds handed him the bottle. He took a long drink.

"Everyone's bettin' how long Joe'll get," Olds said.

"No sense of decency."

"Tom Arnold bet ten he'd get life."

"Hunh. Everyone's having a fine time—reporters and all. Like a county fair. Like soldiers shootin' craps for Christ's coat."

"Listen, let's fish. I promised Velma some for supper."

Russian peered into the river. "Not a bloody fish in the place."

Olds laughed. That Russian was a card, a wonderful, gloomy guy. He began to think of the garden. He'd plant big, floppy red flowers around the bean bed. Velma'd like that. If things got tough it would help to have the garden. Didn't look as though they'd give him any relief unless he worked. Kinda hated to leave Velma. Anyhow, Smut'd come home; no sense going around to the relief office. Something'd come up before then.

From her office, Kay could see the courthouse, hear the drone of the men's voices as they stood on the lawn and on the steps. Johnnie Evans sat with his feet on her desk because it annoyed her, and he had to have his own way sometimes.

"They've got something to talk about, to occupy their time," she said.

"So they won't think about your precious factory?"

She shrugged. "Of course. Darling, I know it was terrible about Mike—and maybe if I could have given Joe some work, he might not have been involved in this. But Joe's not alone. And now it gives the men something to think about." She smiled her friendly, innocent smile. "You seem in a bad mood today."

"Do I?"

"Yes."

"Kay?"

"Umm?" She leaned back in her chair, fixing a cigarette into a long red holder. "What now?"

"What if I decided not to pull off this deal in Chicago?"

"I don't think you will."

"No. Guess not."

"I know your kind, darling. Every so often, you hear the wee, small voice of your conscience, and you want to be an angel in the town. You never will be. It's either too late or you're too tired or you have too much else to do at the time."

"Yeah."

"Oh, I know," she soothed, "you'd like to be another Gene Wimmer, only you'd feel foolish."

"If he ever ran for mayor here—"

"Oh, now, Johnnie."

The Long Year

"All right," he said with an edge to his voice, "I'm not backing down."

She rose and kissed him. "Of course not."

He put his arms around her. When he kissed her, he forgot his crazy ideas.

She moved away from him. "Run along now. I've got a million things to do."

"Will I see you tonight?"

"Sure."

"Is that a promise?"

"Oh, heavens, Johnnie—"

"Okay," he said. He went out. The newspaper reporter was waiting. He recognized him because he had seen him in the *Dispatch* office talking with Mrs. Amos. The reporter got up and walked slowly toward Kay's office, looking at everything. Johnnie saw Kay turn and heard her voice.

"Come in, Mr. ——"

"Stohl," the reporter said. "Fred Stohl." He was small and wiry and wore a shabby trench coat. There was a rim of bitterness around his mouth. He was tired of looking at everything and telling about it, tired of never being deceived by the bareness in towns and cities. For once, he wanted to see one good place, one good man. "Yes," he said. "Fred Stohl. I'm covering Connaught's trial. The whole case."

"I see," she said. "I had no idea Joe was so important."

He sat down, took a cigarette, relaxed. "He's not. It's the times, we got cases like this all over, but this one seems to sum up the times better than any of them." He kept looking at her. "You were married to Prokosch, weren't you?"

"Several years ago."

"I was in Prague in '28. Had an interview with him. He's done all right for himself and his people, one of the best diplomats in the world."

"He's worked hard," she said. "What can I do for you?"

"You know this Connaught?"

"Not well. He came in here with my nephew, Michael Hasswell. He thought if he could get work here everything would be fine with him." She shrugged. "Naturally, we have no work except for about thirty-five men—all of them old-timers. You can understand that."

"Yeah. But what was he like?"

"I don't know."

"Desperate?"

"No."

"What are the people like here?"

"They're conservative and honest and hard-working people."

"They were never without work before. This is the first time you've closed the factory?"

"Yes." She didn't like this man. Newspapermen, nosey and with some sort of intuition which allowed them to find out whatever they desired to know. She was used to them, tough and poetic, always trying to find a perfect place, in need of sleep, liquor, women, money, rootless and omniscient.

"It's not easy to handle, is it?" he asked.

"There's nothing to worry about."

"Un-hunh." He rose and picked four cigarettes from her case, putting them into his packet. "Thanks, anyhow," he said. "You busy tonight?"

"Yes."

"That's what I thought," he grinned. He wondered if she knew how the people talked about her—about her clothes and sex life and how she had tried to run the teacher out of town. He supposed she wouldn't care even if she knew.

In a short time, he knew what these people thought about Joe and Joe's family and about themselves. They expected Joe to get the book thrown at him unless Mrs. Leroy's money could help. They had a deep, bloody feeling of excitement that showed in their faces. It was as if they had forgotten for a moment their own lack of work and fed upon this affair richly.

The Long Year

Might as well go up and see the kid, he thought. He hated cases like this, but he always got them because he did them well, having a feeling for the people, telling of the town and those involved. That was the trouble—he'd seen so much and none of it pleased him, and the germ of despair was planted in him and flowered day by day. Everything here fed this germ well.

Rocky went up to the jail to play poker with Joe. Marth was always busy with Kay, doing her errands, going to the city. Besides, he wanted to be with Joe all he could. The reporters spent a lot of time there trying to get him to say something. He looked small to them, sitting there in the cell, being so quiet. They wandered around the old building, drank the sheriff's whiskey and listened to his stories, walked down the hill and used the typewriters and telephones in the *Dispatch* office. Sometimes, they tried to get Rocky to say something. They knew him and had seen him fight.

"We've been friends since we were kids," he said. He was friendly with them, but he had nothing to say. "Ask Joe."

"Jesus God," they said, "this is a job trying to get anyone here to talk sense."

Marth looked at them in awe. Her tongue felt thick in her mouth, and her mind made a silent, slotting sound, like a coin dropping far and landing on the sidewalk. When they asked her what Joe was like, she couldn't remember except that time on graduation night when he kept saying he had a bellyache. She looked at Rocky for the answer. "What was he like, Rock?"

"Like everyone else," Rocky said.

"Was he a crazy kid?" Fred Stohl asked.

"No."

"Did he talk tough and big?"

"No."

"What was he like then?"

Marth said, "Sad, I guess. Joe was always sad."

"Probably needed money," Fred said. "That was at the bottom of this. Still, he had a girl. She's well-off, isn't she?"

Rocky said, "Her mother's Mrs. Leroy. You'll have to ask her how rich she is. I wouldn't know."

"Don't get snotty, Rocky. I've got to get the whole picture here, that's all."

"Well, a girl'd be only part of it for Joe."

"Was Mike your friend?" He wanted to see this clearly. He smoked too much and bit his nails to the quick, but he had a look of innocence that was stronger than his air of bitterness. He walked up the hill with Rocky and stood outside the cell trying to talk to Joe. Joe sat on his cot and looked back at them and blew smoke rings. Someone asked him if Mike was his friend. They knew this, but they wanted him to say it. Sometimes they got wild stories out of jail characters. They couldn't print these, but it gave them a lead to something they wanted to know.

"Go away," Joe said. "Everyone knows Mike was my friend."

"Don't get mad, Joe," Rocky said.

"Let's play cards, Rock. Tell them to scram outta here. You guys get out. This is my affair, and if I'm headin' for hell I'll do it without you guys spyin' on me. Scram, now."

One of the reporters said, "We represent the people, Kid." He was putting on an act, trying to look grand, but he looked shabby and cold in his old trench coat. "They want to know about this."

"It's bad for them to know. They've got enough useless stuff in their heads," Joe said.

"You scared, Kid?"

Fred Stohl said nothing. He watched Joe, pushed back his hat, a little runt of a guy with pale green eyes, looked like a gangster. He had stomach ulcers, and everything was different to him since he knew about them.

Joe said, "Whaddya think?"

"Maybe you'll get a break. Think about that."

"I got no luck."

"Listen, Kid—"

Joe got up and lit a cigarette. His hands trembled. They saw this. "Get outta here. I'm gonna play cards. I don't know anything. If I

The Long Year

knew anything, I wouldn't be here, see? An' if you guys were wise, you wouldn't be here either, pickin' at the bones of guys like me. Go write poetry. Go find a girl. Stop bulling around here."

"Thatta boy, thatta boy," Fred Stohl said softly. "You tell them."

They went down the hall to the sheriff's office. Joe watched them. Then he sat down and dealt the cards on the cot. He and Rocky played three games.

"That's twelve thirty I owe you, Rock." He scribbled on a piece of yellow paper. "I been losing lately."

"You don't concentrate." He stretched himself. "Guess I'd better go down and do some footwork. If I don't do it every afternoon, Macbeth almost pees in his pants, sits there and waits for me. Wants me to skip around like a bathing beauty and show everyone how good I am."

"You better go then. Everyone kinda waits for it."

"Yeah. Say, Joe, anything I can do for you?"

"No."

"Suppose not." He stared at the wall thoughtfully. There ought to be something he could do now that he was the only one who had a chance. He ought to do something big and right to make up for Joe's inability to do anything, for Mike being dead. The idea would come to him, yet. "Say, Joe—you get a lot of time to think in here?"

"Sure," Joe said.

"What you think about?"

Joe rubbed his bad arm. "Well, I tell you, Rock, we don't make any effort to be alive. I mean we just are, but we don't have a feeling for it. I think about that. I'd like to be sure I'm alive."

"I know what you mean. Sometimes I'm alive. Sometimes I'm not, just sleeping or dead or something."

"Then I think about Mr. Wimmer. We ought to do something for him."

"Sure."

"And I think of you and Mike and me and how we got on together. I don't have fancy ideas about this thing. I don't want them to give me anything. I can take what I got coming—only I wish it had been me instead of Mike."

"It just happened this way," Rock said. He went outside the cell. The door was always open. Sometimes Joe walked out in the hall and then back into the cell. He did that to see if he could do it every time.

"See you," Joe said.

"See you, Joe."

Joe stood by the window watching Rocky cross the lawn and vault the iron fence. As he stood there, he could see two people come up the steps. They walked stiffly and slowly. He recognized his mother's black hat with the gray feather. Empress Eugenie, they called it. She had worn it for a long time, changing the feather. "Geez," he said. He took out a comb and ran it through his hair and lit a cigarette, pushing the butts under the cot and smoothing the army blanket. He sat on the straight-backed chair, resting his heels on the edge of the cot. He didn't want them to worry any more than they had to. But when he saw them, he knew how they felt. They wore their best clothes, and his father opened the door for his mother. She kissed his cheek, her lips trembling, and he stood very still and let her do it, not touching her. His father made a gruff, impatient sound and they shook hands.

"Sit down," he said. "Sit down."

They sat on the cot carefully. His mother had a big paper box. "Your clean shirts," she said.

"Thanks. Thanks a lot."

His father said, "You look fine, Joe."

"I feel okay."

His mother said, "You really feel better now, don't you? They wouldn't let us come until yesterday, and then Parnell had a spell so we couldn't come until today." She kept looking at his arm. "You feel all right?"

"It's nothing. How are things?"

"Fine," his father said. "The kids say hello. Lindy wanted to come, but I said we'd ask first."

The Long Year 215

"I don't want him here—or Barby, either." His voice grew loud, and he lowered it. "How's the kid?"

He's at the newspaper office. Runs errands for the reporters. Yesterday he made five bucks."

"Yes," his mother said. Her lipstick was too orange, and it made her look slightly drunk. He felt angry when he looked at her, so poor and tired. It was the same when he saw Lindy.

"That's fine. Five bucks."

"They want him to do a lot of things."

"He oughtta stay home and be a baby. That's all he is—a baby."

"Oh, he's all right," his father said. "He's going to be okay."

His mother leaned forward, her mouth trembling. "Joe, you think the trial will be soon?"

"Spring term of court. They haven't found those two guys yet."

His father said, "Lots of folks say there weren't two guys, Joe."

"King," his mother said.

"They'll find them," he said.

His father shook his head. "I wish I could do something, Boy."

"No—no, thanks."

His father lowered his eyes. "Maybe we could've helped. We've got a lot of little bills, but we could've helped, I guess—"

"I know, Pop," he said, but it wasn't true. They could help him now when it was too late but not before when he needed it.

"Would you like a cake—a chocolate cake, Joe?" his mother asked.

"Swell. That'd be swell."

His father said, "We'll come tomorrow. We can leave Parnell at the pressers. He does okay."

"Thanks for coming. Thanks for everything."

They stood, confused. When he saw them like that, he remembered how they had always worked hard, never knew about Wilma, nobody'd ever sprung that one on them. "I'm sorry, Mother," he said. He shook his father's hand. "I'm sorry." He wanted to make it as easy as he could, not loud-mouthed or worried or anything but calm and sorry. He watched them going down the hall and heard his father talking with the sheriff, like he was a sick child and his father was talking to the doctor. He sat down and opened the box of shirts. The sheriff's wife would come and take them away and hang them in her closet. When he wore them, they would smell faintly of lavender water.

He began to relax, thinking without effort. Now he understood what Macbeth did every day, watching the red ant, the flowers in the sun, the dust on the street, sending his soul to Chicago, watching the birds. It was a kind of thinking that was in the blood, not in the mind at all—so he lived that moment sweetly and wisely, with the seed of thought germinating in his blood . . . You think all your life jail's a terrible place, jail is hell. It's not hell, it's just a place like any other place, only it doesn't give you life or happiness. Everything fades in a place like this, but it's not hell. You got nothing to do but laze around like a rich man on a fat income or something cushy like that, nothing to do today or tomorrow or any day. Let your damned nose drip if you want. Outside, every guy you know's eating his guts out for this or that. You sit in your best suit chewing on a cigarette you're too goddam lazy to light. It's warm and dry, outside the wind cuts them to lace curtains. Jail is a place that hurts inside you, deep inside you—God, it hurts!

You get an eyeful of yourself.

Everybody ever grew up gets a hurt inside himself, likely as not to kill him if he lets it. The whole world's got a bellyache, damned thing began with the first man and'll end with the last one, not before . . .

Take a cigarette, a little thing, not as large as your finger, mite bigger'n a needle, rolled fancy and convenient, smelling sweet and enticing. Guy could go clean nuts wanting one. I'll go nuts, though, every time I see a door, opening on a road, road leading to the river, Barby, Lindy, Wimmer's farm, anywhere. What does that kid Lindy think of me up here in this Christ awful place? All the tongues wagging, crows on a telephone wire, but if I went out this door, they'd get me—the men, cops, someone, and I might not even get to see Barby, the kid . . .

Gee, she's a swell one, a nice girl, doesn't give it away, a real lady,

The Long Year 217

always so clean, smelling of nice soap, doesn't talk hard or anything like that. Most of them, like the summer girls, talk like that, bragging, but not her. I don't want her here, no place except on the cliff and those times in the kitchen and that lousy hot chocolate she always made in the winter. Well, I know what I am, no matter how Mike tried to make it easy for me out there on the bridge, and I know, I always knew . . .

Sun, now, is a funny thing, moves kind of like water even through the littlest room, inside walls, under the earth and all around it, never a night everywheres. A thing like sun doesn't get into places where it can't get out. If you're sun, you could get out forever. Gee, a guy never knows about sun, though, like when Barbs and I were on the cliff those times, then I was sure of everything and warmer inside than I'd ever been all my life. Could look at everything afterwards and see how it was made exactly and even know why it was. Like a tree, now, a tree was swell, inch by inch of it, each leaf, the scales of bark, the pith, roots, sap. Water was great. Everything I saw I knew about, and it belonged to me. A guy should have one whole thing belong to him, a whole day, a blade of grass, a moment when he was a genius like a painter or something. But then I was pretty full of sun—and it won't happen ever again. Trouble is, when you kill someone, you do it to yourself, too, never know if you're killing another Christ, like the priest said at graduation, maybe another Robert E. Lee or Einstein . . .

It's crazy to be alive—animals and stuff that goes under water, they got it easy, not knowing about killing someone. Wish I was like that kid Lindy again and didn't understand, because once you know, you know the worst. Wouldn't want Barby to know what it means, either, swell, lovely kid, Barby, ought to have parties all the time, dance off her heels, nothing like this. Now it's over for us, no matter what she says, I know it's over. You never get a chance like that again, couple years from now, maybe ten or twenty, maybe for life, and then I'm different and so is she. Maybe they'll only get me on burglary, not second-degree murder, but you can't count on it; the law makes switcheroos. No chance for me. I know it. No chance for me, ever. Not ever . . .

CHAPTER TWENTY-ONE:

BARBY SELDOM left the house and the garden and had no interest in what happened in the town. She sat in a white lawn chair wearing jeans and Joe's football sweater. A little snow still crusted along the wall where the sun never touched. She stared at the willow tree still bare against the leaden sky. Sometimes, she dressed beautifully, gloves, black pumps, sheer stockings, and she sat in the chair with her hands carefully folded over her patent-leather bag. Lindy often sat with her, not talking. He made piles of sodden twigs, dead leaves, stones and weeds, stuffing his pockets with whatever pleased him.

Everything had stopped for her. All she needed was herself and Joe together. She felt there was something she ought to have done for Joe, something that might have helped. That was no life for him in jail. She thought of that and how her own life was nothing with him. Once in a while, she could say something to Lindy or touch his cheek, not hearing her own voice or his answer. She was confused. Where do we go from here? she kept asking herself. Where, now?

"Cleaned the Intertypes," Lindy said.

"What?"

"I cleaned the two Intertype machines."

"Fine."

"We had aigs for supper."

"Oh—eggs."

Sometimes, Marth sat with her. It was always bare and cold in the garden, the last place to feel Spring. The wind came off the river, hissed along the wall, shuttled the bare branches of the willow. Barby's face was pinched and cold, but she did not move. Whenever Marth left her, she felt terrible, wondering when Barby would snap out of it. "Kay, go up and talk to her. Mrs. Leroy asked me again if you wouldn't talk to Barby."

The Long Year

"I'm no genius, darling," she laughed.

"But, she'll listen to you. You always know what to do. She looks terrible, and Joe doesn't want her to go to the jail to see him. It's a mess."

"She thinks her life's over. I know how she feels. But she'll love fifty men like this before it's over for her."

"Barby's not like that."

"How do you know, you pigeon?"

"Anyhow, someone ought to help her, and she'll listen to you."

"All right," Kay said. "I'll try." She didn't care for such things, but she was tired of hearing Marth worry about Barby. Once, she had thought it was the end for her, too—that time with Prokosch—but she knew now there was never an end. With looks, money and guts, a woman could recover and go on. Barby would learn that, too. She'd tell her that.

"Oh, dear—Kay," Mrs. Leroy said, "we had no idea about that boy, and then poor, darling Mike. I tell you, some things are so—so awful. I just cannot let Barby go on like this. She won't leave town. That Joe—things like this shouldn't happen to young girls. Why, he's like all the Connaughts, you know, handsome, but too much inside himself, I always said, too much . . ."

"I don't know what I can do for Barby."

Teresita came in from the kitchen and put the tea things on the table. "Hello, Miss Kay," she sighed. "Ain't that the cutest little ole suit, though?"

"Teresita, you're part French. You have a sharp eye."

"Yes, Ma-am," she giggled.

"Maybe when my house is ready, you'll work for me. You'd like that, wouldn't you?"

"Howard won't let me," she sulked.

"Oh—pooh. Howard."

"Oh, dear," Mrs. Leroy sighed, "I wouldn't know what to do without Teresita. But, Kay—about Barby, you've been around, you should tell her something."

She stirred her tea thoughtfully, crushing the lemon hard into it, like crushing a flimsy yellow flower. She smelled the lemon and the hot tea. "You used to know your way around, Maida. I always envied you."

"I had to give it up. And now it's too late. To tell the truth, Kay, I'm quite afraid—of fast cars and being out late and dark places, really scared."

"Maida, really."

"I know, isn't it silly? And now I'm petrified about that poor baby. If you had a baby, you'd know what I mean. It's a desperate sensation, like drowning."

"I'll talk to her," she said. "I'm not sure what good it'll do." She went out through the kitchen. Teresita was taking nips from the sherry bottle. She poured some tea into the thermos. Kay took it and some paper cups into the garden.

"That Barby's gonna be sick as a cat," Teresita called after her.

Lindy sat near Barby, kicking the hard crust of earth with the toe of his sneaker. Barby, wearing Joe's sweater, huddled in the chair, scarcely seeming to breathe. She sat in the dim, wavering shadow of the willow tree.

"Hello, there," Kay said softly.

"Hello." She did not open her eyes.

Lindy grunted. Kay put the thermos on the picnic table and poured three cups of hot tea. "Here," she said.

Barby looked at her. "Oh—Kay—"

"Take it."

"All right." She put it on the arm of her chair. Lindy drank his quickly, wiped his mouth on his sleeve. Kay dragged the other lawn chair near Barby and put her feet against the wall and drank her tea slowly. "Barby?"

Barby did not hear her.

"Do you intend to sit here all your life, darling?"

Lindy said, "She likes it here. We both like it."

"Barby, dear, listen to me."

"No. Please, Kay." She shook her head. The wind came off the river, rattled the willow tree. Kay shivered.

The Long Year 221

"No one thinks Joe killed Mike. Believe me, no one would think that."

"Mike's dead. Maybe he wanted it that way when Wilma left him. Maybe he was dead all the time after she left."

"Don't be silly. Everyone wants to live."

"I don't."

"Darling, you're young, and this isn't the only place on earth. There's a lot left for you. Remember Bix Lawrence? You said you liked him."

Barby turned her head. "Don't be silly," she said roughly.

"But, you did. You'll see, Barby. You loved Joe. Now, you are sure you can love someone, and so you'll love someone else again."

"No. It doesn't end."

"Certainly it does. It changes, and then you find you're free to go on to something else." Except that Prokosch never ended, that dark man sitting in the bedroom in Prague on a summer night telling you he's through, he's taking nothing more, and please be kind enough not to slam the door on your way out. That never quite ended.

"You mean—some day Joe won't mean anything to me?"

"Yes. I mean that exactly."

Lindy put his hands into the pockets of his torn leather jacket. "Joe didn't mean to do it."

"S-ssh, Lindy," Barby said. "We know that."

"I don't want him to die, neither."

"He's not going to die," Kay said.

"Come back tomorrow, Lindy," Barby said. "Nobody wants Joe to die." She watched him go. "God knows, though, what they'll do to Joe."

"Darling, you can't live his life. It's enough to live your own."

She raised her arm over her eyes. "I can't stand it, Kay," she said. She let her arm fall, and the cup of tea spilled on the ground. Kay bent down and picked it up and put it beside the thermos. "Maybe, it would be easier—for me—and for him, too, if I didn't care—so much."

"A woman is practical by nature," Kay said. "Even if he does get a short sentence—everyone seems to think that he will—even then people will know about him, and you're used to freedom, to moving among any kind of people you choose. It won't be good for you, darling. This is something you have got to outgrow. Joe understands that. He won't let you see him. He probably knows that you've got to get over it—even if he gets a short sentence. The reporters seem to think he has a good chance for one."

"My God," Barby said. "One day is too long for him in there. He's been in there almost two weeks, and I can't stand it."

"You'll know what to do in the end," Kay said. "It will work out."

"Do you think it will?" She sat a little straighter. "Do you think I'll have fun again?"

"Certainly. You always had fun with Marth and me those times when Bix Lawrence took you dancing. Joe wasn't around then, and you had fun. Believe me, a woman loves many men. She has a capacity for it. Especially someone like you, Barbs, and you're only a girl now—it's too soon to care this way for anyone."

Barby unfolded her handkerchief and blew her nose. "Did you ever—did you ever love anyone like this?"

Kay smiled. "Several. But I always had some good laughs later." She rose and looked over the town. "Love is more than a lot of weeping. Keep it calm between you and Joe, calm and gay." But when she looked down at Barby, she thought: They don't remember the same things we do. They never had much, and we had too much—big, booming years, people were gay, there were lots of cars, lots of money, cruises, champagne, sable wraps. We had all of it, the world of Scott Fitzgerald. But they never had any of it.

"Besides," she said, "Joe wouldn't want you to be this way. You can't sit here forever. You'll turn into something the school children laugh about. They'll call you names."

Barby smiled. "I guess so."

Kay pulled her silk peasant scarf from her pocket and tied it under her chin. "I'll come around this evening, and you and Marth and I will go for a drive."

The Long Year 223

"Kay—will you talk to me like this often? Will—will you be my friend. You know—"

"Of course, darling." She went into the house, smiling. Teresita was doing a dance in the kitchen.

"Barby oughtta come in now," Teresita said.

"She'll be in later."

"Oh, dear—Kay," Mrs. Leroy said. "Do tell me, what did you say to her? You are so wonderful to come, and she *does* adore you—"

"I didn't say much. Mike's dead. Joe's in jail. There's nothing to say, Maida. But, she'll be all right. I know that."

"But you will come again, won't you, Kay?"

"Of course. Eventually, Barby will want to go to the city with us. I ought to know. She'll listen to me in time and see that I make sense because it will be easier that way for her. She'll get over Joe. Poor baby—both of them—poor babies."

"Yes," Mrs. Leroy sighed. "Maybe things won't be so bad with him. If only he'd be pleasant and polite to people. Do you think—just looking at Barby—do you think there was anything—I mean, between her and Joe?"

"She loved him, Maida," she said. God, how could people be such fools?

"Oh, dear, I'd hate to think anything would happen, but well, really—" Her voice trailed off. She held Kay's hand tight in her own. "Thank you for coming, my dear."

"I didn't do anything," she said.

She drove toward the factory. Of course, Barby was attractive and gay, but it was curious that whenever you did anything for people, they were so seldom grateful. Yet, there was a fascination in doing things so that people moved in a pattern which you made for them, in which their days belonged to you as well, so that in a way you lived through them. She'd go down to the office, and when Marth came, they could go up to see the house—that was going to be a wonderful place, and she could have Fonn and LeGrand and Marvin Meyers and Laura and Kurt Hardacker, all the people she loved around her—that was what she wanted now.

CHAPTER TWENTY-TWO:

Johnnie Evans walked around the courthouse several times that afternoon. He saw Kay turn up the hill toward Leroy's and then come down again with Barby and Marth. Finally he grew tired of his own hesitant nature and went inside and asked the sheriff to see Joe.

"Haw," the sheriff said, "he's no customer for you, Johnnie."

Joe was sitting on a small kitchen chair, leaning against the wall. He looked very young in there, and for a moment Johnnie found nothing to say. He felt sad and helpless. "Let me talk to you, Joe," he said.

"Scram."

"You'll need a lawyer."

"Maybe." He crossed the cell and sat on the cot. He was neatly dressed, his shoes shined, and his wrist was bandaged so that only the clean white edge of the bandage showed. He tried not to move or touch that arm. He looked at his shoes and pulled the creases into his trousers. "I got enough troubles, and I can talk for myself. I know what I did and what I didn't do."

This meant a lot to Johnnie. He had been thinking about it for two weeks. All his life he'd wanted a case like this. If he should die tomorrow, he would have done nothing for himself except make a little money from sour-faced clients who never mattered anyhow. He hadn't used what he learned those years studying. He dreamed a dream that was young, innocent, full of faith, and he wanted to do one thing right. "You'll need a lawyer," he said.

"Go to hell."

"Joe, I mean this."

Joe looked at him. "Go peddle Kay's papers. Get some contracts you can cheat on, make bad pulleys, poor frames, and then the

The Long Year 225

factory'll never have a chance again. But you don't care. Guys like you never care."

"Neither do you care."

Joe took a long drag on his cigarette. "I care. Just because I got into a jam is no reason for you to stand there throwing turds on me." I never knew how much I cared till now. I never knew a lot of things, but now I know.

"All right," he said. "I thought I'd try." He wondered how the news got around about those contracts. These people always knew everything.

Joe rose and stood against the bars. "Listen, Johnnie, I need someone the jury will believe."

"You think they won't believe me."

"They won't."

"I see."

"Everyone in town liked Mike, and almost no one—except my best friends—liked me. Now they want my blood. They wouldn't believe you."

Johnnie was silent.

"I suppose you know the reporters've been giving this a lot of publicity?"

"Yeah. Maybe that's why you want in," Joe said.

He pushed back his hat, shaking his head. "No. It's not that. Ever since I got out of law school, I've wanted to do something big. That's a human need. I came to this town and got the cold shoulder because it's that kind of town. Walt Purdy was here before me. I gave up too soon and started messing around with smarty guys. You know. Right now I'd give my right eye to be your lawyer, Joe. But, I can see how it is, too. Maybe you're right." He turned and walked down the stone hall and out onto the courthouse steps. Mr. Wimmer was coming up the street. He waited for him.

"H'lo, Gene," he said.

Mr. Wimmer walked along in his own golden light, tagged by the old dog, Jawrge. He looked up, nodded and stopped. "Joe won't have you?"

"No. Guess not. He's right, too." He thought: There it is again, the people always know. I go in and out of here every day, but now they know about this, too. "Gene?"

"What?" He turned his head, and Johnnie looked into the clear, blue, dreaming eyes. He looked down at the ground. "I wanted this case. I was willing to do anything to get it."

Mr. Wimmer's eyes narrowed. He saw a handsome, youngish man in a light-colored topcoat and an expensive hat. He saw the nervous eyes, the tired, bruised sag of the body, the skin without light to it. "I'll talk to him, Johnnie," he said. "Joe's smart and knows what he wants, and we know you're a clever fellow."

"No. I wouldn't want you to—"

"I'll talk it over with him, anyhow."

"I don't want you to put yourself out on a limb."

"No trouble," Mr. Wimmer said. "And say, I'd like to buy the old Purdy place if you could get Sis Purdy to sell. The title's kind of complicated. Land doesn't seem to have much to do with what's on paper, it's just land to me."

"Sure," he said warmly. "Sure—only it's not a very good farm, is it?"

"Good barn."

"Why, sure, Gene." He smiled, kicking a small stone with the polished toe of his shoe. "Be glad to look into it and let you know."

"Thanks, Johnnie," he said.

Johnnie walked down Chestnut Street. In this moment, he had found his place. And now he had Gene Wimmer for a client, a man of considerable importance, the one Kay Hasswell wanted to be rid of, Joe's friend, a deep thinker. Really someone. He'd have to explain this to Kay. He was going to take her up to see her house this afternoon. She wouldn't like having him quit the Chicago deal and then when she knew he was taking this case where there was no money, nothing except an interesting case—she'd like that less. She had a tongue like a whip when she wanted to use it, but he'd tell her. "What a woman—always wants to show what she

The Long Year

can do, build a house while they starve, hang by her teeth from the Empire State Building . . ." Just the same, he would tell her . . .

During the hot days of that first summer, during autumn and winter, Kay had walked along the river looking for the place she could build her house. "I need roots," she kept muttering. She wanted a house near the river where it widened, not near the cheap little places of the artists. She wanted no Bohemia mushrooming near her. She took Marth with her, leaving the big red car at Brown's Creek and walking along the river paths.

Marth loved this. Something was always happening when she was with Kay. Kay knew exactly what she wanted, too. "I want a place within the sound of water." She wanted nothing drab or dull but bright and imaginative where nothing mattered except to have a good time. It would be simple to attract people she admired, creative, important people like LeGrand and big, simple, famous ones like Fonn Kelly. It would have something of Paris so that they would say, "This is like that wonderful house outside Paris where we watched LeGrand throw knives at the dancer." Maybe, it would have the color of Spain so that they could relax as she had done in the hot color and wide sun of Spain. And it would be like New York, only it would be what New Yorkers had forgotten of their first beginnings—eating in a big, friendly summer kitchen.

In February, before Mike's death, they found it. Marth was walking along the lower river path where the snow had drifted away and the path was clear. She could hear Kay walking higher along the cliff for a time, and then she could hear no one but herself. In all the woods there was a terrible stillness, unmoving and ominous. She felt silly standing there, frightened, calling in a whisper to Rocky. It was childish. The river was here as it was in the town, and there was nothing to fear. She came to the fence of old, rotting poles. When she kicked at the bottom one, it splayed open revealing the rotting inner core. A light cloud, smoky and harsh, rose from it. She crawled through the break into a clearing made around five old oaks. She thought the snow was so thick and bright it might never melt here even on the hottest days. She pushed through the bramble hedge and stood on a rise of ground and saw the house with excitement. The shutters hung flapping from the windows. The long, rambling place seemed to sag, and the winter air was sultry, heavy. "Gosh," she said. She called to Kay, and the call echoed and died, and then she heard Kay running. She saw her green suede jacket. Kay stopped in the clearing and put her hand to her mouth.

"We-eel," she said slowly. "I'll be damned, darling."

They pushed open the heavy front door. Inside, the floors rotted away, the house leaned to the east, there was nothing but one long, dusty, bare room after another. "This is it," Kay said emphatically. "This is what I want."

"It smells funny."

She sniffed. "How?"

"Like moss and stuff—you know, like muck off the top of dead water."

"Oh, that. It'll go away when the place is aired and redecorated."

"It's swell. But it smells awful."

Kay laughed. "Imagine what we can do here." She walked through each room, examining the woodwork, speculating as to how it could be changed or renovated. "Hoyt will know about this place. Someone's sure to know." She had to have it. Her mind was set on that. "You'll see—the men want work. Let them come out here and work."

"But, Kay—" Marth said. She made a worried face. She supposed it could be made to look like something, but it did not seem very pleasant, and the smell was terrible.

"You wait. Why, darling, don't you know I can do anything?" She laughed and put her arm around Marth, and Marth nodded. "You'll see."

After that, she went to look at the place every day and would not let Hoyt rest until he had the title cleared so that she could buy it from an old, forgotten estate. A crew worked there tearing

The Long Year

down the back wing, putting on a new summer kitchen. The sounds of their work went through the woods, and the new spring birds flew off over the water. No matter how much they tore away, the house remained dark and damp to Marth. A crew of twenty men worked there during the first part of March. The people resented the entire project.

Marth used to talk to Russian about it when he came to the dock. "I don't see why she can't have that house if she wants it."

"She don't want it to keep warm—not her. She wants it to show off. People like Olds got to crawl on their stummicks to the relief office for coal. They feel bitter about it an' she knows and don't care. She can do anything."

"It's her money, Russian."

"Money, money—you talk like the lead lady in a whorehouse. If we're hungry, we can't eat ten-dollar bills. Anyhow, she didn't come by it herself. She had to marry all those times to get that money."

"The factory—"

"Pooh. That's only part of it, girl."

At first, though, some of the men were glad to have work. They were paid promptly, and Kay acted as if they were doing her a big favor. She sent cases of beer out to them and called them by their first names. One of the Hickory boys worked there the first days in March, but when a pillar from the front porch fell on him and broke two ribs, he said he wouldn't work there again.

"Got nothin' against the house," he said. "Mind you, it's a good house if there ever was one, but that pillar was new—just put it in ourselves—and nothing short of a tornado shoulda knocked it out."

"Oh, really," Marth said, "they have no right talking like superstitious country folks."

"Maybe," Russian said. "Hickory was purt near crazy to get that job. A lot of them was crazy to get one, but he got it because he did her a favor on the school board. Helped to get Wimmer out."

"She didn't have anything to do with that."

"Okay," Russian said, "but you do a dirty deed, and everything like gravity and nature works against you. I know. I helped her to get Wimmer out of there, an I wish I'd never done it."

"Get on with you, Russian," she said. "You can't blame her for everything. Olds says you want to blame her for everything in the world."

He laughed. "You're a nice girl, Marth."

Still, after the accident with the pillar, many of the men would not work there. Others went with reluctance. The work moved rapidly because of their desire to get through, and a veil of silence came over the men whenever Kay was there. They kept telling her another heavy snow was due any day, a March blizzard was in the air. They wanted someone or something to get them out of this work.

In the late afternoon, Johnnie drove to the factory. As soon as he turned in the drive, Kay came out, pulling on her polo coat. She sat close to him, reached into his pocket and took out two cigarettes and lit them.

"Where's Marth?"

"Oh, she's down on the beach timing Rocky. The men sit on the cliffs watching him. He's their most valuable piece of property." Her voice was scornful.

"He's a good fighter. All the sports writers say he is."

"Ummm—maybe."

"Feels like snow."

"Oh, damn. That's what the men've been yelling about. I want everything ready by June, and Marth and I have so much we want to do."

"You like Marth, don't you?"

She smiled her slow, warm smile that always made him believe in her. "We're alike. That's part of it, and then I don't want her to be confused the way I was. I don't want people to get in her way or involve her in their lives. She ought to stay calm and find out what she can do and travel and get some good ideas about

The Long Year   231

clothes. She thinks that boy matters to her. It's just a fling, and she'll get over it. I keep telling Barby that, and Barby's beginning to see that she and Joe weren't meant to be."

He looked down at her. She always seemed young to him, fruity and wild and sweet, and she had a fragile look, so that he expected she'd snap sometimes, but she never did. "You've got it planned. You'll fix the house, have a lot of people there, get the factory under way, travel this winter and take Marth with you."

"Yes," she said. "And next week in Chicago we'll pick lovely plums at that convention." She smiled at him, making her mouth go soft. "What's the idea of cross-examining me like this, darling? You know me. You know I want Marth. I told you that. She adores me, really, and she shouldn't stay here. Look at what this town did to Maida Leroy. She was once a startling person. Now look at her—a silly maternal butterfly."

"She likes it here."

"Naturally. She's forgotten everything else. She's become provincial."

He turned off the highway. Above the sound of the motor, he could hear the men at work. A stiff, gray wind came off the water, and the sky darkened. He felt a snowflake on the back of his hand. "Snow," he said.

She frowned. "I despise winters. This is the last winter here for me. It makes me ill."

He swung the car into the open space behind the house. One of the men was standing on the roof looking at the sky. He was a small, dejected man, and she called to him. He came down the ladder and stood with his hands in his pockets listening to her.

"The snow will die down," she said. "After all, it's March."

"No," he said.

"Why not?"

"It's a spring blizzard like we had eight years ago."

"How can you tell that?"

He took a deep breath. "I remember how it was then."

"We'll see," she said.

The man moved beside her as she turned toward the house. "The men want to quit today—until better weather anyhow."

"It's much too soon."

"They say they want to quit tonight."

She looked at him sharply, but he would not give way. "All right, only it's pure craziness. They shouldn't act like children. Tell them to pick up their pay at the factory tomorrow."

"Yes, I'll tell them," he said quietly.

Johnnie followed her into the house. The walls had been stripped and repaired, new floors were laid, but the stairway looked precarious to him. "This house still slants," he said.

She sat on the stairs and emptied a stone from her green walking shoes. It fell to the floor, rolling toward the fireplace. He picked it up. It was still warm.

"That's an idea you and Marth have. She says it slants, but it doesn't."

He sat down beside her and took her hand. She looked at him, inquiringly. The fox, he thought, the quick brown fox and the lazy farmer. "Kay, listen to me. I want to talk to you."

"Certainly, darling."

"I'm—I've decided not to go to Chicago with you. I don't want to be in on this deal."

She waited, her eyes full of amber lights. He had seen this look before—in the eyes of a ballerina one time in New York, the year he went there for Christmas vacation. He was sitting in the first row, and when the dancer moved upstage, his eye had met hers over the footlights, and in hers had been the same look—of waiting, of knowing, of searching.

"I'm going to handle Joe's case if I can."

"I see."

"I want to do that more than anything."

She took away her hand, moved across the room in that curious, single way she had when she was thinking. She had a very beautiful, elegant back—really a very elegant, beautiful everything. She stood by the windows. The men were getting into the green jitney.

The Long Year 233

They were quiet, climbing in quickly and sitting with their knees pulled up for warmth.

"Kay, I'm crazy about you."

"Yes. You're acting as if you *adored* me, Johnnie."

"Please, Kay. I want you to see it the way I do. I don't want to be alone. I don't want you to be alone."

"Alone," she said, dully.

"Maybe—"

"No. Don't try to explain. I suppose this is important to you."

"Yes."

"Did—did you happen to talk this over with Gene Wimmer?"

"No. Not before I decided. Afterwards I saw him outside the courthouse."

"You think I don't understand."

"I don't know."

"You haven't learned yet what it is to be alone. You talk about it easily, but you don't know—"

"You don't have to be alone, Kay."

She shrugged. "It's hard for me to be anything else." She put her hands in her pockets, moved her feet apart and looked at him. "Do you believe the people here will be glad because you helped Joe? Do you think they like me or are glad because I re-opened the factory? No." Her voice was low and harsh. "I know how you feel. I know how terrible it was about Mike and now it's bad for Joe and it wasn't easy for you to decide this. You've always been a clever, shady young lawyer and now you want to be a clever, good young man. But, can't you see, no one cares, it doesn't matter? In the end, all these kind, Christian people will hate you as they hate everyone who is stronger than they are."

"It's—it's that I want to get on to myself." In the bare room his voice sounded squeaky and futile.

"Maybe you will."

"I wouldn't be much help to you anyhow. You can get whatever you want in Chicago. Let's go home, now, Kay. It's cold here." He put his arm around her.

"No. Things are going to work out for me—exactly as I want them. Everything." But she was thinking of Prokosch saying nothing would ever work out for her.

"Gene wants to buy Purdy's place."

"Why? It's nothing—good for celery and lettuce, that's all. He's no farmer."

"He wants it, though."

"Listen, Johnnie. I'll give Sis Purdy two hundred more than any price he'll offer."

"No. That won't do. You can't hound him forever. The man's free, and he won't leave this town anyhow. Besides, she'll sell to him where she might not sell to anyone else." He wondered why she was always against Gene. Maybe Russian was right when he said she was in love with him. "I'm crazy about you, darling," he said softly.

"Oh, Johnnie, let's not start that again—"

"I'm really in love with you." He had to find out now. "You think it's some kind of joke, but it's true. I *do* love you."

"No. It won't last, anyhow. It's fun for a while. Believe me, I'm not what you want. I'm hard to live with, and I'm old inside, and I try to change people. I spend too much money. I keep running around all the time."

"But, maybe we could—"

"No. You're sweet, but I don't love you."

"Kay, you can't tell me that—" His voice rose, insistent.

"I can tell you *anything*," she said flatly.

He sighed. "Do you want me to wait for you?"

"Don't be so kind, Johnnie, it only makes it harder for you. And don't be humble. It's not like you."

"Well, you can't stay here all night."

"I want to stay here all night. Tell Marth or Howard to come to get me in the morning—only get out of here now, Johnnie."

He moved toward the door and stopped. "It's over between us, isn't it, Kay?"

"It never began," she said.

The Long Year

"That's all right."

"I mean it."

"You lie."

"Oh—go away. Young men—young men are very tiring sometimes. I don't feel young or even interested in you. All I wanted was a smart, attractive young lawyer."

He left her, but he wanted to stay with her more than anything. When he was near her, he always had a good time, laughed a lot, felt that she cared what he had to say. But now, when he left her, he felt as if he died. "She thinks I'm a fool," he thought. She had never loved him, he knew, it was all an act because she had to have someone and he was the one who fitted into her plans. No doubt a lot of young men had fallen for her and she had used them—he felt bitter because she had never loved him. He understood how Mike Hasswell had turned into the town's bum. He got into his car, driving over the bumpy road. He stopped when he reached the highway. He thought he was going to cry, felt like a kid of seventeen. "Damn fool," he thought, "that's what I am, a damned fool to let this happen to me."

She had never told him he had a chance, and he always thought she was thinking of someone else, probably Prokosch. She liked to talk about him. Maybe she still cared, if she could care about anyone. His hands tightened on the wheel, the dream died in him and was lost, he felt empty. "God, she's wonderful," he kept muttering softly.

CHAPTER TWENTY=THREE:

A WEEK BEFORE the trial, a State patrol, wandering in the woods near the river, found the two men whom Joe had described living in a shack. They had almost run out of canned beans and were grisly and bellicose and immediately began to whine and shout curses at the cops. Joe identified them without making any conversation with them. They stood glaring at him, looking dejected and amateurish, prickly-faced, red-eyed, their mouths hanging open. They were two bank clerks from Savannah.

During the first day of Joe's trial, Fred Stohl, the reporter, sat in the courtroom and watched the people and thought: This is the country, the whole saddened face and spirit of the country in this one place, everything we are is here, gathered together like the wheat of the world gathered into one storeroom. There was the calm air of the boy, Joe. The paternal, undramatic, modest air of the lawyer, Johnnie Evans, who kept pushing back his hair and speaking in a low, confidential way to the people being examined for the jury. There was the old guy, Hoyt Hasswell, in a dark overcoat and a derby watching with interest as if it had nothing to do with his son's death, a pageant to entertain him. There was the woman, Kay, in a red coat, and the niece, a young girl confused and tender-mouthed, always with her aunt, turning toward her with delight and affection. There was the boy, the soft-stepper like a precious, wild animal moving through an alien woods, the prizefighter, Macbeth's boy.

He saw this as the realest day he had ever known. It was the temper and strife, the deceit and grandeur of this country in this time. And through all of it, he was looking for one person, nameless, unknown, who would in some way make him believe that this was not all—the country was even more than this. He knew already

The Long Year 237

how the trial would go. He knew trials. The boy would get it on a burglary rap. The other two, the amateur gangsters, would get the book. The boy would go to prison in his own town—they might forget him, they might talk of him as if his had been a great adventure.

He went outside where the men stood on the steps, sat on the terrace under the statue. He read the inscription on the base of the statue and grinned. "Wouldn't you know—some damned fool polo player." He wondered if they cared at all for the kid himself, a kid without a job, lost in the troubles of his family. They seemed interested only as, for the moment, it gave them excitement. He walked slowly down the hill and ate at the Cafe alone. Afterwards he went to Macbeth's. He could see the old guy sitting in his store on the floor behind the rack of tweed suits.

Macbeth was getting drunk. He had not done this in years. He held the bottle closely to warm it. He talked to it. Beside him on the floor was a clean glass. On the other side was a big flashlight and a copy of *Hamlet*. He was profoundly impressed with the Order of Life, so he had developed a system. First to drink, then cork the bottle, put the bottle beside the glass, turn on the flashlight, open *Hamlet* and choose a line and read this aloud: "'Sleep rock thy brain.'"

He read it again: "'Sleep rock thy brain.'"

He closed the book, put down the flashlight and the book, picked up the bottle, took a good pull on it and held it a little away from him. "'Sleep rock thy brain,'" he said. A wonderful thing to have written. A man wrote it, a poor guy a little more than a monkey, a little less than a blade of grass, a man under the curse of life. He corked the bottle, returned it beside the glass and picked up the book again, reading by the light of the flash: "'I have words to speak will make thee dumb.'"

He assumed a crafty look, smacked his lips: "'I have words to speak will make thee dumb.'"

Fred Stohl pulled aside the twenty-nine-fifty tweed suits and saw him sitting there. "Hello, Mr. Macbeth," he said.

"Hello," Macbeth said. " 'I have words to speak in thine ears will make thee dumb.' "

"Shoot." He sat down beside him.

"I'm no drinking man," Macbeth said. "As you can plainly see, I'm a man of literature and mysticism." He held up the book and flashed the light on it.

"I can see it plainly."

Macbeth lowered his voice. "Never been afraid like this before. Everybody standin' around waitin' for Joe's blood. Makes a man afraid."

"Yes," the reporter said.

"My friend, that is as good as any reason I know to get pickled. The world is tottering. Not the whole damned big world but the little world, size of a dime, right here in this town."

"Yeah," the reporter said and took a good drink from the bottle. "I can hear it toppling."

"Do not laugh, Boy."

"I'm not laughing, Sir."

"Everything looks bleak. I'm tired of being an old man of literature and mysticism. I want to see one good man again. I used to see 'em all over the place when I was a young man like you. I would like to see one now."

"That's what I want to see, too," the reporter said. He was sober and lonely, and he had come to talk to the old man out of his own loneliness.

Macbeth flashed his light into the reporter's face. "Come here to find out what I know about Joe? I told you all I knew."

"It's my job," the reporter said.

"That's true," he said after a moment of thought. "That's quite true." He stood up slowly, unsteadily and looked around himself and then touched his worn suit. "Can't go see a good man lookin' like I slept with the hawgs." He pawed along the rack and found a blue serge suit and put on the jacket, which hung around his knees. He looked like a sad and aged clown. "Nice," he said, smoothing it. "Good fit."

The Long Year 239

"Fine," the reporter said. He tried to help him out of his trousers, but every time he had a good hold of them, Macbeth sat down. He did this slowly, unwillingly, for his spirit desired that he should fly. Finally Macbeth sat in a chair and pulled on the blue trousers over the old ones. This gave his thin, wiry body a square, muscular look. He flashed the light unsteadily into the three-sided mirror and surveyed himself proudly. Then he said: "Ought to drink some toasts."

"Toast someone," the reporter said.

"I toast my son, the best damned fighter in the world."

They each drank.

"I toast you," Macbeth said. "Fred Stohl, may your soul and all the souls of the faithful departed through the mercy of God rest in peace, Amen."

"Thank you," the reporter said gravely. He felt his world wheel and settle in a golden pasture. "Now, I toast you, Duff Macbeth, a good man to come to the aid of the party."

Macbeth drank to Chateau Thierry. "That Christly place no one remembers now. So, we drink to remember."

"Ought to toast a woman."

"Fine," Macbeth said. "Only one woman to drink to. Texas Guinan."

They drank to Texas Guinan, to Babe Ruth, to Gentleman Jim and to the super-salesman, Henry Ford. Then, while they groped for another toast, the night cop rapped at the door and opened it.

"You gimme an awful scare, Macbeth," he said. "I thought it was burglars again." He put his gun back into the holster.

"Guns," Macbeth said. "You'd run a mile if it was anyone."

The cop laughed and looked at the reporter. "Macbeth never drinks," he said.

"He's drinkin' now."

Macbeth said grandly, "This is my friend, newspaperman from the city, a journalist. Such as Shakespeare."

"Howdyado," the cop said.

"Fine," the reporter said.

"You got a car?" Macbeth asked.

"No," the reporter said. "You?"

Macbeth shook his head. "Look here, Finney, you take us in the patrol car. We pay taxes. No use lettin' the senators get all of it."

"No," the cop said. "I can't take you guys unless I'm makin' an arrest or it's official business. It says so on a paper pasted inside the car. Go an' look if you want."

"You're a liar," Macbeth said. "I seen you plenty of times with guys in there."

The cop shrugged.

"We pay taxes," Macbeth said.

"We also vote," the reporter said.

"You are a servant of the people. *We* are the people," Macbeth said.

The cop scratched his head. "It's not often you drink, Macbeth. I guess I could celebrate, too."

"We're *not* celebratin'," Macbeth said firmly. "Mike's dead. Joe's in jail. My son—my son's in love with the Hasswell girl. We're not celebratin', see?"

They went into the street and crawled into the back seat of the patrol car, and the cop started the motor. "Where to?" he asked.

"Uh—" Macbeth turned to the reporter. "Where we goin'?"

"Don't know," the reporter said.

"Yeah," Macbeth said. "To see a good man. To Mr. Wimmer's, Finney."

"I can't go way out there."

"Lord God Above, don't worry about inches, go as far as you can," Macbeth said. He braced his feet against the front seat. The reporter slouched and drank. It was very cold, now, and the reporter felt it through his trench coat.

The cop said, "How's the trial look, would you say?"

"Wouldn't say," the reporter said. "All trials stink."

"You been around much?"

"Here and there."

"This town's pretty big when the factory's going."

The Long Year 241

"It's no better than it is right now," Macbeth said. "Same people. Same town."

The cop drove as far as he could and then stopped by the grove along the highway. "You can see Mr. Wimmer's light from here," he said. "You go right down that path through the woods."

"Fine," the reporter said. He helped Macbeth from the car.

Macbeth stopped and put his head through the window. "Lissen," he said to the cop, "go home an' take care of all the precious, darlin' people."

"You old bastard," the cop said affectionately and began to turn around and nose the car back to town.

The moon was very bright even in the grove. "Tell you somethin' about Wimmer," Macbeth said. "He's crazy about Kay Hasswell. Know her?"

"Sure."

"Used to be married to Count Prokosch. Know him?"

"A little."

"Poor Wimmer."

"Yeah," the reporter said, "like being in love with the Mona Lisa."

They crawled under the fence, making a long, slow journey of it. They crossed the farmyard. "S-ssh," Macbeth said.

"S-ssh," the reporter hissed.

They looked in the kitchen window. Mr. Wimmer was sitting with his stocking feet on the stove, and the old dog was lying beside him. A kerosene lamp stood on the table, and the room looked warm and bright. Mr. Wimmer wore his black Stetson and was playing his accordion, but they could not hear what he was singing.

"A man of many talents," Macbeth said proudly. He knocked, and Mr. Wimmer came to the door.

"Come in, Macbeth," he said. "It's too cold for you to come way out here."

"Got a ride," Macbeth said. The room was very warm and clean. The old dog did not move but lay watching them, sniffing a little.

"That's Jawrge," Mr. Wimmer said. He went into the bedroom and came back with two unpainted chairs and put them by the stove. "You're drunk, Macbeth."

"Yes," Macbeth said gravely. "It's so. And Fred, here—he's drunk, too."

Mr. Wimmer laughed. "What happened?"

"Nothing," Macbeth said. "Everything."

The reporter leaned back in his chair. "How old is Jawrge?"

"I don't know. But he's a good dog."

"Got a lot of stock here?"

"Not yet. Two cows and a broken-down horse and some chickens."

"Fred—Fred here's writin' a book about what makes things go," Macbeth said with pride.

"That so?"

The reporter thought about it. "I been around a number of years kind of snooping."

"Going to write on metaphysics," Macbeth said. "Like studyin' air and water." He took off his shoes and stockings, his extra trousers. He hung these on the back of his chair and wriggled his toes and scratched himself with pleasure. The reporter watched and seeing it was a good idea, took off his shoes and stockings, too.

Macbeth said, "Now they want Joe's blood. Tomorrow, they'll want to shoot the county attorney."

"They'll calm down later," Mr. Wimmer said. "It's that they have nothing to occupy their minds."

The reporter closed his eyes and thought this was like Vermont when he was a boy. Mr. Wimmer played his accordion. Macbeth and the reporter sat there very drunk, forgetting whatever it was they so desperately set out to do. After a time, Mr. Wimmer walked them into the bedroom and covered them with an old quilt. "Don't leave this town," Macbeth said. "Don't ever leave us. Everybody leaves us. You stay, Gene," Macbeth said and snored peacefully.

"Sure," Gene said. He went into the kitchen and slept on the table. He wondered why they had come all this way and what they searched for and what they saw in their drunkenness that they

The Long Year 243

obviously could not have seen while they were stony sober. They were seeing horses in the sky, faces in the stars, he thought. He sighed. What he needed was a good drunk for himself and one of those light-haired ballet dancers from the Orpheum up in Grand Forks. He grinned. "Cripes," he said in amusement, "I wonder what those two drunks came up here to talk about. They'll probably never remember what it was."

Russian Peterson saw Kay come out of the house and get into her car. A few minutes before that he had seen Howard carrying the bags and putting them in the trunk of the car. "She's goin' to Chicawgo," Howard had said. Russian saw the big car roar down the street and turn up toward the highway. He thought, She'll do it alone without Johnnie Evans, without anyone. She doesn't need us, any of us, just herself.

He walked up to the courthouse and sat leaning against the base of the statue. A few people had jammed into the courtroom and into the halls, but most of the men sat outside and waited. Every few minutes someone would come out and say something. "Johnnie's askin' Joe was he ever a Boy Scout . . . Looks like those two guys'll get it . . ." Russian was not interested in this. He was interested in one single idea: Kay Hasswell. If there was some way he could fix things so she would stay in Chicago forever. If there was some way— That was how the trouble started—when she came and everyone sat back and said, Let her take care of everything, she'll take care of everything.

Olds said, "Got a card from Smut this mornin'."

"Where's he?"

"Gone out West to Montana. He heard there was work there but there ain't. Ain't work anywheres. Guess maybe Smut'll come home now."

"He's crazy if he does," Russian said.

"What's eatin' you today? Joe's gonna get off just like you said. You ought to've taken a bet on it."

"I'm not betting on things like that," he said.

"Ever since you and yer wife been at odds, a body can't talk sense with you, Russian."

"Kay Hasswell left for Chicago."

"Yeah?"

"I'll bet she'll get some fine contracts. She says she's going to do that."

Olds said nothing.

"If she does, you'll probably get back to work."

"Don't mind if I do," Olds said, "but I'd rather Smut got back. Tell the truth, a body can take onny so much and Velma's got enough on her hands. I don't mind stayin' home to help with the kids. Robert's comin' along fine, pulls hisself up easy."

"You seen Joe in there?" He nodded toward the courtroom.

"Un-hunh. He don't carry on none, answers questions real polite and seems to know what he's sayin'. The other two guys—you know they found 'em hidin' away in that shack up-river just like Joe said all along they was gonna do—them two guys is sure gettin' it hard. Johnnie, he don't take no back sass from that other attorney. He jus' says right out Joe didn't have nothin' to do with the killin'."

"Seems like Johnnie's doing fine by himself."

"Jist fine," Olds said.

"Where's your eye, Olds?" Russian asked sharply. "You don't have your eye in."

"Jesus," Olds said, touching his empty socket, "I give it to Robert to play with. Jesus." He got up and began to run up the hill toward his house. Russian leaned against the statue and laughed hard, holding his belly. By God, he felt better. The minute she got out of the town he felt better. He'd go down on the river and do some fishing. Kids loved sunnies fried in cornmeal and deep fat. He got up and patted the bronze rump of the horse. "Giddap," he said and spat in the grass.

Rock lay on the dock alone. Russian squatted down beside him. "What's the matter, Kid?"

"Nothing," Rock said. "I was just kind of sleeping."

"Where's Marth?"

"Chicago. She went with Kay. Barby went, too."

"Barby?" He whistled softly.

"They talked her into it. They said what good was it to hang around here. Maybe they're right."

"Kay?"

"Kay and her mother. But I hope Joe don't hear it. He wouldn't like her going off that way even if she *couldn't* do him any good." He sat up. "I don't get it. Women, I mean."

"Women." He picked up his oars from the wharf. "Got to get some sunnies for my tribe today."

"What I mean is, Barby was so damned crazy about him, and now she thinks it's hopeless. She says she still cares, but there's no sense sitting around moping over it and she can do more good going away and keeping calm. God, I hate calm women. I like them to break out in a rash and call me names or anything. Calm. They keep it inside themselves and it gets rotten there."

"Uh-hunh," Russian said. He poured the minnows into his pail and laid a quarter on the wharf beside Rock. "What's eatin' you is that Marth went. You think she should take you along?"

"No! She can go, I guess. Her father wants her to go, and then she has a good time. But, geez, the town feels empty now. I guess if I didn't know she went, I'd feel it."

"Come on fishing. It's a swell day. Lock up the house and come with me."

Rocky shook his head. "Thanks," he said. "I'll stay here."

Russian shoved off. He felt free and lucky. He'd bring in a good catch. He looked back at the wharf where Rocky sat alone, not moving, staring into the water. "That's her doing, too, talking those girls into it. She just better let Rock alone, though." He spat into the water and muttered an obscenity about her. After a time, he heard Rock call across the water to him, and he rowed back toward the boathouse. Rock stood on the wharf waving his arms. They must've closed the trial, he thought. He stood up in the boat and made a megaphone of his hands, but he could not hear Rock's answer. He rowed quickly into the dock bay.

"Joe got two years," Rocky said. "They got him on a burglary charge. He pleaded guilty to it."

"Not bad," Russian said. "What about the other two guys?"

"I forgot to ask," Rocky said. "They got the limit, though. I heard someone say that, but then I had to send Barby a telegram, and I forgot to ask about those two. I promised Barby I'd let her know."

Russian nodded. "Not bad for Joe."

"He'll hate it. He'll hate every minute of it up there."

"Could've been worse."

"Joe won't think about that. Every day will make it worse for him. Wish I could do something for Joe. I don't seem to do anything for anyone."

Russian laughed. "You just fight the way you've been doing. That's all you need to do, Rock."

Rocky shook his head. "I've got to do something else," he said. "I've got to make it up to them. Joe and Mike." But Russian had already rowed out of the dock bay again. He was singing a loud, tuneless song that he had once sung to his children as a lullaby. He couldn't remember the words and so sang whatever came into his head.

"May she rot in hell," he sang, "my true love, my true love . . ."

CHAPTER TWENTY=FOUR:

When Kay returned from Chicago, a few men at a time went to work at the factory to make pulleys and frames and sashes for the government contracts. Soon, over a hundred men were working there, and in the mornings they hurried along the streets, swinging their chipped lunch buckets, feeling a pressing need to get there and be at work before anything happened to change it for them. They were convinced that Kay Hasswell could do anything. But there was an uneasiness in them as if they did not believe their work would last long.

Marth used to watch them from her bedroom window. "They're so quiet," she said. "They used to wake me up in the mornings, they made so much noise."

"You're a worrier like your father." Kay laughed.

"But, Kay—"

"Poof," she said and touched her cheek lightly. "Do something to your hair, angel. It's terrible."

Every morning, since going to Chicago with Kay, Marth got up early and ate breakfast with Kay and her father. Sometimes, Barby came, and they went down to the factory with Kay and did errands for her, drove to the city or went up-river to her place. Most of the time, they zoomed around town in Kay's red car, played tennis on the new courts on Kay's lawn.

"What'll I do today?" she asked.

"Don't worry," Kay said, "you always find something to do. You and Barby."

"I sort of promised Rock I'd go down on the beach with him."

Kay smiled. "That probably bores you, darling. Seems to me your father mentioned going somewhere today. He might like to have you go with him."

"I suppose so." She was watching the men. There was something wrong with the way they walked, quietly, hurrying along the street.

It was true that they felt a curious uneasiness, and Russian Peterson didn't help them to rid themselves of it.

"It's a trick," he kept saying. "It's a big, lousy trick."

"God," Olds said, "you're a Christly old doubter."

"Who cares?" the men said. "We've got work. Soon enough we'll be out of this stinking Depression. We'll all have work. And we've got her to thank for it."

"Shut up," he said. "Already you guys are startin' to buy new wash machines and clothes—God knows what. Do you see Gene Wimmer walkin' around like a rich man? You don't care what happens to him any more—before this, you were mad as hornets when I told you how that happened to him. You were ready to kill me for takin' part in it, and now here you are lickin' her boots. Gene Wimmer says a couple lousy contracts don't mean there's a boom."

But the men laughed and called him stupid for worrying. At the same time they hated him because he would destroy what peace they had. Nor could he explain his own unrest. He wished he had read just one large, informative book, that he would have some kind of learning so that he could stop them dead with a single, powerful statement the way Macbeth often did. "Man does not live by bread alone" or words like that.

One afternoon in early May he went outside the main building where the men worked at the saw. He was foreman now and walked around looking at everything, jealously watching the men at the big rip saw. That day he crossed the gully to the foundry. This building was long, made of stone with a huge furnace at one end. The air was full of metal dust, very thin and sharp to make the eyes water. The men worked stripped to the waists. The ones who worked on the floor were in pairs—the molder and the molder's helper. He had once been a molder's helper, a nasty, hot job. The men got up a good sweat that dripped off them as they bent over the molds. The floor was thick with fine, soft clay dust from the

The Long Year 249

molds. There was a kind of glory here as of animals who worked near the hot heart of earth, while in the factory itself, there was poverty of effort, motion and nature.

The mixers worked at the furnace. One worked the stopper, a long stick with a plug at the end. The hot metal burst from the furnace so that it seemed like a living, breathing creature. Russian went up to one of the mixers. "What the hell's that?" He pointed to the gravel-like pile near the dipper.

"Pig iron," the man said. "That there's plain pig iron."

"And what the hell's that?" He pointed to the mountain of old fenders, stove lids and iron pipes.

"Scrap iron. We use scrap iron now. We don't need to mix."

"An' clay molds. You use goddam clay molds."

"Yeah," the man said. He felt nervous and ashamed, but he kept his eyes on Russian's face.

"I should live so long. Where are the dies?"

"We don't use any. She said to do it this way."

"Lousy pulleys." He picked one off the stake truck and examined it. It felt light and false. "Cheap. Chip like china, rust all over the place."

"She says frames don't need pure die pulleys."

"She does, does she?"

"I'm onny tellin' you what she says."

"We never did cheap work around here." He stuck his finger through the core of the pulley. "When I was a core maker, they were smooth. We used good steel. We had dies. We didn't cheat."

"It ain't my fault," the man said.

"You guys make me want to puke," he said angrily. Still holding the pulley he went out and threw it against the stone wall. It splintered. "Jesus God in Heaven." The world was coming to an end.

At four o'clock he washed his face and hands and rolled down his sleeves. He went to the office. Hoyt was going out to play golf. Most of the time, he puttered around his flower garden, and whenever Russian wanted to talk about the factory, he paid little attention. "Perhaps I never cared, anyhow," he said once.

"Hoyt," Russian said, "they're making the lousiest pulleys out there."

Hoyt rammed his hands into his golf knickers. "Oh, now I'm sure the men wouldn't do that," he said.

"It's not the men. You got to do something, Hoyt." Usually, his speech was slow and flat, but now in his excitement and anger, the words came to him easily. "I tell you, they're making them from molds. Not a sign of a die. I threw one against the building, and it busted easy as anything."

Hoyt pulled at his lower lip. "You see," he said slowly, "I don't really have anything to do with it. Miss Hasswell got the contracts and knows what material they call for—so—well, I wouldn't know about this." He indicated Kay's office. "You talk it over with her, Russian."

Russian looked at him curiously. "But, she'll listen to you."

"You talk to her," he said. He was going to play some golf, and afterwards, he'd go home and take a good nap before dinner.

Kay was getting ready to go up to her house. She leaned against her desk, clasping on her wide silver bracelets. "Can I do something for you, Russian?"

"You can," he said. He had forgotten how young she looked. Her wrists were thin and brown, and her smile was friendly, like the smile of his younger child. "I been in the foundry and saw the pulleys they're makin'. They stink."

"So?" She sat at her desk, facing him. "Look, Russian, you must not believe that because we do things differently, we are wrong."

"The pulleys break and rust."

"For frames, it's not necessary to make pure die pulleys."

"We always did."

She shrugged. He felt an urge to slap this clean, fashionable woman who knew so much, sticking her nose everywhere. In his mind, he saw the frames loaded in the box cars, the pulleys dropping from them and the frames swelling with dampness, splitting from heat.

The Long Year

"We are fortunate to have these contracts," she said smoothly. "It means a good profit for us."

"If these frames aren't good, it'll be tough to get orders later. We never cheated. We've always—everyone here did good work."

Her eyes narrowed. "You've been talking to Mr. Wimmer."

He shook his head. "He's no trouble-maker. I'm tellin' you what I seen." He stood over her, and for a moment, he looked into her eyes. She did not seem to breathe. But the moment passed, and she rose and put her hand on his arm. Marth opened the door.

"We're ready, Kay," she said.

"Just a moment, darling."

"Hi, Russian." Marth came into the small office. He thought: They look alike, sharp and pretty. I never noticed it before, but they look alike. He nodded to her.

"You're a good man," Kay said. "We like having you here. You're reliable, and the men will listen to you. Let it go at that."

He knew it was no use. He went out. Mary Connaught spoke to him, and he answered. He felt sick and old. Nothing he had done had really ever mattered. His wife was right—he had an evil sickness. That was what made trouble at home, why the kids tried not to show how they felt about that business with Mr. Wimmer. Hell, the world was built upside down. His feet felt heavy. He had a shuffling, blind look walking like that, his hands trembling slightly at his side.

Hoyt felt nothing at all concerning the pulleys. He knew then with a strange awakening that it had never mattered to him because he had paid other people to worry about that. He still tried to go to the office two or three times a week, but there was nothing to do when he was there. It was difficult for him to miss Mike or even to believe that Mike had been his son. There was only a dull loneliness which he had never felt before. Marth was always busy with Kay. She was sure of herself, very gay and pretty and full of activity. He guessed she'd be all right. Only, he wished he had someone besides Maida to talk to, and yet, when Russian wanted to talk, he shied away from him.

The decorators had come from the city to work on Kay's house. In the mornings, she went to the factory very early and then often stopped in at the hotel to have late breakfast with the decorators. There were two men and a youngish woman who laughed a lot. They were fascinated with Kay's house and with Kay. They admired her energy, her clothes and even the new way she wore her hair. She had cut her hair this way because of that morning when she had become increasingly aware of the ugliness of the town. "I used to think of it as a green place under green trees, wide lawns, clean people." She went into Marth's room and stood by the window. Even in the coldest winter nights, she wore sheer nightgowns —usually yellow—and now she stood by the window, and the March wind whipped around the house. The timid edges of snow lay along the dirty walks. "I hate ugliness. If there is a God, He has no right to do this to us. It makes me want to scream."

Marth was too sleepy to look out the window. "Mr. Wimmer says ugliness, age and health are like the weather—states of mind."

"Oh, Mr. Wimmer! He's impervious to it. Look at this house— even with the living room done over, it still looks ugly, unchanged. When my house is ready, everything in it will be beautiful—beautiful people, everything the way it should be. No whiners. I hate whiners—whiners about pay and morals and pulleys and everything. Oh, I ought to do something." She prodded Marth. "Lazy one. That's what you get staying out all night with Rock. When ever in the world are you going to get over him? You've had your youthful fling, angel, now let's put it behind us."

"Uh."

"Have you a scissors?"

"Umm—in the drawer." She sat up in bed watching Kay snap the scissors together sharply. Kay sat at the dressing table and began to cut her hair straight across the front into bangs. Marth held her breath with admiration. Kay picked up a brush and with great

The Long Year

energy began to brush her hair to her shoulders. It was fine and bright and snapped as she brushed. Then boldly she cut her hair shoulder length. It fell on her satin dressing gown and on the floor, and it looked like the wings of grackles.

"There," she said.

"It's marvelous."

"Yes—I think so. I used to cut it when we were in Africa. There was no one else to do it." She shrugged. "You have to do something desperate when you feel bored." She was proud of her hair and loved to have people rave over it. The decorators could not keep their eyes off her. When Marth saw them sitting around the table talking and smoking, she thought how right they were for each other. In many ways, she tried to talk their language, but she could not. It was Barby who became one of them and learned their language and understood them.

"You're too shy, Marth," she said. "You're so easily shocked."

"I am not."

Barby laughed. She pursed her mouth with amusement, looking at Marth as if for the first time. "You know, Marth, you're a small-town girl. You act like one. Even in Chicago, I kept thinking you didn't really like it even though you had a good time. I mean, you were glad to get home."

"So were you." She wondered if it was because of Joe that Barby had changed—or perhaps Barby would have changed anyhow. She wondered if she had changed, too. She kept feeling sad and confused and turning to Kay for help. But Kay was absorbed in her house. In no time at all it had taken on an appearance of richness and charm. She and Barby unpacked the big crates and put things where they belonged and found new places for the odds and ends. Bix Lawrence went in and out of the house freely with his friends. They had a sailboat on the river and Kay had a long speedboat painted red and white. Even before the early days of summer, there were parties in the unfurnished living room. They sat on the floor beside the fireplace and sang while Kay played for them. Rock would lie on the floor a little apart from the others, admiring Marth.

She always wore pale sweaters pushed up to her elbows and a small string of silver beads and old moccasins and pale socks, and there were times when she looked altogether new to him—more like Kay, in a way, only that her hair was lighter, and she had a more childish voice, and her movements were slower. Often she would stop singing and look for him, and then in the thin, eerie light of the room, they would look at each other. She had a way of smiling and standing very still as if waiting for him, and when she did that, she was the same as always, not like Kay at all, no real resemblance, not even in her coloring or in the shape of her face.

But most of the time, he didn't go there. He sat around the store or helped Mr. Wimmer or worked down at the docks getting the canoes ready for summer. Sometimes, when he did not want to train or help in the store, he would go up to the house. He usually sat in a big yellow leather chair in the bar off the living room. The bar was decorated with Swedish designs and a Swedish toast over the mirror. He could sit there and count Kay's collection of steins and decanters. From there, he could see anyone who came in the front door or down the stairs. He worried about this place because he would never be able to get anything like it for Marth. He felt that he shouldn't worry about such a thing, now in his lifetime he could have a wonderful time and not worry, later to have a place of his own and some kids who'd like to hear about his fights. He disliked trying to make sense out of the way Kay and Marth were when they were together. He preferred to think only of himself and Marth.

She came into the room and stood by the bar smiling at him. Already, she had begun to tan. Her skin was always very smooth, and even in the winter when he moved the neck of her sweater, he could make out the faint markings from her bathing-suit straps. She wore her hair a new way, very straight and curled a little at the ends, and she wore a blouse thing with a low, round neck and embroidery on it. She liked that blouse. It came from Mexico,

The Long Year 255

she said, and she always said the exact name of that place. He could not remember it. She wore a striped skirt, quite short, and flat sandals and pink earrings. The earrings were what he kept looking at.

For him, there was no one else. He had grown up with her, and all the days of his life were tied with hers. When he looked at her he remembered the Saturday afternoons playing baseball in the vacant lot and how she always stood up to it, and then seeing her in the hall at the parochial school and the red plaid dresses she used to wear and how childish and clean her face looked above the round, starched collars. Now, under her smile, he felt troubled because there was nothing he could give her that she wanted. He feared losing her.

"You see, Rock, it's amazing what these people can do."

"Sure. Grow lilacs in December."

"What's the matter?"

"Nothing."

"Yes there is. Tell me."

"How can I tell you?" He looked at her impassively. "You wouldn't understand. I just feel—unhappy and powerless. I can't give you anything she can give you, and you like being with her all the time, and—"

"Please, Rock. I know you don't like Kay."

"I'm not saying that."

"But you make it sound frightening, as if when I'm with Kay it's wrong. It scares me when you talk like that."

"Everything's kind of scary—the way I see it, to be alive is a pretty dangerous thing. Things like sun and air—why, grass is so amazing that if you took a real look at it, it ought to knock you crazy."

"Oh," she sighed, "it's what Mr. Wimmer said to you."

"No. I don't know. Maybe he did. Listen, Marth, why can't you marry me? We could live with Paw for a while—you like Paw."

"Sure, I do, but it's too soon. And I'm not sure—"

"Sure of what?"

"Maybe I don't want to live here. I've never seen anything else. Maybe I'd like South America or France better."

"Maybe. I don't see that it matters. You live wherever you are."

Kay came into the room. "How do you like my place, Rock?"

"It's nice."

She smiled. "Be a big fighter like Fonn Kelly and some day you can have a place like this."

He shook his head. "I'm just a guy. I got no big ideas like that."

Marth said, "You shouldn't talk that way. Everyone knows you're a wonderful fighter."

"I like to do it, but I don't think it's my kind of life forever."

Kay said, "Did you ever see Fonn fight?"

"In the newsreels—that time with Barney Jaris."

"Yes," she said. "That was fast. Everyone thought it would last three rounds, but he knocked him out in less than a minute. You know, Rock, he's coming here this summer. He's a very strange person. You must get to know him."

"There's no one better." He had to admit that when he was talking to Kay, he liked her, liked what she had to say. "No one can get the crown from him."

"Some day you'll fight like that," Marth said.

He didn't think anyone but a fighter knew what kind of life it was. He didn't know many of the fight people except a few old-time handlers who were mostly rummies and punchies. He never went to the training camps and sat around with the crowd. He relied on the old man to tell him, and the old man was clever and hard to beat. Whenever he was fighting, he stayed by himself until it was time to go into the ring. After the fight, he returned to his dressing room and had himself fixed and showered and dressed. Usually he and the old man had a couple of hamburgers and went to bed. That way it was easy to keep his mind on one thing. He didn't want to lose any of the feeling by sitting around talking shop and letting it go down inside him. The old man said if you gassed about it, pretty soon you didn't have enough wind to do

The Long Year

anything but talk. He wondered how Fonn Kelly felt about it. There was never a fighter before him that could have touched a glove to him—maybe Corbett, but he didn't think so. The worst part was before the fight. Usually he and the old man went to a French movie. They couldn't understand the lingo, but they liked the faces and the way the camera showed everything exactly the way it was. The faces were sad and betrayed by life, and it was all as if the people were trying to show how true this thing was for them. Once there was a street fight, and he knew from the clumsy, careless way the actors handled themselves they weren't professionals but the actors themselves. It was a good fight, too. With your mind always working like that, you could never talk about it except with another fighter. So it was easy for Marth and Kay to chatter like this because they didn't understand.

He said, "It's okay to fight when you like to do it and can take care of yourself and give all you've got—but maybe I don't want to be a big-time fighter."

Kay wasn't listening. The woman decorator who was called Lili was trying to find a good place for the coffee table. They both looked at it from every angle, standing away from it and then moving closer, making a big thing of this.

"But, Rock," Marth said, "I thought you'd be awfully excited to know Fonn Kelly's coming and you can meet him. Kay's doing it just for you."

"Why?"

"Well, really Rock—you aren't very nice to Kay."

"Besides, you can never talk to someone like that when you feel the way I do."

"Are you mad at me, then?"

"No. Not because you and Kay get together and gang up on me. That's women's sport." He kicked the door shut and drew her to him. "Let's get out of here."

"I can't Rock. I promised Kay I'd stay for supper, and—"

"Hell." He sank into the leather chair again and drew her with him. "We don't have fun any more."

"Oh, yes we do. We always have fun."

"Yesterday when I came up here, you'd gone to the city with Kay. Day before that, we had a tennis date, and you had to drive your father up to the country. I never see you. I would have gone to the country with you."

"I know, but Barby went, and you know how you act with Barby. You act as if she's being terrible to Joe, but really, Rock, she can't sit around and mope just because Joe's in prison."

"I know it. It's just that she doesn't seem to care any more."

"She sees him whenever she can."

"Yeah." He knew that was true, and he knew you couldn't blame Barby if her feelings had changed, only he felt that if Kay and her mother had left her alone, she might still care for Joe—that was important to Joe. "Anyhow, it seems to me you're always with Kay lately. It's as if you care more for her than you do for me."

"Oh—it's different. If you really knew Kay, you'd understand, and I think it's unresaonable of you to act so small about her."

"Marth. Look at me."

She looked at him steadily. She loved these times when they could be together. She kept telling herself that he was a marvelous fighter even if Kay didn't think so—and some day he would be like Fonn Kelly and live in Kay's world and they could be together.

"Darling, you're not a baby any more."

"Well, I know that."

"Kay won't stay here forever. She's crazy about this place now, but it won't last. It matters too much to her where she lives. She ought to live in one place or else she ought to live in every place at once. She doesn't *live* here—or any place—the way things are now. She just *goes* all the time."

"But, Rock—"

"No, listen to me. She hears no one but herself. She sees people in a mass, never one by one, and if she ever truly saw the face of one person, she'd fall down in a faint."

"Now you're picking at her just because she's different from everyone else you know."

"I'm not picking at her. I'm telling you. And once she goes away from here, you'll be alone, and everything she's stood for will go with her. This town won't change because of her."

"I'm going with her, too."

"No."

"But, Rock, I told you all about it. I want to see things. Some day I'll see you fight at Madison Square Garden."

He said nothing.

"I thought you understood. Daddy thinks it's a good idea for me to travel."

"There's nothing anywhere that isn't here. It's okay to go places—after you've found your own place. Otherwise, it's stupid."

She bit her lower lip.

"Let's not talk about it now," he said, tightening his arm around her. Her body turned under his touch, and he held her lightly, kissing her. It was different for him now. He missed Mike, and when he thought about Joe, it made him sad. When he went to see Barby, it was as if he sat before her ghost. He wondered if Joe felt like that, too, or if, when he was with her, everything was the same. Now, holding Marth, he needed her and wanted her.

Kay knocked lightly and opened the door and saw them like that. "Very pretty. Very pretty indeed."

"Go away," he said. "Scram, Kay." He hadn't begun to say any of the things he wanted to say to Marth. What was it he wanted to say? Something about time going too fast and how the people looked that morning outside Woolworth's hugging their futile little bundles to them, shivering in the hot sun, their eyes blank, their tongues thick with useless words. What was there to say except they had to make everything right because this was their time. I'm trying to tell you that night is a black bird flying and day is a single golden moment dropping from sight, dying. So much that ought to be said—give us this day, stay with me here, arise my love, all sorts of truthful, beautiful things that went with loving her and wanting her to know them, too. But his mind kept them imprisoned. No one could ever say these things.

"Scram, Kay," he said lightly.

She flicked him softly on the cheek. Her red nails glittered, alive with redness. Everything she wore was singly alive, the green eye of her ring, the red buds of her nails, the butterflies glittering in her ears, the swish of her skirt, the flower-scent and mellowness of her.

"We're having cold supper in two minutes," she said.

"Oh—food." Marth sat up in his arms. "Kay, Rock doesn't like the idea of going away from here and being a rich, famous fighter."

"Probably just as well. You want to keep your neck, don't you, darling?"

He grinned. "Sure."

"He doesn't want me to go away, either."

"Naturally," Kay said. "He's in love with you and wants to keep you here forever."

"You have a nasty mind, Beautiful," he said. He pushed Marth from him and wiped his mouth on the back of his hand. "You want Marth, too. You want her because she's a good kid and you can live through her—so you'll have it all to do over again. You think she's like you. But she's not. Everyone's different."

Kay smiled. "You're a big baby. Come and eat something."

"Okay. But don't think I'll like it if you take Marth away. My old man says every place is the same only people've got different names for it. People together—that's all. This is where Marth belongs."

"Where do I belong?" She was looking toward the garden where her father walked with Mrs. Leroy. He looked heavier, slower, older. She linked her arms with Kay and Rocky. They walked toward the dining room.

"You belong to me," he said.

"Such talk," Kay said. She was getting everyone seated, talking about the color of the walls. "They make me feel like we're living under wonderful green water. Marth, be an angel and call your father and Maida." Everything here was hers, carefully planned, cleverly designed for her own purpose. Now, the conversation would go as she willed it to go, everyone turning toward her, her manner quiet and gay and friendly.

The Long Year

Rock sat in silence, scarcely eating. He listened to their talk, and it meant nothing to him, and he wondered how these people could spend so much time doing nothing. He felt shy and clumsy with them, and whatever he had to say seemed vulgar or stupid. They listened to him with a kind of shocked, incredulous expression as if they did not believe anyone like him could exist.

"Don't pout," Marth whispered.

"I'm not pouting," he said. "I know what Joe meant when he said he had a goddam bellyache. I've got one, too. I thought this was going to be a date like the ones we used to have—just us, alone."

Her face had a wise, clever look, he thought, and then she looked like Kay again, only younger, of course. She laughed softly and put her hand on his arm and turned toward him. She acted as if he'd get over this in time. "Be nice. Please be nice, Rock."

He leered at her. "How's this?"

"Eat a lot, Rock," Kay said. "You need it."

"Umm," he grunted.

"Rock's angry with me," Kay said. Her eyes laughed at him.

Everyone looked at him. He flushed. His round, boyish face, under his freckles and tan, seered hot with anger. His big, gentle hand tightened on his fork. A piece of cold ham skidded across his plate and clung to the tablecloth. Painfully, he picked it up with his fork and returned it to his plate. He could feel the blood in his head, roaring and swirling there. His ears felt as if they would snap off his head, and his short hair stiffened.

"You see," Kay laughed. "He thinks I'm a terrible woman of the world. A dangerous type, wallowing in wickedness."

The woman, Lili, laughed softly. "Not you, Kay! Oh, really, how precious!"

His food stuck in his throat. Marth giggled. He knew what Kay was doing to him. She was making him into a clown, a country bumpkin, a kid in knee pants, sweating and red in the face. She always watched to see if he pushed out his soup and used the right fork. Every chance she had, she showed him up with Marth. Maybe he wasn't rich and clever and full of city ways and city ideas, but he was as good as any of them.

"Yes," Kay continued, "I've asked Fonn Kelly here. Perhaps he and Rock can put on a match for us. I know Fonn would adore to do it. But, can you believe it, the suspicious boy believes I'm an evil woman with some terrible, hidden motives."

"I didn't say that," he said. His voice sounded thick and guttural.

"He was joking, Kay," Marth said. "He doesn't think that at all. Rock was just joking." She looked at him and waited for him to say something, to stop sitting there like a shamed schoolboy. Everyone at the table was caught in this pattern.

Hoyt cleared his throat. "Now, Kay, you let Rock be," he said.

"I wasn't joking," he said calmly. He looked at her, and he felt rude, mannerless, out of place. He should have known better than to come here. It was never any good. If he wanted to see Marth, he ought to see her in the old places and in the old ways, without Kay. He rose. His chair fell against the wall, and he clutched at it and put it in its place. "Excuse me," he muttered. He bolted through the French doors, across the garden, toward the river path. He walked very fast, and the air was cool against him, and he heard Marth running behind him. As soon as he gained the hill, he waited for her.

"All right. So, I was rude. But she had no business needling me like that. I know what she's trying to do. She wants—"

"Rock," Marth said. She stood away from him, breathing fast from running, and her voice was low, without anger. The stuff of her blouse and skirt was very cool and soft under his hand. "She was teasing you. I don't know why you're so touchy. You used to be all right with Kay. You seemed to like her. Now, everything she says to you, you take as an insult. She's really terribly fond of you and teases you for fun and I don't see why you can't act the way you are. You aren't like—like that."

He wet his lips. His forehead wrinkled, and he ran his hand slowly across his mouth. "I don't hate her or anything, but she gives you ideas, and she wants to break us up."

"She doesn't. Oh, Rock, I've always loved her even before she

The Long Year

came home and used to write letters from everywhere and send me things. You've got no right to change it now. Can't I love Kay and you, too? Why you want to make it so hard for me—I don't understand. You're not nice any more to Barby, either. And now Kay feels terrible because she teased you. Oh, really, Rock—"

He could see Kay in the garden. She came to the foot of the hill and called to him, "Rock, please come back, darling. You poor fellow."

"You see?" Marth said eagerly.

He opened his hands and closed them. He was sweating. He felt rooted to the earth. He wanted to stay out here where it was dark and cool and quiet, and he wanted Marth to stay with him.

"Come down, Rock," Kay said, laughing. "Is he all right, Marth?"

"Sure," Marth said. "He's okay." She put her arm through his, holding herself close to him. "Don't be mean. It just makes it harder, Rock."

"God, oh, God," he said.

"Come on," Kay said. "I'll let you beat me at tennis tomorrow."

They were going to laugh it off. But, it wasn't any joke. Kay just won again. She was too clever for him. He'd go down there and make an apology and everyone would think he was a lousy kid, big and clumsy, with no sense of humor. Then, what would he get out of it? He could sit around waiting for Marth, and after a while, he'd see less and less of her because all the time she'd be in that house crowded with people and she and Barby'd have all those little errands to do for Kay, for her father, letters to write, journeys to the city. Maybe if he sat very still and waited like the patient saint, he might win yet. He was not without hope. He moved toward Kay standing in the garden, her pale dress fluttering around her, her laughter coming low, sweet, young across the garden.

"I'll be good, Rock," she said.

"No," he said. "I shouldn't run off like that."

"It was my fault. Marth, it was really my fault, you know."

"No," he said. "I ought to get some sense." He walked between them, toward the house. Someone turned on the radio. "Saint Looie woman, with her di-a-mond rrrings . . ." He thought: Joe must've felt like this when he walked back there, to that place. Goddamit, why can't I figure things out for myself and act on them the way Kay does and then have them go the way I want them to go? What's the matter with me and with the rest of us, I mean, Joe and Mike, what's the matter? Even Mr. Wimmer's got troubles. Maybe she's right—I'm just a crazy small-town guy thinks he can be a fighter. I'm probably no good at all. End up in this town without a decent suit on my back, slap-happy, rummy, poor and full of old, dead dreams, a real dead-beat. He put his hand over his heart and felt it going strongly under his shirt. For a moment there, he hadn't felt very much alive, the way Joe said—really *being*. He hadn't felt it, lost it somewhere. But now he was alive, he could feel the beating again.

CHAPTER TWENTY-FIVE:

In the spring, Joe worked in the warden's gardens which sprawled along the cliff around the warden's stucco house. Below these, the river swamps stretched for over two miles to the river. All spring there was a thin blue mist there. Joe worked with Zack, a lifer. Whenever Barby could, she came along the river path and she and Joe sat behind the thick hedge talking. It was different, now. There was nothing to say after the first few minutes of hurried questions and answers. They kissed and tried to pretend there was nothing to worry them, and Barby told him that she was having fun—really, she wasn't moping. He believed her, but it saddened him, too, to know she could live pleasantly without him—or at least seem to live that way.

"But, you want me to have fun, don't you?"

"Yes. But I don't want you to forget me. Is that Bix Lawrence around your place?"

"No. He's at Kay's, though."

"Everyone's at Kay's. Does Rock go there?"

"Sometimes."

"But not often?"

"No. Not often."

"Why?"

"How should I know?"

"I wonder why he doesn't go there. He has a good reason, I'll bet."

Zack said the prison was better than most. He said they were safe. "Outside, no one's safe," Zack said. Joe didn't feel safe. He hated it, and he was constantly trying to find out what was going on in the town. He was afraid he would get like the others—so that he didn't care any more. He looked at the town and saw that the factory had a good steam up and the box cars moved in and out regularly. He saw it far away from him, unobtainable.

"Anyone ever get out of here?"

"Aw now, Joey. You'll get over talkin' like that."

"*Did* they, Zack?" It was true that even though Barby loved him, she was changing. It was natural. If he were out, they'd change together like everyone else, but he had to get out before she forgot that she loved him. It was natural she could forget with all the fine times she was having with Kay and Marth. He had to get out before it was too late.

"Guy got out but they caught him less'n five minutes," Zack said.

"You could do it, though." He watched the two box cars from the C. St. P. M. & O. move along the tracks, two men running beside them into the warehouse. He had a terrible itch when he was out in the open like this. It seemed like such an innocent, easy thing to slide over the cliff. "Could do it," he said softly.

"You hearin' violins," Zack said. "Don't blame you, though."

"I'm not kicking," Joe said in a tough voice.

"Sure, sure." He watched him, though, saw how he was after the girl left him, how he was when he waited for her. "You ever see God, Joe?"

"Naw."

"I saw him."

"Yer kiddin'."

"I saw Him plain as I see you now."

"In the daytime?"

"Sure. Like now."

Joe was serious. "How did He look?"

"Well—the first time, it was just like you'd think. Me and my ole daddy useta walk in cemeteries down East. We walked in any which kind of one, an' they're awful old. The damnedest things wrote on the tombstones, sad like songs and some of 'em nasty an' no respeck in 'em. This day we was walkin' there readin' about some young girl which had died in 1842. I remember the year an' everything—nice, neat lil place. Girl's name was Abbot—Abbot Conway.

The Long Year 267

Guess I was half in love with her myself with a nice name like that an' a nice lil grave. While we was there lookin' at this place, an ole man come along, see? He had a bushy beard an' real ole clothes but clean, clean as a white mouse. His beard was white an' silver an' his eyes was even silver an' he had a big, deep, slow, terrible voice."

"How come you know it was—it was Him, though?"

"Didn't know at first. This old man was real p'lite an' ast us questions an' we answered an' we stood aroun' talkin' like friends. Best lookin' old guy I ever seen. Then he shakes hands with us and walks off. I felt kinda funny, big inside, like I was a balloon growin' an' ready to bust enny minute. So I asks Paw who the hell it was, an' my ole daddy says it was God. He never lied to me. He was crazy kinda, used to write poems. Said it was his life's work, bein' a poet. He wrote stuff for papers like For Joe, For Harry or For My Beloved Wife. Course he didn't know Joe or Harry or enny beloved wife. But he had it printed in the paper an' then he clipped it out an' saved it. Made him feel real smart."

"Maybe it was God."

"Sure it was. I never forgot that old guy. Always useta think before I done somethin', not wantin' to hurt a real swell Joe like that one with the beard."

"When was the other time?"

Zack looked at the ground. "I seen him the day I killt that dame."

"Did he look the same?"

"He was a little boy."

"Aw, now, Zack—don't gimme—"

"Honest, Joe, he was a little boy standin' inside a wicker fence watchin' me do it, all the time lickin' on a big red-an'-white sucker. He watched all the time I was doin' it. It made me feel sick inside with him watchin' even though she wasn't worth gettin' sick over. A real little black-haired boy in a blue suit. Suit had a yella elephant on the front. I kept tellin' him to go away, but he never until the cops come. Then he went."

"Where?"

"Don't know. Wasn't any wicker fence, no boy with a sucker

when I come to, but I knew it was so. You believe me, don'tcha, Joe?"

"Sure. I believe you."

"Mostly the cops laughed at it so I never tole it to anyone again."

"It's yours to tell. I'm glad you told me."

Zack moistened his lips. "You fixin' to go, Joe?"

He nodded. It was high noon, shortly before the noon meal. He put his hoe against the wall and smoothed down his hair. Dust and loam was thick on his tan broadcloth jacket.

"I'll stall fer ya."

"You come, too."

"Naw—I wouldn't like it."

Joe saw it was no use. "Okay," he said. He slid down the embankment and hit the stone beneath the garden wall. He slid on his belly, breathing fast, working toward Mr. Wimmer's. Barby would come, he knew, that was part of the plan, and anything he said would be okay for her. That was the kind of girl she was. He was a kid again crawling through the muck, clinging to tufts, going under the hot sun like he was playing the old games. Only this was a big, deadly game, and he was spending all he had on it to get away from that stinking prison where he had been rotting. It was no place for even an animal—away from sun and air and people he knew and the town where he was born.

His progress along the swamp, through the hot beds of water, was an eternity of a rock, a leaf, a bush and then lying flat to hear the roar of his own breathing. He trampled the swamp violets. His uniform was covered with swamp muck. He was thinking that the guards could see the smallest movement from their towers, and to them his life was no more than the color of a stone, the width of a leaf, the depths of a bush. Then he saw the tree toad and the toad stared back at him with horizontal, blank pupils, his left leg flapping at his side. Joe touched him. He was dry and rough except for the smooth spot of his belly. The toad blinked. "Boys been throwing rocks," he said. He gently lifted the toad and put him

The Long Year

into his pocket. It did not move. He eased himself along slowly, being careful not to lie on the side where the toad was.

The guard who missed Joe in the garden was another of the Hickory boys. He shot into the air three times and sounded the alarm. The steel-barred gates closed over the railroad yard. The factory whistle blew. Kay walked from the office building into the main warehouse where the men had been loading a box car. She stood outside the paint shed.

"Joe Connaught's escaped from the prison. He may want to hide here or in the swamp." They looked at her and waited. They had almost forgotten about Joe. "The guards are searching for him now. I want men at every door around the factory and in the swamp."

They nodded, a soft murmur beginning among them. They stared at her retreating figure. Russian moved toward the door and stood there. Something was happening again around them, and they were a part of it. They took off their work gloves and ran outside. The sirens were still whining. Two big patrol cars went up and down the highway. The men in them were young and adventuresome and wore dark blue guard uniforms with gold buttons. They carried high-powered submachine guns and pistols, and they looked as if they had an easy time of it.

In one car, Tony Ruiz, a young man with reddish hair and a foxy face, kept singing, "Come away with me, Lucille, in my merry Oldsmobile." His voice was strong and rich, and he sang from his boyish heart. The other man was Phil Hickory, from the town. He sat with his gun across his knees, frowning.

"Stop it, Tony," he said.

"Well, gee, Phil, it's exciting."

"You make me sick."

"Get *him*, will you?" Tony laughed. They'd catch that fool kid, and he wanted to be there to see it.

"Kind of hope he makes it," Phil said.

"Hey! You want the kid loose?"

"Maybe I do."

"Nuts."

"Look, Tony—the kid might've had a reason. He's had a hell of a time. He never had a chance. Look at them down there in the swamp. He couldn't hide under a thistle."

"He's dangerous, though."

"Maybe."

"Sure, he's dangerous."

"Lotta guys outside are more dangerous. Don't worry, though. I know what I got to do." Suddenly he was bitter and wanted to get out of the car and let the kid get away. He remembered Joe when he was Lindy's age, and he didn't like the idea of shooting him.

"You beat the Dutch," Tony said. In a big, clear, manly voice he began to sing, "Come away with me, Lucille, in my merry Oldsmobile."

The sound went across the swamp, and the guards picked it up and hummed it as they made their slow way through the swamps holding to their guns. It was hot, and they began to sweat and get red in the face. They called to the factory men to help. At first it was exciting but then it became bothersome because nothing happened. They didn't think the kid could get far. They'd just as soon catch him now and end this mess. One by one, they went into the factory for a drink. They hung their uniform jackets on the stake cars inside the main warehouse. They went out bareheaded and in their shirtsleeves. After they reached the river, they turned around and looked back over the swamp.

The deputy warden, a pasty-faced young man, came down the river road in a black patrol car. He wore a light summer uniform and looked worried and kept his hand on his pistol which was carried in a new holster. "Go back, boys. Go black slow and easy," he said.

"How'd he get out?" Russian asked. "I thought you guys were so damned smart."

The deputy warden shrugged. "Hell," he said. He went over to talk to Kay.

The Long Year

"It was stupid," she said. "I'd never have let him work in the garden."

"We have our reasons. I don't blame the kid."

"You seem to hope he'll get away."

"I didn't say that, Ma'am."

"You do hope it, don't you?"

"Maybe."

She shook her head. "They'll get him."

He got into the patrol car. Some of the people grinned as they stood on the sidewalk. "He's not so smart," Velma Olds said. She rocked Robert in his buggy. The other two children played in the gravel drive. "That Joe's smart. The deputy warden's not so smart."

The deputy warden didn't feel smart. He had the driver stop when they reached the cliff. He spoke to Tony Ruiz and Phil Hickory. "Try the farmhouses on the swamp road," he said.

Howard stood outside Macbeth's store. Macbeth sat barefooted, his chair leaning against the hot building. Inside, Johnnie Evans was hastily trying to find a cooler suit. "Where's the cool stuff, Macbeth?"

"Use your eyes, Boy. If you hadn't spent the best years of your life buyin' in the city, you'd know how to find things. You got an important date tonight?"

"Yeah," Johnnie said. He was taking his secretary to dinner. His secretary was pretty and sharp and merry. It was important, all right.

"He'll find one," Howard said. He jingled some loose coins in his pocket. "Reckon he's in the swamp, Mr. Macbeth?"

"No. Don't think he's in the swamp, Mr. Jackson."

"No, sir," Howard said softly.

Macbeth narrowed his eyes. "Just about everyone's out huntin' him with a stick or dingbat or somethin'."

"Guess so." Howard kept jingling the money in his pocket.

Marth came up the street. "He's not in the swamp," she said. "Gee, I hope he gets away, and maybe he and Barby—"

"He won't," Macbeth said.

"Everyone's lookin' fer him," Howard said.

"You going, too?"

"Nope. Not me."

"Me, neither," Macbeth said.

Marth nodded. "It's terrible, isn't it? I wish Rock was here."

"Rock's gone to Sandstone to fight tonight. Didn't he tell you?"

"I didn't see him," she said. "He never tells me. He never tells me anything, Macbeth."

"Un-hunh. Well, this is the first time I stayed home. Thought he might as well get used to goin' by himself."

"Wish they'd stop looking for Joe."

Howard said, "Kid was born in this town and grew up here and got hisself into a bad jam. Maybe lots of folks helped him one way or 'nother. It's not fer me to say, but I don't go huntin' down a pore boy from my own town—like he's a bad animul or terrible, killin' man."

"That's right," Macbeth said.

Marth blew her nose. Her handkerchief still smelled faintly of new perfume, Lovely Despair. She sniffed. Lovely Despair. Some of the people were crowding down toward the swamp. The guards would not let them into the swamp except the few whom they knew well. Two cops went whizzing down the street on motorcycles.

Johnnie Evans came out of the store wearing a new white linen suit. "Not bad, Macbeth."

"Umph." He looked out of his narrow, calculating eyes. "You're a lawyer, Boy. Seems to me you could learn a lot just going around now and listening and looking at people's faces. Look at them, though. They're scared he'll get away, scared they won't see all of it. They want to see everything."

Johnnie looked at the people going by. They were very quiet, running softly in their thin dresses, pale in the summer light, haunted in their faces. The women were crying or laughing quietly or waiting with their arms crossed over their breasts. There were few men in the streets. Most of them were around the swamp

The Long Year 273

or in it or along the highway. The women wanted to go away, but they could not. Some of them talked quietly. There was nothing for the women to do in the town but talk a little and go home and fry fish or cut up bacon to make it go around, call the children off the streets. The children didn't know what it was all about, but they thought it was fun, like a parade.

One child stood with his hand over his heart. "I'm beating," he said. "I'm really beating." Then he laughed, half-frightened, half-savage.

But no one knew where Joe was.

"I—I wonder," Marth said. "I think I'll go down to the office and see if Barby's there."

Mr. Wimmer's old dog, Jawrge, came up the sidewalk, working his way deftly among the people, seeming to know exactly where he was going.

"Look at that old dog, now," Howard said. "Look at him." He spoke softly, blinking his eyes.

"Yeah," Marth said. She went up the street following the old dog. Macbeth called something to her, but she didn't wait to hear it. The funny old dog—the funny old dog knows where Joe is . . .

Joe wore a faded denim shirt of Mr. Wimmer's. He sat in the kitchen eating a cheese sandwich, talking. "I don't know what I'll do. I'll go West, I guess. Barby's been drawing out some money, and we can do it."

"She going with you?"

"Sure." He would not look at Mr. Wimmer. He twisted the cigarette between his thumb and forefinger—a cigarette is such a little thing, enough to drive a man nuts if he sits in a cell every day hanging on to it like it's driftwood. "It's what she wants, too. Lissen, Gene, naturally I can't take Lindy, so will you look out for him now and then? He gets pushed around. No one cares but me."

"All right," he said. Outside, the old dog scratched on the door. Mr. Wimmer let him in, and he lay down, panting, looking at Joe out of sad, brown eyes. "Any ideas about getting a job out West, Joe?"

"There's no work. Did Smut Olds get a job? All I want is to get away and have something of my own."

"I see."

Joe hit the table with his open palm. "Don't try to discourage me, Gene."

"No," Mr. Wimmer said. He put his accordion under the table. "You do whatever you must do, Joe."

Joe stood near the window. He saw the big red car drive up to the gate. Barby got out, running across the yard, her black hair flying about her small, excited face. "It's her," he said. "Marth brought her."

Mr. Wimmer opened the door. His face was tender and sad. He went out to help Marth with the car. Barby slipped past him and into Joe's arms. She was still breathing hard from running like that, and he saw at a glance that she was pale and thin. He'd never let her go again, she was his life. Something inside him that had spoken all those times in the cell now said, "What are you looking for, Boy? A dream of love? A rock, a pebble, a star in the sky, a blade of grass, a seashell?"

"Oh, Barbs," he said. Tears came into his eyes. He was young again in the world. He was not dead, nor full of rotten thought. He was a boy in the world. "Hello, Blue-eyes."

"Hello—hello, Joe."

"It's all right," he soothed. "Everything okay." He looked quickly through the window and saw Mr. Wimmer and Marth standing beside the car which was parked near the silo. Then, they went into the barn and sat near the door, straddling some empty crates.

"I love you so," she said and held tight to his shirt so that her knuckles were white.

"You look wonderful, Barbs, really swell."

She smiled and moved away from him, laughing her low, gay laugh. She was his old Barby. "Will they come here?"

"Yes." He kissed her. "Don't worry." He wanted to believe that

The Long Year

with Barby here nothing could go wrong. "Wimmer's our friend. He won't say anything. Let me look at you, Barbs."

"Oh, Joe!" Everything was working out for her. If he hadn't done this now, it might have been too late because she had to have him with her to remember how she felt about him. When he was away all the time, she forgot, and she had to fill her time with parties and going around with Kay and Marth so that it wouldn't hurt quite so much. But now he was here.

"Honey," he said, "let's not talk. Let's not say anything."

"I know."

"Honey. Blue-eyes." She came against him, and he smiled and caressed her, and he saw her under a golden light. All the world stood still in time and light. He felt himself turning away from whatever had once been. "Gee, Barbs . . . Gee, honey . . ."

The dusty patrol car came down the road. Phil Hickory got out and crossed the yard, swinging his gun as he walked. He looked at the well, the windmill, the house and the barn. He bent over the car door and examined it carefully.

"Hello, Phil."

"Hello, Mr. Wimmer." He waved to Tony in the patrol car. "I'll take a good look." Tony stuck his head out the window and took off his sun glasses to peer around the yard. "Okay." He sat back in the car singing in his carefree, bar-room tenor.

"What are you doing up here, Marth?"

"I came to tell Mr. Wimmer about Joe."

"That so?"

Mr. Wimmer sat on the crate mixing paint with a long wood slat. "What do you think of my place, Phil?"

"It's beginning to look swell, only you'll make a hell of a farmer. Where's Jawrge?"

"In the house somewhere."

"Find Joe yet?" Marth asked.

"I wouldn't be here if we did."

"I only asked."

"I'm sorry. I don't like things like this. I'm coming down here some evening, Mr. Wimmer, and borrow those books you offered me."

"Any time, Phil."

Tony called to him, "Step on it, Sonny Boy."

Phil said, "Don't suppose you've seen Joe around, Mr. Wimmer?"

Mr. Wimmer looked at him. "I'll tell you, Phil. I've been painting the silo all day. Almost anyone could've come through here."

"Yeah," he said. "I'll take a look."

Marth held tight to the barn door watching him open the kitchen door and stand there a moment and then close it. He walked around the house, lifted the well cover and looked down the well. He looked through the tall grasses around the barn and then he went into the barn and peered into the stalls and kicked at the hay.

"Want any help?" Mr. Wimmer asked.

He shook his head. "Thanks. Anyhow, a regular patrol will go through here all the time. Probably get him."

"I see," Mr. Wimmer said, meeting his eyes.

"Okay," Phil said and went back to the car. "Nothing here," he said.

"Wimmer'd report it anyhow. You should've looked in the house."

"I looked. There wasn't anything to see."

"Damned smart kid to hide this long."

Phil grunted. He wasn't sure the kid was not in the house, but when he stood at the kitchen door, he could not bring himself to go into the house even if it meant finding the kid, and now if anything went wrong and the kid was caught around Wimmer's place, it would go bad for him—still, Mr. Wimmer would have said something. Anyhow, he couldn't go into the house and face the kid if he was there. The car turned down the road among the green summer trees. The kid didn't have much of a chance. Still—still, he had done it now.

Barby stood before the mirror in the kitchen combing her hair. When she raised her arms like that, it made him think of Lindy

The Long Year

in the mornings standing before the washbasin in the kitchen and brushing his hair in the front. There was something innocent and defenseless about both of them. They made him want to do big things to keep them the way they were. Barby hummed under her breath, holding the bobby pins in her mouth. She looked at him in the mirror and laughed.

"You devil," she said.

"Shut up."

"You know, I think we'll have a fine time."

"Good God, how you talk. If your mother heard you—"

"I didn't mean that. I meant we have five hundred dollars, and we can go West and pick a new name and make new friends."

"What name?" He had to smile. It was a picnic for her, but his mind had begun to work again. If he was going to be afraid he might as well quit now because he'd be sure to make a mess of it, and he couldn't do that with Barby on his hands. But she was his good luck. "What name, Blue-eyes?"

"Oh—something American. Brewster or Hale or Hopkins."

"You pick it like it's a new dress."

She bent over him, rubbing her cheek against his hair. "I love you, Joe."

He reached for her. "Uh-hunh. Look out the window."

"Mr. Wimmer's painting the silo. Marth's standing by the car. No one in the road."

"We can't do anything until it gets dark." He opened the kitchen door.

"Phil saw you, I think," Marth said, coming in.

"Phil Hickory," Joe said.

They sat around the kitchen table. Mr. Wimmer opened some cokes. "I don't think you should go away like this, Joe."

Joe was startled. "Come out of it."

"You heard me."

"I thought you were on my side, Gene."

"I am."

"We're going West," Barby said.

"It's a big dream," Mr. Wimmer said.

"Now, look here—"

"I'm not going to inform on you," Mr. Wimmer said calmly, looking at Joe in a friendly manner. Joe grew red and angry.

"Please, don't talk about it," Barby said. "Let's go." She looked to Marth for help, but Marth didn't know what to say. Mr. Wimmer was too calm and sure. She shook her head. Barby twisted at her skirt. "I want to go, Joe."

"Sweets—just a minute now."

"You can go away," Mr. Wimmer said. "I guess a man can go wherever he wants to, it's his affair. Only when you think of Johnnie Evans working himself thin to get you off easy—he believed in you—and now you want to throw it over."

"Yeah," Joe said softly.

"I don't blame you for not wanting to listen to me. Joe, tell me seriously now—was there something in class last year I didn't make clear to you?"

"No," Joe said thickly. "There wasn't anything."

"Oh, stop talking," Barby said.

Joe put his arm around her. Her eyes were deep, troubled. She was remembering all the times she had with Kay and Marth in the city, Millner's shop, dancing in the low-lighted casino at the Beldon. It was safe and beautiful, the way Kay said it was, the kind of thing a girl her age should have. She loved Joe, and she could give it all up if she and Joe could have a life of their own—otherwise, she wanted to go back to it, to playing tennis with Bix Lawrence, to being with Kay and Marth.

Joe suddenly began to laugh, holding her to him. "Honest to God—it's a big joke. I got out of there and now you want me to go back. I got to figure out a way to get back there without getting shot to bits. It's crazy—go back and pitch for the Alley Cats and work in the twine factory and maybe go to night school. All the time I'll know I could've been out in Idaho or Oregon if I hadn't listened too long."

He knew he couldn't bear to be running all the time, living in

The Long Year 279

cheap flop houses, hiding out with Barby. And he knew with deadly certainty that now it was over forever for him and Barby and that she sensed this. He could not bear to look at her. He put his arms around her and kissed her mouth. "Gee, Barbs—it's terrible without you."

"No, Joe. Let's go. Let's try to get away. We can do it—together."

He shook his head.

Barby turned on Mr. Wimmer. "I despise you utterly, Gene Wimmer."

Mr. Wimmer said, "When it gets dark, Marth can drive you around the swamp road to the main entrance. That way, they can't get a shot at you."

Barby said, "It's not fair. I thought we'd settled it, Joe. I mean about the money and the new names and the rest. You said it was settled."

"It is."

"No. You've changed everything."

"It won't have to change anything between us," he said. But these were small, lost words of hope. Before this, he could take it, but now, because of her, he was afraid. She could not look at him. She sat there taking deep breaths to keep from crying.

The patrol cars went up and down the road at regular intervals. They had powerful lights and kept turning these into the trees and across the land. In the darkness, Marth drove close to the house. Joe, wearing his uniform, crept into the back of the car and lay on the floor. Barby sat in front with Marth, half turned, shivering in the damp swamp air.

"You'll be okay, Joe," Mr. Wimmer said.

"I feel terrible."

Marth swung the car onto the swamp road. They drove in silence until they reached the patrol car parked between the swamp and the highway. The driver turned the light on them and then turned it away, whistling softly through his teeth. "Go ahead, beautifuls," he said. "Hi, there, Barbs."

"Hi, Tony," she said.

"You all right, Joe?" Marth asked.

"I'm fine. Only I feel silly down here. Barbs?"

"What?"

"Don't be sore."

"I'm not. I just hate all of this."

"I hate it, too. It had to be this way, I guess." He raised himself a little. "You ought to love someone else, darling. Love some nice easy guy who won't bring you a mess of trouble."

"You don't choose like that," she said.

"Jesus," he said. "I want to get mad about all this, but there's no one to blame but myself."

Marth was trembling. She wished Rock was driving—or Kay—someone who could do things right. "We're almost there," she said. She could see the guards walking near the prison entrance. Barby turned a little. Joe reached up and she bent her head, and he kissed her gently. "Don't forget anything," he said. He lay on the floor with his eyes closed.

In this minute that was left to him, he wanted to cry because here in his youth, lying on the floor of a car, he was going back to prison. The rest of his grief was that now he knew it was surely over between Barby and him. "Barbs, I want you to promise me something. Promise me you'll go away where it's sunny and nice and you can have fun."

"I was thinking—"

"Listen. Promise me. Do that for me."

"Yes," she said. "I've been thinking about it."

He thought she would argue with him. Even though he talked this way, he still wanted to think of her near him in the town. "Okay," he said.

Marth slowed the car. "Go now," she said as the two guards turned at the entrance and began to walk toward the other end of the yard. "Go now, Joe."

Joe kicked open the door. One of the guards saw him and ran with his gun lowered, calling to him. Joe seemed to turn, hesitate, and run from the bright light into the darkness. He heard Barby

The Long Year

call to him. There was no sound after that except the magnified beating of his heart. He faced them when they caught him in the floodlight. A man called to him. He felt the small, sharp prick of the bullet in his back as he fell. The stickiness was on his hands —like that dream he had of his blood flowing around him. He waited for God to come to him in the image of a child with a peppermint sucker, in the guise of a beloved old man. God did not come so easily.

The sky was seven stars wide.

The earth was a deep bowl of red wine.

"I forgot the toad," he said in a slow voice. He saw the green toad clearly in that instant lying dead wherever he had dropped it from his pocket. He saw the horizontal pupils of the toad's golden eyes. He saw the greenness, the amber, the seven stars broadcast like seeds across a night sky. In this way he died and saw himself dying as if he stood above himself looking down without sadness.

CHAPTER TWENTY-SIX:

Now THE house was finished, and the five old oak trees shaded the lawn around it. Beyond them was a rock garden and a flat cleared for tennis. The house itself was white with green shutters. When the sun struck it a certain way, it was so white it hurt to look at it. Marth said it still smelled like moss and old wood, but Kay said she was foolish. "It's an idea you have," she said.

"Rock smells it, too."

"Oh, really, darling," Kay laughed.

They went to the city several times a week. There was always a clutter of boxes and little hats and sharkskin dresses and lamp shades in Kay's bedroom or on the porch facing the river. Usually they sat in the bedroom and opened boxes. There were blocked linen dresses and black sheers for evening and perfumes in bottles with crusted gold stoppers. Underneath everything was a strong, twisting current of a promise of better things to come. Teresita loved all of it. Despite Howard's objections, she had walked out on Mrs. Leroy, and even Barby's half-hearted pleas would not budge her.

At first, Barby could not believe Joe was dead even though she had seen it happen. She mouthed the words, "Joe's dead now," in her room at night, she said them aloud as she walked in Kay's garden or swam in the river near Kay's wharf. The words did not make a difference. She thought that Kay would understand because of Robert Richter's death, but Kay hardly remembered that. "You'll get over it," she said. "We can get over everything." Kay was right, of course, and after all, Joe had wanted her to have a good time. It was something ugly that had happened to her, and if Joe were alive and free, she would love him just the same. But he wasn't alive and he hadn't wanted to be free, really, or he would never have gone back there.

The Long Year

Her face was very thin and small. She wore too much lipstick, and she had begun to wear some kind of mascara that made her look drunk with grief or drunk from some inner gnawing fever to keep going. She said, "I'm famished—but starved, really," yet when there was food before her, she picked at it, talking all the time and seldom eating.

After all the packages were opened, they'd go downstairs and sit on the porch and Kay would lie back in the wicker-and-chintz lounge, smoking in a slow, lazy fashion watching Marth and Barby through half-closed eyes. She smoked with a red cigarette holder and wore red sandals. She had been playing tennis in the mornings with Tony Ruiz from the prison. Now, when she met Johnnie Evans on the streets, he tried to talk to her, but she smiled and left him standing there. She was very happy. The house was as she wanted it to be. The factory was going better and better each day.

Sometimes Barby would mention Joe. "I knew I'd never see him again. I knew it down there in Mr. Wimmer's kitchen."

Marth said, "There's something going on in this town. There's some kind of war, like Mr. Wimmer says."

Barby was not listening. "I can't sit here forever. I guess—I guess maybe Joe and I didn't have anything special. I mean, I always thought it was something no one else had, but it wasn't. I was pretty much of a kid."

"I tried to tell you that, darling," Kay said.

"I don't think Joe felt like that," Marth said. "I think he knew it was over, but I think it was always a big thing with him."

"That's because Rock says that. You always believe everything Rock says." Her face looked old and bitter. "You never liked Joe."

"I liked him," Marth said.

"You always thought it was terrible I cared for him."

"Did I?"

"Don't you remember, for heaven's sake?"

"No. I can't seem to remember that."

"Well, Joe wouldn't want me to carry on about it," she said. She bit her lip. "Listen, Marth, there just wasn't any more feeling left in me when Joe decided not to go away. I think it all died then."

"I don't know," Marth said. "I don't know about things like that."

"Oh, darling," Kay said, "you're much too gloomy. I can't be gloomy on days like this. I'm going to have a wonderful house-party this summer, and afterwards, in the Fall, we'll all go away—to Cuba, perhaps."

Barby sighed. She kicked off her shoes and wiggled her toes. "Cuba," she said.

"Then we can forget the town and its darkness," Kay said.

"It *is* dark," Marth said.

"Black, utterly black," Barby said. "No one does anything."

"Yes," Marth said. She had never thought of going to such a place, speaking a new language, living away from America.

"What are you thinking, Marth?"

"I—I don't know, Kay. Would we stay in Cuba a long time?"

"Until we became bored," Kay said.

"You mean—just keep on going as long as we wanted?"

"Why not?"

"That's wonderful," Barby said. "We'd never know where we'd go next."

"I don't know—" Marth said.

"Honestly, Marth," Barby sputtered, "that's all you say these days—you don't know, you don't know—if you and Rock would just have it out instead of having it like this. You don't know, you don't know!"

"Well, I don't," she said.

Kay laughed. "We'll see," she said. "All of a sudden you *will* know, Marth."

Rock sat on the front porch smoking. He seldom smoked because he did not really like it, but now he felt the need of doing some-

The Long Year

thing with his hands. Marth sat on the porch swing. Inside the house, her father was listening to the radio. Every few minutes she would give a hard push and then let the swing die down.

"Cuba," he said.

"Havana, Cuba."

"I guess that's as good a place as any to start wandering."

"You aren't busting with joy over it."

His kind, boyish face was bewildered and little lines of bewilderment came between his small, quick eyes. "Maybe I'm jealous. Perhaps I'd like to go to Cuba, too." Down the street, a few children were rolling old tires. When they fell, the children laughed and picked them up and rolled them again. He kept moving his toe over the pattern of the grass rug. Little bugs buzzed at the screen and around the patches of light that came from inside the house. She wore a red-and-white cotton dress, very tight at top and full and loose so that it moved full and loose when she walked, and now, sitting on the swing, she held herself very still, like one of those little, glossy figures people kept on the end tables or on their mantels.

She moved her head slightly. "Say it," she said.

"No. Only it seems like an awful waste of time."

"You think Cuba'd be a waste of time for me." She gave the swing a push. It made a squeaking noise. Someone's radio blew loud, hot, red strains up and down the quiet street.

"Not for Barby and not for Kay, but they don't care about this town. They got different ideas. They think my old man's crazy and they don't like the people here and they don't think much of Mr. Wimmer, but you do, Marth. And so Cuba's wrong for you, and I think any place is wrong when we're not together."

"No," she said. "You just want your own way." She bit her lips. She hated to talk to him like this because it made her feel dirty and afterwards she always wanted to cry. He was calm and gentle and everyone loved him, so that maybe he was right. He could be right and she could be wrong and Kay and Barby could be wrong. "But, Rock, I don't want to stay here forever."

"Don't you want to stay with me?" His voice was low, and the words did not come easily.

"Yes. Sure, but—"

"Maybe I've been wrong all along." He would not look at her now, sitting there with the ribbon in her hair, all calm, clean, quiet, still soft—he was not going to look at her. "I don't belong with Kay and her crowd. My food doesn't sit right when I eat up there, and I never get any other chance to see you any more. I need someone who'll like this town and let me live here the way my old man does. I want to matter here the way Gene Wimmer matters. I'll find out what I can do here some time—maybe work in the factory or make something out of the store or even find a business of my own. But, you would have to be happy here and not make me feel like a big fool all the time, or else—"

"It's just that I want to see things. If I go away, it won't make any difference with us, will it?"

"Everything makes a difference."

"I mean—you'll still be here, won't you?"

"You want your cake, and you want to eat it, too. I'll be here, but it might be too late then. I keep thinking of Mike and Joe." He rubbed his hand slowly over his short hair. "And you know, they never had a chance to do anything for themselves, and so I really ought to. Do something for myself, I mean."

"You can do anything," she said. She smoothed her dress over her bare knees. She wanted him to sit on the swing with her the way he usually did.

"I wasn't thinking of fighting. I was thinking of something else."

"But you like to fight."

"I haven't decided about that, yet." He rose and stretched and touched the ceiling. "Guess I'll go down and run a while."

"Want me to come?"

"No. It's late."

"But I can go even if it's late."

"No. Not tonight."

The Long Year

She moved toward him. "Rock, I'm sorry if I acted terrible to you."

"You got a right to go to Cuba if you want. You don't have to make excuses for that."

"I'm not making excuses."

"Okay."

"All right!" she said. She went inside and slammed the door. When he was like this, it frightened her that he would go away and she might never see him again. It wasn't fair to make her choose like this. There was no reason why, if you were born in an ugly time, you had to lead an ugly life.

"You all right, dear?" her father asked. He looked up from his newspaper.

"Yes," she said. "Nothing's wrong, Daddy."

In the late afternoon, Marth went down to the office. She stopped to talk to Mary Connaught about Kay's house and the people there. Afterward, she tapped on her father's door. He looked up from his desk and called to her to come in. She sat on the corner of his desk. "C'mon home, Daddy," she said. "You look hot and tired."

"Guess so," he said. "What's doing up to Kay's?"

"Nothing," she said. "Some people are coming tomorrow."

"You look tired, Baby."

"No."

"Something the matter? Need some money?"

"No, Daddy," she said. She felt like crying. He always wanted to give her something, do something for her, and there was no place where they truly met, where she could tell him how it was with her. Even though she loved him, there was no way to tell him.

"You know, you can tell me if there's something the matter."

"I know, Daddy."

"So, if you want to tell me anything, I guess I'll understand it."

"I don't know what to tell you," she said.

"All right, Baby."

They walked slowly up the hill toward their house. From the swamp road, she could see the house plainly, white and red brick and the patch of green lawn. She could see Howard out there in his white coat moving the sprinklers.

"You and Rock have a fight?"

She was staring at their house, at Howard moving on the lawn. "What—what, Daddy?"

"You have a fight with Rock?"

"No."

He smiled broadly. "*He* have a fight with you?"

"I don't know, Daddy. It's just that he doesn't want the same things I do. And now, he's busy all the time."

"Maybe you said something—you often do, you know." He was concerned about this. He had never understood Mike and now he thought he ought to try to understand Marth and what she wanted to do. He wanted her to be young and happy, to go away to school or to travel, but he didn't want to force anything. It seemed strange to be the father of a grown daughter. He always felt like a boy—young Hoyt Hasswell, going into his office, trying to run a big factory, living in the town. He couldn't manage to feel like anything but a boy.

"Oh, Daddy," she said, "I don't know what to do. I want to go with Kay. And then, Macbeth says it's the same no matter where you go. Barby's going with Kay, and it seems right for her, but somehow, I just don't seem to feel the way other girls do—"

"Oh, now, maybe you do."

They turned down the street. She held on to his hand, walking close to him. She wished he wouldn't go down to the office. It was like playing a joke on himself, sitting at the desk, reading the *Saturday Evening Post*. What did he find there? Maybe a moment now and then for himself, living in the same routine he had always known—nothing more for him.

They saw Olds coming down the street wheeling the buggy, his shabby shirt hanging out of his trousers, his head bent. They could

The Long Year

hear the soothing, crooning sounds he made over the baby. The buggy had a squeak. The sun was dying in the west. Olds was tired, old before his time, caught for a moment in the wonder of himself going on and on forever in this child and afterwards in the child of this child.

"Hello, Olds," Hoyt said. "Taking the baby for an airing?"

"Yes," Olds said. "Take a look at him. Met Russian. He says the baby's got muscles already."

"What's his name?" Marth asked.

"Robert—Robert William Olds."

Hoyt touched the child's cheek. He opened his eyes, stared, saw something delightful. He sighed and closed his eyes. "He acts like an old geezer," Hoyt said.

"Almost seven months," Olds said.

"He won't see what we've seen, hey, Olds?"

"No. Guess not."

"Remember the war, Olds?"

They looked at each other in silence. There was nothing to say. They remembered it, and they wanted to forget it. "Yuh," Olds said.

"Tough," Hoyt said. "Every time I go to the Legion convention, I try to remember it. It seems crazy then."

"Were you at the Marne, too, Mr. Olds?" Marth asked.

"Sure. I was there. I was everywhere to the end of it." He looked at the baby. "Got to get him home, now."

"Heard from Smut?" Hoyt asked.

"Heard last week."

"Is he coming home?"

"Guess so," he said.

"You tell him to come to see me," Hoyt said. "We can't have a fine boy like Smut going off like this."

"I'll tell him," Olds said.

Marth watched him wheeling the buggy. "I didn't know Olds was there—at the Marne," she said. "I didn't know he was with you, Daddy."

"He wasn't with *me*, exactly. Everyone seemed to be with everyone else."

"I see."

"Now about you and Rocky—"

"Please, Daddy—I guess I don't want to talk about it."

"All right, Baby," he said.

"It isn't that I *wouldn't* talk to you about it, Daddy—it's only that I'm all mixed up. I used to think this town was—different. I guess I never took a look at it. That's what Rock says. He wants me to know things, and he always tries to tell me about everything. But the factory used to be open and everyone seemed happy enough. I don't know what happened."

"This is a good town," he said. "You mustn't think too badly of us because—"

"Oh, I don't," she said. "I understand how it isn't a pink dream. But Rock says I want everything to be a pink dream."

"Maybe you and Rock have grown apart."

"No—oh, no."

"What does he want to do?"

"He doesn't know. He just says he isn't going to work here in the factory and he wants to fight for a while and then do something else. He doesn't want to be a great fighter, he just wants to do it for fun. But Kay says he probably wants to be a very famous fighter only he doesn't know it. But then, she says he can't be very good—big-time, you know—not like Fonn Kelly."

"Well, a fighter's life is precarious."

"Yes," she sighed. "It's all so mixed up."

They turned into their own walk. Well, he'd eat a good supper and then go to Maida's and sit on the front porch and listen to the radio. The day had suddenly grown too big for him—Marth and this business about Rocky and then meeting Olds like that. He remembered when they came back on the boat—Olds, the Hickory boys, Russian Peterson, some of the others. They were going to do big things in the town. Have swell times together. Never lose what they had together. Russian had saved Tom Hilton's life over

The Long Year

there, they wouldn't forget that either. He was going to give them good jobs. The world was green, they sang about it over bathtub gin. They cried over their dead buddies. The thing seemed like a great adventure, then, and they all felt unbelievably young and strong. What had happened? Look at them now, look at the town and the factory. And then there was Kay. He never understood her, and something was going on in her head. She seemed to touch everything and everyone. He shrugged. Something was always going on—around him, under the earth, in the darkness of night, in people's minds. There was no way of solving it.

"I'm hungry," he said. "Come inside, Marth, and eat a good dinner. You'll feel better."

"I'm not hungry," she said. "I'll have some milk or something."

"Tell me about the people Kay's having. It must be fun up there."

"Oh, it is—" She told him about LeGrand and Fonn Kelly and the others. But while he listened, he felt that she looked tired and unhappy underneath her air of delight. He didn't want a daughter of his growing up like that. "Give us a smile," he said. "Give us a big smile."

He walked along the path toward Kay's house swinging his bathing trunks. The thing was, he reflected, that he had damned near loused up that fight with Jaris. It was nothing big, of course, but it could grow bigger and bigger, and there was no reason for leaving himself wide open like that. If Jaris had been quicker and keener, no telling how it might have gone. Afterwards, he had a kind of superstition about it and thought that he might as well be as superstitious as the rest of them. Maybe it was because the old man hadn't been there sticking his red beak into it and giving him what-for every time he went into a new round. And then he hadn't maneuvered it properly to be near his own corner right before the bell to give himself those extra seconds of rest and make Jaris walk all the way to his own corner. It was a fuddled business. He hadn't tuned to it properly.

It wasn't because the old man hadn't been there. It was because his head wasn't clear. You had to be tight inside yourself, away from everything and everyone. Going down on the bus, he kept thinking about Marth and how he seemed like a terrible lout to her and to Kay, and there wasn't anything to fight against. The thing was, too, when he marked Kay down for an opponent, there was nothing to measure except a cool manner and some lush words and a kind of look, but he didn't know how her mind worked or what she wanted except that she wanted Marth and was going to have her because she was lonely and could woo her in ways which he couldn't contest. It was dumb to hang around all the time looking like someone with a bellyache, just to hang around and wait, and he never got to see Marth alone, anyhow. It wasn't like the other summers, and now it was more serious for him, too, because he needed her. He wasn't a kid any more, and he wanted her, and maybe he was getting soft in the head harping on all the luxuries like staying here and having Marth, but it mattered to him all the time. His stomach was all twisted up, and he was having bowel trouble, and he didn't feel right lately. He would catch himself thinking like how about doing it this way or how about doing it like that when, before this, there was always only one way.

He walked more slowly across the garden, his long-legged, easy walk, swinging his trunks. His arms and face were freckled, and his striped jersey pulled tight across his chest. He wore a pair of clean white ducks. He was always careful to wear everything clean and the best he had when he went to Kay's. His nose was red and sore from being on the river so much, and his short, reddish-brown hair had bleached over his brow. This gave him a grave, comical air of a child who never knows quite what to say but always looks guilty. He could see Kay sitting in the small bar. She wore pale blue shorts and a red bandana. She was dictating letters to Mary Connaught, and as she dictated them, she moved her hands and changed her voice so that she acted out what she was saying. She looked up and, seeing him, smiled and called to him, "Come in, Rock."

"Hello," he said. He stood outside the door, swinging his trunks

The Long Year

against the house. "I thought Marth might be here and we could have a swim."

"No," she said. "Is Marth around, Mary?"

Mary shook her head, looking at him all the while. "I think she went off with Barby and those boys from the city."

"Oh," he said.

"Come in, come in," Kay said.

He shook his head. "You're busy."

"No. Really I'm not. We've just finished."

Mary closed her notebook. "I'll type these up, Miss Hasswell."

"Yes—please," Kay said.

He looked at Mary again. She smiled. "Marth said she'd be back soon."

"I'll wait," he said.

"Do you want a drink?" Kay asked when Mary went out.

"No."

"No *thanks*, darling."

"No, thank you," he said.

She tapped her cigarette on an inlaid box. "Mary Connaught's attractive, don't you think?"

"What?" He sat in the yellow chair and pulled his slacks up and sat carefully so that he did not relax or feel drowsy. He never wanted to let go of himself when he was with her and in a way it was like a tennis game, putting the ball back and forth, low or high. All the time, it was fast, and he waited for it, and then when he missed, he could tell that he had missed.

"I said, Mary Connaught's—"

"Sure. Yes, she is," he said. He let his hands rest on the arms of the leather chair, and it was cool, smooth to his touch, everything cool and smooth, soft as cream in your mouth, cool on the tongue, you were wrapped in it. Mr. Wimmer said, We are betrayed by too much ease. This was so here, in this place. "All the Connaughts are good-looking. Wilma Connaught was the best-looking girl ever came out of this town, had nice long legs and a swell face. She looked a little bit like an Indian. Everyone says King Connaught's got Sioux blood. Joe looked that way, too. Mary's a good kid, best of the lot."

"She adores you, you know. But then everyone here in town adores you. I suppose you're quite used to it."

"No," he said, bewildered. "I—why, Mary's just a kid, and—"

"She's older than Marth."

"Is she?"

"Yes. How old are you, Rock?"

"I'm nineteen."

She sighed. "It's wonderful to be nineteen. You can hold the whole world in your hand."

This surprised him. He thought she held the world, all of it that she wanted. "You've got it in your hand," he said.

She shook her head. When she did that, he could see the way her skin was under her chin and in the hollow of her throat, smooth but crepy smooth, and he wondered if she knew it and cared. "Darling, you have no idea," she said. "You're so young, and you don't know how it really is for me. It looks wonderful to you, but it isn't."

"Oh," he said. He wasn't sure what she expected of him. He squirmed a little. The leather was very hot, and his jersey was sticking to his back so that it felt prickly like wool. He scratched his knee. He wished Marth would come now.

"Yes," she said, "it looks very grand to you, and I know that you think of me as cold and unscrupulous, sitting here with everything I want. Oh, I know what you think, darling, you needn't look like that. But I tell you, I have nothing. I'm lonely and certainly getting no younger, and everything turns bitter in my mouth."

He waited. He had heard people talk like this in the movies where no one could take them seriously, but she seemed to want him to take her seriously now and to have pity on her. Some people he felt sorry about—old folks broken to bits and alone, old fighters trying to come back, young kids like Lindy who never had enough of anything. Not her. Because she had too much to start with—

The Long Year

brains and looks and money and good teeth and good food, and she looked strong and wiry like a farm woman.

"You don't understand me, do you, Rock?"

"I don't know," he said.

"You *think* you do, don't you?"

"I don't know."

"You don't like me much—I mean, the way you like your Mr. Wimmer and the others. You don't like me like that, do you?"

"I like to watch you, and I like to talk with you," he said slowly. He didn't know why people asked questions like that. It was as if they expected you to lie, and then when you said what you believed, they took it hard. "But, I wouldn't want to—I mean, well—"

She slapped her bare knee and snorted with laughter. "Oh, you're priceless, darling, you're really priceless. You mean you wouldn't want to have me, would you? Not in any way—not as a mother or a sister or a mistress. I love your frankness, Rock. I hope you never lose that. It would be a shame to lose anything so wonderful."

He was red, and he had to turn his face a little away, trying to hide his embarrassment. "Now you're making fun of me," he said.

She shook her head. "I am not! Besides, you don't really want to listen to me, and nothing I can say would convince you that I love Marth very much and want to do things for her. You wouldn't believe it, would you?"

He thought about it. He had never talked to any woman like this, and he didn't want to be rude, but at the same time, when she asked questions and expected an answer, he was going to give it to her. He said slowly, "If you love someone, you don't own them or show them off like you owned them. It isn't like buying something—land or jewels or houses or cars. I mean, I don't think you can own anyone."

"You really ought to have a drink, darling. You talk so beautifully, and if you had a drink, you'd really get going and tell me all about your young ideals. All young people have these fine ideals."

"I—I don't like this kind of talk very much," he said. He looked out the window past her.

"Do you find me dull, Rock?"

"No—oh, no," he said hastily. "I don't think you're dull."

"Well, we could talk about your fight with Jaris. How was that?"

"It wasn't so good," he said. "I got him in the fourth round, but I should have had him sooner than that. The second, anyhow."

She smiled. "Fonn always says a fighter has got to have a clear mind, nothing on it but the work at hand. You know, Rock, you're very wise. You take the easiest way out. You stick to this town and to your father. That's much easier than going out into a larger pond."

He had never thought of it like that, and he said so. "It's just that I like it here. Mr. Wimmer says all people can't go away from the town. Someone ought to stay here and make the place grow and take on some new life."

She spoke slowly. "Hasn't it occurred to you that Mr. Wimmer has also taken an easy road? He's the most learned man in this town and therefore has little real competition. When people talk about him, they tell you how smart he is and how good and kind and wise. Such things are vastly overrated and terribly dull."

"No." He shook his head. When he talked to her, he always got new ideas and he looked at things differently for a while, and then everything changed again to the way it always was, but if he talked to her enough, he might find everything changed forever. And that was what she did to Marth. "You see, Mr. Wimmer's really someone. You can tell. He walks like someone, and when he talks to you, everything gets very simple." He tried to move his hands to make gestures because the words he spoke never accurately expressed what he wanted to say. Moving his hands made him appear clumsier, bigger, slower in thought. He dropped them to his knees. Mary came in holding the letters so they would not crumple, flat on her open hands. She laid them on the coffee table and handed Kay a fountain pen. He moved the things on the table.

"I thought we could get these off this afternoon," Mary said.

"Ummm," Kay said. She scanned the letters. "I don't think Marth will be back soon, Rock. She always says she will be, but she never is. Would you mind driving Mary to town in the station wagon?

The Long Year

Ummm? And then pick up my things at the cleaner's, will you? We're having picnic supper tonight." She signed her name in a small, firm hand, printing all except the capitals. "Will you do that, Rock?"

"Sure," he said stiffly. "Glad to." He felt she had won some sort of victory over him. He could not name it, but he knew it was so because he felt it inside him.

"And then you and Mary could come back here for the picnic. Drop in the kitchen on your way, Mary. Tell Teresita there'll be two more for supper tonight."

He left his swimming trunks on the bar stool and went out to the garage and backed the station wagon into the drive. He still felt confused. "What the hell!" he said.

"What's the matter?" Mary asked. "Something wrong, Rock?"

She wore a white cotton dress that was too small and tight over her breasts, and when she turned toward him, he thought for a moment it was Wilma. He had a light, sad, confused feeling as if someone had pulled the ground from under him, and he kept seeing Kay's face, tan and beautiful and wise-looking, and he said to himself: She's honest, she may not be anything else, but I know she's honest. He ran the flat of his hand over his wet, hot brow. The station wagon was a big, fast creature that handled beautifully and easily, and he had never driven a car like this. He pressed his foot hard on the gas, speeding down the wide, sunny highway, the wind in his face.

"Rock," Mary said, "I don't *have* to go to the picnic just because she asked me. It was swell of her, but if you'd rather not—"

"No," he said, "I think it'll be fun, Mary. Gosh, I never see you any more, either."

"But, Marth might—"

"Aw, she won't care. You know—" The words felt thick in his mouth, "You know, Marth does as she pleases, and that's okay with me, I guess. She breaks a lot of dates with me. Maybe she can't help it, but she does it—so, she shouldn't care too much. She probably won't even notice anything. I mean—" He stopped talking abruptly. The old man always said you shouldn't give too much of yourself away, talking all the time. The feeling of uneasiness persisted, and he listened half-heartedly to Mary's chatter. The car moved quickly, soundlessly over the road, and he found delight in it and let himself enjoy the moment driving the car. By the time they reached town, Mary had grown silent. When he stopped at the post office, she stood on the curb.

"I don't think I can go to the picnic, after all," she said.

"But, Mary—look, Mary, if you don't want to go to the picnic, why don't we take in a show or something?" He could tell that he had hurt her some way, and he wondered why he hadn't seen more of her—maybe she missed Joe, too, and she worked hard and didn't have very much fun. He put his hand over hers on the car door, but she moved away.

"I guess I'd better not, Rock. I forgot I promised Mamma to help her with some slipcovers tonight."

"Well— Well, then I don't think I'll go either. I'm sorry, Mary."

"Nothing to be sorry about," she said.

He didn't get it. She seemed to like him well enough, but maybe she knew how he felt. It was Marth he had to think about up there with that new fellow he didn't know, sitting by the campfire on the point. He wondered if she acted different when she was away from him, gayer or more serious. He couldn't go and sit there like a big stupid lout—exactly the sort of fellow Kay thought he was, afraid to break into any really competitive circles, hugging to his father and sucking up to everyone in his home town. His tongue moved hard along the ridges of his teeth, his bite clamped tight the way it did when he was circling his opponent in the ring. He'd bring the station wagon back and then go for a swim alone, and in the evening he'd walk up to Mr. Wimmer's and sit in the kitchen and look at the seed catalogues and listen to Mr. Wimmer's songs. That was the best thing to do.

CHAPTER TWENTY-SEVEN:

THE VISITORS began to come to Kay's house in July. The people in the town would see them in Kay's station wagon driving down Chestnut and up the river road to her house. They were clean people in colorful summer clothes, and they spoke in a widemouthed fashion that made the people laugh. "Look like goldfish when they talk," Macbeth said. They wandered into his store and bought old tie racks and willow plates, stickpins, flannel jackets. He charged them twice the original price. "No one with sense'd buy that stuff. They deserve to get clipped." He felt they were happy in the mere act of purchasing. "Blind—they're stony blind," he complained of them, for they walked in a forest of multiple fauna and flora and manifold life, but they saw none of it. They felt superior, but he was no one's inferior. He had seen everything in its own light. He had a son who was a fighter such as none since Corbett. He had a store and a good stomach and all his own teeth. He was no one's inferior.

They came to town on Wednesday and Saturday afternoons, walking slowly and making much of small things such as the mint beds that flourished around the post office, the antique chairs in the newspaper office. They called these quaint. They wanted to buy everything that delighted them. The people offered them quiet, slow-tongued, unbending exteriors. Secretly, they laughed and grew tired of these clean, laughing sightseers. Then they ceased to joke and grew sulky. The visitors on the streets in their spotless, fine clothes, walking in groups, had any amount of money to spend. The people found it odd that there were still people who had money—as one who carries a torch finds it odd there are those happy with love.

The visitors wanted to know the good fishing holes. Fish were scarce that summer, the river had dried above the bridge and now there were many islands of reeds, sediment and driftwood. They would not tell where the crappies, sunnies and catfish were because they had need of these, and it was no sport to go out day after day under a hot sun, sitting where the muggy stench of river mud and stagnant waters was thick around them. And so they appeared ignorant, stupid, sulky, dirty and lazy in their silence.

The visitors talked about a life Marth had only vaguely sensed in Millner's and at the Beldon. They clung to Kay and adored her and brought her small bits of gossip. They lived a moment here and a moment in another place and then after that in still another place, but without any fresh interest. In late July, Fonn Kelly came to Kay's. At once, he changed his clothes and lay on the lawn in a white jersey and grass-stained white shorts. Every afternoon he lay there, staring at the sky and the water, and no one bothered him.

"He doesn't want to talk to anyone," Kay said. He talked to her, though, but seldom to anyone else. The others said he was an artist. One woman who seemed crazy to Marth and who liked to talk about the time she had married an Indian potentate said that Fonn was a poet. Marth couldn't see anything poetic about him. He seldom spoke, and when he did his voice was thin for such a big, powerful man. When others talked, his eyes fled from face to face, but his expression did not change. In some ways he reminded her of Rock—his silence, perhaps, and the way he walked —but he frightened her. It was not his strength which frightened her but the way he sat apart from everyone, watching, and there was neither warmth nor coldness in his eyes.

Downstairs, in the kitchen, Teresita was having a tantrum. She had them when there were too many people. Joanie Peterson was helping in the kitchen. Her father didn't want her to do it, but she did it anyhow because she wanted the money for her schooling in the Fall. She was going to the teachers' college. Upstairs, in Kay's bedroom, Barby sat by the dressing table putting polish on

The Long Year 301

her toe nails. Her hand shook a little so that she had to rest her elbow on the edge of the table. Her black hair fell around her thin, tan face. Marth sat by the window looking at Fonn Kelly.

"Has Rock met him yet?" Barby asked.

"No," Marth said.

Barby kicked her foot back and forth. "This stuff never dries." She looked at Marth with cool, measuring eyes. "What's the matter with you lately? Bix said the other night you acted as if you were sick or something. Maybe you don't get enough sleep. You're always walking around at night—the other night you went down into the garden."

"I'm all right," she said. She was thinking about sitting in the garden alone at night with the house dark behind her and the moonless night dark around her so that the darkness came inside her where she was empty. She touched herself there and found herself totally empty, and even her hands had the feeling of having been empty for a very long time. It wasn't just the garden and the night, it was other times as well—dancing in the living room and on the porch, listening to the people. It was as if she had already gone away from home and left Rock behind her, and she missed him and even when she saw him she could not reach him. There was one time; the evening when she went into the garden late— that evening when Rock had come to the house. It was before Fonn Kelly, and she had danced with Rock and talked to him about trying to be a big fighter, and there was no answer from him, no real answer. She had seen his face in the light, quiet and closed against her because he thought she was mouthing Kay's words.

"I'd be so proud of you, Rock, and it doesn't seem right not to have ambition."

"Ambition? I've got lots of ambitions," he said.

"Well, but what kind?"

"Like this," he said and pulled her against him and kissed her with an open mouth as he had never done before, his body trembling against hers so that she held his shoulders and tried to calm him. This was all very strange because he wanted to do something to her not out of his love so much as to prove something to himself, and she sensed this. Afterwards, because she couldn't sleep, she went through the dark, silent house and sat in the garden and tried to get back a good, solid, measured feeling of being herself, Marth Hasswell from High Falls. The feeling had not returned. Then, while she was sitting there, Kay called to her from the porch, and she saw the glow of Kay's cigarette and went up there and sat with Kay. And Kay had begun to talk of the canals in Venice and the wonderful bookstalls and perfumeries in Paris and the way Waterloo Bridge looked and the sound of the cities at night and the taste of Mexican foods and the pleasant, flat, relaxed feeling of sea voyages.

Instead of growing calmer, the feeling mounted as if she were torn two ways and the voices of her childhood and school years cried out to her and all the sad, small faces of her friends turned waxen, weeping mouths toward her. And there was Rock, and she knew that it was crazy to go on like this. He was growing tired of the way she was and she could never go back to him again because he would not take her now—except to take her *that* way, but not peacefully as it had been before, wanting her to stay in the town and marry him and live with him however he chose to live. And on the other side was Kay with golden apples in her hands. That was the way she thought of Kay. She once had a book with a goddess with three golden apples in her hands, and now she thought of Kay that way, giving her anything she wanted and eager to give it.

"Rock's through with me," she said, and Barby laughed. "Well, he is, and I don't blame him."

"I don't think so," Barby said soberly. "Do you think if Joe was around now, he'd be through with me—no matter what I did? No."

"But, Barbs, do you have to be *with* someone you love, I mean—with him in every way?"

She nodded. "Take me, Marth. I'm not old enough to know

The Long Year

how to love someone I can't be with. I mean, if Joe—if Joe was alive and in prison, I'd forget how it was. I couldn't help it because I never learned how to love someone when they were out of sight so long. But, just the same if he was here now and we could be together, that would be for me. Nothing else would count."

"You mean—you think I should marry Rock?"

"I didn't say that."

"Well, *do* you?"

Barby sighed. "Marth, you used to know what you wanted to do. Everyone said you had a good mind. No one ever said that about me. Anyhow, Rock loves you, and I guess he'll love you for a long time. Good heavens, every girl in town's been after him—Mary Connaught and Joanie Peterson, and almost everyone, but it's always been you."

"It's over, though. I know it."

"What happened?"

"Nothing much—but he's changed."

She sat very still. "I guess no one knows about love. Maybe I'll have it again. Bix Lawrence is sweet, but I don't love him. And maybe if you go away with us to Cuba, you won't be the same and you'll forget Rock. If that's what you want to do, you ought to tell him. You don't want to make a lot of mistakes, Marth."

She watched Kay cross the lawn. Fonn rose and followed her to the wharf, and they got into the yellow canoe. She could hear Kay's laugh, but the big man did not laugh. "I keep trying to make Rock do something with his fighting so he can be rich and famous like Fonn. But when I look at Fonn, I wouldn't want Rock to be *like* him."

"He's scarey. But I like people who scare me."

"I don't." She wondered if Barby would tell her how it had been with Joe, but then she thought it might hurt Barby too much. Barby never talked about it, whether she felt it was safe and right with Joe or whether she just couldn't help loving him that way. Joe wasn't like Rock, anyhow. Joe had a lot of girls, and probably Barby knew it. But Rocky didn't have other girls and he always kept saying he wanted to get married, and it was more that he wanted to have her around all the time and take care of her and be with her in every way and not just to sleep with her. Whenever she thought of being married to him, she could never see the place where they would live or their children or what her life would be like. She could only see Rocky living in the same place, hanging his clothes with hers, always eating at the same table and sleeping under the same roof, and she felt that it was a calm, good life. But nothing told her it was her destiny. No one told her that she was the kind of person who could be happy in that life—it wasn't like doing lessons and having a teacher tell you the right and the wrong. You had to decide for yourself, and there was nothing to go by.

"I don't know what to do, Barbs."

"Oh, Marth! Really, I'm so darned tired of hearing you say you don't know, you don't know. It seems time we both *ought* to know something."

In the evenings after dinner, the people sat around smoking and talking. Kay turned on the radio, and a few danced in the living room and on the porch. Barby and Bix Lawrence went swimming. Their voices came across the water, low and young. Sometimes there were as many as twenty people from Los Angeles, Mexico City, Quebec, New York, Paris and Rio. The earth was small to these and held no wonder for them. They spoke of what they did with small, disdainful shrugs. They liked to talk politics, and Marth was always shocked that they could know so many facts and quote so many people and have so little to say as to what they themselves really thought. The political talk of Macbeth and Mr. Wimmer and her father seemed completely foreign compared with this. They were horrified at the grubbiness of people they saw in cities and said the country was going to ruin. They called Roosevelt a Red, a dreamer, a fool. She had never heard anyone speak of the President with such condescension and scorn.

Fonn Kelly did not talk about what he did. Every evening, he

The Long Year 305

danced with Kay. Sometimes he danced with Marth or Barby. His eyes were very blue, set deep in his head, and his bones did not seem thick but fine and light. He neither liked nor disliked dancing. His left ear was swollen so that the small, purplish-red veins stood out clearly like the clear pattern of a leaf. Marth always tried to talk to him.

"Do you like it here, Mr. Kelly?"

"What?"

"Do you like this town—the river?"

"Fine," he said. He always spoke carefully, each word separate and considered.

"The swimming's very good around the bend."

"Yes. Fine."

Afterwards, he danced with Kay. When anyone cut in, he stood by the stairs and waited to dance with her again. They danced in silence, easily, and they looked handsome and worldly together.

"He adores her," one woman said. She shrugged her thick shoulders, watching with envy. She wore a ruby necklace and her skin was red from the sun. "But who doesn't adore Kay? I said to Bill last night it's no use running away from dear Kay. You like her and you'll do anything in the world for her."

"Fonn's in for a fall," the other woman said. She was tall, thin, and her hair and skin were the color of light honey. She had once been a tennis champion. Now she was married to a bitter-mouthed man who manufactured women's underwear. She was lost in a room full of people. Like Fonn, she had little to say but watched everything. Her husband came into the room looking for someone. "Not you, love," he said and patted her arm. She slipped her bracelet off nervously and held it, her hand opening and closing over it. Marth thought she was going to throw it at him. She turned and smiled. Marth smiled back at her.

"Oh, no, dear," the other woman was saying. "It's been going on for years."

"What has?"

"You haven't been listening. Fonn and Kay, I meant."

"Oh, they say that of every man she's been with."

Marth moved away. She supposed they always talked like this, but she hated to have them say it about Kay. She saw the old man who wore brown-and-white sport shoes with his tux drinking rum. He was a portrait painter, and she could never remember his name. Branesci or Brancheski, something like that. When he was drunk, he developed a lot of nerve and kept tapping Fonn on the shoulder.

"I want to paint you," he said carefully.

"Thank you," Fonn said. His hands hung loosely at his side. They were wide and thin and flat, and Marth noticed he took very good care of them, the way Rocky did.

"I want to do it tomorrow," the painter said. "We can use Kay's barn, wonderful north light, and Kay'd love to have us do it."

"No."

"I am glad to do it."

"No, thanks." He smiled. Kay crossed the room. She tottered a little on her thin, high heels. Her hair had come loose, and she kept turning and calling to Tony Ruiz to follow her. She clung to Fonn's arm, leaning against him. "Come away from Burton, Fonn," she laughed. "He's a terrible bore. He paints rich women with sea-green hair. Besides, I want to talk to you." She led him to the porch and sat on the yellow lounge and drew him down beside her. He sat stiffly, holding her hand.

Rocky came through the house, and when she saw him, Marth who was dancing with Bix Lawrence, excused herself and went to him. "Hello," she said.

"Hello," he said stiffly.

"I was—hoping you'd come, Rock."

"Your aunt called me. She wants me to meet Fonn."

"Oh. They're out on the porch."

He hesitated a minute, looking at her, and she remembered how shy he was. She put her arm through his and led him toward Kay and Fonn.

"Hello, Rock, darling," Kay said.

"Hello, Kay," he said.

The Long Year 307

"This is Rocky Macbeth, Fonn," Kay said.

"Hello," Fonn said, and shook hands with one quick, hard shake.

"Glad to know you," Rocky said. He let his hand fall. In some ways, he seemed larger than Fonn, larger and thinner, but because Fonn was black and self-contained, to Marth he seemed larger than Rock.

"I saw you with Callahan in Chicago," Fonn said.

"Yeah?" Rocky licked his mouth. He held Marth's hand tightly in his, moving his fingers slowly in and out of hers. "I—I only saw you in the newsreels."

"That was a good fight," Fonn said. He sat down again beside Kay.

"Rock's an admirer of yours, darling," Kay said. "I've been wanting you two to meet. Rock thinks the sun sets on you."

Rocky moved uneasily. "That's true," he said.

Fonn said nothing. In that moment, he was looking at Rocky carefully, and Marth could see his eyes moving, and she drew away from Rock. "C'mon," she said. "I want to dance, Rock."

"Okay," he said. "Sure." He nodded to Fonn. "See you again, I hope."

"Of course, Rock," Kay laughed. "Fonn's going to be around for a while."

Marth could feel Rocky holding himself rigid. The trouble was that he wasn't like these people, and it was difficult for him to express himself. Now, Fonn thought he was nothing at all, and it hurt her to think he always put his left foot forward. He wasn't the way he seemed to be, and she knew how he was. She could feel Fonn's eyes on them as they went back into the room and began to dance without talking. There was nothing to talk about. She could say she had a new dress and he would make much over it, but it wasn't the way it had once been. She wondered if he already knew his destiny, didn't have to have anyone help him decide it. Maybe he talked about it to Mr. Wimmer. Maybe he knew it clearly the way he knew about fighting and swimming and running, something beyond himself directing him in these. Perhaps, if she held on to herself and watched and waited and tried not to indulge herself too much, something would also tell her what to do. Barby and Kay always knew—and Mr. Wimmer and Rock, also. She couldn't go around empty forever. Some people did, but she wasn't going to.

Fonn kept looking at Kay in the dim light. "Now, what do you want?"

"Nothing."

"I know better, Kay."

"What did you think of Rocky?"

"I have already told you that. He's young and very good. There are some things that he has to learn, but it is so for everyone. He has already learned much."

"I was thinking, I could give a big garden party and ask everyone from town who would care to come. We could have a ring laid out where the tennis court is. And then I thought—"

"No," he said.

She moved closer to him, but he did not touch her. He sat with his elbows on his knees, his hands clasped. Sometimes he sat like that for hours looking at her and saying nothing. It made her nervous. Now, however, she was feeling wonderful and did not care how long he stared at her.

"What do you see?"

"Nothing."

"You always say that."

"Untilled green fields."

"No. I wish you would tell me something."

"You don't wish that." He waited for what she would say next. Anything outside his own work bothered him. It was as if he preferred to live in a circle of light squared at the edges, and beyond this there was merely darkness and confusion for him. When he ventured into this darkness and confusion, he desired

The Long Year

to turn back into the light and find peace again. Other people talked of being afraid, but he had no understanding of fear. He did what came his way, whatever his nature desired to do. This woman was the only adventure in his life outside his fighting. She amused him, and he looked at her as if she were someone paid to do this—like a ballerina or a blues singer or a cook—and he was grateful to her for being exactly what she was.

"You see," she explained, "I'm crazy about Marth, and I don't want her to stay here forever. I want her with me, but she has some idea that Rocky will be a great fighter like you. You can see how stupid this is."

"No."

"Really, Fonn, the boy is uncertain. He likes to fight, but he has no ambitions, and so long as he never goes very far to find out how good he is, he will believe that he can do anything. He's a small-town boy who is worshiped by everyone here. That's part of his charm for Marth even though she may not know it."

"Listen, what makes you think he's no good? Because he comes from this place? I came from a hole in the wall. My old man was nutty as anything from shell shock. I learned to fight in the places where I used to sit and wait for him. They called me Sleepy Kelly because I slept all the time. I was growing too fast and didn't have enough to eat. That's what I came from. Do you know why I'm telling you this?"

"It's interesting."

"A good fighter can come from any place."

"But he wants to stay here. It's bad for Marth. She's in a terrible rut now."

"I suppose you've given her ideas, too."

"Oh, darling, just say you will or you won't."

"I have to think about it. I have to see how the kid feels."

"Fonn, you're being impossible."

"I'm not like these others. I can't throw myself around and spend myself easily on nothing. I'll talk to him tomorrow."

"Promise me?"

"No. I may be dead tomorrow, and I don't die with promises hanging over me like a ton of bricks."

"You're sweet."

"Don't talk like that."

"You really *are* in a mood, darling." She touched his arm. "I'll take you into town tomorrow and you can talk to him."

"I'll go alone and see for myself. When I've thought it over, I'll tell you."

She smiled.

"I'm no goldfish to show myself to these people."

She laughed softly.

"I'm no clown."

"Of course not. I didn't say that."

"I want to fight a nice, tough kid with cleverness to him. Someone who'll throw his heart into it as well. You don't find many of them like that." Thinking this way made him feel alone because there was no one in the world left to fight.

"Dear Fonn," she said.

He looked at her and put his hand behind her head and kissed her mouth. He had never kissed her except casually because it was something she expected of him, and now the thing inside him that loved to fight came into his throat, and he began to tremble with it.

"S-s-ssh," she said. She smiled, her smile moving under her lips. "S-ssh, Fonn," she said.

Rocky pulled himself up on the float beside Marth. Her skin looked wet and golden in the moonlight and in the golden light that came off the water. He was breathing hard, and he felt very happy because this was like the other times—at the tennis court and walking up to the farm and sitting on her front porch. He felt free of everything. "You know," he said, "some people get their strength from soil or from flying in the stratosphere. I get mine from this stinkin' river."

The Long Year 311

She peeled off her white bathing cap and shook out her hair. "I don't have any strength at all," she said.

"You can have mine. You can have all of it," he said, laughing. She lay flat on the float, and he put his arm over her and kissed her wet, cool mouth. Her lips moved under his in a kind of slow, sleepy whisper. She was saying his name, and then he thought her face was wet from the river, but when he moved his lips over it he could taste her tears.

"Tell me. Please tell me. You can tell me, Marth."

"I don't know," she said. She sounded like an amazed child. "I don't know what it is."

He spoke angrily. "I want to take you away from this business. It's not good for you. It mixes you up, and you look tired, and Barby says—"

"I'm all right. I guess I'm tired, that's all."

He lay flat beside her, his hand moving up and down her arm. "Don't you love me any more, Marth? You can tell me if you don't. I wouldn't blame you much, either. I act like a clumsy boob, and all the people you know here are smooth. They know how to act."

"Oh, no," she said. She turned and lay on her stomach, resting her weight on her elbows. "Oh, Rock," she said eagerly, "I want to love you the way you want me to, and I keep telling myself that I do, but nothing happens. I mean, I *still* want to be with Kay, and it just seems unfair that I have to change. Make a choice, I mean. Why do I have to choose, Rock? Why couldn't I go away for a couple of years and then come back here and we could get married—"

"Tell me," he said, "what do you want from Kay?" In the light, she looked too young to talk like this, like a young, skinny girl in a bathing suit.

"I like being with her. And I want to *see* things and be gay and have clothes and—do things."

"I see."

"No. No, you don't. Now, you're hurt, Rock, and I don't want to hurt you."

He put his arms around her, holding her to him. "It's all right. You can't help it if you don't love me the way I love you."

"But I do love you. I do!"

"Sure," he soothed her because she was trembling, and he didn't want her to cry, and he thought of all the times he had held her, those autumn days behind the school gym, holding her and the soft feeling of her cashmere sweaters and the silkiness of her hair and the way the autumn leaves piled there so that they stood ankle-deep in them, and the hot, dry, reddish smell of them. "Sure," he murmured, "but you love her, too, and you want to be with her and she tells you all the time how much she needs you. That's all right. You've got to do it for yourself. I can't do it for you."

"Do what?"

"Find out what you want."

"Yes," she said. "I guess so." She sighed, and he could see how bewildered she was, and he wondered if there was ever an end to bewilderment.

His hand moved over her shoulder and under her suit where her skin was cool and smooth. She lay very still under his touch, looking into his face. "I love you," he said. "I want you to know it. I think we could have some times together, but I don't want to decide anything except that you should do whatever you want to do."

Her lips moved soundlessly, her face lay in the shadows, and her eyes were closed. Across the water, a fish jumped. He could see a few dim lights in the house. Someone came to the edge of the wharf and called to them. Quickly, she sat up, pulling the straps of her suit into place.

"It's Kay," she said.

He put his hand over her mouth. "Be quiet," he whispered. "She can't see us here."

"Marth! Rock!" Kay called across the water.

She pulled away from him. "She knows we're here."

The Long Year

"Be still."

"I'm here! We're out here, Kay," she called.

"Damn you!"

"I was worried!" Kay said.

"I'll bet," he muttered. He dived into the water, swimming deep under it, curling himself in a ball and letting his arms move slowly, to keep him there. Under the water, he felt light, and when he opened his eyes, the water was dark gold around him, and smelled of moss, wet sawdust and fish. His skin was very smooth to his touch. He rose slowly and broke surface, spraying the water all around him. He could see Kay standing at the end of the wharf, alone, waiting for them.

"You're mad," Marth said. "Oh, Rock—I wanted to stay with you, but I thought she'd worry about us."

"She doesn't worry," he said. "Can't you understand it's impossible for her to worry about anyone but herself? If I had an ounce of sense I'd drown you—or both of us."

"But, Rock—"

Kay held Marth's robe for her. "What were you two doing out there? We missed you, and then I thought something had happened. Rock, you should've let me know you were going."

"Yeah," he said. "I'll remember it next time."

"I couldn't see you out there. Darlings, do rub yourselves well, and I'll have Teresita fix you something hot. Are you staying overnight, Rock?"

"No," he said. "I never stay overnight."

"Do you want to use my car, then?"

"No," he said. "Thanks, though. I'll take the river path home."

"But, Rock—" Marth said. He had already begun to run across the lawn toward the house. She felt cold and pulled her robe tight about her. "He's angry," she said.

"He'll get over it. He's a difficult person, you know. He just doesn't seem to get ahold of himself in public, and he ought to try to do it. He's really very delightful. I've had some wonderful talks with him, but he makes it so hard for anyone to get near him."

"I know. No one knows him because he's so shy, and you think he's dumb or something when he's awfully smart. That's how he is, Kay. I'm glad you know he's not stupid because he *thinks* you think he's stupid."

"He doesn't worry about what I think," she said. "I've been talking to Fonn, and he seems interested in Rock and might even agree to put on a match here. Yes, I think I can promise that he will."

"Oh—Kay." She felt tears come into her eyes, and she threw her arms around Kay. "That would solve everything. If Fonn likes him, I mean—and maybe he might even win. Rock's wonderful. Everyone says so."

"Yes, it might solve everything," Kay said. "I wouldn't be surprised."

CHAPTER TWENTY-EIGHT:

ROCKY SAT on the long counter in the store, his legs crossed in the manner of a tailor. He was reading one of Mr. Wimmer's books —Audubon's book of the birds of America. He liked to sit in the store. A few people came in, but there was plenty of time to read or look at the place and wonder where the hell all this stuff came from and who was going to buy it. It was a good thing the old man didn't spend much energy trying to sell anything. The suits looked skimpy, old-fashioned, except for a few new ones that the salesmen usually forced on Macbeth. The shirts were covered with dust. He had to laugh at this place. The old man loved it more than most men love their women. It was exactly right for him, requiring little, giving him time to sit on the sidewalk, a man of property.

He saw the station wagon stop on the street and Fonn Kelly get out of it. Marth was driving. He watched Fonn cross the street, and he thought he would have known him anywhere, not only because of his face but also because of the way he was built and the way he walked. He slid from the counter and pushed the book under the Stetson hatbox and ran his fingers through his short, crisp hair. He watched Fonn carefully, squinting. He wore a cream-colored linen suit, a pale blue silk shirt open at the throat, carried a Panama hat, and his hair was short, black, curly in front. He was very tan, and the way he walked was like dancing, from his hips without moving his shoulders. Rocky wet his lips. In the daylight, Fonn looked bigger and younger.

"Good afternoon," Fonn said.

"Hello."

"Mind if I come in and talk?"

"Come on back here." He led him to the rear of the store where the punching bag hung from an old rafter. Fonn tapped it lightly with the tips of his fingers and sat in Macbeth's cracked leather chair and put his feet against the wall. "Nice place. I grew up in Manhattan. Know that place?"

"No."

"That was some four rounds you had with Gunner Torklinson."

"The Gunner kept throwing his left."

Fonn nodded. "You were fine. You kept your head."

"Well, he was smart, but he kept edging and backing away. He wouldn't come in. But I don't like it when they're a cinch."

Fonn nodded.

"I—I saw you just that time in the news reels."

"You've got a clean punch. You put everything behind it. That's good." He preferred not to talk about himself except to Manny or Kay. He didn't like the sound of his voice saying "I think—" or "I don't think—" It was two years since he'd been in the ring with anyone who counted. Even Barney, his sparring partner, was slap-happy, almost blind and putting it on the middle. The trouble was there were no takers. It was fine to win, but then you wanted someone to make you keep it. "Tell me—what do you do before the match?"

"Mostly, I go to a movie with my old man. He's the one who taught me. I guess no one knows as much as he does. Anyhow, we go to French movies. We don't know what they're saying, but it's fast and peppy the way folks really talk."

"Un-hunh. You like fighting?"

"Sure."

"What do you do afterwards?"

"I go back and shower and get fixed and dress. No one's ever touched me much—a few nicks on the nose and jaw once and my ear the last time. My old man and I go out and have a couple hamburgers and turn in."

Fonn was not listening to him. "Kay wants us to do a few rounds."

"You mean—I would go in with you?"

The Long Year 317

"That's the idea. She's giving a big party—asking everyone in town."

He licked his lips. A slow, rising trembling went through him. He felt hot and sweaty. "I—do you mind if I talk this over with my old man?"

"Sure. You do that."

Rocky watched him go out and walk toward the post office. Marth came out of the post office and waved to him. They got into the station wagon. Rocky sat on the counter and opened the book to the picture of the scarlet tanager. You couldn't beat a guy like that. You couldn't tire him or make him groggy or do anything to him. You'd be up against a thing that was like a miracle of endless power. There wasn't another fighter like that on the face of the earth. Even if you busted yourself wide open, it would be worth it. It would be like Joe dying, like Mike dying, you were up against something too big to understand. He had to do it. Even if the old man—even if he— He slid off the counter and ran into the street. Olds was pushing the baby.

"Say, Olds," he said, "would you mind the store for me a minute?"

"Sure," Olds said. "Where's the fire?"

"Got to go up to Mr. Wimmer's," he said, and began to run. "Got to see the old man!"

Olds watched him run down the street. He shook his head, sighed. "There's a boy for you," he said, bending over the baby's buggy. The baby wore a pair of diapers made from an old tablecloth and a thin cotton shirt. His skin was fair and sweet-smelling. "See that boy, Robert?" Olds asked softly, looking into the baby's clear, expressionless eyes. "You be a boy like that for me, hunh—you be a boy like Rocky Macbeth."

Every day, the men from the town went to the cliffs to watch Rocky run up and down the beach. They moved their tongues in their mouths, worried. Macbeth sat on a rotting log holding a stop watch. The high, hot winds of summer hardened the beach. Some crazy little birds that were not sandpipers drifted over the sand, very low, tracking it here and there with a light wing mark like the mark of a falling leaf. "He'll do all right. The boy will be fine," Macbeth said every morning. He smoked or ate a raw carrot for his eyes and said nothing to the boy but watched him in the manner of a hawk watching a fish.

Rocky liked to run. Since he had beaten Play Boy Blair that time at the Golden Gloves, he had believed in running. He did not know what happened to him in this running, when he forgot about Joe or Mike or Marth up at Kay's house with all these people—whatever happened he called poetry. The sun was on the water, the water lay along the rims of sand, and the feeling surrounded him. He pulled off his cotton shirt and slacks, folding them neatly on the pier where they soaked up sun and smelled of fish and moss and river water. He stood in his shorts, bent down and touched the sand, flung his arms wide so that his lungs expanded.

He knew the parts of this feeling not in his mind but in that which was stronger, purer than his mind—the hard sand, the speed of himself, digging his toes and starting off and catching a glimpse of his father's skinny, tanned face looking at the stop watch. And the men sitting on the cliff, desiring his speed and running with him, not against him in contest, with the look of running on their faces. He could never explain this to Marth because she thought fighting was only in the ring. The rhythm came easily, and he ran with his arms as well, as the old man had taught him, the pull between the shoulders, the easy way of coming down and then up again and all of it one thing. He ran two miles to the end of the beach where the quack grass grew and turned and ran into the sun toward the old man. When he had gone eight miles or so, he had lived through the feeling again, come from the slow, relentlessness of his body into his second wind, into the whole again.

"Well?" he said.

"Okay," Macbeth said, and wrote the time down on the back of the gas bill. "A running son is worth four cooking daughters."

The Long Year

"Who wrote that?"

"Shakespeare."

Every time he would make up something like that and say it was from Shakespeare or the Bible or Dante, and there was seldom anyone but Mr. Wimmer to argue with him. "I never read that," Rocky said, pulling on his shirt. "What's it from?"

"Button your shirt. It's from *Othello*—yes, I would say *Othello*—first scene, second act, about line two hundred."

"I don't believe it," he laughed.

Macbeth pulled on his pipe. "You are a great unbeliever. If it is not *Othello*, then it is *Hamlet*."

"No."

"Well, if it is not Shakespeare, then it *should* be."

"Paw," he said, "no one can beat you."

"It's true," Macbeth said. "And no one can beat you either, Boy."

Gee, he thought, what a swell old man to have. He walked home slowly, listening to him, and the men in the hills rose and stretched themselves and went away silently.

"You must have no doubts," Macbeth said. "You must think that you will win. Many people say it's impossible, but nothing is impossible, and I know this."

"Paw," he said, "do you think you could pay me a salary in the store?"

"Hey?"

"Well, if Marth and I—"

"It is no time to think of that now. Think of this fight. Now, I've been thinking they might try to pull something. I don't like Kay Hasswell, and I think she's having this party and all to prove to Marth you don't amount to much. But I know and you know and everyone knows you are a good fighter, and what does it matter if you win or lose? You're still a fine fighter. Are you listenin' to me, Rock?"

"Yeah, Paw. But I was thinking that maybe Marth won't go away. Sometimes things happen—"

Macbeth slapped his thigh. "To be a good fighter, you've got to put your mind to it. Marth will come around in good time. Where could she find a better boy than you? And it's not as if you couldn't marry whom you like. You could, so she needn't put on airs."

"She's not putting on airs, Paw. She's just a baby. She wants everything her own way, and when she's with those people, it's as if she's wrapped in cotton all the time. She's scared to look at anything properly for fear it'll blind her or hurt her some way."

Macbeth sighed. "I will give you a little salary. Later, you can get a job in the factory. They need good men there. In due time, it will open as before, and you can work there, and with the sense you have and the wisdom you get from Gene Wimmer, I dare say you will make an important man in the factory. But now about Fonn Kelly, I intend to examine the construction of the ring in every detail."

"Yes," Rocky said. "Don't worry, Paw." He put his arm over the old man's shoulder and listened carefully to everything he was saying.

The party was to be Saturday night. Kay had chairs brought up from the funeral home. Small colored tables were set on the lawn and Japanese lanterns hung from wires stretched between the porch and the five oak trees. Two men from the city worked on the ring to have it exactly right. Macbeth and Russian sat on the lawn and watched them. Macbeth never spoke to these two men —a little man in a sweatshirt and rumpled slacks and old sneakers doing a quick two-step around the ring, putting his face near the ground, touching the ropes and the canvas, sniffing at this and that.

"My boy's heavy," he said at last. "We don't want this thing caving in."

"Hold an elephant," they said.

Russian tested the ropes. "We want this to be fair," he said. "I got a hunch she's gonna pull something."

"Mark you this," Macbeth said with grandeur. "This is a fight

The Long Year

to the end. Ten rounds. I don't want the ropes unravelling when Kelly bounces on them. I want my boy to win fair and square."

The men kept their faces straight. "Yes, sir," they said. "We'll see to it, personal." This man was a madman.

"Yes, see to it," Macbeth said. He had dreamed of this since Rocky was born. He had seen Corbett fight and had never forgotten it. Then his boy had crowded out that dream. He was careful about everything that had to do with the fight and had the scales brought from the express office to his store for the fighters to be weighed in. Kay sent the scales from the factory so there would be no mistake. Fonn brought Dolan, the referee from Cincinnati. Russian was suspicious of Dolan. He was also suspicious of the factory scales even though they registered the same as those from the express office. The men stood outside the store to watch the weighing in. Nothing happened except that Fonn bought a pair of tennis socks, and Macbeth refused to accept the money. "It's on the house," he said grandly.

The men were still standing around when Marth drove up. "She's tryin' to do us dirt," Russian said.

"No, she's not," Rocky said. "She just wants to see if I'm a good enough fighter to have Marth. And I am."

Marth made her way through the crowd. "Hello, Rock," she said.

"Hello."

Russian and Macbeth went outside, still arguing. Russian kept saying, "There's a trick to it somewhere. She doesn't want us to have a good fighter in this town. She wants to make us think Rock's no good—and we know better."

"You'll see," Macbeth said. "You'll see." But he wished the girl hadn't come. She might make Rock nervous. "Damn women, anyhow—young *and* old."

Marth could hear him, and her face flushed. "You scared, Rock?"

"I don't think so."

She touched his arm. "I've never seen you fight like this."

"Scared I'll lose?"

"No."

He sat on the counter. "Don't worry. The old man'll tell me what to do. And Russian's going to be one of the handlers. It's all very important to them. They'll take care of me. Maybe I'll win."

"But, Fonn's *deadly*, Rock, and even though this isn't a decision fight, he'll put all he's got into it. He doesn't *feel* anything. He's just—just a fighter."

"You'll see," he said. "I'm not flashy, but I can hold out, and I can give a lot. There are some points on my side, too."

She tried to make him think she was confident of his winning. She wanted to touch him, to make him know that she was with him no matter what happened. He was all that was left of her life in the town. Joe and Mike were dead. Barby had already moved away from that time into a new time of her own. There was no one to talk to who belonged to the town. Mr. Wimmer never came to Kay's house although he had been asked several times. Kay laughed about that and said Mr. Wimmer was full of crazy ideas that he might be contaminated in her house.

"Rock—you'll win," she said.

"No. I won't win."

"But you just said—"

"It's a lot of talk. People around here like to think Fonn's not in shape. He is. Even if he weren't, there are some things you don't forget. You know as an animal knows."

"I'm scared. I can't help it."

"Scared of everything, hey? Scared of your shadow. Scared to make up your mind. Scared to be a big, fine girl for me."

"Please, Rock—" She was trying not to cry. "Don't be nasty to me. I didn't come here to have you nasty to me."

"Go away," he said shortly. "Go away tomorrow. Go to Cuba or wherever you have to go and get it over with and come back to me."

She shook her head. "I don't blame you for being angry with me," she said. "You're right." She went out of the store quickly.

Macbeth sniffed. "Kind of uppity, aren't we?"

The Long Year

"I'm scared, Macbeth," she said.

"Go ahead," Russian said. "Have a good cry, Marth."

"No," she said. "I'm not crying."

Macbeth pursed his mouth. "Trouble is, Rocky doesn't want a little playmate makin' mud pies. Look at him, Marth. Can lick his weight in tigers. He's no Boy Scout."

"I don't want Fonn to hurt him, Macbeth."

Macbeth shrugged. "What's a little nick here and there? You twist him to pieces. Ever think of that? You think that doesn't kill him."

"I don't—I don't mean to." She walked away and blew her nose hard. Johnnie Evans coming down the street whistled, "La Golondrina." She felt tired. She wasn't going back up to Kay's. She'd go home and have some of 'Phelia's fresh bread and take a nap. She wanted to go home and maybe talk to Daddy and Howard and 'Phelia—and sleep.

The Japanese lanterns made a thin, eerie light over the wide lawn. The people moved in this light laughing and talking, eating all they could. Velma Olds stuffed cold chicken into her handbag. They held the food carefully on paper plates and tried not to look hungry. They had forgotten everything—that soon they would be dead, that the summer was dying as well, that the time of hunger and violence eddied about them. For this moment, their lives hung between two points: the food and the fight. Tomorrow was beyond sight. Lindy Connaught sat in the rock garden picking flowers and putting them in his pockets. He ate nasturtium petals. He ate the leaves of sweet peas. He was not concerned with the fight or the people. His stomach was full and tight as a drum.

In the kitchen, Howard and 'Phelia and Teresita worked. Howard carried food into the dining room. 'Phelia sighed as she bulged over the stove. They had nothing to say to Teresita about her wicked ways. They had prayed and given up the fight. Howard looked at her with a stern face, but Teresita giggled shamelessly. She was going to Cuba with Miss Hasswell. The world was her oyster.

Outside, Russian and Macbeth sat with Rocky and would not let him eat anything. Dolan, the referee, and Fonn sat on the front porch watching the people in the garden, the women in summer dresses, the men and children sitting around the ring at the edge of the spotlight which hung from a wooden arch decorated with crepe paper. "They're too quiet," Dolan said. "Ought to be a gang of them, lousy drunk. This kid means a lot to them."

"I suppose so," Fonn said. He went upstairs and dressed in his room. He wore an old terry-cloth bathrobe over his black trunks. He had never known his opponents well—knew them by name and their methods of fighting, but he had never known about their lives. He kept seeing the girl, Marth, walking back and forth in the living room, trying to tell him something. He felt uneasy. His uneasiness increased when he went down to the ring, walking in the bright light. At first the people merely watched him as if they were unaccustomed to the proper way of acting at fights, but when Macbeth stood up and clapped, the people clapped and whistled. He rose and nodded to them. He could see Kay standing by the porch in a white dress. She waved to him, but he pretended that he did not see her.

He watched the boy cross the court wearing a sweat shirt and a pair of faded green trunks. His father walked with him and the big, slow man they called Russian. The father was a giant with life, the greatest man in the world, cocky and red in the face with pride. Fonn nodded to the boy, and the boy nodded back. The people sat in the pale, orangeish light of the Japanese lanterns. They hooted and screamed at the boy, and he turned and grinned affectionately at them, his lips moving in greeting. Fonn contemplated his shoelaces, bent down and tied them. The thing was too small, too full of meanings new to him. He felt they were suspicious of him.

The girl came up to Fonn. "Uh—good luck," she said.

"Thank you, Marth," he said. He waited for her to say something else. Instead, she kept looking at him and waiting. He wondered what Kay wanted to accomplish in this—to show up the

The Long Year 325

boy, to knock the idea out of him, to make the town think less of him? Whatever it was, it was no good. "Don't worry, Marth," he said gravely. "He is a fine fighter."

"Yes," she smiled.

He watched Macbeth talking to the boy. He looked like a gnome. There was a character named Frank Lennan, used to work out at Quillan's Gym, looked like that old hawk-nosed man, had a fine brain for the game, knew all the angles and how to do everything clean, without any waste of effort. That was who Macbeth looked like. The boy took the old man's hand between his gloves and held it and said something. The old cow bell sounded. The people grew quiet. Dolan called to him, and he went up to the kid and touched his gloves and looked at him and thought that the kid was all right. He went back to his corner and limbered up and looked over the crowd and then when the bell sounded he turned and began to circle the boy, eying him carefully, holding his body in a half-crouch, his shoulders high. "All right, Kid," he said.

Rocky smiled faintly, and he could see him getting the feel of it. He wasn't a dopey kid trying to prove anything. He moved in the heart of it, well, containing this thing of order and method.

"You're okay, you're okay, Kid," he said. But, as they moved together, he ceased to care and held the thing, too—this feeling that was without substance. They shared it, and he felt his own instinctive, mortal skill, and his breathing was easy. The kid got a left to him, and then he knew it was his strong point, that quick left. He had been fighting with those whose tricks he knew well before he got into the ring, but he knew there was nothing the boy could use against him—there was nothing anyone could use against his own cleverness. When Dolan separated them, he said nothing to the boy. He forgot about the crowd, about everything except to get at the heart of his opponent. The boy had no face nor name. He touched him lightly on the shoulder and came in with force against the left side of his head and stood back circling, and waiting. He came in again swiftly, close, striking with a persistent, hard rhythm while the boy got him high in the ribs and then broke away and got him again lightly on his chin. The boy's left eye was bleeding so that his vision was queered and he kept shaking his head a little in an effort to shake the blood out of that eye.

Every time the boy was hit, the crowd rose and moaned softly as if they felt that blow. But Fonn would not think of the crowd —he had never thought of them out there yelling for blood. The only thing was that he was fighting where he wanted to be and had enough power to go on forever. In the fourth round, he could see that the boy was not getting tired but was gaining momentum, and he thought: now is the time. As the apple is ready for plucking, this young one's ready for the kill. He came in again and got him low, under the ear and then again on his shoulder and again with a blunt, high-powered body blow near his wishbone. The boy tried to say something, groaned and fell flat. Dolan stood over him counting. The people rose and yelled to him, calling him by name. "Rock—get up, Rock." Macbeth kept beating his fist against the corner post and cried out to him. Dolan came over to him and held up his hand, and he stood looking down at the boy. The people were very quiet. He heard Kay call to him, and he turned, breathing regularly, and looked at her. Then he bent and lifted the boy who was big and long and a dead weight in his arms. He carried him gently over to his own corner.

"He's all right," he said to Macbeth. "I got him with that last one to his head."

Macbeth nodded and held the salts to the boy's nose. The people stood silent and defeated around the ring.

"You see," he said. "He was good. I had to give him all I had." He could not look at any of them.

"Sure," Macbeth said.

He returned to his corner and pulled his robe over his shoulders and got out of the ring. The people made room for him.

"Fonn," Kay said. She took hold of his arm.

"Go away," he said.

"But, darling, you were terrific."

The Long Year

He waited while Dolan untied his glove. "Sure," he said. "That boy's good. But maybe he doesn't want to be a fighter. You leave him be, Kay."

"But, really, darling, I've never done anything to him."

He went into the house. LeGrand was sitting in the small barroom off the living room. He had come the week before. Most of the time, he sat there drinking or reading. "Well?" he said arching his thin eyebrows.

"What did you expect?" he asked.

"That you'd win, naturally. Drink?"

"No." He went to his room and took a shower and rubbed himself down and dressed. He was careful to wash the cut on his lip with alcohol. He ought to stay long enough to talk to the kid. He stood by the window looking out across the water and tried to remember what it was like to be a boy like that. He remembered Foley's Gym and the day Manny discovered him and how he and his old man went out and bought a turkey even though it was only July. He wondered what the boy would do now and how much difference this would make. Then he knew there was nothing he could say to him because he knew nothing at all about people, nothing about himself, even—why he existed or why there were times when to win did not matter any more. There was a growing desire within him to be defeated expertly, quickly, well by a new young man.

Kay was waiting for him in the hall downstairs. The girl, Marth, sat in the small barroom with LeGrand. She had been crying, and when he smiled at her she looked away. He stood for a moment awkwardly, picking at his fingernails.

"I suppose you're going," Kay said. "It was too much for you, wasn't it? You don't like the idea of knowing anything outside the ring, do you? You just want to be a machine—like a big telescope that observes the stars."

"You are too clever," he said slowly. He saw LeGrand smile and gulp more of his drink. "Listen," he said, so that the girl would hear him, "I'm very tired of all your plans, Kay. You did this boy no favor. It would be better for him to work up all along the line until it was proper he should fight me. It isn't because he lost. It's because you go against Time and hurry up everything. You are not a very good woman, Kay." He saw the girl get out of the yellow chair and come to the doorway and look at Kay, and he knew that the girl was understanding now about Kay and how Kay did things.

"But, Kay," she said, "I thought it was because you like Rock."

"Of course I like him, darling."

"No," the girl said, shaking her head a little. "No. You don't like him at all. He says you don't. I used to think it was an idea he had, but you really don't like him."

Kay shrugged. "Fonn is talking this way because he's scared."

"Yeah," Fonn said. "I'm scared. I don't like to know anything but how to fight. The kid wouldn't like to be the way I am—and that's how it is when you're a champ. You've got one thing. You hang on to it. You got to stay up there because the only other way is down and you don't know you go down every day, all the time."

"But, Kay," the girl said, "you told me it was because you wanted to give Rock something—because Rock always wanted to fight Fonn."

"Exactly," Kay said.

"That wasn't it," Fonn said. "You understand this, girlie. You don't want that kid to be like me. He's a big kid—in every way. I guess I never saw a better kid."

"You hurt him," she said. "I—I couldn't bear it to see him lying there with his knee up in the air. It reminded me of that time they shot down Joe Connaught."

He brushed the back of his hand across his eyes. It was hard for him to make the girl see how it actually was—and all the time that sham-faced LeGrand sitting there and thinking now Kay would turn to him because Kay always had to have someone on hand, as if she were a fighter and all the men she had around were

The Long Year   329

her coaches and handlers and managers or something. "I don't like tricks," he said. "I don't like this fight—no part of it."

Kay patted his arm. "Stay a while longer, darling. You aren't going to blame me for the fight. After all, you won and Rock was in with you. You both got what you wanted—and then you didn't *have* to fight, you know."

"Yes, I did," he said. "Not because of you. Because of the kid." He laid his hand on the girl's shoulder. "You go see him, now," he said. "It doesn't matter if Kay did him dirt. After a while, everyone will remember that he came close to licking the hell out of me."

"Did he?"

"Sure," he lied.

"I mean—could I tell him you said that?"

"Sure," he said. "You go and tell him."

Kay said, "I'll see you again, Fonn."

"Will you?"

"Of course."

LeGrand said, "You're a funny dog, Fonn."

He said nothing. He picked up his bag and went out to where Macbeth and Russian were getting into the police car. He asked for a ride into town, and they looked at him, puzzled but still friendly. Then he got into the car, and as they drove away he saw the three of them standing on the porch—LeGrand, still holding his drink, and Kay beside him and the girl Marth a little apart from them. He thought: Now the girl is through with her, too, and there will be LeGrand. He's a kind of fool, but a foxy fool, and maybe in the end that's what she wants, and maybe she doesn't know what she wants—but, even so, the girl will go to the kid and tell him what I said, and that will help.

The street was dark and silent under the soft, summer night. Rocky and Macbeth stood on the sidewalk outside the store. Macbeth looked down the street. He wondered idly if he should have asked Russian to come in for a beer or something. Russian was feeling awful and probably wouldn't go right home but get soused or something.

"Well—" he sighed. "That's that."

"Uh-huh," Rocky said. He put his arm around the old man. "That's that. It was a damned good fight."

"You feel okay now?"

"Sure. Fine."

"I see Marth sittin' on the porch bawling like a baby. I guess she didn't like the idea of your gettin' hurt."

"She cries at sad movies, too."

The old man rubbed his nose.

"You look tired," Rocky said. He bent down and lifted him in his arms, and he felt light, dry, crisp.

"Hey," Macbeth said.

"I keep remembering the times you carried me home from the depot when you were teaching me down there."

"Damn you, Boy," Macbeth said in a tired voice. He held on to the boy's jacket. He was tired and old and his time was petered out. Everything was getting to be too much for him. Tomorrow he'd move off the sidewalk, sitting outdoors like that wasn't good for the bones. Besides, might as well admit he sat there to brag to everyone about his boy. Now, it would be stupid to brag, not that the boy hadn't made a good showing, but he had been defeated and people wouldn't understand that easily. Of course, Fonn Kelly was a big man and all—

Rocky carried him up the back stairs and laid him on the big, jingling brass bed and took off his shoes, being careful to unlace them all the way down. Afterwards, they both lay in the big long room above the store, unsleeping in the darkness.

"Rock?"

"Yeah, Paw?"

"You were damned good."

"It was tough getting a hand on him. But it was really something. Imagine it—fighting Fonn Kelly."

The Long Year 331

"Corbett was better."

"Geez, that's impossible."

"Just the same, take my word for it. Corbett was better."

In the darkness, the boy was crying. He turned his head and pushed the pillow over his sore, swollen face and saw in the fierce darkness the image of Fonn—dark and intent, moving in a circle, moving inward in a kind of mortal ballet. He wondered if Marth went home or if she was still up at Kay's and if Kay was happy now that he was beaten. He supposed they were having a party up there with Barby and that Bix Lawrence and Marth and someone else, the Parker boy, maybe. That was the new one Bix brought with him all the time. He needed her here with him, to hold her and to have her say something kind to him. After a while when he could not stand it, he put on his shoes and went out on the silent street, walking toward Mr. Wimmer's.

I died back there, he thought, and now I'll never fight again in any real competition. The old man must know that, now—that was what Kay did to him with her fancy plans to give him the big-time too soon, before he was ready for it—still, no sense to blame Kay. It was his fault. Well, we are all unbelievers. Love is a fine dream for young boys. Fame is a small tin god. Skill is a moment that will never last. What lasts? Everything ends in the bones of the earth—Mike and Joe are ended even if Mr. Wimmer says they are not. Nothing lasts. Even if Mr. Wimmer says there are things that last—even so—

His whole body had begun to ache. He was no longer a boy with a big physical ache, in his muscles and his organs, a boy looking down the street wondering about new worlds, passing papers, listening to dirty jokes behind the outhouses. He was a man and had been a man for a long time, and he wondered what men did when they loved a foolish child who did not know what the word meant, when they had nothing to give her, when their friends were dead and a brown taste of death and bitterness came into their mouths. What was the nature and substance of Life?

He would talk to Mr. Wimmer about everything. Mr. Wimmer's

talk was of eternal things—wars, the country itself, the stars—and some place in all this talk he always came across something he himself had known, and it helped to believe that he was not totally ignorant. Like the old man, he admired knowledge. As he walked, he began to talk to himself. He walked past the darkened windows. In one, he saw a model dressed in a bathing suit. She was sitting on a blue rock that looked like painted cardboard. Her bathing suit was white, her legs were thin, waxy in texture, idly crossed. A sign hung over her flat, wooden belly. $3.98 Sale Price, he read. "It's too damned much," he said aloud. He looked at the wooden face. It's expression was that of a sleepwalker—the painted mouth, the painted black eyes, the smooth, lacquered skin. She reminded him of someone he knew. He thought of Kay and the women who came into the store who were visiting at Kay's house. He thought then of Marth and how it was no longer simple for them, always something coming between them—Cuba, a big red car, shopping trips to the city, Kay's friends—everything. Life is too quick, a moment here, a moment there. Life is nothing but a dream. "Goddamit," he said. He turned and began to run away from the window through the silent, dark streets toward Mr. Wimmer's farm. "I love you . . . I love you . . . I love you," he said under his breath as he ran.

CHAPTER TWENTY-NINE:

To MACBETH, it was as if he had written an ode that marked the end of his time—Farewell to the Street, Farewell to Everyone. He took his chair off the sidewalk and sat at the counter. He dusted off the hat boxes, hung the suits in their proper order with price tags dangling correctly from the button holes—the summer weights, the dress serges, the tweeds, expensive, medium-priced, cheap. After work, Russian helped him clean windows. They sprayed them with green window polish and worked without talking. The men stood outside the store, in the street, around the filling station. Almost two hundred worked now at the factory. The others worked only in desperation for the county. When they saw Rocky, they tried not to talk of the fight. They did not know what he was trying to tell them when he said, "Fonn's a great fighter. It was the best thing ever happened to me." They thought he was a good sport and was making it easier for himself and for them.

After the windows were clean, Russian went outside and stood looking up the street. "She done it," he said for the thousandth time. "She wanted him to lose. She done it to prove something—maybe she wants us to think everything else she has is better'n what we have."

"Hunh," Olds snorted. "She's givin' you stummick ulcers."

"Yeah?" He walked toward the cliffs trying to think it out properly, to know what he should do. He sniffed the air like a hound dog. Toward dusk, he came to the clearing where the big house stood. Some people came out and got into the boats. He watched the one named LeGrand, the one Joanie liked so much. The man ran from the house carrying a picnic hamper and got into the boat beside Kay. She sat at the wheel. The motor roared, and the speedboat kicked up a wake of water and nosed ahead of the other boat. She called teasing across the water, laughing. Then he saw Teresita come out of the house wearing a thin white dress, a red straw hat, red sandals. She looked across the river and ran out of the garage and drove away in the station wagon.

"The little devil," Russian grinned. The idea that she was putting something over on Kay pleased him. He walked toward the house that lay in the moving darkness of the woods. Someone had hung the cowbell on the porch door. He took it off the door, holding the clapper so that it would not ring. He knocked, but there was no answer and the front door was locked. He went to the rear of the house. There was no one there. He scratched his head, looking around him on the ground and in the woods. He was remembering a time when he had cleaned a nest of rats out from under his folks' tool house. First he had used a commercial poison, but when the rats died under the house, there was no way to get them out and they sent up a powerful stink. He had finally burned the small, rickety building, and when the ashes were raked away, the grass had come up there greener than in any place—not even the smallest sign of those rats. Fire was the thing because it was clean.

He went into the garage and found some old cleaning rags on the workbench. He took the cap off the Packard's gas tank and dipped these in the tank. Afterwards, he found a can of kerosene and dripped a trail of it around the house. He put the rags in the kitchen and in the living room and sprinkled kerosene in the bar and in the dining room. It had made him a little sick to have to break the kitchen lock, he was no destroyer. He didn't want to take anything from the house. This was something he had to do now, and he was doing it, but there was no pleasure in it for him. A man could take a lot, but there was a limit, and then a man had to fight back.

He went outside and scratched some matches on the soles of his shoes and the house began to go at once because it was old and dry. Before he could reach the rising ground that led to the woods, the house was already full of roaring flames. Once he looked back to

The Long Year 335

make sure it was spreading—then, satisfied, he began to walk along the river path.

It had been a simple thing to do. In all his life he had never killed a fly or broken a chair, but to burn the house had been easy. He sighed. The backs of his hands were oily. He washed them in the river and tried to rub off the oil with dry grass. It would not come off. Well, now it was done. He had no language to tell how much he desired to be at peace again with himself and his wife and his two children, and now he would have peace. His fear had begun when the woman came to the town. It would go away when she left the town. It was as simple as that to him—like the turning of his palm over a hoe, a very simple thing. Everything that arose for him was of the utmost simplicity, good or bad.

The house burned steadily in the silence of the woods. Johnnie Evans, driving on the highway, saw the flames licking the tall trees, and knowing at once what it was, he drove to the first Texaco station and called for the fire department. He said it was Kay's house, he was sure, and he would go back to see what he could do, pick up a few farmers on the way. The air was thick with smoke. By the time he reached the house, it was a shell of fire and charred boards, and the farmers stood around helpless. The siren wailed, the motorboats came swiftly down the river, and under all these sounds was a tone of silence, of waiting, of secret pleasure and wonder. Lindy lay on the bank, blinking his eyes from the smoke. He and Rocky watched it go up. Lindy made a round mouth of wonder.

"Goddam," he said, "there's a piano in there and a lotta food."

"Terrible waste," Rocky said. He wondered if it would make a difference. He supposed it was insured and she could build another —with her guts, she could build a thousand houses, each better than the other. She would never give up. He sighed. He felt terrible lately. Whenever he saw Mr. Wimmer working on his farm or Russian going to the factory or Olds wheeling his grandson, he felt ashamed because they all had their places, but he had none. Nothing that was exactly right for him.

"Boy," Lindy said, "hot as hell." The creatures of the grasses, the hoppers, ladybugs, June bugs, crickets, moved in little swarms toward the deep woods. The trees bent toward the water. The people moved in a widening circle, and when Kay came up the dock, they let her go through. She held on to LeGrand's arm. She could not believe what she saw.

"Everything, just everything," she moaned.

"All my clothes," Barby said.

Mr. Wimmer and Johnnie Evans tried to help the firemen. They sprayed the top story, and the men hosed the ground around the house. The top story fell lightly in black flakes into the inferno of the burning first floor.

"Teresita's in there," Kay said.

"No," Mr. Wimmer said. "I saw her going to town in the station wagon."

"Oh," she said, and moved away from the heat. She did not want to look at this. She and Barby and LeGrand drove the Packard out of the garage toward town.

"You see," LeGrand said, "you should not have come."

"Someone did it," she said.

"Nonsense. The house was old."

"Someone did it. I know it."

"But why?"

"Why? Good God, do you think these people have to find a reason? They prefer to do things without reason. They have some idea about me, and that's all they need. They'd give everything they have to get me out of here."

"Oh, no," he laughed, "people aren't like that."

Barby said, "I don't think anyone would set fire to your house, Kay."

"We'll see," she said sharply. She had been going along nicely, but now this had to interfere with her plans. She saw LeGrand smiling at her, certain that now she would go back with him. She

The Long Year

felt betrayed by everyone—by Marth because she was acting moody and would not come up to the picnic, by Fonn for going away like that, by her brother for not keeping a better hand on the people so that houses got burned like this. She was not defeated. She drove with sureness, around the curve, along the river.

"What will you do now?" Barby asked.

"I don't know. The insurance company will want to look at it. Everything's insured."

"My things, too?"

"I suppose so."

LeGrand put his hand on hers, holding to the wheel. "Come away for a while, Kay."

"No," she said. She was thinking of Prokosch sitting at the desk in that hotel room in Paris saying that she would never find her place because she had nothing to give and so would never be received. What happened here? She came to the town where she had been born, opened the factory, worked hard and desired to live here in pleasure and friendliness. Something always happened. When she was younger, she felt the dislike and aloofness was because of poor Simon O'Dodd that time. But now they plotted against her, and there was none of the radiance of her life in Rio, none of the lushness and peace of Hamilton or Cuba or Mexico. Perhaps there was the solution—that it was necessary for her to live in the sun or to move in the tides of the season. Perhaps LeGrand was right for her—after all.

"I'm sorry," she said, squeezing his hand. "I'm upset, that's all."

"I know," he said. "Have you heard from Fonn?"

She shook her head and looked at him coolly. "That doesn't matter to me, you know."

"It's an awful waste," Barby moaned. "Mamma'd die if someone burned her house like that." She hated to think of all her new clothes burned. She screwed up her childish face in disgust. The innocence was gone—she had not forgotten Joe or Joe's love, the garden and the willow tree. She had put them behind her because they were no longer within her reach. In her sleep, she moved through the curious, airy regions of her childhood dreams. She drifted toward locked doors, walked over high bridges, breathed thin, acrid air. She smiled and sighed, and a crazy song galloped through her head. "Barby doesn't live here any more—Barby doesn't live here any more . . . any more."

"I'm very tired," Kay said. "I ought to go away soon." She pressed her foot hard on the gas. "Where's Marth today?"

"At her house," Barby said.

"What does she do there all the time?" LeGrand asked.

"She mopes," Kay smiled. "She has some idea that I've done Rocky harm. It hurt her—every blow Fonn laid on him, that hurt her."

"She never sees Rock, though," Barby said. She leaned against the seat. "You don't think she's changed her mind, do you, Kay? I mean, Bix says he doesn't think she'll go with us."

Kay laughed. "Poor Marth. Poor me. It is all a big puzzle." But she was thinking that the house was nothing, after all. She could rebuild, if she wanted to. The insurance men would come to look at it, and there was nothing lost except all that effort. It was no big tragedy. She had seen worse ones in the cafes and along the pleasant, fashionable beaches. But she would have to talk to Marth.

The house was cool. Howard came in from the garden and tiptoed through the kitchen, carrying Hoyt's suits from the dry cleaner's.

"Where's Marth?" Kay asked.

"Around," Howard said.

"Did you see the fire?"

"Yes," he said. He looked at her puzzled. "You take it fine."

She shrugged. "What else is there? Did you expect me to throw an hysterical fit over something which I couldn't control?"

"No," he said, "I thought you'd be mad, though."

"I'm mad," she said. "Is Marth in her room?"

"Guess so."

She stopped halfway on the stairs and lit her cigarette. She

The Long Year

supposed Hoyt must know about the fire by now. From the front porch, you could see the smoke and flames and know it was her house. She knocked softly on the door, and when there was no answer, she pushed it open. Marth lay on her bed staring at the ceiling. She bent over her and kissed her forehead, and her skin was dry and hot. "You all right, darling?"

"Yes," Marth said.

She sat beside her holding her hand. "Did you hear about my house?"

"Howard told me."

"Yes," she sighed. "It went up like nothing at all. I don't think they'll save a thing. I just couldn't bear to stay there and look at it so I took LeGrand to the hotel and dropped Barby at her place. Bix was there. That Bix is charming, really one of the most engaging—"

"It's too bad," Marth said. She kept slipping her class ring on and off her finger. "About your house, I mean."

"Well, yes. But there's nothing I can do about it, and the insurance men will come and look at it."

"How did it start?"

"Someone set it on fire." She drew hard on the cigarette and tapped the ashes into a small hand-painted ash tray on Marth's dressing table. "Of course, it is natural for a woman like me to have enemies—especially in this town. And I've known it all along."

"Will you—will you build again, Kay?"

She thought she caught a trembling note of fear in the girl's voice. "Perhaps. Not at once, though."

Marth lay very still except for her hands toying with the ring. She had already begun to lose her tan, and lying on the bed in the small, childish room, she looked like a child who had been taken with some summer sickness.

"Well," Kay said, "there's nothing to keep me here now. I think that by October we can leave. Will you like that, darling?"

"Yes."

She rose and walked into her own room to get another cigarette and a long ivory holder. She continued to talk. "Darling, I'm worried about you. You've been so dejected lately, like a little sick cat, and you never go any place. That sweet Parker boy waited around yesterday for you to play tennis with him, and Barby is worried, too. She says—"

"It doesn't matter anyhow," Marth said. She swung her feet over the side of the bed, slipped them into a pair of scuffed moccasins. Then she sat at her dressing table and brushed her hair. "I said I'd go with you, Kay, and I'm going."

"Why, of course, darling. I knew you'd go, but it worries me, to say the least. I think you ought to go to Rocky and tell him how you feel. I'm sure I don't know what it is, but it's on your mind, and after all, Rocky's a very understanding—"

"You don't know! You don't know anything about him, Kay." Her voice was shrill. She bit her lip and spoke more quietly, tears in her eyes, her hands pulling at her ring. "Please, Kay, just don't try to advise me any more about Rock."

"All right." She rubbed her hand slowly across her forehead. "I guess I'm tired, dear. Really tired. This house business—everything. And then I've been worried about you. I feel responsible."

Marth said nothing.

"If you really want him, it's simple."

"Don't you see, Kay? If I go to him now, he'll think it's pity because he lost the fight. I don't care about the fight. When I saw it, I hated it. It was beautiful in a way, but it scared me stiff. And I don't want him like Fonn. Fonn's nothing except a big, strong guy who's clever with his body. But Fonn doesn't *know* anything. Not the way Mr. Wimmer knows. And Rock *knows*. And—it's too late. I've got to go with you now. I mean, I've got to get away from here because I hate it, and Daddy's hating it, too. He doesn't know what's the matter, and you know—well, he *tries* so hard."

Kay said, "I understand. I know how you feel. I felt like that, too."

"No," Marth said. "You didn't feel like this. You'll never die

The Long Year

without someone. You can always take care of yourself. Oh—I'm sorry about the house, Kay, and I'm sorry—about everything. But I'm not like you and Barby. I *try* to be, but I'm not. Maybe after a while, I'll learn how to be."

"Of course," Kay said. "We'll have a marvelous time, darling, and soon enough you'll forget Rock." She put her arm around the girl, looking at their faces in the mirror, seeing how, more than ever, they looked alike. And she thought: But, perhaps like me, she'll never forget. For the first time, she felt a curious weariness weigh her down, and a prickling sensation of fear and despair moved across her mind like a shadow. It was as if she had done nothing right in all her time, as if her end was one of defeat. "Don't worry," Kay murmured. "You'll be happy yet. The hardest part is a first love, and after that, the rest is well in control." She kissed her cheek lightly, thinking that once she got her away from this silent place, started her well on her travels and adventures, she would be all right.

She did not notice Marth move slightly away from her with a solemn, puzzled look of affection and pity.

Russian sat with Olds on the small, hot, bare lawn outside Olds' house. They watched the two men driving slowly up the street in a new black Ford. They stopped by Olds' gate and called to them. "You Mr. Olds?"

"Who—me?" Olds whacked his chest loudly. "Yeah, I'm Olds."

"I'm Brady from the Northern Insurance Company."

"That so?" Olds raised his eyebrow and turned slightly to wink at Russian.

"Who's that with you?"

"He means me," Russian said, staring at the man sitting in the Ford. "I'm Russian Peterson."

"Either you guys see that fire?"

"Yeah," Olds said. "We seen it. Gave off a powerful lot of heat."

"You see how it began?" His round, red face puckered. His thick lips sagged petulantly. He pushed his cheap straw hat back from his forehead. "See it begin?"

"Naw," Olds said. "We was up here when it begun."

"Any ideas?"

"I didn't see it till it was lickin' the sky," Olds insisted.

"What about you?" He pointed at Russian.

"Well, now," Russian said, "you want to talk to me about it, you get outta that car and come in here and sit down and I'll talk to you."

The man swore and spoke to his companion. "I'll see you later," he said.

Olds tittered. "Big ole fart," he said, "sittin' out there yellin' at us like we was hawgs to be called home. He won't find out nothin'."

"Can't tell," Russian said. His eyes narrowed, but his manner was calm and undisturbed. "What you hear from Smut?"

"Oughtta be home enny day now. I tawked to Hoyt an' he says there'll be a part-time job fer Smut, an' maybe later on he can take him on the old way. He was real nice about it and said not to say much till Smut got here an' I said I'd tell Smut to go in an' see him."

"Yeah," Russian said. "Don't let him see *her*. Anyhow, she'll be gone by then. She's going, all right. Howard told me. I'll be glad. My girl Joanie got a crush on that musician friend of hers. Fancy name—LeGrand. Rich, sissy guy with a face like a hawk. I'll be glad when the whole pack of them clear out. Barby Leroy, too."

"Yeah. Guess so. But Macbeth tole me it'll sit hard with Rock if the Hasswell girl goes. That Rock. He ain't like me when I was his age. I'd have me a good time an' leave them easy."

Russian grinned. "I never heard tell you was popular with women. The other way around, I remember."

Olds blushed. "I had me a few tries."

They sat there smoking and talking. After a while, they went down to Macbeth's. Russian was interested in everything people said about the fire. He couldn't hold the feeling that he had been

The Long Year 343

any part of it. His air of content and outward calm was noticeable only to Macbeth and Olds, and they kept their peace. Where the house had been was nothing more than a black shell that smoked for days. The air around the shell was hot and dusty. You could see where the living-room fireplace had been, and a part of the bar was still there, and the rusted, broken harp of the piano made an eerie sound when you walked there. Mary Connaught said that Kay said nothing when the investigators asked whom she suspected. "She acts like she knows, though," Mary said.

Kay pressed the button that brought Mary to her office. "I want to speak to Russian Peterson," she said.

Mary went out to the foundry herself. Russian stood inside the door throwing pulleys up against the stone wall of the warehouse. "Lookit," he said and threw one hard. It made a popping sound, and the pieces fell like glass on the gravelled path between the buildings. She could see the clutter of broken pulleys all around there. "Miss Hasswell wants to see you right now," she said.

"She can damned well—" He grinned. "Okay, Mary." He went to the men's washroom, still smiling softly, changed his clothes and wet down his hair. He went at once to Kay's office. "Mary told me—"

"Yes," she said. "Please sit down."

He sat facing her. He kept his hands on his knees and waited. She looked old to him—the little streaks in her hair. You could tell a woman's age by her hands and her neck. Now she's aging fast, and she'll hate it. Looks like she's hitting the bottle, looks like almost any old shrew except for the clothes. He saw that the office had been cleared of the file cases. Her desk was bare except for the telephone, a miniature of her mother and a gold fountain pen.

She picked up the pen. "You saw my house, Russian?"

"Sure. At the party when Rock got knocked out."

"No."

"You mean afterward? I saw it after it got burned."

"It was a very complete job."

"Yeah," he agreed.

"The insurance investigators have reason to believe it was arson."

"Arson?"

"Someone deliberately set it afire."

"Oh." He kept looking at her and waiting.

"I'm not asking any questions," she said, rolling the pen between her palms. "Nor do I intend to tell these investigators anything."

"You got something to tell?"

"Possibly."

"You should tell it." He was enjoying this.

"Tell me—did Mr. Wimmer ever say anything to you about me?"

"No."

"It might have been Mr. Wimmer, you know."

He shook his head. "He wouldn't do that."

"How can you be certain?"

"I just know. Besides, no one would believe it."

"Would they believe it if I said you did it?" She was smiling now.

"They might."

"I'm not going to do that, though."

He shrugged. "That's for you to decide."

"Well, I'm not going to tell them you set fire to my house."

"You just said it was Mr. Wimmer. Now it's me."

"It was trick—about Mr. Wimmer," she said impatiently. "I know, you see. I might even be able to prove it. But I don't choose to do that. You believe I'm beaten, don't you? If I told you I'm going away, you'd think it was because I'm afraid to stay here any longer. Wouldn't you?"

"Everyone says you're going away."

"To Cuba. But I had planned to do that all along. No one burned me out of this town. I was going anyhow."

"Sure," he said. "That all, Miss Hasswell?"

"That's all." She threw the pen on the desk. It rolled and hit

The Long Year

the base of the telephone. "I suppose after I'm gone, you'll get together with Hoyt and make die-cast pulleys."

"Sure," he said. What did she expect?

"You know, don't you, that I was the one to get those contracts and to open the factory again? You know that."

He nodded, silent. Mr. Wimmer had told him the whole business wasn't over yet. She wanted him to feel grateful. He didn't. She had enough people licking her feet now, and he wasn't soft inside. He was a man who worked hard and had a family and didn't need to have anyone do his thinking for him. When he went out, he could hear her laughing, and he felt like laughing, too. He was at peace with himself, and he would never have to do a thing like that again. He began to think about the pulleys and how they should be made, and he decided that tomorrow he would talk to Hoyt about it. Hoyt was okay. He whistled "Yankee Doodle Dandy." On his way home, he would stop in at Sid Butler's and pick out a good steak and maybe some fresh dills and celebrate. He would think of some way to get the school board to offer Wimmer a contract. There was still that vacancy in the sociology department, and everyone was ripe for a change—well, it was over with. Everything would *look* the same as soon as she left, but for him nothing would ever be quite the same.

Three days a week, Mr. Wimmer worked with the road crews. The rest of the time, he worked in his house where he was preparing for the winter. He put weather stripping on the windows and doors, installed a vegetable bin under the kitchen drain board and washed down the walls with a solution that was not supposed to mar the old wallpaper. In the afternoons when he was free, he went into town and worked on his thesis. The library was usually very quiet, and the librarian let him work in the small reference room. From there, he could see the school. The janitors were working in the yard and on the roof. Well, he was not a good farmer. He was a teacher, and he ought to teach. He thought of Kay Hasswell and how her house burned and the way she had shrugged it off. He didn't know there was a woman who could stand unweeping while her house and possessions burned to nothing before her eyes. He smiled. He felt paternal toward her. He no longer dreamed his dream of a poor, adolescent boy's love. When he thought of her now, it was with tenderness, afraid that she would be rootless forever. Now, when she left the town she could no longer think of it as a place to which she could ultimately return. She would never come back.

"Hello, Gene," Rock said. He came into the reference room and sat at the end of the table. "You working?"

He shook his head. "Daydreaming."

"Yeah." He frowned and wet his lips. "Looks like a good fall. How was your tomato crop?"

"Okay," he said. "They grew, anyhow. What's the matter?" He smiled, watching the boy closely.

"Nothing. Why?"

"I thought there was something the matter."

"No."

"I suppose Marth and Barby are getting ready to go."

"I wouldn't know."

"Well," he said, "if you aren't going to be talkative, I think I'll walk down to the factory. Hoyt called and asked me to drop by."

"At the factory?"

"Yes."

He stopped at the desk to check out his books. The librarian, a gentle, plumpish woman with dyed hair, smiled at him over her steamy glasses. "My, you are a reader, Mr. Wimmer. We always say, Mr. Wimmer's our greatest reader. People get a hunger for books, and they just never lose it. I always say, you can't get too many books in a library."

"You're quite a reader yourself, Miss Molly."

She flushed. "Why, yes, I am, but no one ever *thinks* about it. I mean, almost no one ever asks me what to read, and do you know I've read almost everything? Yes, almost everything, and no one asks me—ever."

The Long Year

"Why, now," he said thoughtfully, "it was you told me to read that fine book on farm life by Ruth Suckow. Don't you remember that?"

She tittered, clutching his books to her and then in a fierce, surrendering gesture, thrusting them across the glass-topped desk. "I'd forgotten. Truly, Mr. Wimmer, you *are* so clever about remembering books and every little thing. I don't know what this town would do without you. I keep telling people—"

"That's kind of you, Miss Molly," he said.

Rock followed him outside. "This town's got more nuts in it than any town in the world," he said. "Like Miss Molly. She doesn't live at all except in her books. I keep thinking Marth will get like that if she doesn't watch out. Miss Molly's not the only nut."

"What's the matter? You lame or something?"

"These moccasins are ripped and stones get in there—that's all."

Wimmer looked at him sharply. "You ought to look out for yourself more. You've been lazy and sloppy lately. Do you think it's all over just because Fonn Kelly whacked you to pieces?"

Rocky flushed. "That's not it."

"Well—what then?"

"It's Marth. Honest, Mr. Wimmer, I can't fight anyone else because now I've fought the best one there is. It's like you dreamed of going to Paris and then, through some miracle, you get there. That's all you want. You can go home and be in peace. That's why it's over for me. Sure—I'll fight around for fun, but it's not my life work."

Mr. Wimmer smiled gently. They passed the fire hall, and he waved to the men dozing there, playing cards, rubbing the shiny red truck that was their passion. "What *is* your work, Rock?"

Rocky squinted into the sun. "I guess it's to stay here and maybe work in the factory some day and help the old man in the store. Gosh, it's fine for some folks to leave this place, but I don't want to. I just want to stay here and work and try to have a happy time here."

"A happy time," he said slowly. He was thinking of the woman in her red coat, like a red flower inside a house and himself on the outside looking in, and he knew it was too late for him to have her. Perhaps he didn't really want her—only the *idea* of her, and now when he knew that he could love someone like that, perhaps he could find someone who would love him, too. He didn't want someone to love him as much as he wanted to love someone now, in this time, here in the town with himself as a schoolteacher and his wife the same as the wives of his friends, clean and gay and sorrowful and full of the business of living as his wife in the town. "Look," he said, "did you have a fight with her?"

"No," Rocky said, "It's just that I never see her, and she doesn't go anywhere. I went up there to talk to Howard, and he said she mopes and reads. He says she feels awful sorry for Kay losing her house, and I suppose Kay wants her to feel sorry. She wants Marth. Maybe that's right, but gosh—" he shook his head, "whenever I meet her on the street, she looks scared, and when I start to say something, I feel like a big boob. She always thought I was a pretty big fighter. You know how everyone makes her think that— and now, well, gosh— Gene, if you know anything about women, you know how it is. You get to a place where you don't know what to say."

"You have a meek, timid heart," Mr. Wimmer said. "The thing to do is to tell her all of this. Don't tell me. It bores me a little."

Rocky grinned. "I ought to kick you."

"Yeah," Mr. Wimmer said. He looked at the boy, and the boy looked at him fondly, still grinning.

"I'll bet Hoyt wants to ask you to come back to the school."

"Maybe."

"Will you?"

"Sure—if he asks me. Now, go away. Go about your own business."

"Okay," Rocky said. "See you later."

He watched him go off at a steady lope. He thought: She ought to have let him alone—him and Marth. She shouldn't be tossing

The Long Year 349

golden apples at their feet, just out of their reach. She ought to believe in innocence and the adventure of living with love and friends and patience. He went into the office building. Hoyt came at once to the door.

"Will you come in, Gene?"

He did not sit in the chair but on the window seat where he could see the men loading the last box car. He knew it was the last one for this week because Russian had told him so.

"Things are better, aren't they?" Hoyt asked. "We have two hundred back to work, and if our contracts hold out, it will mean part-time work all winter."

"Fine," he said. He saw her come out of the warehouse. She wore something yellow, all yellow, yellow flowers in her hair and yellow sandals, and he watched her and kept his face blank, without softening.

"Nothing changes you, does it, Gene?" Hoyt asked. He was thinner now, and he no longer sat with his fingers bridged and an air of calm authority. His hands lay idle on his desk, and he kept turning and watching the men as if he expected them to disappear any minute.

"I don't know. I guess I'm not very changeable. I see things and I think about them."

"Tell me something."

"Sure." She stood for a moment watching the men. Then she came into the building and went past Hoyt's office. His eyes met hers, and she smiled and moved her lips, soundlessly. "Sure, Hoyt."

"What do you tell the men?"

"When?"

"Up at the filling station and around the courthouse. Do you tell them to strike or to burn down someone's house—anything like that?"

"Why, no," he said, surprised. "I just listen to them. They like to talk about the last war. The whole history of their lives. And they like to ask questions about the Civil War and the Democratic platform and who was Marion the Swamp Fox and was Grant really an old souse? I don't tell them anything except to answer their questions when I can."

"Oh," Hoyt said.

"And I'm no Communist," he said. His voice was thin with anger. "I don't know about labels. Everyone wants to label everything and everyone. I'm just a guy who wants to keep things going. We've got to change because the way we lived twenty years ago is outmoded, and we've got to change a lot of things, and I want to help do that. If that's Communist, then I am one."

Hoyt frowned. "I don't know, Gene. I used to think you had to do everything the way it was done before. That seemed enough proof. But lately, I've been watching and thinking. Well, I don't know."

"What did you want to see me about?" He kept thinking the old boy had changed a lot, even his uncertainty and speculation was a healthy sign. If he could see there was something new happening, then that was a help. Before this he'd always been so blind and insulated.

"Oh," Hoyt said. "I was thinking about the school job. We all talked it over, and we want to make it right for you. We can't make it exactly right, I guess, and it's been a long time, but we'd like to have you come back."

"Sure," he said at once.

Hoyt raised his eyebrows. "You mean, you will?"

"Sure," he said. "That's my job, isn't it?"

"Yes—yes, I guess it is."

Kay came to the door and opened it. "Private conference?"

"No," Hoyt said. He rose, but Mr. Wimmer sat by the window. "Come in, Kay."

"I was wondering about shipping my things. Did you arrange for them to call for my trunks?"

"Yes," he said. "This afternoon."

"Where you going?" Mr. Wimmer asked. Her lipstick was so bright, it made her face look pale even though she still had a good

The Long Year

summer tan. He could see that she wanted him to make some comment on her departure.

"Cuba," she said.

"Ever been there?"

"Yes." She sat on the edge of Hoyt's desk. "Several times."

"Why do you want to go there again, then?"

"Well—mostly because I liked it."

"It won't be the same."

"I know that," she said.

Hoyt cleared his throat. "You can stay here, Kay. You don't have to go to Cuba or anywhere."

"No," she said slowly. "I can't stay here, and I won't ever come back."

Hoyt said, "Gene's coming back to the school, Kay."

She smiled. "I'm not surprised. You really are a tough man, aren't you, Gene Wimmer?"

"No," he said. "I'm not so tough."

"A lot tougher than you look. I know your kind with the meek, sweet, boyish spirits and the lovely look of Sunday school on your faces, and you've all got guts like steel and heads as hard as obsidian."

"That so?" he asked. He leaned forward to light her cigarette. She looked at him, and their eyes were very close, and she raised her hand and held his wrist so that the flame was steady. "I'm sorry to see you go," he said. "You could learn to like it here if you wanted to."

"Think so?"

"Sure."

She shook her head and dropped her hand and turned a little away from him. "No. I'm not the kind. I always keep going."

"Has Marth everything she needs?" Hoyt asked. "She doesn't say."

"She has everything." She went toward the door and looked at him, and he rose and went to the door and opened it. "Good-bye, Mr. Wimmer," she said.

"Good-bye," he said. He stood watching her go out and get into her red car, and he thought that she was very tired, walking in a tired way, her hair falling about her thin face, and he wondered if he ought to have said something to her that would in some way tell her how he felt about her.

"Don't worry about Kay," Hoyt said, sitting at his desk and looking through the window. "She's like that red car. She can take a lot of wear and tear and still come up with her lipstick on." He felt that was a clever thing to say. "She's had three husbands. She'll have a fourth. She knows a lot of people and there's enough to keep her busy."

"Yes," Wimmer said. Hoyt began to talk about the school and his job there, and he listened, his mind already beginning to move along an old, familiar pattern. There was always someone to teach. That was the thing.

CHAPTER THIRTY:

THE MORNING was a bell, the air was thin as splintered glass, the sun was brighter than ever before, and the earth turned more slowly, grinding itself in an ecstasy of brightness and fair weather. It was October in the town, and so to the people, it was October everywhere.

Lindy Connaught, lost without his brother, had become in the space of a finger's breadth, a wanderer. He wandered in his sleep among the stars, under the earth, through the intricate molds, levers, oils, tubes and cams of the Intertype machine. But in the daylight of this October, he walked by the river. He saw some carnelians under the water where the sun struck at them. He picked up one, but when it dried, he saw that it was drab and like anything else in the world, and he threw it back into the water, touching it in farewell. He remembered Joe's voice—"Everything has a place and belongs in it—leave it there, Kid." He sat on the bank and pulled off his shoes and stockings and lay staring at the sky with his feet moving in the water. Two cloud shapes passed over the sun. He sighed and stretched himself and waited for them to drift beyond his sight.

Marth walked around the room. Her three bags stood at the foot of her bed. They were new and had her initials on them. She looked into her purse to see if everything was there. She had her traveller's checks, compact, pen, lipstick, comb, mirror, piece of gum, keys to her bags, pack of cigarettes, small nail file, change purse, handkerchief and a match folder. Howard came up and took the bags into the hall. Every few minutes, Barby called. She was full of chatter.

"Marth, I ought to come down there to help you. The trouble

is that you're not one bit excited, and I'm frantic. To think I'm really going to get out of here at last and I won't have to think of this place— Oh, Marth—listen, don't sit down there like a dope. Where's Kay?"

"She went down to the office with Daddy. She'll be back in about a half an hour."

"But, Marth—listen, have you seen Rock?"

"No."

"Well, aren't you *going* to see him? I did. I went down there and said goodbye, and he was really very sweet. He said he thought it was all a fine idea because—well, because of everything. If you don't see him, you'll feel terrible all the way to Chicago. I know you."

"He knows where I am. If he wants to see me—"

"Aren't you going down there?"

"No. I don't know. Look, Barby, I've still got some things to do."

"You're packed, aren't you?"

"Yes, but I want to check and see if I've got everything."

"All right. Only you checked a few minutes ago."

"I'll call you as soon as Kay comes."

"Okay."

She bit the hard callus around her nail. Howard came up for the last bag. "Just the same," he continued his argument of the morning, "that Teresita's goin' to get into trouble. Marth, you ought to watch her."

"I can't watch anyone, Howard. Not even myself."

The room was stripped of her things. Tomorrow, Howard and 'Phelia would clean it. Suddenly, she could not bear the idea of leaving this place. She ran down the stairs and out into the street. Kay was just turning up the drive. "Hey!" she called.

"I—I want to say good-bye to Macbeth," she said. She heard Kay laughing gently, still sitting in the car. As soon as she reached the corner, she began to walk more slowly. Macbeth was crossing the tracks toward the river, his fish pole over his shoulder. He saw her and waved and shouted something to her. She stood by the door.

The Long Year

Her new suit felt very hot, and she smoothed it. In the window, her hair looked wonderful. She looked like a well-dressed traveler.

"Oh," he said. "Going today."

"Yes."

He got down off the counter. He wore rumpled shorts and a dirty T-shirt, and she thought that he had never looked messy before, and she knew it was because of that fight.

"When?" he asked.

"Soon. Right away, I guess."

"Oh." He scratched his knee. "Well, I'll keep the home fires burning."

"I—I just wanted to say good-bye."

"Good-bye," he said. He ticked his fingers nervously on the counter. Outside, a few people went past carrying bundles. Olds, wheeling his grandson, walked toward the filling station. The smell of swamp water was very strong, like molding ferns and stagnant river water. He could feel the hot October sun against his back. "Swell day to start out," he said.

"Yes." She moved a little toward the door. Her body felt hollow and heavy, the way it was in the garden that night when she felt so lonely and then later went up on the porch and sat with Kay and the loneliness had slowly broken inside her. She felt as if she had been taken apart, looked at and left lying in useless pieces for everyone to see. Worst of all, she was going to cry. That would make a fine mess when she had spent all that time trying to look like something. "Guess I'd better go now."

"Sure." He scratched his knee again. "I suppose so."

"Will you fight any more, Rock?"

He shook his head.

"I'm sorry."

"I'm not sorry. There are a lot of things to do here."

"Like what?"

"Well, I can work for the old man, and then some day I can work in the factory and learn about that. Russian says I'd be a good worker, and I've been talking to Gene about it, and he says—"

"You mean, stay here forever?"

"Yes. You see, I keep thinking about Mike and Joe and how they liked it here, and I don't know, but I kind of want to do something—is that crazy, Marth?"

She shook her head. "Oh, Rock—oh, Rock, I—"

"It's all right," he said gently. "It's better like this, and you can send me postcards from wherever you go. You'll have fun. Kay always has fun and so does Barby, and then when you come back, I'll still be around."

She looked at him. Her tears made him seem bleary and far away. "I thought you were mad about it—the fight, I mean, and how Kay fixed it just to make you lose—and everything."

"Hell, I'm not mad. I got no call to be mad." He held her wrist. "You write to me—understand—no matter where you are."

"Oh, Rock—I don't know what to do."

"I can't tell you," he said.

"It's just that she wants me to go with her and I really want to see things and have some fun, but I don't know—" He stood very still, waiting. "I always had fun with you, Rock, only everything changed here. The factory and the men and that terrible accident and then Mike—and Joe. All of it."

"It always changes," he said.

"Yes. Yes, I know."

"Even if you stayed, it would keep on changing, and I wouldn't have anything much. Paw says he could give me a regular salary."

"Yes."

"And we know the same people. This is really our town, Marth. We could play tennis and do all the old things, and we wouldn't have to leave each other any more—at night, I mean. We could always—"

"Yes," she said.

He touched her tweed suit, running his fingers over her arm. "But I wouldn't want you to feel—"

"No," she said quickly. "I wouldn't—Rock, I wouldn't *ever* feel,

The Long Year

only I thought you were mad because of the fight. I didn't like it. It was all so terrible."

"S-ssh," he said. "Don't talk. Let's get out of here, quick."

She laughed. They called to Olds, and Olds came in, pushing the buggy. "Okay," he said. "You crazy kids."

She ran beside him. The air was light, the air was a bell of jazz, the town was a dream come true. Her heart was a hammer rising inside her. She belonged with him, and she was a reflection of no one. There was no one like her in the world and there never had been anyone like her—not her aunt or her father, no one. She was herself, moving as herself and loving as herself.

They ran down the street. Mr. Wimmer called to them. Macbeth, still standing beside the railroad tracks, saw them running down the street toward the river cliffs. The street was full of their laughter. Fran Connaught came out and stood for a moment in the open air and watched them running. She smiled a slow, knowing smile. Johnnie Evans opened his window and watched them, the girl with her hair loose like that and the boy, running easily holding her hand. He turned and spoke to his secretary. "Look, angel," he said and kissed her mouth. Olds sat in the store, cackling, feeding his grandson expertly, dangling his Croix de Guerre for the baby to reach for. Down by the river, three boys lay in the river grasses watching a tree toad on the bark of a tanny, molding tree, watched the clouds in the sky, heard the river in the deep listening ears of their boyhoods. The season was golden. The earth turned slowly, grinding on its phantom axis.

Kay stood in the kitchen. Howard was peeling potatoes carefully with thin, twisted peelings. "She just went out," he said. "You saw her."

"It's almost an hour," she said.

"She's with Rock," he said. "I always knew she'd go with him."

"You always know everything."

"I oughtta warn you, too, 'bout Teresita. She's not honest, an' she's been in trouble an' you ought to make her work like sin else she'll never work."

"Teresita's all right," she said. She looked at her watch. She sighed. "Well, maybe you're right. I'll call Mr. Hasswell. He was coming up to say good-bye."

"He'll be glad. He's mighty lonely as it is."

"So—everyone's glad." She made an elaborate gesture of despair and humor. "Let me speak to Mr. Hasswell, Mary," she said.

"He went out," Mary said. "He's in the foundry. Shall I call him?"

"No," she said. "Just tell him I'm leaving. Marth's not going, so he won't want to come up here to say good-bye. Just tell him that, Mary."

"Is—isn't Marth going?"

"No," she said. "She changed her mind."

She looked at the house for a long moment. She picked up Barby and Teresita and drove down the highway. It was the same road she had used before. The big car turned up a flurry of hot dust. There was a tipsy, gypsy air about the three of them. Teresita giggled, her eyes round with delight, her fruity lips puckered with amusement. She wore a green silk dress and a green flower in her hair. She kept clutching the flower, sitting among the heap of hatboxes, cosmetic bags, trifles of luggage and tennis rackets, golf clubs and ice skates.

Barby slouched in the front seat beside Kay, her eyes closed. She was already dreaming of what she would see. The world was neatly put together in cities, counties, towns, the mountains in their rightful places, the buildings along the streets. The neatness of this was already beginning to grow on her, and she trusted in it and was pleased by it. "Wonder what Marth'll say when she finds out we left her."

"Nothing," Kay said. "She wants it this way."

"Oh, she'll say something. She always has something to say."

"Leave it be. She's obviously changed her mind."

Teresita giggled. "It's that Rocky Macbeth. I always knew he'd get her to stay."

The Long Year

"Howard'll be mad at you," Barby said.

Teresita sighed, "He can't do nothin' to me now."

Barby smiled, "Isn't it wonderful, Kay?"

Kay said nothing. She kept her eyes on the road, the big car hummed and sank deeper into the roadbed, gathering speed. She had not expected to feel sad about leaving the town. It proved that no one should go back to the old places. She kept thinking of Gene Wimmer as she had last seen him standing outside the post office, the dog beside him. Anyhow, the town would never be quite the same. Not even Hoyt. It was curious how easily he had come back to the factory and taken up the reins and waited for her to leave—even so, he was not the same, either. He lacked his old assurance, and he had some new ambitions and in a way, she liked him better than she had ever liked him.

Well, it was marvelous that the world was so big that there was always a place to go. She was through with all of it, and she had sent LeGrand off to New York, uncertain as to how much he bored her or how much she needed him, that little, clever man with his sharp eyes. But now, in this moment of departure, she felt for the first time a nervous tick of fear. It was running through her mind like silent mice, down her spine, through her, under her heart, under her secret pulse, beneath her skin. She put her fear into words that stood out clearly in her mind. Now I'm thirty-eight, and I'm afraid of that, being old, without power, full of wrinkles, decay, slowness, fat, the voice too high with eagerness—I've seen it everywhere—thickness around the hips, all the light, fragile spirit lost inside me. And now where is there to go? And I can no longer harbor the thought of going back to this town. That's over.

"Dammit," she said aloud.

"What's the matter?" Barby asked.

"Nothing, darling," she said. "Everything." But it was Time playing this trick on her. No one person could make her feel so broken, flat, helpless. Time passing over her and leaving her this way. It was a joke. This was the thing she shared with everyone, the passing of Time.

"Look—there," Barby said. "That's Smut Olds coming home. Look at him, will you?"

She passed the thin, slow young man in a hot cloud of dust. She looked at the October fields lying faded and golden behind the crooked fences. She tasted road dust, she tasted bitterness. She felt like weeping or shouting or spitting. The world was full of glamour and magic, full of stink, full of a thousand sad betrayals of blood and conscience, full of delight. Going to Cuba with Barby and Teresita, to all the little, gay parties, love in the gardens of Havana, the ocean and the stars and the scent of the Cuban night. And somewhere in all of it, she might see Prokosch. Some patterns repeated themselves successfully. She drove faster—faster—faster—to get away from the town, smiling a little because the town would never be quite the same again. It occurred to her, momentarily, that she herself might never be the same, either. She drove seventy miles an hour up the highway, into the warm, dusty noontime.